The
NEIGHBORHOOD

WARREN DRIGGS

Also by Warren Driggs

Crossing Lines
A Tortoise in the Road
Mormon Boy
Swimming in Deep Water
Old Scratch

The wicked flee when man pursueth.

Proverbs 28:1

1

THE BOYNTONS

BRUCE WORE HIS ADIDAS EVERY DAY. He would have worn them at night but his mom would not allow it. She told him to set them on the oval-braided rug next to his bed and put them back on in the morning. So that's what he did, every morning. Three stripes—three stripes that meant he was popular. He bought them with his newspaper-route money because his dad, frugal as he was, would not spend lavishly on a new pair of sneakers when the old Keds still had some tread. The Adidas were worth every penny, too, even though they were a half-size too small and gave him a blister on his heel.

After he died, his mom eventually boxed up his clothes and dropped them off at Goodwill. She gave his baseball-card collection to his best friend, Timmy, and his mitt to a cousin who had accepted the charity gingerly, for it felt disloyal somehow. But she would never give away his Adidas. She'd done her best to scrub off the tire-track marks and the dried drops of blood before setting them on the rug next to his bed, the laces neatly tied in bows.

The family had tried to move on, as if moving on was something that could actually be done. His mom, Darlene, remembered what it was like to be normal, so she offered an impression of that for others. His dad, Earl, was the same way—he put on his face and did his impression. Within a year's time, people thought they were getting over it but it was not the sort of thing you get over. Their heartache may have peaked, may have broken like a fever, but still it loitered and was bound to loiter forevermore. Besides, they couldn't dwell only on the tragedy when there were other neighborhood entanglements to deal with.

Darlene and Earl's other two children were temporarily left without functioning parents after Bruce was killed. Eighteen-year-old Carl and fifteen-year-old Becky hoped their parents would eventually regain their equilibrium. In the meantime, they'd tried to comfort their parents who could not be comforted, rotating as they did between anger, guilt, and despair in no particular order.

Carl and his high school buddies pooled their money to fund a reward for information leading to the arrest of Bruce's killer. Because that's what he was to Carl, a killer whose conduct was both willful and demonic. It seemed unlikely, however, that the robust bounty of $180 would be enough to lure the villain out of hiding. And as the trail grew cold, the reward money was eventually spent on weed.

As for Becky, she didn't obsess over the ultimate ruin of Bruce's killer like Carl did, plotting his suffering down to the finest detail. Instead, she consoled herself with food. This had been easy in the weeks following Bruce's death because the neighbors had delivered more casseroles and trays of enchiladas than the Boyntons could possibly eat. As the heartbreaking news grew stale, the death meals inevitably petered out and the pantry thinned. And because Darlene was in no mood to shop for groceries, Becky shoplifted a supply of Hostess products which she hid in her bedroom closet behind her tuba case.

The year was 1970 and the Boyntons lived in a rambler on Orchard Drive, a drive that had never hosted a single fruit tree. Orchard was located in a middle-class neighborhood with cachet hovering somewhere between St. James Place and Marvin Gardens. The red brick rambler with white trim had excess mortar spilling out between each brick. The oozing mortar had been fashionable in the fifties and sixties but now, more than a decade later, it looked like the brick mason had been too generous with the mortar or simply too lazy to scrape it off. A basketball hoop without a net was bolted to the roof above the garage and a rusting flag pole stood barren in the front yard. The flag pole had been installed by the original owner in a fit of patriotism but had long since lost its flag.

Darlene now stood in her small kitchen with the cuckoo clock and faded spoon-and-fork wallpaper, her homemade apron stretching just to the edge of her childbearing hips. She was trying to muster enthusiasm for the batch of cookies she was baking for the neighborhood. This was something she did several times a year because Darlene was a charitable woman. She wasn't overly showy about her charity, but neither was she entirely anonymous because there was always a note. Perhaps that is why the neighbors went overboard with the casseroles.

Darlene wore an auburn bob around her plump face like a fitted bed sheet. This snappy bob was the only fashionable thing about her, for she was rather plain looking, having thrown in the towel after three kids and all that baking. And now she'd become a forty-something-year-old mom who wore a cross-your-heart bra and dutifully fed her children from the four basic food groups because she was a good mother. She played the role of matriarch as if history had written it for her. It was impossible to tell Darlene's actual age. She could have been thirty-five or fifty-five—a thin person ballooning up with age, or a heavy person slimming down from her never-ending list of domestic obligations. Her knees were dimpled and her legs were pale and unshapely like the flour-dusted rolling pins she used in her baking. She artfully hid her figure under a collection of floral muumuus.

An hour later she was leaning over the suds in the kitchen sink, going to town on the baking pans with a ball of steel wool. Her fingers were scarred from slipped knives, broken dishes, and pulling weeds from the small vegetable patch next to the backyard shed, weeds that seemed to grow at twice the rate as her zucchini and tomato plants. A gold wedding band fit like a torniquet around her thick ring finger.

The preceding five years had seemed like a dream—a dream that had become a nightmare and would eventually settle into the simple monotony of survival. Her mind drifted as it so often did to the happier years before Bruce's death and all that had happened in its aftermath. She'd become an expert on the past, memorizing and embellishing it to suit her conviction that Bruce's life had been a happy one, for living in past tense had become her only place of refuge.

———

Darlene tidied the house, for soon Earl would be home and he didn't like a mess. Like his own father, Earl was exasperated by a household chore. He probably couldn't find the vacuum in the hall coat closet, he didn't know where the spare toilet paper rolls were kept, and his cooking repertoire consisted of pushing the lever down on the toaster if Darlene's hands were tied up with the laundry.

Thirteen-year-old Bruce was glued to the black and white television set in the living room watching re-runs of *Gilligan's Island,* vacillating between Ginger or Marianne and eventually concluding that either one would do. The Boyntons had considered upgrading to a larger color console, one like the Batemans had. The Batemans lived down the street and could afford such luxuries because Phil Bateman was a lawyer and impressed with himself because of it. Indeed, there was no one else Phil wanted to be.

"Turn off that racket and go get your homework done," Darlene called from the kitchen. "Your father will be home any minute and I've made a yummy casserole."

"But, Moooom, it's almost to the good part." Bruce was a fairly intelligent boy but had yet to embrace the likelihood that the dense crew of the Minnow would be stranded on that goddamned island for at least two more seasons.

"Oh, all right, but at the next commercial I want it turned off and your room straightened. Do you hear me?"

When she overheard a commercial a few moments later, Darlene marched in with a dishtowel swinging from her fist and turned the knob herself. She already knew that four out of five doctors recommended the unfiltered king-sized Viceroys.

Bruce was their youngest. He was a pudgy kid ("hefty" according to Darlene) and pale, nearly wedding-cake white. He had a snarl of red hair and his face was plastered with so many freckles they merged together in brownish clusters. He was well known at school but tended to be annoying by always raising his hand and knowing the answers, which everyone knows is just asking for it. He had only one real friend—the Bateman's son down the street named Timmy. Darlene didn't particularly care for the Batemans and their snobbery but she worshipped Timmy for liking her son.

Bruce had retreated to his bedroom where he spent a lot of solitary time. He could usually be found there with the door locked, lying on his twin bed with the maple headboard, fantasizing about Ginger or Marianne, or possibly Lori Wilcox, an exotic eighth-grader who wore a skirt and white knee socks and had no idea who Bruce was. The poor kid had so many triggers. He found additional material by rummaging through the stack of National Geographics in the garage. There were the dog-eared photo spreads of topless African women with rings around their long necks and the women of New Guinea who only wore grass skirts.

Darlene had been horrified when she was changing Bruce's bed sheets and found evidence of his chronic preoccupation. Did this solitary exercise make her son sexually deviant? Was he headed for one of those Watch Lists? She'd been too embarrassed to talk about it with anyone, not even Earl. My goodness, what would she even *say?* The only time the boys' maturation had come up, she'd awkwardly asked Earl if he, you know, when he was a teenager, if he'd, you know, ever "experimented" with himself. He falsely denied he had, which Darlene interpreted to mean that her son was indeed a budding pervert.

Earl was a conservative man of routine. He came home from the office every day and sat in his recliner in the living room with a glass of scotch and Walter Cronkite. The scotch was cheap, for Earl was frugal, indubitably so. He didn't even like the taste but endured it because he thought it lent an air of sophistication to his otherwise unsophisticated life. He'd experimented with a pipe for the same reason but Darlene put her foot down because of the smell. Now the only pipe in the house was hidden at the bottom of Carl's sock drawer.

Earl was short with an extra thirty pounds that drooped to the middle third of his body. He looked an awful lot like Mr. Potato Head. And like Mr. Potato Head, he'd lost most of his hair, leaving only a few wispy stragglers to float above his shiny scalp. The smallest current of air would set them to swaying. More hair sprouted from his ears than from the top of his head. In fact, a secretary at his office once whispered that if you peered inside his ear you might see an entire nativity scene. He would have mortgaged his soul to have Phil Bateman's thick mane.

Earl was an accountant whose slog up the corporate ladder had petered out on a middle rung and if you saw him you'd know why—he was ordinary and didn't command the same cachet as, say, You-Know-Who with the great hair and color TV down the street. His appearance gave little indication that he was destined for greatness. He wore polyester suits, white short-sleeved shirts, and dark ties (including the occasional clip on). The white shirts had been purchased before his metabolism slowed and now the pressure against the buttons had a tendency to make him look upholstered. He'd tried to blame Darlene for shrinking them in the wash but she'd reminded him they were polyester. She's done so gently because she was a kind person.

There had been little spontaneity in the Boynton household except where the kids were concerned and none of their children provided more fireworks than Carl who was wild and unburdened by experience. Carl was the firstborn so naturally his parents thought he was a prodigy. He could name all seven continents when he was only four-years old, and most of the state capitals when he was ten. Darlene and Earl had the wistful suspicion that he might be a genius. Unfortunately, he never made the honor roll because he whiled away his study time rolling other things instead.

Carl was also very handsome, having hogged about seventy-five percent of the family's looks and leaving the other four to divvy up the remainder. He had long blond hair that feathered back from his face in a Farrah Fawcett sort of way and grew weed in his bedroom, confident his parents wouldn't know marijuana from alfalfa. A Rolling Stones poster was thumb-tacked to the wall next to a dartboard which was surrounded by holes in the sheetrock from errant throws. Honestly, the wall looked like the Milky Way. A stolen BOYNTON AVENUE public street sign hung above his bed—the same bed where roughly half the cheerleading squad from Woodrow Wilson High had nervously allowed themselves to be adored.

Carl had saved his lawn-mowing money to buy a motorcycle—an especially loud one with an orange flame painted on the gas tank. The neighbors were relieved this hoodlum racing up and down Orchard on that obnoxious contraption didn't belong to them, especially Mrs. Hobson who trolled the sidewalk every afternoon with her Pekinese pulling on its leash, contemptuously eyeing Carl as he'd ride by with his hippie hair trailing in the breeze.

Fifteen-year-old Becky was forced to fend for her share of the remaining twenty-five percent of the family's looks and, sadly, her cut was only in the seven-percent range. She had a pimply face and no thigh gap. She was round and her best friend, Marjorie, was bony thin—so skinny that her hip bones jutted out like furniture under a sheet. So they made quite a pair. It's not that Becky and Marjorie didn't *want* to be popular. They bought the right albums, ratted their hair, and drenched their necks with Yardley perfume. Becky even suffered through a week-long carb-free diet and wrapped her thighs with Saran wrap but it simply wasn't enough. Therefore, she joined the less popular kids in the school band and could often be seen after school at the bus stop sitting alone on the curb behind her tuba case.

Everyone assumed Becky was a goodie-two-shoes. After all, how much mischief could a chubby, tuba-playing, fifteen-year-old girl cause? But she was prone to shoplift and had also been caught cheating on an algebra test which resulted in her being grounded for a week. Carl would have been traumatized by a grounding but Becky rather enjoyed it.

The family of five sat around the dinner table that evening while Humphrey waited beneath them for the occasional scrap. Humphrey was a dog of indefinite breeding who took comfort with his snout in someone's armpit, or preferably their crotch. The Boynton family had inherited him from a dead uncle. They didn't particularly want the dog but had been guilted into it. And once they got it, they didn't have the heart to take it to the pound. It was surprising that Earl hadn't insisted on changing the dog's name because this particular uncle had been an outspoken Democrat who'd named the dog after Hubert Humphrey. Whenever Earl addressed the dog it was with a hint of distain because of its politics, even if it hadn't actually voted.

Bruce attempted a stealth nose-pick but was caught scooting a finger out of a nostril with a sticky booger attached.

"Eww, you're disgusting," said Becky.

"I'm not disgusting, you are," said Bruce.

"You're both disgusting," said Carl.

"Well, your face is disgusting."

"At least I don't suck."

"Language," Darlene said. "Please."

"Well, if they suck, they suck," said Carl.

"Stop it! All of you," said Earl.

"But she started—"

"I said stop it, and I meant it."

Meanwhile, Bruce had no specific plan for the booger. He rolled and rolled it before trying to flick it under the table but it was still stuck, so he wiped it under the table.

A few moments later Becky dared to ask who had taken the bag of M&M's from her bedroom—M&M's she'd recently shoplifted.

"I did," said Carl. You see, Becky was so insignificant that no one even bothered lying to her.

"But that's stealing!"

No one came to her defense.

"Eww, somebody farted," said Carl.

"Language!" said Darlene.

"I can't smell it," said Bruce who was himself rather gassy and prone to declare he could never smell them.

"I bet it was Humphrey," said Becky.

Earl put down his fork and glared. "If I hear one more word."

Over dessert, Darlene asked the kids about school and friends. "School's lame," said Carl as he peered up through his bangs. "They don't teach you jack." Becky, who was trying to fit into a pair of bell bottoms, ignored the questions and reached across the table for seconds because eating was not something she did casually. She applied herself. And Bruce simply said too much, for why would he so eagerly confess to spying on the Hobson's teenage daughter?

When they looked back in time, they would remember those days as happy ones—those days before the homicide, the assault and battery, the prison sentences, and the new fish. No one could say exactly when it started to go wrong but the turning point might very well have been the skinny dip.

2

THE BATEMANS

PHIL BATEMAN DIDN'T KNOW who the boys had been, only that they'd deserved to be shot. His pampered wife, Mitsy, thought the same thing. Neither one of them believed the trespassers ought to be actually killed, of course, but perhaps a maiming or at least a temporary wounding would be in order to teach them a lesson.

It was late, nearly midnight on a Friday night when Mitsy heard them outside. The noise was coming from their backyard swimming pool. "Phil! Wake up! Phil!" She shook him from dreams of his legal secretary until he finally came to realize with profound disappointment where he was. "Phil!" she frantically whispered, "I heard something in the backyard. Listen!" She froze and cocked her ear. "There's somebody out there! I think we're being robbed!"

Phil leaped out of bed in his boxer shorts and grabbed Timmy's pellet gun from the hall coat closet before creeping back to the upstairs bedroom window overlooking the swimming pool. He parted the curtains a few inches to peek just as Mitsy turned on the bedroom light.

"What are you doing!" he hissed. "You'll scare them off!"

"Sorry, I was just trying to be helpful." Mitsy felt wounded by his criticism but she shouldn't have taken it personally because Phil was critical of everyone. Everyone, that is, except his buxom secretary who typed poorly and knew virtually nothing about the ordinary requirements of a good legal secretary, but could otherwise do no wrong.

Carl Boynton and his high-school friends saw the bedroom light flicker on and off. "Shit! They're awake!" The naked boys, who'd hopped over the Hobson's fence to go skinny dipping in the Bateman's backyard pool after the high school football game, now flew out of the water and grabbed their clothes just as Phil emerged from the sliding glass door with the pellet gun firing. Pellets pinged off the wooden fence and the tool shed in the corner of the backyard.

Carl was the last one to the fence. He threw his clothes over and had begun pulling himself up when a pellet hit him squarely in the ass. It was a lucky shot because Phil was hardly even aiming—just shooting in the general direction of the clatter. Carl was able to climb over the fence and fell awkwardly into a pyracantha bush on the other side. His naked body was scratched and bleeding in spots as he limped through Hobson's backyard with his clothes wadded up in his fist.

When Phil returned to the bedroom, he found Mitsy sitting up in bed, terrified to move until the criminals were either dead or safely in jail where they belonged. Mitsy was an attractive woman—more cheerleader cute than traditionally beautiful— but she looked dreadful that night with her dark hair in sponge curlers and Pond's cold cream smeared over her pixie face. She felt traitorous using the Ponds because she was an Avon lady and made her weekly rounds in the neighborhood. Ding-Dong! Avon Calling!

"Who were they?" she asked.

"A bunch of vandals, that's who," said Phil, still holding the pellet gun to his side.

"Did you scare them off with the gun?"

"No, I shot one of them."

"You *shot* one?" Mitsy was horrified. She envisioned a dead vandal sprawled out in their backyard. She believed a good whipping would have been justified, or maybe a week in jail, but her heart was not so cold as to want the trespassers killed, and especially not on their new terracotta patio.

"Yeah, didn't you hear him yelp?" asked Phil. "I thought he was going to wake up the whole goddamned neighborhood."

Mitsy stared at her husband in disbelief. She did not know this man—this man who could murder a semi-innocent vandal and be happy about it.

"So, like, where . . . *is* he?" Poor Mitsy couldn't decide what would be worse; having her husband handcuffed and hauled off to prison for life, or having to scrub stubborn blood stains from the new patio tile. Both were genuine probabilities in her mind because she didn't know the difference between a pellet gun and a bazooka.

"I think he made it over the fence into Hobson's backyard."

"Shouldn't we call the police, or an ambulance?"

"Hell no, I've got court tomorrow and I need to get my sleep."

No, Mitsy did not know this man who could casually drift off to sleep while vultures circled above their backyard.

"Where did you shoot him? I mean, where was he?"

"Over by the fence."

Well, *that* was a relief. Hobson's fence was nowhere near the new patio.

"So, what should we do?"

"What do you mean, 'What should we do?' We should go to sleep, that's what."

"But what about the body?"

"What body?"

"The vandal's."

"Good God, Mitsy, I shot him with Timmy's pellet gun. That couldn't *kill* him."

"So, do you think he's still out there?" Mitsy was still processing the fact that there hadn't been an actual killing and couldn't quite decide how she felt about it. "Maybe he'll come back for revenge."

"You worry about the most goddamned ridiculous things."

Mitsy had largely become immune to Phil's disapproval, like a woman who's come to expect that she's going to be criticized from time to time whether it was justified or not. In fact, she idolized Phil and his embellished accomplishments so much that she would endure almost any insult from him. After all, he was utterly handsome—six-foot-two with perfect white teeth, a well-defined jaw, and silvery squares of gray at the temples. He wore only the most stylish suits with the wide lapels and pleated pants with cuffs. He commanded more closet space than Mitsy and whenever he stood still it was hard to escape the suspicion that he was posing for an unseen camera.

Phil believed he had the superficial ingredients to justify his self-importance which extended to everything about him—his house, his car, his career, and his looks. Even his erections somehow registered a degree of arrogance. Indeed, it must be said that Phil had a rather indecent obsession with himself.

The Batemans owned the nicest home on Orchard Drive with a swimming pool and two-car garage. When they'd moved in a few years earlier, Darlene Boynton had welcomed them with a casserole and lovely bundt cake but the Batemans made no effort to become part of the neighborhood. They'd auditioned a few couples at the country club, like the Montgomerys for example, but Orchard Drive was only meant to be a weigh station until they moved to a fancier suburb after Phil made partner at the law firm, for his successes were easily anticipated.

Mitsy had been raised in a mobile home park by a single mother with brassy hair who spent her welfare check on Pronto Pup corn dogs and cartons of Chesterfields, leaving barely enough to fill the propane tank on the side of the doublewide. Mitsy had been determined to break the cycle and marry well. Surely she was pretty enough with thick, dark bangs hanging to the cusp of her eyebrows. A cousin had lined her up for a blind date with a law-school student. The cousin had said this handsome student was destined for great things, a ringing endorsement for a fairly average law student who'd plagiarized his way to the middle of his class.

Mitsy had cold feet in the lead up to their wedding because Phil was intolerant of her common imperfections. But the wedding congregants unanimously gushed over the handsome couple as they walked down the aisle and no one was more impressed than Mitsy's mother who was quick to remind every-one that her daughter had married a lawyer. It may have been her mother's lack of refinement that ignited her admiration for such a shallow achievement. When Mitsy called her mother in tears two weeks after the honeymoon, her mother had told her to toughen up. You're lucky to have him, damned lucky, she'd said. Just be glad you didn't sign one of them pre-nup thingees.

Now, fifteen years later, Mitsy had become accustomed to being second fiddle to Mr. Phillip Bateman, Esquire. She was a timid soul and even though her tastes had become more indulgent as Phil's career took off, she remained a timid soul—so timid that she obediently fawned and hardly ever complained. And with her timidity there came a certain politeness, a politeness that was extended primarily to those in the neighborhood who were also members of the Riverside Country Club.

On the night of the skinny dip, Carl Boynton had limped across the Hobson's backyard on the other side of the fence and met up with his buddies who'd gathered in the dark beneath an elm tree a few doors down. When he came hobbling up, scratched and complaining about having been shot in the ass, the other boys fell to the grass with laughter.

"Hey, this isn't funny! I coulda died!"

"Let's see," they said.

Carl turned his back to them and bent over. The moon gave off just enough light for the boys to see a quarter inch-sized red welt a few inches from ground zero. Even Carl had to admit it was funny and before long he was recounting his dramatic tale of the leap, the shot, the shrub, and the hobble with cinematic embellishment.

Unfortunately, he woke the next morning in terrible pain. The pellet was still lodged underneath the skin and the redness had expanded to include half his left cheek. He made the difficult decision to show the welt to his mom.

"Uh, Mom, I, uh, well, I have this thing on my butt."

"What thing? And you know I don't like that language."

"This sore."

"You have a sore on your behind?"

"Yeah, and it's killin' me."

"Let me take a look." She hadn't seen his butt for a full decade and was now shocked to see that it was hairy, like a grown man's.

"What on earth! Why, it looks like you've been shot!"

"Well, it's like, okay, see, last night me and some guys were walking around and some guy shot me for no reason."

"But that could have put your eye out! You could have been killed! Let me get some ointment."

Carl jumped from the pain when she began smearing the ointment.

"I feel a bump and I think the bullet's still in there. We need to get you to a doctor."

Carl sat cocked to his right on the front seat of the Boynton's burgundy station wagon with the faux-wood paneling on the side. When they arrived at the clinic, he lay face down on the exam table with his Naval bell-bottom jeans puddled around his sneakers as the doctor poked and prodded, first with his finger and then with a knife. The disposable paper crackled as Carl arched his back and clenched with each poke. The doctor then attacked the pellet with the X-Acto knife like it had been buried in cured concrete. Two minutes later he held the pellet up in a pair of tweezers like a jeweler examining a diamond before dropping it into a stainless steel bowl with a ping. He then produced a syringe filled neatly to the brim with penicillin and jabbed it into Carl's right cheek, the only good one Carl had left.

Carl limped out of the clinic and lay face down on the station wagon's backseat. Darlene knew she hadn't been told the full story.

"You say someone just shot you in the rear-end for no reason?"

"Yeah," Carl winced from the back seat as if he'd been shot in the mouth, too.

"But I checked your pants and underwear and there wasn't a bullet hole in them." The thought of his mom scrutinizing his boxer shorts was distressing.

"The bullet was pretty small I guess."

"Carl, I'm your mother and I demand to know what happened. This could have been a matter of life and death."

And so most of the truth dribbled out. He'd had the good judgment not to mention the beer but he did confess to the skinny dipping (which he emphasized hadn't been his idea, at all), the fence, and the shrub. Darlene believed in second chances and tended to offer them freely, mindful as she was of the Golden Rule. Therefore, if the shooter had been anyone other than Phil it might have ended there. But if that snobby Phil Bateman thought he could shoot her son like a common criminal, well, he had another thing coming.

———

Mitsy had a busy schedule the following day. First there were her Avon deliveries where she'd roll her tote into neighborhood living rooms and spray her Eau De Parfum followed by all the wrist sniffing. She'd already reached Avon's Ambassador level, which was nothing to sneeze at, and was now gunning for the Rose Circle. There was also a committee meeting to plan the Labor Day social at the club. Phil had no idea how much work went into a successful social. She also had to get a pedicure and take Cocoa, their obnoxious Chihuahua, to be groomed. This dog yapped constantly—utterly vain without a rational basis—and yet Mitsy treated him like he was Old Yeller. She even wiped his butt. Phil was appalled. "My God, did you just wipe his *ass?*" But, alas, Mitsy loved Cocoa even more than she loved Phil, so the dog stayed and had its ass wiped.

All of this left precious little "me" time for Mitsy. Fortunately, they'd shipped Timmy off to summer camp. He hadn't wanted to go but Phil and Mitsy had insisted on it. For his own good, they'd said. And here's a new pocket knife for being such a good sport! So, Timmy spent six homesick nights in the Camp Kawanhee bunk room, tossing and turning while the other boys masturbated under their covers as soon as the lights were turned off.

Timmy's conception did not reflect on the Bateman's pent up desire to breed. Frankly, he'd been the result of an untimely fornication. Mitsy was relieved he'd been a boy, fearing as she did that Phil would resent having another female in the house who could not throw a proper spiral or mow the lawn.

Timmy and Bruce Boynton became best friends in kindergarten, a development that pleased Darlene who worried about Bruce's malnourished social skills. The boys spent most of their time at the Boynton's because Mitsy didn't want them at her house—too loud and messy she said. Bruce was leery about spending time over at the Bateman's anyway, ever since he'd gone over to play and Mitsy had casually informed him that Timmy couldn't play because he was tied up. Bruce envisioned poor Timmy tied up in his dark basement, somewhere near the furnace most likely, struggling under the weight of a rope and double half-hitch.

The boys had more fun at Bruce's house anyway. They spied on Becky and snooped through Carl's record albums—Black Sabbath, Cream, Led Zeppelin, and more. They performed musical armpit farts and ran through the house with bandanas tied around their mouths and noses. And Bruce's mom didn't flip out like Timmy's mom would have when an errant football knocked over a plant stand in the living room sending a philodendron flying.

Mitsy began her busy day by slipping into her polka-dotted bikini. She was pleased with what she saw in the full-length mirror on the back of the closet door—how her petite figure had kept its cheerleader shape and how her smallish breasts asserted themselves. She turned to the side to admire her firm and shapely rear before grabbing a towel and bravely walking out the sliding glass door to the backyard, barely daring to look at the area by Hobson's fence. There was no bloody corpse, thank god, but a few bushes had been trampled. This made her lose whatever compassion she'd once had for the wounded vandal who'd got what he'd deserved.

She was anxious to get back to her romance novel in peace without Phil criticizing her for reading fluff—one more demerit on her list of general unworthiness. She'd been determined to read the meatier classics to impress Phil and others with her cocktail chatter but quickly realized no one gave a shit about Wuthering Heights or Moby Dick. After dousing herself with Coppertone because she'd been moved by its slogan—Don't be a Paleface!—she lay on her stomach and reached back to untie the string on her bikini top.

Two blocks away, Darlene Boynton stewed, pacing the kitchen floor in her floral muumuu and house slippers. She didn't like conflict but by late afternoon she'd convinced herself that a confrontation with the Batemans was necessary. She didn't want to do anything to jeopardize Bruce's relationship with Timmy, but Phil had shot her oldest son in cold blood and hadn't even called to see if he'd survived.

"Earl, you need to call Phil Bateman this instant."

"Why?"

"*Why?* He shot our son, that's why."

"Well, I'm not calling him."

"You're not intimidated by him are you?"

"Of course not," Earl lied.

"Then why won't you call him? He shot our son with a loaded gun."

"Darlene, you need to calm down. Carl was trespassing and I probably would've shot him too."

"I don't believe this. You're telling me you would have shot an innocent boy?"

"He wasn't innocent, Darlene. Let it go."

"Well then, if you won't call him then I will because I'm his mother and what that Phil Bateman did was wrong. Dead wrong. And I refuse to live in a neighborhood where people resolve their differences with gun battles."

Darlene would privately blame Kent for the skinny-dipping episode. Kent was Carl's best friend and there was just something about him that made her uneasy. It wasn't the long hair or the tie dye. It wasn't even the puka shell necklace. It was his over-the-top politeness, a hippie Eddie Haskell. She also noticed how often he'd whisper to Carl in her presence. Why all the whispering unless he was up to no good? Darlene liked Carl's other best friend, Alejandro the Mexican, much better. He'd become Alejandro the Mexican because no one in the Boynton household could properly pronounce his last name. It was Zepeda or Zapato or something else that started with a Z. At least she thought it started with a Z but it could have been a Q, or maybe a Y.

Darlene waited until after the dinner hour to call the Batemans because she was a courteous woman. She stood in the kitchen, stretching the phone cord as far as it would go, nearly decapitating Becky who'd walked in for another helping of Swedish meatballs.

Phil Bateman was in his kitchen admiring his reflection in the window when he picked up the phone. Darlene skipped the pleasantries and got right to the point. He had willfully shot her son and she demanded an apology. Rather than show an ounce of regret, however, Phil had refused to pay the medical bills or even offer a weak apology. He even had the gall to demand that she and Earl replace the trampled shrub. He even threatened to sue them!

Phil's threat to sue should have come as no surprise because he sued everyone, furiously dictating his legal retribution to his buxom secretary who pretended the lawsuits were justified. Take the lawsuit he filed against the Drake's who lived next door. They'd mistakenly built their fence five inches, five *inches*, onto his property and you'd have thought he'd been sexually molested at gunpoint. And there was the time he sued the neighbors across the street because their Christmas lights were too bright.

The stalemate over the bum welt ended two weeks later. Carl's wound had healed nicely, at least according to Carl who would not allow his mother another personal inspection. Darlene was a church-going woman and had been moved by a sermon about turning the other cheek. Therefore, she'd left a plate of cookies and a lovely note on the Bateman's front porch. Phil would not formally acknowledge the truce because he was never wrong, but Timmy began showing up at the Boynton's house again.

3

THE MONTGOMERYS

"THANK YOU, IT WAS A LOVELY EVENING."

"Well, thanks for coming," said Jean Montgomery. "We raised a lot of money for a good cause. But I'm afraid it's late and time to clean up, so . . ."

"Say, we're thinking about hosting a fundraiser of our own in a few weeks. Will you come?"

"Perhaps, but I'd hate to commit because Lawrence has a medical convention in Sun Valley coming up, and his surgery schedule is booked solid."

"We'll send you an invitation and hope you can make it."

"Thanks, and please drive safely."

It had indeed been a lovely evening for the privileged crowd with big trays of small food but now it was late and the guests, especially those who'd had too much to drink, stayed too long. When the last couple finally left, Jean leaned her back against the door and kicked off her high heels. "My Lord, I thought they'd never leave."

"Some people have no clue," said her husband, Dr. Lawrence Montgomery, who wore a navy blazer with gold buttons over a cream-colored turtleneck.

"Tell me about it," said Jean. "I was cornered half the night by that Shirley Thompson who carried on about her grandchildren, like anyone cared. Why, I couldn't get a word in edgewise." And no one should've been allowed to hog the conversation from Jean. That had been her pâté! Those had been her deviled eggs!

"And who was that woman with Vaughn?" asked Lawrence. "My god, she looked like a walrus. She must be loaded."

"You think that's bad, how about that dress Mitsy Bateman was wearing?" asked Jean. "I don't know why these women think they need to flaunt it." Jean's black chiffon cocktail dress was tighter and skimpier than any other dress at the party and she was anxious to get out of it.

"I didn't notice what she was wearing," Lawrence lied with ease. "I was too busy listening to Phil drone on about a divorce he's handling for some woman who's probably paying him on the side, if you know what I mean."

"I highly doubt it," said Jean. At least she hoped that wasn't the case, for she'd had her eye on Phil Bateman for some time. And she had his.

"By the way," Lawrence said, "I saw you talking to him for quite a while. What was that all about?"

"I was?"

"Yes, over there by the minibar. You two were whispering about something."

"Oh, that. It was nothing. He was just telling me about one of his cases."

Lawrence let it go. "Well," he said, "at least we raised some money for charity." Lawrence actually didn't give a shit about the money they'd raised. Not one iota. He didn't even like the symphony.

They both sat back and listened to the soft jazz background music still playing on their new HiFi console before Jean picked up a few empty wineglasses and crumpled cocktail napkins from the coffee table and headed to the kitchen. "They asked if we'd like them to put up a donor plaque in the lobby of the concert hall."

"A plaque's the least they could do."

"Well, I *am* on the Board," said Jean as she returned to the living room, the back of her dress unzipped halfway. She dropped into a chair next to the flagstone fireplace where a clock in the shape of the sun was hung. The bookcase behind her was crammed with books—a combination of a few unread classics and the rest fillers. She burrowed her feet into the high-pile rug. "You know, you're right about the plaque," she said. "I'll call them first thing tomorrow. They'll probably want to know how to engrave our names."

"Let's keep it understated—something simple like: 'Dr. and Mrs. Lawrence C. Montgomery.'"

Understated indeed. Lawrence wasn't on the board and hadn't been to the symphony in years. He wouldn't know a Bach from a Bernstein if there was a gun to his head. Nevertheless, the plaque should be emboldened with his name, and it was imperative that his doctor status be recognized. In fact, every note he ever wrote, every check he ever signed, indeed, every time his name was ever mentioned, he'd made sure it began with "Dr."

Lawrence was a tall and imposing man of forty-eight years who had narrowly missed being handsome but, alas, his nose had jinxed him in the end. It was long, thin, and sharp as a shark's fin. In profile it looked like the billowing sail of a ship.

He had a designer wardrobe but preferred wearing his scrubs so that everyone would know he was a physician (and the scrubs tended to hide his paunch). He could usually be seen at the neigh-borhood grocery store in those scrubs buying wine or imported cheese. Earl Boynton swore that Dr. Montgomery came home from work, changed into his scrubs, and then roamed the neigh-borhood to be seen. Darlene tried not to judge because she was a kind, church-going woman. "He probably just needs to be ready in case of emergency."

When he wasn't wearing the scrubs or the occasional turtle-neck, Lawrence wore a bow tie. This bow-tie-wearing business started when he was an undergraduate at USC. His frat broth-ers gave him a hard time about it because, really, who wears a bow tie in college?

Even though his given name was the rather pompous Lawrence Charles Montgomery III, he'd gone by the name of Larry until he enrolled in medical school. In fact, the photo board in the hallway of the Sigma Chi frat house had listed him as "Larry Montgomery, President." Not surprisingly, he was the only fraternity brother photographed with a bow tie and if you looked at the photo closely you would probably conclude he was destined to become either a professor or child molester. Once he'd been accepted to medical school at Yale, however, he insisted that he be called Lawrence. Even his mother had to make the adjustment and was reprimanded every time she'd slip back to the occasional Larry.

Lawrence disingenuously played down his Ivy League cred, but only after he was certain you knew he'd gone to Yale. He'd steer the conversation in that direction and then, once it was properly commented upon, he'd allow the conversation to change to another topic he wanted to talk about. For example, if they said: "We just returned from a trip to New York City," he might say: "Yes, I've been there several times. It's fairly close to where I studied medicine at Yale."

Jean put her head back and let out a sigh to reflect the onerous weight of charity. She wasn't a fan of the symphony either but it looked good on her country club resume. And it must be said that she could throw a fabulous dinner party. This was a talent so modest, however, that it conjured up the vague suspicion that surely there must be more.

"Can I get you a night cap?" she asked.

He checked his watch. "I think I'll have another vodka soda."

The Montgomerys were both starting to fray at the edges. This fraying was not dramatic, for they were a handsome couple, but there was the prelude to aging. This depressed them so they drank. Indeed, their evenings revolved around the cocktail. They'd sit in their expensively appointed living room with the colorful vinyl wallpaper and heavy draperies, swirling their alcohol and cataloging the weaknesses in others. They might have sobered up but they appeared to be content with their bad habits.

After Lawrence offered a few more criticisms of their guests, including a couple more jabs at Phil Bateman's haughty lawyering, Jean lifted herself from the chair and walked back into the kitchen holding a few more empty wineglasses by the stems.

Jean was an attractive woman with ginger-colored hair and a stunning figure. She'd attended Gateway Community College in New Haven, Connecticut where her principal objective had not been to graduate cum laude but rather to snare a gifted husband. Every afternoon following her classes she'd drive her rusting Pontiac over to Yale University and troll the campus hoping to lure a budding medical student. Her strategy paid off when Lawrence took note. Because he was focused mostly on himself and his bow tie, he didn't realize that Jean was a Yale imposter until after he'd become smitten by her long legs and high cheekbones.

Jean was image conscious despite her low-rent apartment and functional used car. In fact, she may have been the only young woman in New Haven who wore a mink stole. Of course, the other students considered this accessory to be the height of pretention because what student wears mink? And they really would have rolled their eyes if they'd known it was actually muskrat, for even though her tastes were indulgent, garish even, she was cheap. Once having snared a husband, Jean dropped out of the local community college to the disappointment of virtually no one and bought a real mink, again without the unanimous support of other women her age.

Jean's frugality was something of a puzzle because she was rumored to be a trust funder who would one day become very wealthy. She'd started the rumor and allowed it to flourish, trading on it for years without ever specifically denying it. It was supposedly a grandfather or perhaps an uncle—a phantom industrialist who apparently chose to pull his anonymous levers of wealth from afar.

It was Dr. Lawrence Montgomery who'd removed the pellet from Carl Boynton's ass with an X-Acto knife. He knew who Earl and Darlene Boynton were because they lived in the same neighborhood but he had an irritating way of not remembering your name or that you'd met. It remained unclear whether these slights were intentional or simply the result of disinterest. He was determined, however, that everyone would remember *his* name, and that he'd gone to Yale.

"The offending projectile appears to have lodged beneath the epidermal surface and must be excised and debrided," he'd said to Carl as if his teenage patient were a chief resident instead of a C+ high school student with only the vague knowledge that the hip bone was somehow connected to the thigh bone. Lawrence would have preferred to squeeze in some unnecessary Latin but then realized the Boyntons might not have been worth it. None of this is meant to suggest that Lawrence was an inferior general surgeon. He'd done a fine job with Carl's pellet extraction and could competently remove an appendix or gall bladder, even when it wasn't necessary. And often times it wasn't because Lawrence could charge more for surgery, so it was rare that a teenager with a tummy ache escaped with his appendix when a tablespoon of Pepto Bismol probably would have done the trick.

The Boyntons, Batemans, and Montgomerys all attended the same church—the inestimable Tower of Power—but the Boyntons were the only ones who went more often than Christmas or Easter. The other two couples had no room for another Messiah. They believed in God on some primal level but they thoroughly disliked Him and His nosey rules. And when thirteen-year-old Bruce was killed, the Boyntons were the only ones who prayed for relief.

4

REVEREND JIMMY
AND THE THERMOMETER

IT WAS 7:30 ON A SATURDAY MORNING and the Boynton's phone on the kitchen wall was ringing off the hook.

"Hello?" Darlene's voice was still sleepy, an octave lower for the first few words of the day.

"Oh hi, Darlene, it's Mitsy. I didn't wake you, did I?"

"Of course not," Darlene lied. "We've been up for a while."

"Oh, good. Say, could Timmy come over to your house this morning? I've got a doctor's appointment and Phil has an important golf match." Mitsy actually had an appointment to get her hair tipped but that didn't have the same oomph as a doctor's appointment. And surely Phil should not be inconvenienced.

"Sure, we'd love to have him."

"Great. I'll send him over. And, say, it was sure nice to have Brucey over the other day." Darlene knew that Mitsy was simply trying to take credit for watching the boys, once. For an hour. And why was it always Brucey? Just because Tim was Timmy did not mean that Bruce should be Brucey.

Darlene shuffled over to the kitchen table in her pink bath-robe and slippers where Bruce sat hunched over a bowl of Fruit Loops in his tighty-whities.

"That was Timmy's mom. He's coming over this morning."

"Can I take off my headgear before he comes?"

"Fine, but I want it back on the minute he leaves. We've spent a fortune on those braces."

When Timmy arrived, Darlene noticed that he and Bruce hardly said a word to each other. There was only a Hey and a Hi. This silence between them was not a symptom of strife in their relationship. How different it had been with Becky and her few friends who chattered endlessly and the end result was usually drama.

Earl walked into the kitchen in his bathrobe that was untied around his pot-bellied waist exposing a T-shirt and a glimpse of his own stretched-out tighty-whities. A pair of reading glasses peeked out of the bathrobe pocket. His face registered the early morning puffiness around his eyes and the few hairs on his head had no organized direction.

"Who calls at 7:30 on a Saturday?"

"Oh, that was Mitsy Bateman wondering if Timmy could come over."

Earl only grunted. He poured a cup of coffee and sat at the kitchen dinette set in front of the purple ceramic ashtray Bruce had made at school even though no one in the house smoked. Dishes from the night before had been set to dry in a rack next to the sink. The miniature door of the cuckoo clock flung open and the bird came out, squawking seven times. Earl looked up at the contrap-tion, annoyed, for no matter how many times he pulled down the chains to raise the pine cones, the damned bird was never on time.

Earl sipped his coffee noisily and then farted. Darlene tried not to be irritated but Earl, please, this was the kitchen table. The fart was loud enough for Bruce and Timmy to hear it from the living room where they were watching the Saturday morning cartoons. Timmy laughed nervously and Bruce pulled his T-shirt up over the bottom half of his face. Earl sipped again, squinting the way you do when the drink is hot, then looked out the kitchen window to the small patch of grass in the backyard. There would be another fight between Carl and Bruce over whose turn it was to mow and Earl knew he'd end up doing it himself.

"Turn that TV down," Earl hollered from the kitchen to the boys in the living room.

A few moments later *Rocky and Bullwinkle* ended and another telecast began. And what a telecast it was.

"We now bring you the 'Tower of Power!' And here's the host of our show, Jimmy Monson!"

"Hey," said Bruce, pointing at the TV, "that's the guy from our church! Mom! Come look! Our preacher's on TV!"

"Omigosh," said Darlene as she and the boys crowded around the black and white television set.

"Look, Earl, it's Reverend Jimmy! He's on TV!"

"Well I'll be darned," said Earl as he made a minor adjustment to a rabbit ear. "It sure is."

Reverend Jimmy Monson and his longsuffering wife, Betty Mae, sat on the dais in matching upholstered wingback chairs. He wore a polyester suit with wide lapels and a tie that hung no lower than the bottom of his rib cage. The tie's knot was bulky owing to the thickness of the fabric. Betty Mae wore a conservative dress and her hair was piled high on her head in the shape of a beehive.

A chorus of women stood behind Reverend Jimmy and his lovely wife. They wore matching peach chiffon gowns, high school prom-like. They hummed and swayed in lethargic rhythm to the organ music like a white ensemble of Gladys Knight's PIPs. There were two banquet tables off to the side where volunteers sat in front of telephones, ready with sharpened pencils. This was Jimmy's telethon and he was raising money for Jesus the old-fashioned way; he was begging for it.

Reverend Jimmy had come a long way since the Boyntons first met him. He'd worn a reversible suit back then—an unapologetically functional navy blue on one side and powder blue on the other. Fortunately, he'd since upgraded to the more traditional, and fancy, one-sided polyester courtesy of the widow's mite. He'd also upgraded his hair, for when the Boyntons first met Reverend Jimmy he'd been mostly bald, employing a desperate comb-over that fooled precisely no one. One Sunday, however, he appeared with thick black hair—too thick and too black. When Jimmy had returned from the wig shop, so hopeful and expectant, Betty Mae had said it looked natural because she knew he would've been crushed to hear otherwise. "Maybe adjust it a little bit. Here, like this," she said and reached up to slide it forward a half inch as he winced. "There you go. That looks much better."

"Do you think anyone will notice?"

"I'm not sure," she said.

Church goers collectively held their breaths whenever he'd tilt his head to consult his prepared remarks on sin, urgently hoping the glue would hold. It was terribly awkward and made worse by the fact that no one said a thing. There was no acknowledgment from Reverend Jimmy that he'd glued a pelt to the top of his head, nor did his flock tell him it looked good, or bad, or natural. Nothing. Not a single word. Regrettably, Jimmy took the silence to mean that no one had noticed.

Reverend Jimmy now stood and made his way to the podium. *"Brothers and Sisters, welcome to the Tower of Power! We all have sin in our lives but we can be saved through the love of our Lord and Savior, Jesus Christ!"* The studio audience obediently delivered well-timed Amens! *"But who among us can stand with Jesus knowing we gave all we had to our Savior?"*

The television camera panned to the studio audience where parishioners looked forlornly down and shook their heads. It appeared not a single one of them was completely free from sin.

"Jesus wants us to prove our love through sacrifice. For it is only through giving that we can be saved." A few more Amens! and one very distinct Hallelujah! from an enthusiastic sinner who hoped to compensate for stealing office supplies from his work and fantasizing about the babysitter. *"We know it is easier for a camel to pass through the eye of a needle than for a rich man to enter the Kingdom of Heaven because the rich man didn't sacrifice his money to God. Is there any among you who can say you gave all you could to the Lord?"*

The audience members frowned and dropped their heads providing credible, and damning, evidence of their guilt.

"Pray with me." The Reverend bowed his head and raised his arms. *"Dear Lord, soften our hearts and rid us of our selfish greed. Let us surrender our money, the root of all evil, to Your humble messengers, that they may proclaim the gospel! Amen."*

Jimmy's message was simple and compelling: Money was evil, so give it to him.

"Brothers and Sisters, the Lord's servants are standing by to take your Pledge for Jesus." The camera again panned to the phone bank

where a few of the volunteers awkwardly lifted their telephones and pretended to be taking donation pledges. *"For a small donation of $15 we will send you this pamphlet on the story of Jesus' crucifixion. And, for an additional $50, you will receive this handsome medallion in the shape of a cross."* Reverend Jimmy held up a cheap gold chain and cross in front of Betty Mae's décolletage as the cameraman zoomed in to inspect it resting just above her plump bosom.

"Jesus has promised that His sheep would hear His call. Operators are standing by. Dial 272-2930, that's 272-2930." The organ music played again and the church ladies in their colorful chiffons began swaying anew.

The phone lines are open! Call now! And the phones started ringing, for the sheep were answering the call from the Good Shepherd, anxious to receive the handsome gold medallion. And Jimmy was there to fleece them.

When the TV cut to a commercial for Folgers, Darlene looked at Earl. "What do you think? Should we donate enough to get the medallion?"

"That's a lot of money, but it's probably the right thing to do," Earl said as he stood in the middle of the living room with a hand on his hip and the other still holding the cup of coffee. He didn't want to part with the money, stingy as he was, but he fantasized about showing up at the next church service wearing the medallion. Talk about commitment! Talk about righteousness!

Becky wandered into the living room to see why the family had woken her at 8:00 on a Saturday morning. She wore an oversized Mickey Mouse T-shirt and her hair had been yanked into a high ponytail. "Look, Beck," said Darlene, "it's Reverend Jimmy on TV. Pretty neat, huh?"

"I'm going back to bed. Wake me up when Marjorie gets here."

Becky and Marjorie were lumped into the same category of unpopular girls who didn't have much to offer the in-crowd. Neither one had a deep bench. They reluctantly accepted this arbitrary banishment, both having an infectious discomfort with their own skin. They'd spend their Saturday afternoons strolling the mall and splurging on Orange Julius instead. Marjorie was skinny but thought she was too fat. It's not that she didn't eat, she ate plenty, binged actually. It's that whenever she did she'd excuse herself to use the nearest bathroom and come out smelling like Scope, or worse, vomit.

The Boyntons decided to drop off their donation in person the next morning because Reverend Jimmy and Betty Mae lived only a few blocks away. Darlene assumed Jimmy would be up early on a Sunday morning preparing eloquent remarks on the dismal fate of mankind. She was holding a plate of cookies and a check for $50 when she rang the doorbell. No answer. She rang again and waited.

The door finally opened to Reverend Jimmy who stood on the other side of the screen door wearing a silk paisley bathrobe and Betty Mae's wide-brimmed gardening hat. Jimmy enjoyed the youthfulness and vitality his pelt gave him but it was too hot to sleep in and he hadn't had time to glue it on when the doorbell rang. Therefore, he'd grabbed Betty Mae's hat because, on balance, he thought he'd look better standing in the doorway wearing a paisley bathrobe and woman's gardening hat than with no hair on his head.

"Good Morning, Reverend," said Darlene. "I wanted to catch you before you left for church."

"Uh, yeah, Betty Mae and I were just doing some early morning Bible study and weren't expecting anyone."

"Well, we saw you on TV and, well, that was so exciting! I brought you some cookies and a donation of $50."

Jimmy opened the screen door just wide enough to snatch the plate of cookies and check. The smell of coffee and bacon wafted out. "Thank you, Sister Boynton." He then made a move to close the screen door.

"Um," said Darlene to stop it from closing. "I was just wondering if, um, you have one of the, you know, medallions. But only if you have one handy."

He looked confused for a moment. "Oh, you mean one of the giveaways? Shoot, I don't have any here with me. But I'll be sure to get you one."

"Oh, it's not that important. It's just that, well, I just thought seems I was already over here and all it might be less trouble to just pick it up now, you know. But I guess if you don't have one then . . ."

Bruce was sitting on the kitchen counter when Darlene got home, kicking the cabinets with the heels of his Adidas. There was the scent of orange and a peel lay on the linoleum floor next to the kitchen trash can.

"Do I have to go to church today?"

"It will be nice."

"But how come Carl doesn't have to? It's not fair."

"That's different. He's older and it's his choice."

"Then why can't it be my choice? All they do is talk. It's boring."

After negotiating a fudge bar as compensation for going to church, Bruce retreated to his room and locked the door. He lay on his bed with the fudgsicle contemplating the injustice of having to go to church when Carl didn't. He could hear the barbell's rhythmic clanks on the other side of the wall and the occasional grunt. Carl had cut the sleeves off most of his shirts because his workouts were paying real dividends but Bruce would rather have a fudge bar than endure a weightlifting session followed by a protein shake.

Reverend Jimmy had become a local sensation overnight, having tapped into the erogenous zones of greed and guilt, and he was radiant at church that day. A few sinners in the congregation even asked for his autograph. Oh, he desperately wanted to sign something, too—a napkin, program, hymn book, anything really—because that's what celebrities do. He humbly refused, however, because the glory belonged to Jesus even though He'd never been on TV. Jimmy's feigned humility, and it *was* feigned, caused his flock to adore him even more. This adoration allowed for more fleecing.

The sermon that morning was another clarion call to donate. Reverend Jimmy had drawn a large thermometer on a poster which had been propped on an easel near the pulpit. It looked like a gigantic erection with a single engorged testicle at the base. The poster was labeled TOWER OF POWER. Numbers with dollar signs were written up the side of the thermometer in $50,000 increments. The numbers gradually rose up the shaft to $1,000,000 at the very tip. Jimmy had previously filled in the bottom third of the testicle with a red magic marker to prime the pump.

5

JOHN WANG AND THE ORIENTALS

IT WAS THE DOG DAYS OF SUMMER and the Little League baseball season had ended. Bruce and Timmy were on the same team—the Giants—and game days had given them something to look forward to. They'd put on their pinstripe uniforms two hours before the game started and were always the first to arrive at the neighborhood ballpark where advertisements for local businesses lined the home run fence. There was Larry's Burger Den, Floyd & Sons Automotive, and McDougal Tax Services, courtesy of Eric McDougal's dad who was an accountant and had been pressured to advertise there.

Now the boys were bored. Bruce's measly back-to-school budget had been quickly spent at Sears with acrimonious debate. Darlene couldn't understand why he'd spend his entire wad on just one pair of pants, but he had to have them because of the small logo on the back pocket. Timmy Bateman, on the other hand, had no budget and Mitsy practically *insisted* that he wear the logo pants because it would not do for a Bateman to be caught wearing a logo-less functional pair of jeans from Sears.

The boys had spent the morning in their tree hut. The hut was top secret, a small lair in the crotch of a maple with five square feet of living space. Their parents didn't even know it existed, or that it was on the property of an annoying neighbor who didn't know about it either, which was something of a mystery because the boys had nailed four rather conspicuous horizontal slats of spare wood to the trunk of the tree to access the hut. This neighbor would have had a conniption fit had he known the boys conspired on their mischief there, mischief that included doorbell ditching the poor man to the point of insanity, or threading a rope through a tumbleweed before hiding on either side of Orchard Drive and lifting it up whenever a car drove by so it looked like the tumbleweed was suspended in midair.

After conspiring in their tree hut for an hour, the boys went to Timmy's house. Bruce liked it there because Timmy had an electric train that wobbled through a miniature town with a depot, trees, and tunnel. He had an Erector Set and a lot of model airplanes too, even a replica of the Apollo 11 spacecraft that'd landed on the moon the summer before. Timmy's mom left them alone when they were at the Bateman's, ignored them actually. Mitsy had only reprimanded Bruce once a few years earlier after he'd shot the paper cover off a straw, hitting Timmy in the temple. "You're nearly ten years old and it's time you act your age!"

They'd been at Timmy's house for a half hour watching the train wobble around the track while Mitsy was in the kitchen painting her toenails, her foot on a chair with the phone cocked between her ear and shoulder. The cord was stretched so tight it had lost the coil. "Oh my God, they're on *sale?*"

She lowered the receiver to her chest. "Why don't you boys go over to Brucey's house now. You've been here for nearly an hour."

"But we don't have a train," said Bruce.

"Then you can go play outside."

"It's too hot," said Timmy.

"Hey," said Bruce, "wanna go spy on the new neighbors? I saw a moving van in front of the Rhinehart's old house."

"Then you could go to Brucey's after," Mitsy said as she lifted the receiver back to her ear. "Honestly, I can't get a moments peace with these kids."

The Rhinehart's bitter split had caused a stir in the neighborhood. All Bruce and Timmy knew was that Mr. Rhinehart had been caught with a "floozy" so the Rhinehart's had to move. They'd overheard their dad's say that Mrs. Rhinehart overreacted when she'd thrown him out. The two boys agreed she was a classic overreactor because of the way she'd spaz out whenever they cut through her yard on the way home from school. They concluded Mr. Rhinehart might have been better off with a floozy.

They parked their bikes a few doors down and hid behind a row of junipers, hoping the new neighbors had a teenage girl they could spy on. Unfortunately, all they saw was a middle-aged Chinese couple and their teenage son. The Wangs had already caused a scene in the pious Christian neighborhood. "What are they doing here?" Earl had lamented when he heard through the grapevine that an Asian family was moving into the neighborhood. "Don't they want to live where the rest of them do?" Most of the neighbors agreed with this sentiment without coming right out and saying it. Well, some of them did—the ones with Nixon-Agnew bumper stickers—but the remainder just privately fretted over their property values.

That night over dinner, Bruce reported on his afternoon adventures. "We spied on the new people who moved into Rhinehart's old house. They're Orientals." The rest of the family understood that in no way was Bruce suggesting the Wangs were area rugs.

"Exactly what I was afraid of," said Earl. "Now we've got a bunch of Chinks in the neighborhood."

"Earl, please. Your language. Not in front of the children."

"I don't care if they're Orientals or just normal people," said Becky.

"Me neither," said Carl. "I don't care if they're not normal."

"That's because you don't pay the mortgage," said Earl. "You're too young to understand how this works. When one of them moves in, they all start moving in. There's no getting rid of them. It'll be like Chinatown around here in a few years."

"That's ridiculous," said Darlene. "We don't even know where they came from. They might not even be Chinese. Maybe they're something else."

"Darlene," said Earl as patiently as he could, "Chinese, Japanese, Koreans—you name it. They're pretty much all the same."

"Well, that may be," said Darlene, "but I intend to welcome them to the neighborhood. It's the Christian thing to do. In fact, I think I'll take them the carrot cake I made for dessert. They must be exhausted."

"That's bullshit," said Carl.

"Carl! I will not tolerate that language. And I don't appreciate you cutting the sleeves off your shirts."

"What's the big—"

"You heard your mother," said Earl.

"But carrot cake's my favorite," said Bruce.

"No fair," said Becky.

———

The burgundy station wagon with the wood paneling rumbled down the street to the Rhinehart's house, forevermore now known as the Wang's. Becky had agreed to go along out of curiosity. When they arrived, they saw a U-Haul parked in the driveway and boxes strewn on the front lawn.

A petite woman wearing a Chinese cheongsam dress came outside for another load. She dabbed the sweat from her forehead with her sleeve. She smiled and bowed slightly to Darlene and Becky who stood on the sidewalk leading to the red brick rambler.

Darlene reciprocated with a bow of her own. The woman bowed again in response to Darlene's bow. The situation had quickly escalated into a bow-off before Mrs. Wang awkwardly stopped after three.

"Hi, my name is Dar-leeeen," she said slowly and too loudly, patting herself on the chest for emphasis. "And this is my daughter Beck-eeee."

"Ah, fank you. My name Ming. Ming Wang."

"We (another chest pat) are your neigh-bors and want to welcome you (pointing at Mrs. Wang) to the neigh-bor-hood."

"That bewy kind to you."

"Do you have any child-ren?"

Becky could hardly even look at her mom whose mouth contortions would have stumped an expert lip reader.

"Yes," said Ming. "I get now. They be wooking bewy hard and need west. Chawee! Jian!"

A handsome man appeared along with a tall teenage boy with short-cropped hair that stuck out like he'd just woken up from a backyard sleepover.

"Chawee, this Daween and her daughta Beckeeee."

Charlie bowed.

"And this our son, Jian. He seven-teen yer owed."

Jian stood awkwardly holding a box labeled Garage.

"It's nice to meet you Chawee and Gee-on," said Darlene.

"It Chawee," said Charlie. "My name Deng but my fwends in Amerweeka call Chawee."

The Wangs had moved from China to San Francisco a few years earlier and had now relocated to southern California to open a Chinese restaurant, arriving at their new home on Orchard Drive in time for Jian (pronounced "John") to enroll for his senior year at Woodrow Wilson High where Becky would be a sophomore.

Earl was in the living room reading the evening newspaper when Darlene and Becky returned home with their report.

"The Wangs, you say? Do they even speak English?"

"Yes, but they have an accent because they've only been here a few years."

"That's great, just great," said Earl. "For all we know they could be spies from Vietnam."

"Don't be ridiculous," said Darlene. "They're not spies from Vietnam."

"I didn't say they were. I said they could be."

"Well, I don't care what you say," said Darlene. "I like them."

"Me too," said Becky.

"What's the kid's name anyway?" asked Carl.

"Jian," said Becky. "It's spelled J-i-a-n, but it's pronounced John."

Earl put the newspaper down and laughed. "You've gotta be kidding me."

"What's so funny?"

"John Wang?" He re-lifted the newspaper and shook it open with a snap. "Now we're living next to a celebrity. I take back everything I said."

———

Darlene and Earl were having coffee the next morning after another restless night of worry over Carl and his hippie heresies.

"Earl, I'm worried sick about Carl, just worried sick. All he wants to do is sleep and play that silly guitar. And I haven't heard a word about college."

"Kids are lazy these days. All they do is gripe about the 'system,' whatever the hell that means."

Carl wasn't lazy in the strictest sense. In fact, there were times he displayed energy that surged with ungovernable force, like a high-pressure fuel hose swishing back and forth without direction. It's just that the hose hadn't yet pointed in Earl and Darlene's preferred direction of an accounting degree and white picket fence.

"Well, it could be worse," Darlene said. "At least he isn't taking drugs and having pre-marital sex."

"He could be and we just don't know about it."

Darlene prided herself on her motherhood intuition. Therefore, it was a mystery that she could know her honey-glazed rump roast would be cooked to perfection by 5:35 p.m. on the dot but not know that Carl was a stoner who routinely had sex in his bedroom, or that Earl hid a girlie magazine behind his stack of out-of-style sweaters on the top shelf of his closet.

"What he needs is some military discipline," said Earl. "In fact, it might do him some good to go to Vietnam—might make him grow up and see that there's more to life than rock and roll."

Earl had always been gung-ho on the war, any war for that matter. Darlene tended to agree. They preferred the known establishment and thought the anti-war protesters were naïve. Why have the best military if you weren't going to use it? War wasn't the only thing these hippies protested either. There were sit-ins and women with hairy armpits were burning their bras. Who would burn a perfectly good bra? Darlene wondered. And why? There were campus riots and a few months earlier, up in Ohio, it'd gone too far when the student demonstrators were shot by the police, providing fodder for even more anti-war rock and roll anthems which just inflamed everyone. It seemed the world was coming apart at the seams.

Earl's list of targets kept growing. So far, he'd shown an inclination to drop the A-bomb on Vietnam, Russia, the Democratic National Headquarters, and Hollywood.

"I just worry, that's all," said Darlene.

Carl walked into the kitchen where Earl sat in front of a cup of coffee watching Darlene do the dishes. Carl wore his bell-bottom jeans and a tight T-shirt with the sleeves cut off. The T-shirt had the image of a man riding a motorcycle and urged all others to "Put something exciting between your legs."

"I heard you guys talking about Nam."

"Well, no. We were only—"

"I was just telling your mother we need to wipe out the Viet Cong once and for all," said Earl. "It's the only way there'll ever be peace."

"And," Darlene said, "you know darned well I don't like that T-shirt. It's inappropriate."

Carl looked down at his shirt. "It's only a Kawasaki motorcycle shirt. You don't need to freak out."

"Don't talk back to your mother."

"Wow, sorry I'm such a criminal for wearing a shirt."

"Let's not start."

Carl walked over and opened the fridge. "War's supposed to bring peace, huh. That's far out, man."

"Listen," said Earl, "I don't want to bomb them any more than you do, but it's the only way to make them listen. It's the only thing that'll work."

"Just so you know, there's no way I'm going to Nam. I'm moving to Canada if I get drafted."

"Not if I have anything to say about it."

"Hey, I'm eighteen."

"Now you listen to me, young man. We need to stop communism and if it means war, it means war."

"Easy for you to say. Nobody's talking about drafting you. Besides, I'd be a lot safer here than in Vietnam."

Even Earl would have to acknowledge that an American teenager would be safer in a small town in southern California than the rice paddies of Dinh Tuong eating Kipper snacks with rain dripping off his poncho. To suggest otherwise would be to engage in careless understatement.

"You're not moving to Canada. You'll take a stand for American freedom and democracy, just like I did in the Pacific!"

"That's some insane logic right there," Carl said and made a finger pistol to shoot himself in the temple. "And, besides, you didn't go either."

Earl shoved his chair back and stood, red-faced. He was touchy about this subject, and for good reason, because he didn't actually go.

"I would have fought for my country!"

"Listen," Darlene interjected, "why don't I make some more of those yummy blueberry pancakes and we can watch—"

"Not now, Darlene! Our son here needs to understand a few things." Earl then reminded Carl for the umpteenth time that kids had it easy these days, unlike the days of yore when men were men and worked their tails off before gladly marching off to war with a spring in their step.

Neither of them was hungry by the time they finished shouting over each other—Carl calling his dad a chicken hawk and Earl calling his son weak and unpatriotic. In the aftermath, they both brooded, rehearsing in their minds all the zingers they should have used to close the case.

Carl retreated to his room and pulled a chair up to the window. He cracked it open and lit a joint. His parents were so out of touch.

———

Earl had been poor as a child, spawned in a meager house with a disabled father and an overworked, ornery mother who darned socks, took in laundry, and saved spare pieces of cloth and rubber bands. Their misfortune demanded that they be humble. Twelve-year-old Earl sold newspapers on the corner of Main Street in a ragged, oversized wool coat, stamping his feet to stay warm. They flailed about like upended turtles, trying to cobble together just enough to make it work. Earl had told his kids how poor they'd been so many times that Carl had begun to look for his dad's gaunt face in all those grimy black and white photos of bread lines during the Depression.

Earl also worked at the Starlight Bowling Lanes, manually stacking the pins. It was this pin-setting job that altered the course of his history.

It was hot and noisy in his cramped work space that was about the size of a cockpit. He had to be on his toes because the bowling pins flew chaotically within the cockpit, smacking him on the shins or landing on his feet. It was hard work for a scrawny kid.

The accident happened toward the end of his shift—a shift that would pay sixty cents toward the family treasury. A metal hinge was bolted to the wall that opened and closed to allow stray bowling pins to fall into a basket. A bowler threw his ball hard, causing the pins to fly. Earl jumped back and braced his right hand against the wall and into the hinge. Before he could regain his balance, the hinge closed like a giant pair of shrub trimmers, methodically severing his pinky and ring finger. His hand looked like a pistol spurting blood from the trigger.

The doctors wrapped his hand with so much gauze it looked like a white boxing glove. Earl was the toast of the town with his hand elaborately bandaged. Kids at school wished they could have a painless, temporary amputation, too. Before long, however, the dramatic finger amputation had become passé, even to his mom. He was back to school where the kids had moved on to gush over another boy's broken leg. It was gush-worthy, too, because the boy had tripped over a sprinkler one night after drawing a gigantic penis over a hop scotch pattern on the elementary school's blacktop with blue chalk. And surely Earl's work-related injury couldn't compete with that.

Earl finished high school and then enrolled at the local community college. He was studying for his semester finals when the radio crackled with the exhilarating news that Japan had bombed Pearl Harbor. Earl lined up with the other volunteers to repay those little bastards for what they'd done, but he'd been 4-F'ed due to his missing pinky, sent home along with the paralyzed, the blind, and the homosexuals.

He was privately relieved but feigned outrage that he hadn't been allowed in a frontline foxhole lest people think him an irredeemable pansy-waist. When he'd walk down the street, an otherwise healthy twenty-year-old man without a uniform, people thought he was unpatriotic or, god forbid, an outright queer. Whereas before he'd hide his hand because it looked funny, now he practically flaunted it to rebut the presumption of his cowardice.

He met Darlene as the war was winding down. She was taller than Earl and outweighed him by two dozen pounds but she was goodhearted and adored Earl and his thin-gripped handshake. The decision to marry him had been easy because he was, after all, her only suitor. There'd been no need to draw a line down the center of a yellow legal pad to list the Pros and Cons and neither had it been an internal struggle—a life-or-death-for-all-mankind decision over which wire to cut to defuse the nuclear bomb. *The blue one or the green one! Only five seconds left! Decide or else!*

So, Carl had poked his dad in a tender spot because Earl was defensive about the subject, having long forgotten the private relief he felt when he'd been declared ineligible. He'd come to remember only that he'd been on his hands and knees, begging to be stationed as close to the gunpowder as possible.

6

BOMBS FOR PEACE

EARL SAT AT HIS STAINLESS-STEEL DESK looking out his window to an overcast sky. A spitting rain tapped the window. He saw a colleague running from the parking lot with a briefcase over his head. He swiveled back to face his desk where there was a coffee mug crammed full of pens, a rotary-dial telephone, and an adding machine the size of a cash register that was operated by pulling its lever like a slot machine. On the credenza behind him there was a family photo and a plastic bowling trophy topped with a miniature golden man stuck forevermore in his perfect bowling pose. The photo needed updating because Carl still needed braces and Earl, with a fuller head of hair, was holding Bruce in his arms, a boy so young his teeth were still breaking through the gums.

Earl was annoyed that despite his years of dedicated service to the accounting firm, he'd been passed up again when it came time to award the corner office. He was a mere widget, just another middle-aged man in a white short-sleeve shirt and skinny tie. He'd slog through another fifteen years crunching numbers for richer clients before boxing up his photos, the World's Greatest Dad coffee mug, and the bowling trophy. A personalized sheet cake—*Good Luck With Retirement, Earl!*—would be on a table in the office breakroom and a few balloons would hang from the ceiling with strings like the tendrils of a jelly fish. Then he'd carry out his cardboard box of treasures and head to the pasture to be replaced by a younger widget who would eventually transition to a longer belt. All in all, a rather modest career and utterly exploitable.

"Good morning, Earl," said his secretary. Joy had been at the firm for years and it stuck in her craw that Earl was her boss simply because of his gender and accounting degree. Joy dressed in the latest fashions with the shoulder pads even though the desired effect was undone by her full figure. It looked like she'd been poured into her dress or pantsuit and kept forgetting to say when. She wore enough makeup to frost a tray of cupcakes and her hair was sprayed with so much Aqua Net it was as sturdy as a football helmet. Her cheap perfume wafted around her like an aromatic moat as she roamed the halls of Baxter & Ellis in wobbly heels looking for someone to gossip with.

"Good morning, Joy," said Earl. "Bring me some coffee, please."

"Certainly. Oh, and that Bob Neely keeps calling," she sighed as if her martyrdom for taking Earl's messages would never end.

Bob Neely was a gullible hustler with an investment scheme and wanted to bring Earl on board. Bob knew Earl was teetering and hence all the phone calls.

"I'll call him," said Earl.

"Oh, and I may need to leave early today," said Joy. "I've been battling this nasty bug but I'll try to soldier through it as long as I can." Joy was always soldiering through illnesses, cycling through her inventory for the benefit of telling others about them.

For example, if someone saw her walking with an exaggerated limp she'd say, "I've got this awful bunion, but I guess I'll just have to tough it out."

She stepped into the office breakroom to get Earl's coffee where Margie was holding forth with other secretaries. "I'm just so darned busy I can't get a thing done," she was saying as she sat blowing on her coffee at 9:45 in the morning.

"I'm busy, too," said LouAnn, not to be outdone. She took a drag from her cigarette and tapped the ashes into her empty coffee cup, then casually opened the newspaper which was on the breakroom table.

"At least you get to work for Richard," said Joy. "I'd take dictation from him any day of the week."

"He's handsome but he knows it," said LouAnn. "I swear he spends more time fussing with his hair than I do. And the way he struts around here . . ." she took another drag and blew a contrail of smoke to the ceiling. "Let's just say he's got an ego on him."

Joy got along with everyone at the office, at least publicly, but there were a few irritating employees who were hated by everyone. Take Rose in human resources, for example. And of course there were the employees who appeared to like everyone—those too-happy souls who were unanimously reviled precisely because of it.

The secretaries at Baxter & Ellis were a mean bunch and Joy may have been the meanest one of all. Take her feud with Rose. Rose had accused Joy of taking an extra-long lunch break. When Joy confronted her, Rose apologized for the accusation but then cheerfully kept repeating it again and again to anyone who would listen. Joy retaliated by finding Rose's toothbrush in the women's restroom and then dipping it in the toilet bowl. She swished it around to make sure every bristle was thoroughly soaked before wiping it for fingerprints and placing it back into the toothbrush stand. When Rose didn't skip a beat, Joy took a scoop of Chicken a la King from her Tupperware container and hid it in the bottom drawer of Rose's desk underneath a stack of never-read office memos. After all, she felt no satisfaction when her victim didn't even realize she was a victim. Naturally, Joy was overjoyed when she caught Rose sitting at her desk a few days later sneaking a quick pit whiff, wondering where on earth the smell was coming from.

Baxter & Ellis was a petri dish of humanity. Workers retaliated against each other in a vengeful cycle, employing their anonymous villainy with fake smiles. Their gossip was so chronic it was considered to be involuntary and largely incurable.

Meanwhile, Earl sat in his office waiting on his coffee as he stared at the stack of pink "While You Were Out" messages. Joy had added some complimentary doodling to Bob Neeley's message and at the bottom she'd written: *This man calls way too much!!!!*

Earl was tired of being taken for granted—tired of working for regular wages when all the other Jones' were buying new Cadillacs and built-in Maytag kitchen appliances. He'd always played it safe but now it was time to do something bold. It was time to act!

He hoisted the receiver and dialed. "Say, Bob, it's Earl—Earl Boynton."

"Good morning, Earl. Good news I hope?"

"Well, I've been mulling this over and I think I'm in."

"Why, that's fantastic! You won't regret it, Earl. This thing here's a no-brainer. We'll need to raise about two million but I've already raised nearly $95,000 from my family."

Indeed, the incipient San Juan Uranium Mine Company was radiating with promise. The Cold War was in full swing and the United States wanted to build as many nuclear warheads as it could, to keep the peace. Because the Cold War was so hot, Bruce and his classmates were taken single file to the basement of their school for the monthly bomb-shelter drills. In the unlucky event the kids didn't have time to sprint to the bomb shelter, they'd been taught to hide under their desk and put their hands over their heads to shield them from the atom bomb. The whole mess had been Kennedy's fault, at least according to Earl, but it was hard to blame him for *everything*—especially when he'd been so handsome, and so recently assassinated.

Uranium is an indispensable ingredient to make an atom bomb and speculators found it in spades on the Colorado Plateau. The ore was there for the taking, hidden just below the surface—a bonanza for peace on earth.

Bob Neeley's brother-in-law, a fellow named Harvey Pratt, owned the mineral rights on a few acres in the area and watched his neighbors grow rich while he'd dilly dallied. Now his "gut instinction" told him it was time to cash in.

"Listen, Bob," Harv had said, "alls we need is enough money to dig 'er up. I'd be willin' to let you in on the deal if you go and round up the money we're gonna need for the diggin'."

"How much are we talking?" asked Bob.

"I'd say about two mil." This was a number Harv had come up with on the fly because he didn't have a nose for business. Or numbers. Or drilling. "I'm sick and tired of sittin' around takin' my land for granite. I can damn near smell the stuff." Potential investors would have been wise to go out and take a whiff for themselves because the smell was faint, and it didn't linger. Indeed, Bob Neely and his brother-in-law, Harvey Pratt, were Exhibits A and B to prove that fertile brains did not sprout in the family tree. This dubious genetic trait extended even to the in-laws.

Bob's assurance that he'd been picky about who he'd let into the deal was a farce, for he'd called everyone he knew, even casually, starting with the A's. He didn't tell Earl that all the A's and B's up to Boynton had politely declined, as had all the C's, D's, E's, F's, and G's. The only investments so far had come from the N's and P's, but the Neelys and Pratts were not wealthy people.

Once he'd made the courageous financial plunge, Earl couldn't wait to tell Darlene about his decisive action and their forthcoming bounty.

"So, here's the deal," he said as he sat at the kitchen table that evening while Darlene busied herself with dinner. "We make money off our own investment plus we make money off everybody else we get into the deal. Basically we can't lose."

"Oh, that sounds nice," Darlene said. Earl wanted her to be excited but high finance wasn't Darlene's thing.

"So," said Earl, "I did some checking and we've saved about $12,000."

"Uh-huh."

"We can pull that out and invest it."

"Uh-huh," she said again as she crouched to look through the oven door.

"It's stupid to have all that money just sitting in a bank earning five percent when we could quadruple it in a year." These were numbers Earl made up as he went. He should've known better as an accountant but his naive hope doused every smoldering ember of reason.

"Whatever you say, dear." She grabbed a hot pad and opened the oven door. "Carl! Becky! Bruce! Time for dinner!" She placed the pan on the counter. "Go on, I'm listening."

"I think we ought to get your mother in on it, too."

"Oh, this looks yummy," she said, leaning over the casserole for a sniff.

"Yeah, I think your mother should be in the deal, too."

"My mother?" She turned to face Earl. "But she's only got her Social Security."

"No, she's saved a little."

"But that's all she's got. Are you sure that's a good idea for her?" She turned toward the hallway. "Beckeeeeee! We're waiting for you to start!"

"Darlene, it's a no brainer. She's saved about $10,000 which could really get us started. We ought to use the kids' college funds, too."

"The kid's college funds? Are you sure?"

"Sure I'm sure."

They all sat for dinner around the dinette set, passing to the left as was the family tradition.

"Carl, would you please offer the blessing on the food?"

"Sure. 'God, help us eat this.'"

"Carl, is that tone really necessary?"

"Sorry. 'God, please help us eat this.'"

Earl would have normally chastised Carl for being a smart ass but he was deep in thought over the investment.

"I thought Marjorie was coming to dinner," said Bruce.

"She has to work," said Becky.

"Got a crush on her, don't you," said Carl. "That's hilarious."

"No I don't," Bruce lied because he actually had a crush on nearly every living female between the ages of twelve and twenty-five, even a few cartoon characters like Wilma and Betty. The last time Marjorie had come to their house for dinner, Bruce had desperately tried to tamp down his under-the-table woodie and had to stop himself from following her into the bathroom as soon as the meal was finished.

———————

EARL'S OPTIMISM WAS MATCHED by the Wang family's down the street because Riverside now had another option for egg foo yung.

The Wang's new Ming Chinese Café was located in a strip mall flanked by Dooley's Dry Cleaning and The Top Dog pet store. Photos of all the dishes they served at Ming's were taped to the bottom half of the windows on either side of the front door. The bench seats were covered in plastic and the tables had the usual array of plastic flowers, soy sauce, chop sticks, and paper placemats promoting the Chinese calendar. There were pictures of dragons on the walls and photos of not-at-all-famous patrons, including the local TV weatherman, standing next to Charlie and Ming. A framed dollar bill hung on the wall behind the cash register.

Their son, Jian, bused tables on weekends but was otherwise expected to concentrate on his school work. When he wasn't doing that, he hung out with his new best friend—sophomore Becky Boynton from down the street.

Jian had not been accepted by the Woodrow Wilson High class of 1970. There was his accent and the fact that his jeans and shoes were all wrong. And it didn't help that he buttoned his shirt clear up to the neck. But mostly it was his eyes that were too squinty. Jian was oblivious to the ridicule. He didn't even know that Woodrow Wilson had just beaten Jefferson High in football. And Jefferson was their rival! It was no wonder they bullied him.

Becky Boynton had her own issues. Her upper thighs touched and she always had several pimples on the verge of eruption. She'd experimented with hot pants but her keg-like figure didn't allow for it. Within fifteen years she'd probably be wearing a muumuu, too. She'd recently overheard her parents discussing her prospects.

"We've got the college funds set aside for Carl and Bruce," her dad said.

"What about Becky?"

"Hopefully, she'll just get married."

This humble assessment of her worth should have depressed Becky but it's all about expectations, and Becky had low ones. She'd been groomed to cook, clean, and breed, grooming that had yet to take root by the looks of her messy bedroom and appetite for junk food.

Becky entered the lunchroom on that first day of high school facing the ugly prospect of eating alone because Marjorie was out sick with her "digestive issues." She walked the perimeter with her tray before finally spotting Jian sitting alone at a far table in the corner.

"Hi. Mind if I join you?"

"Okay," he said.

"It's Gee-on, right?"

"Yes, it Jian but pronounce John."

"Okay then, hi John," she giggled.

Becky noticed the other students were staring at Jian. These students were all endowed with the vague knowledge that Jian was different, and the certain knowledge that this difference made him inferior.

"Hey, look at the Chink!" one of them hollered. "Where's his chop sticks?"

"They're just being stupid," said Becky. "Don't listen to them."

"Hey, Jap boy!" said a boy wearing a navy-blue letterman's jacket with white leather sleeves. A prominent white W had been embroidered on the breast. He was the school's quarterback who could adequately read a zone defense but couldn't distinguish between a Japanese, Chinese, Swede, or Navajo.

"Ah So! Ching Chong Chinaman," said another boy as he put his index fingers on either side of his eyes and pulled the skin to give himself that authentic Chinese look.

"Come on, Jian, let's just go," said Becky.

When Jian stood, the wunderkind in the letterman's jacket shoved him in the chest causing Jian to fall backwards. The gym teacher saw what was happening and rushed in to break up a potential fight. He told Jian to mind his own business and then patted the wunderkind on the shoulder. "Go easy on the Chink, huh? It's not worth getting expelled over and we're gonna need you this week against Cedar Hills."

Becky and Jian became inseparable, forged as they were in the club of the unpopular. Jian was the first boy who'd ever paid any attention to her and Becky clung to him like a pimply barnacle. They were alone after school a few days later, standing in Wang's kitchen near the sink, when Jian finally made his move. Becky had turned to inspect the contents of the refrigerator and when she closed the fridge door and turned around he was just *there*, a few inches away, nearly in heat.

There was the usual fumbling and none of the fluid romance Becky had recently seen in *Love Story*. She had never kissed a boy before, hadn't even played spin the bottle, so there was some catching up to do. Several more make-out sessions followed, rolling around on the shag carpet in the Wang's rumpus room for hours at a time, rubbing, grinding, yearning.

Even though Becky was in love with Jian, she wasn't ready to go all the way. Second base felt about right to her. Jian, however, had his sights set on a triple, at least. Becky tried to slow him down as he rounded the bases, his jeans bound around his knees.

"We shouldn't," she whispered, but Jian had neither the desire nor the conviction to hear her and Becky had neither the desire nor the conviction to stop him.

The end came quickly, for it wasn't well choreographed—just a mad dash to the finish. Becky felt guilty once Jian had rounded the bases and slid into home. The guilt lasted until they did it again the following day and the day after that. In fact, they went to Jian's house after school for three straight weeks while his parents were cooking chow mein at the café. Becky was like a mare backing into the fence and Jian could think of nothing else, guided entirely by the radar of his loins. They had become accomplished fornicators by Thanksgiving, banging against the itch with alarming regularity.

Darlene and Earl knew only that Jian Wang helped Becky with her geometry. They must have assumed the hickeys that dotted her neck and throat like a rash were unresolved pimples because it was inconceivable to them that their daughter had been busy every afternoon in the Wang's master bedroom, laundry room, rumpus room, and even once in their garage. And Jian's parents would have been mortified to know their son was spending more time with the anatomy of the fleshy high-school sophomore down the street than with his *Essentials in Biology* textbook.

Becky's pregnancy was rather predictable.

7

A HOLE IN THE BATHROOM WINDOW

MITSY BATEMAN KNEW IT WAS A SHAME that her beauty was largely going to waste. Phil was so busy working and looking at himself in the mirror that he hardly seemed to notice her anymore. She suspected he saved his best for the buxom tramp in his office who wore practically nothing in the summer and tight turtlenecks in the winter.

Mitsy had fallen hard for Phil years earlier. And why not? He was so handsome and smart. But now after fifteen years of marriage she'd been cursed with the knowledge that he was human. It was the familiarity that bred the contempt. And perhaps contempt is an exaggeration because they still enjoyed each other's company from time to time, but their wild love-making in the early years had now become rather domesticated.

Mitsy would be the first to acknowledge that feeling ignored by Phil did not justify her dalliance but she'd become haunted by the knowledge that the best years of her life, the years when she could cash in on her beauty, were expiring. There were a few streaks of gray which she colored with Clairol hair dye and she knew it wouldn't be long before her high school cheerleader outfit no longer fit. Therefore, when Phil had phoned to say he'd be working late again, she'd gone to the Parent/Teachers conference alone, determined to flirt back with Timmy's argyle-vest-wearing principal.

Mr. Gooding mistakenly believed Mitsy's attention was the direct result of his sexual charm, and perhaps the new grapefruit diet he'd been on. He fancied himself to be a nine or a nine-point-five on the scale, an overly exuberant appraisal that allowed him to believe Mitsy Bateman wanted to run off with him to the suburbs. Any impartial scale, however, would have put him snugly in the three category. Take away his sleeveless argyles and the sensible, thick-cushioned shoes he wore and maybe he stretches to a four-point-five.

Their little fling had been so-so, at best. The sex had been decent for the forty-five seconds it lasted except for all the awkward noises Gooding made. Mitsy didn't know if he was in pain or simply having an epileptic fit. It even crossed her mind that he may have been the unfortunate victim of a sexually induced form of Tourette's. The affair was short lived because Mitsy quickly became disenchanted with the sweater vests, all the talk about school budgets, and the constant yammering over the many injustices his ex-wife had foisted upon him. The ambiance at the Westward-Ho Motor Inn was lacking, too. How was she supposed to feel sexy in the Westward-Ho?

It was out of character for Mitsy to have cheated in the first place. It wasn't so much her moral code as it was her politeness. It was this very politeness that allowed for the affair to continue as long as it had because she didn't want to be rude. Besides, this was only meant to be a casual shag resulting from boredom. Simply put, their relationship was not forged in everlasting romance. Therefore, Ray Gooding was stumped when she abruptly ended it. How could she dump him so easily? He was the principal for god's sake!

Mitsy justified the tryst in part on her reasonable belief that Phil was doing the same thing, and most likely with that secretary of his who threw herself at him at every opportunity. She'd lean over his desk with a fresh set of interrogatories, her lacy bra straining to contain her plump breasts and only extending to the edge of her areola. And at the law firm's Christmas party she'd gone out of her way to ignore Mitsy. For all his self-absorption and chronic flirting, however, Phil had technically been faithful to Mitsy. He may have ignored her, may not have felt amorous whenever he saw her on the toilet, and may not have noticed the new silk teddy she'd auditioned for Ray Gooding. But he didn't formally stray, as in have full-bodied sex with others.

Well, actually that is not entirely true. Phil was a divorce lawyer and many of his clients were in rebound mode. But it wasn't his clients so much, or even his buxom secretary that tempted him beyond reason. It was Jean Montgomery—the very one he'd whispered sweet nothings to at the Montgomery's dinner party to raise money for the symphony. His wife, Mitsy, was still a perky, dark-haired doll, but the grass looked greener over at the Montgomery's house because Jean was so . . . *different*. Tall, exotic, curvy. Jean was Ginger to Mitsy's Marianne. And Phil was Phil so he believed he should be allowed to have both.

Phil was in shock when he found the bouquet of red roses in the trash along with the Thank You note with all the X's and O's—complete shock that Mitsy would have the audacity to cheat on him. It was inconceivable. And she'd done so with Ray Gooding no less, that dull, low-paid principal who wore argyle sweaters and sensible rubber-soled shoes. When he confronted her, Mitsy had simply said: "It's complicated" which politely interpreted meant: "I don't feel like telling you, and you're going to be lied to anyway."

What traumatized Phil was not so much the possibility of losing Mitsy but rather the unimaginable notion that she had been motivated to cheat on him in the first place. He was Phillip T. Bateman of Johnson, Sterns, & Bateman! He was a prominent lawyer! Had she lost her fucking mind?

Even though nothing was said on the matter (after a few days of everything having been said, repeatedly), it was simply understood that Mitsy owed him one. Maybe not a weekend at the Four Seasons with his secretary, but owed him *something*. And something fairly big. He cashed in on the debt whenever it suited him, wielding her affair like a moral club. Mitsy was obliged to take it, too, because she had no proof of his own cheating.

Phil's relentless memory would not allow him to simply forget the sordid affair, no matter the amount of contrition and apology. There was the smug satisfaction that he was morally superior to her—an insufferable look that communicated his bigger-than-she willingness to forgive. However, to the debatable extent that he actually forgave her, he did so in small pieces and never completely. The injustice loitered in the periphery.

All of this added to the contention in the Bateman household. There was also emerging evidence that their once perfect child was having behavioral issues having recently discovered the various uses of his new BB gun, an early Christmas present to motivate better behavior in the run-up to the big day. Timmy's belief in Santa was wavering but he hedged his bet, what with Christmas so close.

On the afternoon of December 16, Timmy and Bruce Boynton were target shooting with Timmy's new Daisy in the Bateman's backyard. They'd placed an empty Malt-o-Meal box on top of the fence separating the Bateman's and Hobson's backyards, fairly close to the spot where Bruce's older brother, Carl, had been shot in the ass trying to escape Phil Bateman's shooting spree. They eventually grew bored shooting at the box and set their sights on a few sparrows. Unfortunately, the birds flew above the fence and the boys hadn't considered the fact that the Hobson's house, and specifically their bathroom window, was directly in their line of fire.

They missed the bird and hit the window instead, then ran into Timmy's house and hid the BB gun in the hall coat closet.

Sadly, Mrs. Hobson, who was a crotchety woman with no sense of humor, was in the middle of doing her business when the BB hit the bathroom window. She would later describe a massive explosion that had literally scared the remaining shit out of her. But the window did not burst. The window did not even crack. The BB left only a small round hole in the center of the window with a few fissures stemming from it like a Daddy Long Legs.

The Bateman's doorbell rang a few minutes later. Mitsy was out having her nails done, so Timmy reluctantly answered it to find Mrs. Hobson standing on the porch next to the inflatable Frosty the Snowman which seemed out of place in the seventy-degree southern California weather. She wore her house dress and slippers, the complete absence of Christmas spirit in her glare. Meanwhile, Bruce hid in the kitchen, wiping his sweaty palms on his logo jeans, desperately praying it wasn't the cops at the door.

"My mom isn't home."

"I did not come to speak to your mother, young man."

"Then why did you come over?"

"You know exactly why, Timothy Bateman, so don't you give me that *why* business!"

"We didn't shoot your window with my BB gun," he said. This fairly illustrates why lawyers routinely urge their clients not to speak.

"Oh, so you know *exactly* why I'm here."

"Um, not really."

Bruce remained frozen in the kitchen, wedged between the refrigerator and the garbage can, hoping responsibility for this crime might be borne by Timmy alone.

"Where is Bruce? I saw the two of you out in the backyard shooting that gun."

"He's in the kitchen."

Bruce was disappointed that Timmy had sold him out without a proper fight. He slithered out of the kitchen in shame and stood in front of Mrs. Hobson with his head down, his arms folded, and his hands tucked into his arm pits.

"Do your mothers know you were out shooting?"

"Um, I think mine does," Bruce lied, trying to beat Timmy to the punch.

"You tell your mother, Timothy, to call me the minute she returns!" And with that, Mrs. Hobson stepped off the porch and marched back across the lawn to her house.

"Crud, I'm dead meat," said Timmy.

"Me too," said Bruce.

For the next hour, the boys solemnly reflected on their misdeed as if they were to be hanged at dawn. They decided to get it over with as soon as Mitsy walked in the door. And that's exactly what they did, having already vacuumed the part of the living room carpet that showed.

"We shot the Hobson's window," said Timmy. No preamble. Short, honest, and to the point.

"What?" Mitsy was busy unloading the large paper bag of groceries onto the kitchen counter and wasn't paying attention.

"We shot the Hobson's window." Timmy felt doubly sorry for himself for having to confess it twice.

Bruce was sent home post-haste and Timmy was told they would deal with it when his father got home.

When Phil walked in the door a few hours later with a suspicious floral scent, Mitsy immediately escorted him to their bedroom and closed the door, leaving Timmy to sweat it out in his bedroom. He lay on his bed and looked up at the mobile of paper airplanes rotating lazily with the current of air. A blue and white Dodgers pennant was thumbtacked to the wall above a framed illustration of Timmy they'd commissioned at the county fair—the kind where the head is ten times larger than the little body drawn beneath it. A Batman poster was scotch-taped to his closet door and an Uncle Milton's Ant Farm was forgotten in the corner.

Timmy hoped the entire ordeal would blow over quickly because his parents tended to focus on their own dramas. He was surprised, therefore, when they told him they were considering juvenile detention. *Juvenile detention?* Just for being a bad shot? But he knew better than to argue and looked forlornly down as if juvie might not be punishment enough. Even Cocoa, their bratty Chihuahua with the ass-wiped bottom, looked up at Timmy as if he'd been a major disappointment to the entire family. It was finally resolved they would go over to the Hobson's house after dinner to apologize and discuss the cost of the window repair.

Bruce, meanwhile, had gone home to pace, practically jumping every time the phone rang. Nothing. Maybe this would be resolved internally between Timmy and the Hobson's. If so, he would never forget the debt he'd owe to Timmy, especially since Bruce had been the one who'd pulled the trigger.

Darlene had just returned from a fundraising drive at the Tower of Power and didn't have time to make dinner so the Boyntons sat in the living room watching the *Hee Haw Christmas Special* with TV dinners on folding tray tables. A festively decorated tree with tinsel and a construction-paper chain Bruce made at school a few years earlier stood in the corner. Wrapped presents were stacked around the skirt.

Earl became bored and changed the channel to a basketball game.

"But that's not fair," Becky said. "I like *Hee Haw*."

She was ignored.

Bruce also preferred *Hee Haw* over the basketball game but had neither the rank nor the necessary disrespect to outwardly challenge his dad. Besides, he was on his best behavior with an ear cocked to the kitchen in case the phone rang.

Carl didn't care either way. "Who you rooting for, Dad?"

"The Celtics."

"Why them?"

"Because they have more white players."

"Are you being serious right now? Cuz that's some messed up racism right there."

"I'm not a racist," said Earl. "One of the accountants at my office is black and I go to lunch with him sometimes." But Earl *was* a racist, of course he was. To admit to such a thing, however, would have been to deliver a deep moral blow to himself—a character assassination of the ugliest kind. Therefore, all his energy would go into defending the scandalous charge that he was racist and none of it would go to introspection.

Darlene winced over Earl's comment but dared not challenge him because she knew nothing about sports. For Carl's part, he simply began rooting for the other team to protest his dad's naked bigotry.

Becky was in her bedroom writing furiously in her diary about a popular girl at school who'd mocked her for her acne. This was the same girl who had invited Becky to go trick-or-treating several weeks earlier as a ruse to further humiliate her. Becky had stood by the picture window in the living room for two hours dressed like Dorothy and holding a stuffed brown terrier until there was no use denying that she had been ditched. So, Becky had plenty to write about before closing the diary and locking it with the small key she kept poorly hidden in the jewelry box on the nightstand next to her retainer. Whenever the jewelry box was opened, a little ballerina twirled to *Für Elise*.

Meanwhile, Bruce could focus on nothing but the Hobson's window. While his dad and brother watched the basketball game and Becky lamented in her diary, he waited for the phone to ring. Around eight o'clock that night it finally did.

"It's for you, Bruce," said Darlene. "It's Timmy."

Bruce was relieved it hadn't been Mrs. Hobson. He took the receiver from his mom and then stalled until she was out of earshot before putting it to his ear. "Hello?"

"Um," said Timmy, "my mom and dad said you need to come over so we can talk about what happened."

"Are they mad?"

"Sorta. I think they just want to talk about how much it's going to cost to fix it and stuff like that."

"My mom and dad don't even know," said Bruce.

"You're lucky."

"Do you think I should tell them?"

"Heck no, I wouldn't," said Timmy.

"Maybe I'll just say I have to go over to your house to do homework."

Bruce hung up and grabbed his Social Studies notebook that was covered with doodling. "Um, I have to go over to Timmy's to do some homework."

"But, Bruce honey, it's after eight," said Darlene. "Are you sure this is something you need to do tonight?"

"Yeah, it's pretty important because Mr. Fenton said it's due tomorrow."

"Well, okay, but come home soon. You know we don't like you out late on a school night."

"I know."

"I love you, Bruce."

"Yeah, I know," he said.

Darlene replayed that brief conversation at least a thousand times. She'd close her eyes and concentrate on exactly where he'd been standing in the living room and the tone of his voice. He'd been wearing a red-striped T-shirt, navy-blue hoodie, jeans, and the Adidas he wore every day. She would have traded him places, she would have given any amount, she would have agreed to burn for eternity, if only she had known to stop him from walking out the door into the dark that night. She would have given almost as much if only she could hug him just once more and smell that early teenage scent in his bright red hair, or kissed him on his freckled cheek.

8

URANIUM!

THESE WERE HEADY TIMES at the Tower of Power. The sinners in town loved Jesus and proved it by giving their money to Reverend Jimmy. The coffers were overflowing, so bigger coffers were brought in. Jimmy had rationalized a healthy cut because he was doing most of the work. In the words of a less deferential biographer, Reverend Jimmy had real issues.

In his overworked imagination, Jimmy had become a prelude to the Second Coming. He'd already been approached by a man who wanted to publish a book about Christians making it big in the business world. This, the would-be publisher believed, was a faith promoting topic. After all, if Jimmy could make it big as a Christian, that implied Christians had a knack for making it big.

The book was titled *My Favorite Stories of Jesus* because even Jimmy knew he didn't yet have the universal cachet of, say, Jesus. The publisher recommended a nice portrait of the Savior for the cover, perhaps one showing him pulling off a miracle, but Jimmy decided that he should grace the cover instead. So, he posed for a number of portraits.

In one photo, he sat at his desk in a poofy leather chair, a picture of Jesus on the credenza behind him next to a golf trophy. In another, he stood in front of the pulpit, arms outstretched and looking heavenward. That photo, however, was shot from below and made his face look fat. He ultimately chose a shot of himself in a navy-blue suit and red tie, his arms folded across his chest in a satisfied "I'm Christian and I'm rich!" sort of pose. By all accounts he looked awfully handsome. And what better way to promote Jesus than with a good photo like that?

The Tower of Power enjoyed tax exempt status as a religious organization. This allowed it to sell its merchandise tax free. Jimmy's book was a pricey $17.99 but the leftover medallions went for the blowout price of only $15. This legal chicanery also allowed him to keep the financial books private. After all, what Jesus did with His money was no one else's business. Jimmy, however, could examine the books at his whim. And he did— combing through the ledgers at a rate of ten-to-one over the Bible.

Jimmy's clever Theology for Capitalists angle was catchy and God-fearing people were seduced by the sales pitch, for who wants to belong to a crummy church that focuses on sacrifice and suffering?

The "Build The Kingdom" campaign was Jimmy's creation and he was deeply proprietary of it. In fact, he liked the slogan so much that he asked an elderly parishioner to embroider a pillow with it. She was tickled when he held it up in front of the television camera. The campaign was producing nice returns but Jimmy needed to add more pizzazz to the weekly church fundraiser. That's when he arranged for audience members to stand and describe their sad afflictions and the stunning effect a simple donation had produced. These were souls he could count on—volunteers who happened to be on his staff like Melva, Glenna, and Reed.

"My husband lost his job," said Melva, dabbing her eyes with a handkerchief. "We made a donation to the building fund and he got a new one within three weeks."

Glenna stood next in a floral dress with puffy sleeves. "I had a terrible bladder infection. It was awful—you can ask Myron. But we made a donation and it went away within a week!"

Reed was next. He looked like he'd just come from Alabama with a banjo on his knee, his overalls hanging by one strap. "The missus and me," said Reed nearly weeping, "were struggling to make ends meet but we made us a donation anyway and the next thing you know we went and got our tax refund sooner than we thought we would."

These miracles and more could be yours for as little as fifty dollars, tax-deductible.

The Lord's sheep wanted to believe, of course they did, and if a donation could heal ailments ranging from hay fever to a stubborn yeast infection then they were all for it. These miracles of perversion were inspiring and their influence could not be exaggerated. "Why, I've known Brother Dilworth for five years and if he says his allergies are down, well, then I believe him!"

Reverend Jimmy and Earl were chatting next to the church organ following the services one Sunday. The cameras had stopped rolling and Jimmy was in a satisfied mood. Darlene was clustered nearby with a gaggle of other church ladies all of whom wore at least one of Jimmy's medallions around their necks. Bruce stood next to her in an ill-fitting sport coat that had previously belonged to Carl. He held his clip-on tie in one hand and pulled at his tight collar with the other.

Jimmy and Earl were making light conversation about all the killing in Vietnam and how it'd all been LBJ's fault. The guy was a moron and a communist. Raising taxes to give to the poor and needy? Please. And his obsession over civil rights was morally corrupt. Enough was enough.

Earl would never admit it, of course, but he was star struck by Jimmy's new celebrity status. If he could persuade the Reverend to invest in the San Juan Mining Company he could parlay that into investments from other star struck parishioners.

"Say, Reverend," said Earl. "I have a little investment opportunity you might be interested in."

"I'm listening," said Jimmy, leaning in.

"You know how uranium is so valuable these days?"

"Uh huh."

"Well, I know a fellow who happens to be sitting on land that's loaded with the stuff. All he needs is some seed money to start excavating. I'm going to invest $15,000." Earl was proud to declare he had an extra fifteen grand of discretionary money to invest when really he didn't.

"Let me pray about it," said Jimmy. It did not appear to faze either one of them that the widow's mite would be used to buy atom bomb ingredients. "I'll get back to you. Probably by tomorrow."

It should not be taken as an unkind slight to suggest that neither Earl nor Jimmy were well informed about the ins and outs of atomic weaponry because not many people are, but it must be said that neither one of them had been graced with scientific savoir-faire.

When Earl arrived at work the next day, Joy told him that a Mr. Timmy Minson was holding on line two. Joy's tenure allowed her to be complacent with names.

"Hello?" said Earl.

"Yeah, say, Earl, it's Jimmy. Jimmy Monson."

"Oh, yes, of course. How are you doing, Reverend?" His pulse quickened because no one else he'd pitched the investment to had bothered to return his call.

"Say, I've been thinking about that uranium investment. We're gonna need a lot more nukes as long as the Ruskies keep pushing their godless communism. So, yeah, let's go ahead and put me down for fifty."

Did he say fifty? Fifty what? Could he have meant fifty *thousand?*

"Okay then, Reverend. It's good to have you on board. So, let's see, you want to invest fifty . . ."

"Yeah, fifty grand. I'll get a check over to you in a day or two. I feel good about this one."

Earl hung up the phone and swiveled his chair around to look out to the parking lot. He put his hands behind his head and leaned back contentedly, nurturing the wistful suspicion that God's capitalistic grace would finally shine upon him and his courageous financial wit.

It seemed like everyone in the neighborhood was fundraising. Darlene was organizing a PTA bake sale to rustle up money for the school, the Montgomerys were collecting for the symphony, and Reverend Jimmy was going to the mat for Jesus. Darlene actually cared about the school, but Dr. Montgomery didn't give a shit about the symphony, and Reverend Jimmy's genuine devotion to Jesus was rather iffy.

Jimmy assumed Jesus didn't actually *need* the money, so there was some skimming to do. This skimming was necessary because of the church's bulging overhead. After all, it would be a slap in the Redeemer's face if Jimmy spoke on His behalf wearing a cheap polyester suit. Who would join a church like that? Who would donate?

The proof was in the pudding because the temperature was rising up the Thermometer of Giving. It wasn't yet red hot, still only mid-shaft, but it was filling in nicely and hope was high that it would soon spew from the tip. The highlight of Jimmy's week was filling in the shaft in $50,000 increments with a red magic marker, preferably a thick and smelly one, during each Sunday telecast while his chiffon-wearing PIPs serenaded him and the telephone operators looked on in radiant awe. Rack up another fifty grand for Jesus!

The imitation-gold medallions were flying out of the church's broom closet where they'd been kept in cardboard boxes. Some of the most righteous church members collected gobs of them around their necks like they were strolling Bourbon Street. Yes, the Tower of Power was enjoying a bull run.

Jimmy was in bed next to Betty Mae, an opened copy of *How to Raise Money in a Down Market* propped against his chest. "I need another secretary," he said. "The one I've got is a real dingbat."

"What about Maxine? I bet she'd be good."

"Yeah, maybe," said Jimmy, "but I'm considering Susie Gilmore." Susie was the most beautiful woman in the congregation with a physical anomaly that caused her breasts to swell.

Many of the men in the congregation privately wished their wives gracefully bore such an affliction. It was this very swelling, however, that caused Betty Mae to dislike her.

"But Maxine is a widow and I know she could use the money."

"I just think Susie would be a better fit," said Jimmy. "I've prayed about it."

Jimmy returned to his book. "Says here we should give special recognition to our donors."

"But we already offer them the medallions," said Betty Mae.

"Well, I've been thinking about a special fundraising drive so we can build a nicer church because ours is pretty rundown. Maybe it could have a built-in television studio."

"Couldn't we just remodel the one we've got? A new church would cost a fortune."

"The price of salvation has always been high, Betty Mae," he said as he absentmindedly tapped a pencil to his mouth, thinking. "Everyone who donates $1,000 or more gets their own pew."

"That's a lot of work, Jimmy."

"That's why I'll need to work closely with Susie to monitor how much we've collected. Maxine could be her assistant."

Jimmy went back to his book, doing his homework for Jesus with a calculator in hand.

"I heard from Darrell today," said Betty Mae. Darrell, their youngest son, had been banished from the house when he was eighteen years old for sins that were unspeakable, even between the two of them in the privacy of their bedroom.

Jimmy put his book down again. "What did he say this time? Does he think he's coming home?"

"He doesn't want to come home unless he can be himself," she said.

"Be himself. And what the hell is that supposed to mean? Does he think he can flaunt his so-called 'lifestyle' right under my nose? I'm a Reverend for god's sake! I can't have some queer running around my own house." The word "queer" shot out like a slung dart.

Betty Mae looked at her husband. There was repugnance, even loathing, in her look. She got out of bed and ran to the bathroom. When she slammed the bathroom door, the Styrofoam head that stood on the countertop next to Jimmy's toothbrush toppled over sending his toupee into the sink where it remained splayed out like a shiny black loofah.

"You can cry all you want," Jimmy yelled from the bed, "but it's not my fault he's a homo! He's like your Uncle Gene. Trust me, there aren't any of those on my side of the family!"

They'd first become suspicious of Darrell's sexual preference was he was a child but they hadn't really *known* known. He threw like a girl and would rather decorate the new tree hut than pound a nail. Jimmy rode him constantly, even about his gait. He said Darrell had a girlish way of walking because he didn't swing his arms like men are supposed to. This, at least to Reverend Jimmy, was weighty circumstantial evidence of homosexuality. Jimmy had taught Darrell from the Bible and had hauled him to church every week. What more could he have done? That's why he insisted this perversion had migrated to Darrell from Betty Mae's side of the family. He also thought it might have had something to do with an effeminate kid named Kerry who hung out with Darrell in the sixth grade and was always angling for a sleepover. This Kerry kid was also fond of showing his "thing" to anyone who may have had even passing interest, or not.

Betty Mae finally emerged from the bathroom with smeared makeup. "How can you be so calloused toward your own son?" She turned around to face the dresser because she could hardly look at her husband. "How can you be so coldhearted?"

"I'll accept him as soon as he accepts the Lord."

She swung around. "He can't *help it*, Jimmy!"

"The hell he can't! He just needs to get married and have a family. Enough of this nonsense. It's embarrassing. If word of this leaks out, we're finished. Do you hear me? We're finished!"

"He's our *son*."

"I didn't make the rules, Betty Mae. God did. And He's been crystal clear on this."

Betty Mae was a devout church-goer but this was an issue she simply could not accept—that God would be cold enough to punish her son for his sexual orientation. For his part, Darrell patiently bore the burden of his elusive masculinity.

9

A TENNIS SHOE IN THE ROAD

DR. LAWRENCE MONTGOMERY NEEDED A DRINK, and preferably a stiff one, because he'd had a rough day. A patient had developed an infection following gall bladder surgery and had the nerve to blame it on him and now threatened a lawsuit for her pain and suffering. Pain and suffering my ass, thought Lawrence. He now wished he'd nicked a small organ with his scalpel, nothing lethal of course, but something that would've given the ungrateful whiner an awful case of diarrhea.

His day got worse when he came home to find the country club's $400 assessment to remodel the women's locker room. Was this a joke? Why in the hell did the women even need a locker room? They'd already bellyached about reserving Wednesday mornings for Ladies Day, and now this.

He kicked off his loafers and walked over to the liquor cabinet in the living room where a few expensive bottles and crystal tumblers were displayed. The expensive liquor was only for show because he was too cheap to drink it. He drank the cheap stuff hidden in the cabinet below instead.

"How was your day?" Jean asked.

"Don't ask."

Using tongs, he picked a few ice cubes from a silver bucket and dropped them into his crystal tumbler with a clink. Lawrence always looked forward to the clink because it meant he'd earned another drink—a Pavlovian response that would water his mouth. He allowed himself a generous pour with a splash of tonic. There was always *something* to justify a stiff one.

"Well," said Jean, "then this is probably a bad time to tell you the landscaper gave us a bid on that broken sprinkler and it was over $200."

"Goddamned Mexicans. Bunch of lazy crooks." He took a gulp of Smirnoff and waited for it to warm his throat. "Tell him you'll pay $150 and if he doesn't like it he can start mowing someone else's lawn."

"I tried to tell him we couldn't afford that kind of—"

"Dammit, Jean! I don't want him to think we're poor, I just don't want him gouging us." He took another gulp and leaned back in his favorite chair. His hair was slightly tussled and his bow tie was askew on his throat like a twisted propeller. "I work my ass off and some lazy Mexican thinks he can pull one over on *me?* I don't think so. Maybe he should've gone to medical school like I did instead of taking the easy way out." Lawrence had convinced himself against all reason that he was self-made when he'd actually squeezed through the birth canal gagging on a silver utensil. And now this . . . this . . . *Mexican* who hadn't even gone to college wanted to be paid for fixing his sprinklers.

Lawrence hid his stinginess well. His booze was bottom shelf, the turtlenecks and blazers were Italian knock-offs, and it galled him to pay a $5 golf bet, so much so that he was obliged to cheat. His only authentic spending spree had been for his beloved Mercedes. It was a splurge, especially with gas inching up to forty-five cents per gallon, but surely the Mercedes would rebut any presumption of his stinginess. (Jean was the same way. She wore clothes with the tags tucked in before returning them. Or consider the mink she picked up at the thrift store. It was designed to impress her friends at the club but they whispered with unrestrained satisfaction that it wasn't the same quality as the one Shirley Weinstein wore.)

Lawrence shook the ice cubes in his tumbler and picked up the newspaper. Remodel the ladies' locker room my ass, he thought. What next? A woman on the board? All these injustices caused him to require another drink, and then one more.

By 8:00 that evening he had a most pleasant buzz. He hoisted himself from his chair to pour one more but the bottle of tonic was now empty. He debated driving to the supermarket before deciding it was worth a go.

"Jean!" he yelled down the hall to the bedroom where she was watching television, "I'm running to the store to get some tonic! Be right back!"

"Pick up a gallon of milk while you're there!" she yelled back from the bedroom. "Oh, and pick up a box of Kotex if you don't mind."

He only grunted.

"Are you okay to drive?" she hollered.

"I'm fine. I've only had a couple."

He staggered out to his garage and slumped into his Mercedes which still emitted the new-car scent. The tan leather seats and wood-trimmed interior were extras but he deserved this bit of luxury. Of course he did—he was Lawrence C. Montgomery, *M fucking D!* He turned the key and let the car idle, losing himself for a few moments in the fog of inebriation before backing out of the driveway.

There was a slight chill in the air that December evening. Bruce was wearing a hoodie over a striped T-shirt and his favorite pair of jeans, the ones he'd worn every day since August when he'd blown his entire back-to-school shopping wad on them. And, of course, there were his Adidas. He carried the notebook in his backpack; a simple prop to fool his parents.

Bruce had walked the two and a half blocks to Timmy's house so many times he could have done it under anesthesia. A sidewalk led the entire way from the Boynton's to the Bateman's house except for a stretch of about twenty yards in front of a vacant lot where a new house was under construction. The basement for this house had recently been excavated and a large pile of dirt maybe eight feet tall spilled from the vacant lot onto the sidewalk, blocking the way. The dirty-yellow backhoe that had dug the hole had been haphazardly parked for the night next to the curb.

Orchard Drive was a flat residential street with no hills or curves. It was fairly well-lit, too, thanks to a fanatic in the neighborhood who'd hounded the city council into submission. This was the same insufferable neighbor who, unbeknownst to him, had a secret hut in the crotch of his backyard maple tree where Bruce and Timmy conspired on their mischief. He would sit on a folding lawn chair in his driveway and jot down the license plate numbers of speeders. The neighbors hated him. But at least he'd been responsible for the street lights which pleased most everyone in the neighborhood. The nearest street light, however, was at least one hundred yards from the vacant lot, making the area near the backhoe fairly dark.

As he walked down the sidewalk, Bruce was scheming for a way to keep this messy broken-window business from his parents, especially with Christmas so close. He calculated how much he had in savings, knowing he'd have to pay half the cost of a new window. And it was one of those frosted kinds so it was probably going to cost a lot more than a normal one. Then he pictured that ugly old Mrs. Hobson sitting on the toilet when the BB hit the window and he smiled to himself. One day he and Timmy would retell the story and get a big laugh from their buddies.

Darlene was back at home finishing up baking her home-made ginger cookies and doing the dishes while Earl and Carl were in the living room watching the basketball game and Becky was holed up in her bedroom. The house smelled of ginger, a smell Darlene would forevermore associate with the tragedy.

The booze had taken the edge off Lawrence Montgomery's sour mood. Let the ladies have their goddamned remodeled locker room if it'd shut them up. He drove west down Orchard. He noticed his headlights were off and reached down to turn them on. Once they were illuminated, he saw a yellow backhoe parked oddly on the right-hand side of the road, maybe fifty yards ahead. It looked like it'd been parked by a drunk who'd veered off the road and onto the curb, lurching to a stop after hitting the pile of dirt. The rear-end of the backhoe protruded out into the roadway about the width of a parallel-parked car.

Bruce, who was walking in the opposite direction that Lawrence was driving, saw the headlights approaching from about one hundred yards away but thought nothing of it. He and Timmy had climbed the mound of dirt after school that day to watch them dig the hole. They'd sat atop it for a few minutes, chucking dirt clods at other kids walking home. But he didn't want to climb over the pile that blocked his path that night, so he stepped off the sidewalk to walk around the dirt pile and backhoe.

When Bruce reached the rear of the backhoe, he was forced to step into the road but stayed as close to the backhoe as he could. The headlights were now only twenty-five yards away. Bruce expected the approaching car to move to its left, to give him extra room and not cut it so close.

Lawrence saw a dark figure step out into the roadway from behind the backhoe but it took a few seconds for this sorry development to take root in his foggy brain. Unfortunately, he didn't have the luxury of a few seconds. Making matters worse, he'd been hugging the right side of the wide residential road in his contented buzz.

It is impossible to know what was going on in Bruce's mind in that split second before he was hit, in that nanosecond when he realized the right headlight was going to do him in. Did his whole life flash before his eyes; the birthdays, his mom, and slinking out of Timmy's kitchen to face Mrs. Hobson? Or perhaps there was nothing but the unrealized hope the car would somehow miss him.

Lawrence saw the look on Bruce's face before the thud. It was a look that became stored in Lawrence's hippocampus forevermore, deep within the temporal lobe, a look that would haunt him for the rest of his days. He jerked the steering wheel to the left but it was too late, coming as it did *after* the thud. Bruce's body flew up onto the hood like a rag doll and then slid off to the right.

Lawrence slammed on the brakes, threw the Mercedes into park, and jumped out of his car. There was an immediate, unpleasant onset of sobriety. He'd hit someone. A boy. But where was he? It was dark as he frantically looked around hoping a kid would crawl from his knees and mumble something like, "Hey, Mister, watch where you're going!" But it was silent.

Then he heard a moan, a sound so soft that it was almost un-hearable. Bruce was lying next to the gutter, his leg grotesquely bent like a snapped twig. A pond of blood, almost like mud, was beginning to congeal with a few decaying maple leaves in the gutter. The boy was alive but unconscious and his breathing was shallow. Lawrence, a man who'd been trained for this very moment, reached for Bruce's pulse which was faint. The boy was losing ground in his fight to survive, and Lawrence knew it.

This was the moment when Lawrence's true soul was exposed like a raw nerve, when his irresolution and cowardice were laid bare, when doing the right thing might evaporate in favor of doing the selfish thing. There were no witnesses. Would he stay or would he flee? This was his moment.

Lawrence stood and looked around. No one. He bent down again and felt Bruce's weakening pulse. He stood again and walked quickly to his car, looking around to see if anyone had seen him. He turned off his headlights and drove down Orchard for a block, then turned his lights back on and took a circuitous route back to his house, not daring to look back at the enormity of his transgression.

———

It had been nearly an hour since Bruce left the house and Darlene began to worry. Maybe she'd go pick him up at Timmy's so he wouldn't have to walk home in the dark.

She called the Batemans.

"Hello, this is the Bateman's residence? How may I help you?" Mitsy, polite as she was, always answered the phone like she was auditioning for lead receptionist.

"Hi, Mitsy, it's Darlene."

"Oh, hi, Darlene. We've been expecting Bruce."

"You mean he's not there?"

"No, we haven't seen him."

"But he left nearly an hour ago. He was walking to your house to do some homework with Timmy."

"Oh my gosh, let me double check, but I'm pretty sure he hasn't come yet. Hang on. 'Timmy!'" she yelled into the background, "'Have you seen Bruce!'" A moment later she was back on the line. "I'm sorry, Darlene, but we haven't seen him. I hope everything is all right."

Darlene hung up the phone and went to the living room where Earl had given up on the game and was nodding off in his recliner, his head back and his mouth gaped open like a Pez dispenser. Meanwhile, Carl, who'd left the house a half hour earlier, was in the process of crawling out of the trunk of Kent's Pinto at the Motor Vu Drive In after having sneaked in to watch *The Planet of the Apes*, and Becky was holed up in her bedroom practicing her tuba as Humphrey sprawled on her bed patiently farting.

"Earl!" Darlene said as she wiped her hands on her apron. "Earl, wake up!" She shook him on his shoulder. "Bruce walked over to Timmy's house nearly an hour ago and they still haven't seen him. Something's wrong."

Earl woke up all at once. "I'll drive over there and see if I can find him."

"I'm going with you."

They headed down Orchard in the station wagon. The headlights illuminated what was in front of them, but the sides of the street were dark. Where was he? Where was Bruce? Two blocks down the street they saw it; a lone Adida in the middle of the road fairly close to a backhoe that had been parked in front of the vacant lot. The station wagon's headlights glared off the shoe as they slowly approached it.

Darlene and Earl were terrified, for they knew the shoe belonged to Bruce. They stopped the car in the middle of the road and jumped out. It was quiet and dark except for the illuminated pavement directly in front of the car. Earl saw him first, lying next to the curb. His twisted body looked like a stuffed Halloween dummy that had been thrown from the window of a moving car.

"Bruce! It's me! It's dad!" He looked up, hysterically. *"Help! Somebody help us!"* Darlene stood in the middle of the dark street. A neighbor later recalled that her wail could be heard for blocks. They said her shrieks were inhuman.

"He's alive!" Earl yelled. *"Somebody help us! God, please help us!"* A porch light turned on, and then another. A neighbor opened his door and then ran back inside to call 911 for help.

"Is he breathing? *Please!"* she begged.

"He's still breathing! *Bruce, it's me! It's dad! We're here! Please, Bruce! Stay with me!"* Earl looked from the broken little boy in the striped shirt up to Darlene and back again. The faces they made cannot be fairly described.

Earl's face would never be the same. There would always be evidence of inexpressible pain, the kind that would register on his face forevermore if you knew what to look for. He would smile again, but he'd never again be happy without reservation. There would always be an asterisk. Darlene's suffering may have been even worse, for her pain had no analogue. She collapsed to the curb where she sat with her feet in the gutter. Her head was down as she hugged her knees, her upper body bobbing up and down like an airline passenger waiting for the plane to crash.

The ambulance arrived and paramedics hovered over the crumpled boy lying next to the gutter. He looked like he'd lost most of his stuffing. The entire neighborhood was now either on the street or on their porches but it was surprisingly quiet. Officers were stringing up yellow caution tape, lifting it up and ducking back and forth beneath it, taking photographs and measurements in the orange light of the strobes. They asked for witnesses. There were none.

No one touched the lone tennis shoe which stood upright, forlornly in the middle of the road like a monument to the calamity. A circle of chalk had been drawn around it. Bruce's notebook and mimeographed homework papers were scattered—his juvenile penmanship littering the large pile of dirt.

The police investigators knew Bruce had been hit by a car that night because of the nature of his injuries and the angle in which he'd been found. There was also a scuff mark on the roadway that corresponded with a bumper to the boy's right leg and hip. A trail of blood ran from the point of impact in the roadway to the right-hand side of the road where he'd been found. Skid marks just beyond the backhoe suggested the driver had skidded to a stop before fleeing the scene.

The neighbors gradually finished with their gaping and retreated to their homes. They were excited by the drama because trauma is always exciting, provided it is safely inflicted on someone else. They hugged their kids and read them an extra bedtime story that night resolving, at least for the moment, never again to take them for granted.

10

THE PALL BEARER

DARLENE RODE WITH HER SON in the ambulance. She would not be taken from him, not then, not when his precious life (and by extension her own) hung in the balance. She knelt next to him, wedged between two paramedics and all the wires and tubes, stroking the back of his hand. Earl drove the station wagon behind the ambulance in a blur as he tried to make sense of this awfulness. They rolled Bruce on a gurney through the sliding glass doors of the hospital, Darlene hunched at his side, mascara smeared, reassuring her unconscious son that he would be all right.

He lived for another hour.

When the doctor came out of the operating room to interrupt Darlene's prayers, she knew from the look on his face. She'd promised God every conceivable thing she could think of, condensing it all into one jam-packed plea. She realized, however, that she hadn't promised enough when she saw the doctor's face.

The doctor wore his gray surgical scrubs and a matching scrub cap tied in back. His white surgical mask was pulled down to his throat. He sat next to Darlene on a chair in the waiting room. She and Earl held hands, searching the doctor's face, clinging to each other as the only people on earth who could possibly understand the overwhelming grief. But still there was hope, hope that maybe they had mistaken the look on his face.

"I'm sorry, Mr. and Mrs. Boynton." And he really was. "We did all we could but the loss of blood was just too much."

What else could he say? That Bruce was a fighter? That it was God's will? That they'd just saved a bundle in college tuition? This doctor was himself a father.

Darlene fell from the chair to her knees and covered her face with her hands, rocking back and forth. Earl sat, numb. The doctor waited another interminable minute without saying a word because he didn't know what else to say. He finally stood from his chair, touched Darlene on the shoulder, and walked back into the operating room with his head bowed.

Across the waiting room, a woman sat next to an adolescent boy with long bangs. The boy's arm was wrapped in gauze and he was holding a skateboard. The woman bowed her head, only peeking at Earl and Darlene from under her brow as if she were an intruder who had no right to be there in the Boynton's moment of private suffering. The boy simply gawked.

When the nurse came out in her sad, sterile duty, Earl asked her if they could see Bruce.

"Of course you can," she said.

She led them back to the operating room where Bruce lay under a sheet pulled up to his neck. His head was roughly bandaged but he otherwise looked like he was merely sleeping. Darlene sat down on the edge of the bed gingerly, with one hip, careful not to disturb him. She was sobbing and there were purple shadows under her eyes, racoon like, almost as if her nose had been broken. She held balls of waded tissue.

"Oh, Bruce honey," and then an uncontrollable, shoulder-racking sob.

Earl leaned against the bed for support. Every muscle in his face was at work trying to hold back his tears. His chin quivered, his jaw flexed, and there was subtle rapid movement all about his eyes. His voice was nearly a whisper. "We are so sorry. We are so sorry."

They gently peeled back the thin white sheet that covered him. His shirt had been removed to expose his small pale torso. Darlene sobbed uncontrollably when she saw that Bruce was still wearing his favorite logo jeans, the ones he'd worn every day, the ones she'd tried so hard to deny him. Why hadn't she bought him two pairs? They were blood stained but she would never throw them away. She'd later washed them before neatly folding them and putting them in a shoe box which she stored on the shelf of her closet. His Adidas would remain on the floor next to his bed.

She held her son's hand which was already rough and calloused from holding baseball bats and sticks. There was dirt in his fingernails from throwing clods and building forts, even though they'd been chewed nearly to the nub. She didn't want anyone to clean him up or groom his careless mop of red hair, for this is the way she would remember her son.

The nurse who had pulled the curtain around the small section where Bruce lay to give Darlene and Earl a modest amount of privacy now stood on the other side of the curtain. She and a few colleagues in their scrubs and hairnets looked at each other and bowed their heads for they had seen trauma, they had seen heartache and pain, but never more awful than this.

———————

The days somehow passed. There were moments when the pain was so deep it seemed easier to just swim down. Bruce's death was a tsunami that swamped them, and kept swamping them, with wave after wave of despair.

Darlene would not remember much about planning the funeral. Her sister had flown in from Texas and had taken charge. She's the one who had called the funeral home and gathered the pieces of Bruce's life that were displayed on the small table in the foyer of the funeral home next to the sign-in book with the fancy pen in its holder. There was his Dodgers pennant, his baseball cleats that needed a shine, and his geode collection. There were photos, including one taken on his last birthday standing next to his new bike and another one of him fishing with his dad and Carl. He stood on the lake's shore with a fishing pole in one hand and a wiggly trout in the other. The smile on his face was so wide it broke Darlene's heart, again.

There was a viewing an hour before the funeral. Friends and family formed a line to witness Bruce in the casket, dabbing the corners of their eyes with wads of tissue. Standing sprays of lilies and mums were next to the casket where Bruce lay peacefully with his baseball mitt on his chest. Darlene and Earl stood at the end of the line to receive the well-wishers like the bride and groom in a wedding line. They watched Darlene carefully to keep her from crawling into the casket with Bruce.

After seeing the dead little boy and his mitt, the sympathizers milled about in clusters. The country-club set, including Phil and Mitsy Bateman, formed one cluster and the Boynton relatives in their polyester and sensible shoes formed another. Kent and Alejandro the Mexican stood awkwardly in the corner with their still-damp hair combed and shirts tucked in while Becky, who could not bear to look at her little brother in the casket, clung to Marjorie who wore a black dress and combat boots. Her black eyeliner, dark gray eyeshadow, and lipstick signaled the beginning of her gothic stage. It was a macabre event—gawking over this innocent dead child.

Darlene would remember only bits and pieces of the funeral. There was all the lyrical prose reserved for such an ugly and mundane thing as death—the somber speeches that dull the senses and deaden the heart. And, of course, there were the boiler-plate recitations that Bruce was in heaven where he belonged. But, of course, no one wanted Bruce in heaven. She would remember the pall bearers, including thirteen-year-old Timmy Bateman who stood on the right side of the casket between two of Bruce's uncles and tried to hoist his share of the casket which listed in his direction as they solemnly lugged it out to the hearse. Timmy was so small and innocent. It was a blatant injustice that he should carry his best buddy's casket before he'd even graduated from the seventh grade.

Darlene would not remember, however, what was happening in the lives of her two other children. She did not know, for example, that Carl had formed a vigilante group to find the murderer. He was so *angry*. Some of that anger was absorbed by his relentless weightlifting, the sounds of clanking barbells interrupting the quiet sobbing of his parents. He claimed in moments of high-minded principle that he only sought justice but it really wasn't justice he sought, it was revenge.

The Boynton house had become a refuse of quiet grief. No one spoke much. There was no arguing. There was no laughter. All the energy had been zapped. The doorbell and phone didn't ring very often either. There'd been the obligatory "If there's anything we can do's" and the "We're so sorry for your loss's" from neighbors and friends but they had dwindled. These expressions had been genuine but it seems rather impossible not to be trite on these occasions. And there'd been the "How are you holding up's?" and other painfully absurd questions. It was inevitable that the meals would taper off, too, leaving the Boyntons to be all alone in their sorrow.

The quiet was punctuated by the rock and roll coming from Carl's Magnavox record player in his bedroom. Jethro Tull, Deep Purple, and Grand Funk Railroad nearly shook the walls. His parents heard and even felt it, of course, but said nothing. Carl mourned for his little brother, it is true, but his mourning took the form of vengeance. How he yearned to find the killer! How he fantasized about what he'd do to him once he was caught! He would tie him up and calmly talk to him as he systematically tortured him with pliers, clippers, and knives, smiling sadly as he detailed all the reasons why he'd been left with no choice, no choice, but to kill him slowly and painfully because that's what he deserved.

This was the fantasy that sustained him in his grief. Maybe he'd start by cutting off the killer's finger, and then perhaps a thumb. He would force the coward to look him in the eye the entire time as he patiently emphasized that he was dutybound to administer the punishment. The villain would cry and beg for mercy and when Carl finally took him out of his misery there would be a bitter aftertaste because the sonofabitch hadn't suffered enough—that his suffering could never be as awful as what he deserved.

Darlene tried to keep up with the laundry but there wasn't much in the hamper because no one left the house much. She'd put a load in the washing machine and not notice the drops of blood on Carl's shirts with the cut-off sleeves. Or the occasional rip or lost button from his fistfights—fistfights Carl was drawn too in his rage. Often times they were consensual assaults with other boys who were angry too, but other times it was violence simply for violence sake.

And neither would Darlene remember what Becky had been up too in those first months following Bruce's death. She generally knew Becky went to school and spent her solitary diary and tuba time, but she didn't know Becky had been sleeping with Jian Wang down the street on a daily basis. And she certainly didn't know that Becky was pregnant.

Darlene's mother stayed for two weeks after the funeral to help. Unfortunately, she was no help at all—just one more person to take care of. Adding to the mix was the well-known fact that she was an ornery woman who spent her days chronicling her various ailments to anyone who would listen. She appeared to take great pleasure in boasting about her spells. There was her gout and her arthritis to flaunt, among others. She was also hard of hearing, or at least she pretended to be, for one aspect of her pending deafness was her ability to choose when not to hear. So, for example, she never heard a word Earl said. Earl took comfort in knowing she was in her eighties and about ready for one of those dying places where they serve dinner at four o'clock and women outnumber men four to one—where a man who has a driver's license is worth more than a headful of hair or the ability to sustain an erection. Maybe she could snag one of those men to annoy.

As the days somehow melted into weeks, Darlene became tormented by guilt for allowing Bruce to leave the house that night. She suffered even more when Mitsy Bateman let it slip that Bruce had been summoned to their house because of the broken window. She was haunted to know that Bruce's final moments had been filled with fear of punishment from Earl and her, or from that dowdy old Mrs. Hobson. The boys had shot the window, this was true. And Darlene had no reason to doubt that Mavis Hobson had been on the toilet at the time and was genuinely startled. But she didn't need to yell at the kids.

Mrs. Hobson would not connect the dots that her broken window had somehow spiraled into young Bruce Boynton's death. She was sad for their loss, of course she was, but she was also unhappy that her window remained unrepaired. After a week, she called Phil Bateman to follow up. Phil had debated calling the Boyntons to split the cost, or at least telling them he had paid the entire thing all by himself, but then thought better of it.

There arose a neighborhood patrolman in the aftermath of the hit-and-run. The patrol was the brainchild of Don Rigtrup, a retired cop who lived one street over. He drove an out-of-service squad car and slowly patrolled the neighborhood like a shark cruising for a wounded seal. After two weeks and a tank of gas, all he'd spotted were two teenage boys who'd been toilet papering the Livingston's house. Unfortunately, he'd been unable to apprehend them given his bum knees. His nightly vigil petered out for good a week later.

11

THE BALL PEEN HAMMER

LAWRENCE MONTGOMERY HAD DRIVEN HOME that night in a state of panic. He needed to concentrate. He needed to think! The accident had chased away the pleasant buzz, but cobwebs still lingered. He'd thought about going to the store for the milk and Kotex lest Jean find it odd that he'd been to the store and back so quickly, and without the goods to prove it. On the other hand, the thought of browsing the dairy aisle at a time like that was unthinkable. Besides, he needed to be off the road as soon as possible.

He drove into the garage and quickly pulled down the garage door before inspecting the front grill of his Mercedes. He dreaded what he might find so he was surprised to find so little damage— only a dent on the right-hand side of the front bumper. There were also small droplets of blood spatter which shook him, but this was no time to fall apart. The lighting was inadequate so he crept into the kitchen to get a flashlight.

"Lawrence? Lawrence? Is that you?" Jean hollered from the bedroom. "You're back from the store already?"

"Yeah, I didn't end up going," he shouted from the kitchen. "It looks like one of my tires is low so I only drove a few blocks and then came back. I'm going back out to take a better look at it."

He found the flashlight in the junk drawer where everything they didn't know what to do with had accumulated—string, masking tape, a lock with an unremembered combination, keys to something, and a few used batteries. The flashlight didn't turn on so he smacked it against the palm of his hand until it did. He then returned to the garage to have a better look.

The two-car garage was small and the Mercedes was large, leaving little room to operate between the front of his car and the dirty cinder-block wall. He crouched down and shone the flashlight up under the bumper. No damage there; in fact, the only damage appeared to be the dent on his bumper.

He went back into the house. "Almost done," he yelled toward the back bedroom. He grabbed a rag from under the sink in the laundry room, got it wet, then returned to clean the droplets of blood from the bumper, headlight, and grill. He tossed the rag into the garbage can when he was finished.

"So, you didn't end up going to the store?" Jean asked when he went back inside.

"No. Like I said, I only drove a few blocks and then turned around because of the tire. I pumped it up using the bike pump so it should be okay in the morning."

A bike pump? It's a good thing he wasn't talking to the FBI.

"Are you okay, Lawrence? It looks like you're sweating."

"Yeah, I'm fine. It's just hot in the garage and I had to pump the tire by hand."

"Well, I hope you've fixed it because I need my car tomorrow. Remember, I have my bridge game at ten."

"Yeah, I think it'll be fine. But I'm exhausted. I'm going to bed."

"Mind if I stay up with the reading light on?"

"Sure. Whatever."

Lawrence lay in bed pretending to sleep. He would have stopped and rendered aid but he'd been drinking and they would have arrested him for drunk driving and manslaughter. His career would've been over. Besides, the boy was probably going to die regardless. Fortunately, he'd been unconscious so he probably hadn't suffered much. And why in the hell did the kid dart out into the road, anyway? Lawrence thought, already rationalizing his abhorrent behavior.

He woke early the next morning and made toast and coffee with slightly trembling hands. Jean wandered in wearing her pink silk bathrobe with the white fur collar. "You're up early," she said as she yanked the carafe out and poured a cup.

"I need to get to the clinic early this morning. I've got a full schedule."

"I hope the car's okay."

"The car? Oh, the tire. Yeah, I checked it first thing this morning and it should be okay."

He drove down Orchard Drive on his way to work because he wanted to see the scene in daylight and to make sure the boy had been taken away, scraped up like the carcass of a deer on the highway.

He slowed as he approached the dirty yellow backhoe and tried to reconstruct how it'd happened. He saw a circle drawn in chalk in the middle of the roadway. What could that mean? He looked to his right to where the boy had been laying against the curb, holding his breath before confirming that the boy was no longer there. There were lines of orange spray paint on the pavement outlining where Bruce had been found and dark stains on the cement gutter.

Lawrence was certain that no one had seen him. And without an eyewitness, who would possibly suspect him? He was the esteemed Dr. Lawrence C. Montgomery III, educated at Yale and on the board of the country club. There were two nagging loose ends, however. The first was the dent on his bumper. He wisely assumed the cops would be on the lookout for cars in the neighborhood with dents on the right front side of their bumpers. So, he'd been tempted to bum a ride to work with a colleague, or even take the bus. But the bus? He was a surgeon for god's sake and couldn't be seen on a public bus.

He considered taking the Mercedes to a repair shop but figured the police might canvas local auto body shops looking for someone who'd slunk in wearing sunglasses and paying in cash. Too risky. Or perhaps he could take a quick road trip to another city, say, Bakersfield, and have the repair work done there. He even thought about doing the repair work himself but he knew he would've botched it so badly he might as well have put a neon sign on the bumper that read: "Hey, look at my dented bumper from hitting the kid. I tried to fix it with my ball peen hammer."

The thought occurred to him to "accidentally" ram the car into a telephone pole in front of several eyewitnesses. He would stumble out of the car and describe how his foot had slipped off the brake and onto the gas pedal before getting their names and addresses. Such a collision would disguise the original dent and also allow him to get it fixed. He finally resolved, however, to simply be on the lookout for cops who were on the lookout for dented front bumpers until he could figure out what to do.

The second loose end was his wife, Jean. This problem loomed larger than the first. His behavior the night of the accident had been suspicious. Maybe he should've gone to the store to cover his tracks with her. Too late for that now.

Jean called him at the medical clinic about ten o'clock that morning to breathlessly tell him about a little boy who'd been hit and left for dead. And it'd happened only a few blocks from their house! In their own quiet neighborhood! He ordinarily wouldn't have bothered taking her call because he was seeing patients but he knew it was imperative that he stay on her good side until the dust settled.

"What happened to him?" Lawrence asked.

"He was found on the side of the road and was still breath-ing, the poor thing. They rushed him to the hospital but by then it was too late. They said he died about an hour after he got there."

"That's terrible," said Lawrence. And indeed it was.

"I can't believe someone would do that," said Jean as she sat in the kitchen filing her nails in front of her second cup of coffee. "My God, can you imagine being so calloused that you'd leave a little boy to die on the side of the road and not *do* anything? Just drive away?"

"Yeah, not good."

"Well, if they find him, I hope they string him up. I'd give him the electric chair if it were up to me."

"So, they don't know who it was I guess?"

"Not yet," she said as she brushed the nail dust from her skirt. "I just saw the Eyewitness News. They had a reporter out here an hour ago."

"Out here?"

"Yes, just down the street. He said they're looking for leads and asking anybody who might know something to come forward."

"But still no witnesses, huh?"

"No, but they usually get to the bottom of these things."

"Well, I'm sorry to hear about that," said Lawrence. "But listen, I gotta run. Are we still on for dinner tonight at the club?"

"I think so, unless Phil and Mitsy decide they can't make it. It was their son Timmy's best friend who was killed—that little Boynton boy over there on Orchard. I think his name was Bruce. He was thirteen, Timmy's age."

The revelation of an actual name socked Lawrence in the gut. He didn't know the boy but he remembered treating his older brother for a pellet wound a few months earlier. This made it more real. He was no longer just a crumpled mess of bones and blood. His name was Bruce Boynton and he was thirteen. And the worst of it was that Lawrence now knew he might have been able to save him. He'd lived for nearly two hours? That was one helluva tough kid, thought Lawrence.

Jean thought Lawrence had been acting strange, and it was surprising that he'd gone to the store and then come back so soon empty-handed. It also seemed a bit odd that Lawrence had used a bike pump on his low tire. But Jean would not even consider, not even dream, that her husband could have been responsible for such an abhorrent act.

A few nights later they were having cocktails in the living room before going to dinner with the Batemans when she decided to put her fears to rest. Lawrence was facing the bar with his back to her, pinching an ice cube with metal tongs when she began.

"Lawrence, tell me. Why didn't you go to the store that night?"

"What night?" he asked. His face was flushed and he needed to compose himself before turning around to face her.

"The night that little Boynton boy was hit. You left and came back without going to the store. How come?"

"My tire was low, remember? I had to pump it up with the bike pump." He was still facing the bar, pretending to struggle with the cap on the bottle of Crown Royal.

"And what about the dent?"

"The dent?" He finally turned around but didn't look her in the eye.

"The dent on the bumper of your car, over by the headlight."

"There's a dent there?"

This put an ugly pit in her stomach because Jean knew how much he loved that Mercedes—practically made love to it from every angle and position. She knew he'd throw a fit if there was a smudge on it, let alone a dent. Lawrence knew that Jean knew this, and Jean knew that Lawrence knew that she knew.

"Lawrence, I need to know. Did you have anything to do with the hit and run that night?"

"I can't believe you'd ask me such a ridiculous question."

This was no denial and Jean picked up on it. "Well, I'm asking, and I need a truthful answer." Actually, what Jean desperately needed was a truthful denial. She needed impeccably reliable alibis. She needed a bold and tearful confession from someone she didn't know, someone who deserved to rot in prison.

He looked at his drink, then out the window, then at his shoes. When he'd run out of places to look, he finally looked at Jean. He had been cornered and saw no way out.

"Can I trust you, Jean?"

And then she knew.

"Oh my God, Lawrence."

"You don't understand."

"I don't *understand?* Oh my God. No, Lawrence. No, no, no," she pleaded. She was standing now, shaking her head slowly from one side to the other.

"Do you want to hear what happened, or not?"

Jean was trembling. She put her glass of chardonnay down on the coffee table before it sloshed onto her hand. Her husband, the father of her children, had hit a young boy with his car and left him to die on the side of the road like a feral dog. It was unthinkable.

"Jean, listen to me! I need to know that I can trust you if I tell you what really happened."

"You need to call Phil. Oh my god, Lawrence."

"I'm not calling anyone. He only does divorce work anyway."

She stared at him for a long moment without really seeing him, and then walked without purpose or direction toward the kitchen and back again, finally collapsing onto the sofa where she put her hands to her face. This would become her nightmare, too. The shameful secret had now been foisted onto her—a secret so horrible that neither of them could ever divulge it without cata- strophic consequences. Her entire life changed in this instant, and she knew it.

"I was driving down Orchard and it was really dark. Okay? I had my headlights on. Sure, I'd had a few drinks but I felt fine, and you know as well as anyone that I can drive when I've had a few drinks. Okay? So, I'm going the speed limit, maybe even a little less than that. Hell, Jean, I was probably doing *less* than the speed limit."

She stared at the wall behind him without blinking. This was not happening.

"I was on the right-hand side of the road, exactly where I was supposed to be, okay? And I was going below the speed limit with my headlights on," he said again to be sure she understood the extent of his innocence. "There was a backhoe parked illegally, very dangerously I might add, on the right-hand side of the road. Whoever parked it that way was just asking for trouble. So, anyway, I was just barely moving along when all of a sudden, this kid jumps out from behind the backhoe right in front of me. There was nothing I could have done, Jean. You've got to believe me."

"You hit him," said Jean. It was less an accusation than a statement of fact—to set the unthinkable record straight.

"Jean, it's not like that. It's almost like *he* ran into *me*, like he jumped out in front of me. There's nothing I could have done."

"Bullshit, Lawrence! You left him to *die!*"

"But it wasn't my fault."

"Not your fault? What wasn't your fault?" She was shouting now. "That you were drunk? That you hit him? That you left him to die? Oh my god, please, this isn't happening."

"Jean, get a hold of yourself! It was an accident, okay?"

"An *accident?*" She stood from the sofa but didn't know where to go or what to do next. "And that's why you didn't stay to help him? That's why you ran? That's why you didn't give him first aid? Because it was an accident? *You*, Lawrence, of all people! You didn't call for an ambulance because it was an *accident?* You did *nothing* for him. *You left him to die, Lawrence!*" She was screaming now—screaming for the little boy, and his parents. She was screaming for their lives that would forever change because of this inconvenient confession.

"Jean, calm down. I know you're upset. But I need your help."

"Oh, *now* you need my help!"

"Jean, please. Be reasonable."

She ran to the bedroom and slammed the door behind her. He could hear her crying from the living room where just a moment earlier they'd been casually enjoying a cocktail. Now everything had changed. He stared at her glass of wine on the coffee table, pink lipstick on the rim, then threw back the rest of his whiskey.

Lawrence experienced some relief when he unburdened his secret onto the one person who had immunity, the one person who had nearly as much to lose as he did if she let it slip. Now they both shared the burden of this sin.

He made his way to the bedroom, passing a montage of family photos on the hallway wall, photos that had been taken at a happier time. He turned the knob on the bedroom door. Locked. They'd installed the lock when their daughter became old enough to know, and be wholly grossed out by, what occasionally went on inside. From the time she was twelve-years-old until she left for college, their daughter had been traumatized whenever she heard the click of the lock, retreating to the backyard or her bedroom with the door closed and a pillow over her face. Lawrence now realized they might never have a need for the lock again.

"Jean, please, open the door. We need to talk."

There were muffled sobs coming from the bed where Jean lay with a pillow over her own face. He'd done it now, hadn't he? He'd pulled the pin on a hand grenade and rolled it under her privileged life.

"Jean," he said as he stood with his hand on the knob. He leaned his forehead against the door and smelled the enamel. "You know I would have tried to save him if I could, but he was dying, okay? He was dying and there was nothing I could've done about it." He waited for some response. Nothing. "What do you think would have happened if I'd waited at the scene, or if I'd called the police? They would have arrested me for drunk driving, that's what. They would've arrested me for manslaughter. And why? Because the accident had been my fault? No, because it wasn't my fault! But they would've thrown the book at me anyway, Jean. They would've thrown the book at me and you know it.

"That family would've sued us and I'd have been a perfect target. Just think about the headlines—how a drunk driver killed an innocent child. Our lives would've been destroyed, Jean. Destroyed. Do you hear me? We would've been sued for all we're worth and I would've lost my medical license. Our friends would've disowned us and we would've been pariahs at the club." He paused again. Still nothing from inside the bedroom where Jean was barely listening to his moving speech.

"I couldn't let that happen to us—to you, Jean. My confession wouldn't have solved a damned thing. He still would've died, only there would have been even more pain. Even our kids would've been targets. And my patients? They'd suffer needlessly because I wouldn't be there to help them."

The sobbing had stopped but the door remained locked.

"Do you really want me to confess to the authorities? Because if you do, I will," he lied. "I just don't understand what good that would do. Sure, the cops could close a case and that family would get their pound of flesh with one of those greedy injury lawyers. And then what? Would it bring him back? My arrest would only bring shame and humiliation to you and the family. That's why I left the scene, Jean. Don't you see? I did it for you and the kids. Maybe it wasn't the right thing to do, but it was the best thing to do. Just think about it."

Lawrence knew the stakes. The cops would call him Perpetrator. His lawyer would call him Client. Criminologists would call him Sociopath. Sociopaths would call him Misunderstood. Jean would call him Selfish. He would call himself Victim. And the Boyntons? They would call him Thief.

12

AN EMPTY PLACE AT THE TABLE

BLOODSHED IN VIETNAM WAS ON THE RISE. For every God-loving American patriot who wanted to drop the A-Bomb on the Viet Cong, and maybe Russia while they were at it, there were three others who were lukewarm about the whole sordid mess. Earl was a Bomb Dropper and Carl was a Sordid Messer. Succinctly summarized, Carl had a fundamental reluctance to be shot.

"Listen, Carl," Earl would lecture, "America fights for freedom. We fight to ensure the peace."

"But, Dad, your argument makes no sense," Carl would say. "You guys think the only way to have peace is through war. That's just crazy."

"It's not that simple," Earl would say. "We only bomb the countries that don't want peace."

"Who doesn't want peace?"

"The countries we bomb, that's who."

"So, you're saying that bombing promotes peace?"

"Sure it does, as long as you bomb the right people."

A truce in their brain to brain combat had developed, however, after Bruce's death. The energy to argue had evaporated. The only energy that remained was packed into Carl's relentless determination to find the killer. He and his friends prowled about for cars with dented bumpers, swearing revenge. Alejandro the Mexican contributed his lawn-mowing money to the $180 reward pot and Kent kept promising he would too. Carl had contributed the rest. Unfortunately, the handsome sum had not been enough to entice a confession.

The Boyntons were sitting around the dinner table in the death-crowded house a few days after Christmas. Darlene was wearing the same floral muumuu for the third day in a row. Bruce's new skate board remained under the tree, still in its snowman wrapping paper now dusted with dry pine needles. An advent calendar made from felt in the shape of a Christmas tree hung from a nail on the pantry door. Bruce had woken early every day that December to count down the days and now the candy cane still poked out of the number 16 pouch, the sad date of his death.

The kids' heights had been recorded at yearly intervals on the wall next to the advent calendar where they'd stood with their backs to the wall. *Carl at 12. Becky at 9. Bruce at 6.* The measurements would never be taken again because Darlene could not bear it. She wanted Earl to paint over it but he never got around to it so their respective heights were frozen in time forevermore.

Bruce's empty spot at the table seemed like space enough for ten. Darlene would catch herself counting out the plates from the cupboard before walking them over to the table and then remember she only needed four, not five. Earl finally removed the table's leaf to make it seem less vacant. Oddly, Bruce's name was never spoken in the house. Instead, they said things like, "I need to straighten his room" or "What do you think we should do with his presents?"

"We're having a pot roast the Barkers brought over." The misery in Darlene's monotone was undisguisable.

"Want me to take the tree down?" asked Carl. He knew his parents couldn't bear a melancholy chore like taking down the Christmas tree, something the family had always done together over hot chocolate and Bing Crosby.

"Let's leave it up a bit longer in case we have more visitors," said Earl.

"Everyone has been so generous," said Darlene. "Last night the Batemans brought over dinner for the third time. The night before that it was the Drakes with the enchiladas. And today I got a phone call from Jean Montgomery. She's that Dr. Montgomery's wife, the one who operated on Carl. She's bringing dinner over tomorrow night and she couldn't have been sweeter. The Wangs have been generous, too."

Becky flinched at the mention of the Wangs, wondering how generous they'd be if they knew she and Jian had been madly fornicating throughout their house.

"We've been blessed," said Earl.

"*Blessed?* What in the hell are you talking about?" asked Carl. "My little brother was murdered."

"Language," said Darlene.

No one had a compelling response to Carl's point so they retreated to the quiet.

Becky was relieved her parents hadn't lingered on the Wangs. The last thing she wanted was a repeat of the embarrassing conversation she'd endured with her old-fashioned parents six-month's earlier. It'd been preceded by a hand-wringing discussion between Darlene and Earl after they'd caught Carl in his bedroom with a hand up Karen Simon's blouse.

"I think we should have a talk with Becky, too," Darlene had said to Earl.

"Fine, but she obviously doesn't want to hear about it from me."

Actually, Becky didn't want to hear about it from either one of them. She figured any modest sexual thought her parents may have once had had long since expired. At least she hoped so. Therefore, she about died when her mom awkwardly broached the subject of birds and bees. Darlene sat with one hip on the edge of Becky's bed and said something about how boys were like little factories and occasionally needed to blow off some steam. "I'm sorry to be so frank."

"Uh-huh."

"And they have certain urges, you see."

Becky would've rather discussed her bowel movements, or her period.

"I don't want to embarrass you but now you're old enough to know these things."

Unfortunately, that factory speech hadn't taken root because now, six months later, Jian's little factory had rolled out its first widget. No one knew yet except Becky, not even Jian. She had meant to tell her mom but then the accident happened and she was not about to barge in with more glad tidings. "Uh, mom, want some more happy news? All that fornicating in Jian Wang's rumpus room has finally paid off. I'm pregnant!"

Once the diminished family had finished eating the Barker's pot roast, Darlene got up to clear the table when Carl, who obsessed about Vietnam when he wasn't obsessing about Bruce's killer, reminded them that he would take a bus to Canada if it came to that, for he believed there was a certain virtue to disobedience—that defiance in the face of an unjust war carried with it an element of honor.

Earl was tempted to remind Carl about the perilous state of democracy but one look from Darlene convinced him otherwise.

That night Darlene and Earl made love for the first time since Bruce's death. It'd come out of nowhere and it was the neediest lovemaking of their lives. It wasn't about the sex; it was about the need to cling and so they did, arms and legs wrapped around each other like tangled vines.

Afterwards, they lay in the darkness, their bruise so deep it colored their marrow.

A few minutes later Darlene heard a quiet sob. She rolled over to face him. He lay on his back with his eyes opened. She reached out and put her hand on his chest.

"Are you okay?"

He only nodded in the dark because if he'd opened his mouth all that would've come out would've been an unintelligible sob. Darlene curled up next to him and they wept.

Earl would never have admitted it, at least not to his friends at the Elks Club, but he was having his own doubts about the politics of war. Carl dodging the draft would've been anathema to him just one month earlier but now things had changed. Earl was a God-fearing patriot, but he would not sacrifice the only son he had left.

13

THE RELUCTANT CO-CONSPIRATOR

JEAN SPENT TWO HOURS BROODING in her bedroom before finally unlocking the door. Lawrence had given up on her and returned to the living room for another belt of Crown Royal. Since the hit and run, he'd alternatively sworn off drinking and then showed a determination to drink himself to death. He'd persuaded himself that he'd done the right thing by leaving Bruce to die on the street and then polishing his bumper. Sure, it may have looked bad, at first blush, but Lawrence believed his role in it had been blown out of proportion. Was it unfortunate? Of course it was—tragic even—but he'd simply been in the wrong place at the wrong time.

Lawrence believed this defense should have exonerated him. The only reasonable punishment should have been a ticket for leaving the scene of an accident, an accident that hadn't been his fault. This slow necrosis of the soul, or at least of reason, may have been obvious to a disinterested passerby but not to Lawrence who was able to discard personal responsibility like a used condom.

Jean had finally emerged from the back bedroom with puffy eyes and smeared mascara. "I can't believe what you've done."

"I'm sorry it happened but it wasn't my fault."

"Please, Lawrence. He was a child. *A child!*"

"He may have been a child but he was old enough to know better than to dart out into the street."

"So you left him to die."

"He was essentially already dead."

"No, Lawrence, he lived for over two hours. Two hours. You could have saved him. So, please, don't try to justify your monstrous behavior. Not to me."

Lawrence had had enough of Jean and her drama. He was sad, too, but all this blame was doing no good. "Think!" he said as he emphatically tapped his temple with his finger. "Think, Jean, think!"

"Oh, I've thought plenty."

"Then you know it was an accident and there is nothing we can do about it at this point."

"I will never be able to understand how you could leave him, Lawrence. Never. But now I have no choice. You've left me with no choice."

"And what is that supposed to mean?"

"You know I can't tell anyone. No one can ever know. No one. Of course, you already know this."

Lawrence nodded, enormously relieved to learn that she hadn't been in the bedroom dialing the Riverside County Sheriff's Office.

He jiggled the ice in his glass and took another sip, a gulp really, then stood and turned to the bar.

"I'll need an alibi," he said. "If it comes to that."

"You were home all night with me, I remember that quite clearly," she said with bitterness, for now she had become a willful co-conspirator, albeit a reluctant one.

Nothing else was said about it. There had been no role-play-ing or rehearsing for when the police might show up. Jean had simply turned and walked back to the bedroom. Lawrence heard the door close again and listened for the click of the lock. Even though he didn't hear it, he knew this was no time to celebrate. He did, however, pour himself another drink.

———

Jean met her friends for brunch the following day at the country club where they gossiped about Shirley Weinstein's outfit at the club's Christmas party. "Honestly, it was ghastly!" And there was the matter of that lush, Barb Gilmore. "The way she flirted with every man there. My God, she ought to be ashamed of herself. Why, I wouldn't let my Frank any-where near her!"

They ordered their array of salads with dressing on the side and idly chatted over the tinkling piano music in the back-ground. The tip jar on top of the piano held only the stale seed money the pianist had contributed to his own cause. "Is it too early for a glass of wine?" The others hesitated to prove they weren't lushes when, really, they mostly were. Jean ordered a glass of chardonnay and the rest of them followed suit. "Oh, why not." After gossiping about a friend who wasn't there and her penchant for calling balls out on the tennis court, the conversation soon drifted to the mystery on Orchard Drive as Jean feared it might.

"Who on earth would hit a child and leave him to die on the side of the street? My Lord, the poor child."

"A monster, that's who. A monster who ought to rot in jail."

"Maybe the driver didn't realize he'd hit him," said Jean.

"Not on your life. The newspaper said he knocked the poor thing over thirty feet. Knocked him right out of his shoes! I can't believe for a second the driver didn't know."

"Well, maybe the boy ran out in front of him," said Jean.

"And so what if he did? You wouldn't stop if a child ran out in front of you? You wouldn't call for help? You'd just drive away? My God, it's the most barbaric thing I've ever heard."

"We just don't know what happened," said Jean, "so it's hard to know what we'd do." She'd crossed a line with these women because normally she would've been the one doling out the torches and pitchforks and rallying the townsfolk.

"Well, listen to you, Jean Montgomery! It sounds like you think he deserves nothing more than a slap on the wrist!"

"No, I just think we ought to reserve judgment until we see if he's caught and then find out what really happened."

A few of the women cocked their heads and frowned, as if perhaps they hadn't heard her correctly. Reserve judgment? These women were accustomed to no such thing. They were like black buzzards circling over a hit deer on the highway, salivating at the chance to devour a mad killer and Jean Montgomery was taking the fun right out of it. How were they supposed to enjoy their cobb salads with Jean sitting over there trying to reserve judgment? Why, it ruined a perfectly good lunch.

The conversation then shifted to another uncomfortable topic for Jean. Mitsy Bateman hinted that her husband, Phil, was working late more often than not. Did she look at Jean a moment too long, or did Jean just imagine it? Did Mitsy suspect something? The others comforted Mitsy. "No, not Phil," they all said. Jean pushed her salad around her plate desperately hoping the subject would change again before they began to speculate who the other woman might be.

They finished lunch and one of them asked to have the bill split equally. Jean knew she ought to lie low but she was too cheap not to mention that her salad was a small one and everyone else got a large. And she only had one bite of the appetizer they'd bought for the table. So they spent five minutes on the math. Jean put her money on the table and excused herself. The others were relieved she was leaving because now they could finish their wine and gossip about her and her stinginess. "And I've heard she's a trust funder to boot!"

Jean and Mitsy were friends and Jean felt bad about the way she'd been meeting Phil recently at her house for romps behind Mitsy's back. Their friendship, such as it was, was not bonded in loyalty. There was a contagious form of envy between the two most attractive women in the neighborhood. So, they were superficial friends who disliked each other with cordial enthusiasm. Nevertheless, despite Jean's aversion to Mitsy's competitive beauty, she actually felt worse about betraying Mitsy than she did about betraying Lawrence. This, however, was a betrayal she had learned to overcome.

Jean drove past the scene of the crime on her way home from the club. The backhoe had been removed along with the mound of dirt, but there was still dirt on the sidewalk and a pick-up truck was parked where the backhoe had been. She almost vomited when she saw the dark stains near the gutter.

Later that afternoon, she paced in her kitchen before finally daring to call Darlene Boynton. She'd previously met Darlene a few times because Jean's youngest son was a year older than Carl Boynton and had been on the same Little League team. But

Darlene wasn't a member of the country club, was fairly frumpy, and didn't hob-knob with the privileged crowd, so it'd been fairly easy to dismiss her.

She'd told Darlene on the phone how sorry she was to have heard the dreadful news and could she please bring them dinner the next night. Jean hung up before she burped up the fact that she slept with the man who'd done it. Darlene had been touched by the charity, especially coming from someone she hardly even knew.

Jean spent hours preparing the meat loaf with homemade tomato sauce for the Boyntons, pouring all her hope for forgiveness into the venture. When she finished, she scrubbed her kitchen down like she was wiping evidence from a crime scene.

14

BECKY'S PICKLE

BECKY HAD A LOT ON HER PLATE. There was her school work and the tuba lessons as well as the sewing class her mom made her take. There was her relationship with Jian Wang that had become stormy of late, and there was her little brother's tragic hit and run. Oh, and she was pregnant at sixteen without ever having been on a date and her teenage lover was a boy from China who had no clue that his little factory had spawned a fetus.

There were many reasons to rue her pregnancy. Up to this point in her life, her greatest desire (aside from having clear skin and an arsenal of boyfriends) was to own The Monkees Greatest Hits album. And now this. She was only a teenager so she'd lose the remainder of her childhood. There was also the question of how she would support the child on her babysitting money. And, of course, she knew her parents would flip out because they were conservative, church-going Christians with a manicured list of Do's and Don'ts's (and a fundamental Don't was getting pregnant at sixteen). They would claim her lovemaking was immoral. And perhaps it was, Becky thought, even though she knew that most of God's creatures did it whenever the itch arose, and appeared to do so without any apparent shame. After all, no one scoffs at the immorality of two goats in the pasture, regardless of their ages.

Becky stressed about the dilemma for weeks. How would she tell Jian? Would he surprise her with a ring? Would they have a spring or summer wedding? What would their colors be? And what about their wedding song? Oh, and the venue, she forgot about the venue. Finally, the stress over her bridesmaids—who to ask, who to exclude—caused her to break out. And she didn't want to tell Jian about their forthcoming marriage when her face was covered with zits.

But she had to tell *someone* because it was killing her to hold it inside. She finally decided to tell Marjorie which was risky because Marjorie was insufferably self-righteous and believed it was a sin to go beyond first base. And with a foreigner to boot? Not good. It was only in private that Marjorie longed for a boy who found her attractive enough to give it a go. And when no boy was forthcoming, she demanded that Becky share her commitment to virginity.

"So, Jian and I, you know Jian, right?"

"Yeah, that Chinese kid who helps you with your homework?"

"Well, yeah, see, how do I put this? Okay, I'll just tell you. I'm pregnant and he's the father."

Marjorie was floored. Jian Wang? *Jian Wang?* When? How? Where? Becky's diary entry that night was perceptive: *Told M my news today. She freaked out like I knew she would. But mostly it's because she's jealous that I have a boyfriend and she doesn't.*

Becky decided to spring the news on Jian when there was a brief clearing of pimples. They'd skipped sixth period and were downstairs in the Wang's spare bedroom where family and friends would presumably stay when they flocked from Changi to see Knots Berry Farm. The lighting was poor because the only window was a dirty piece of glass at the bottom of a corrugated metal window well. If you stood near the window and bent low you could look up and see a sliver of sky.

They were lying on their sides in the queen bed facing each other after desperately re-scratching the itch. Becky's back was to the window well, which was good because it kept her complexion nicely shadowed.

"Jian, I've never loved any other boy as much as I love you and I'm ready to settle down."

"Oh, okay," he said, not comprehending this was how Americans communicated their desire to wed.

"How about you?" she asked. "Are you ready to settle down, too?"

"No. I have biology test in morning so I'm up late to studying."

"No, silly, I mean, do you think you're ready to get married?"

Uh. "Get married?" This was very confusing.

"Well, not like right now, more like in a few months, maybe after school gets out in June or something like that."

"No," Jian said, not yet having mastered the art of subtly, in either language.

"Well, I think we should get married. I'm ready."

Jian stared intently at her trying to figure out what she might be talking about. And the more he stared at her, the more she became self-conscious of the two big whiteheads on her forehead which she'd tried to hide with bangs. This additional stress caused her to begin sweating.

"Well, Jian, aren't you going to say something?"

Jian was unable to speak. He was a kind boy and didn't want to hurt her feelings. Besides, there was the very real possibility that she'd been joking, or that he'd misunderstood her.

Becky turned from her side and lay flat on her back. She awkwardly took his hand and placed it on her stomach, palm down. His hand felt cool and clammy on her skin.

"I know you can't feel anything now, but soon you'll feel her moving inside me. I'm pregnant, Jian, and I think we're going to have a baby girl. I can just tell."

If Jian was speechless before, now he was fully catatonic. Because he was unable to speak, Becky plowed ahead.

"I'm good with pretty much any name. And we can raise her in a Chinese religion too, that is if they have religions in China. If they don't, that's okay, too."

Becky kept talking about strange things like showers and bridesmaids and rental tuxedos while Jian lay on his back looking up at the ceiling. He noticed the acoustic tiles were set in a pattern where each square was perpendicular to the other. He'd never noticed it before, but the smaller pieces of tile around the edges sometimes cheated the pattern, like they were spare pieces the ceiling guy just threw in hoping no one would notice. And probably no one had until this very moment when Jian was lost in his trance as Becky breathlessly yammered on about bibs and formula.

"My parents going to kill me."

"Mine too. But aren't you happy? For us?"

"I can't tell my parents," he said. "What you going to do?"

"Well, this isn't my first choice, but we could just elope and then have a big wedding later. Maybe around Labor Day or something."

"No, I mean about the baby."

"Oh, she'll be so cute. We could decorate her room with Pandas. I heard they grow a lot of those in China."

"I don't want a baby. I don't know what to do with a baby."

"It's not that hard," she said. "I'll stay home with her and you can just work."

"But what about college? This is why we come to United States. So I can study."

"Oh, study schmuddy. You could just eventually take over the café."

Jian was smart but he wasn't a scholar. Everyone assumed he must have been good at math, including his calculus teacher who himself was no scholar but had conquered basic algebra. This teacher had been somewhat intimidated when Jian appeared in his class that first day of school, and was then relieved to learn he knew as much about math as this Asian kid. But, alas, the Wangs hadn't moved to the United States so Jian could drop out of school to become a seventeen-year-old father.

Becky, on the other hand, had no pressure to excel in school. She'd been conditioned to aim for a high school diploma and then become a homemaker. She was jumping the gun a bit, what with this unplanned pregnancy, but that was simply a timing issue. Therefore, it wasn't ideal but it shouldn't have derailed the overall plan.

Becky had assumed she and Jian would sit down to plan colors, polish up the guest list, and decide where to go on their honeymoon (Becky had her heart set on Disneyland). She wanted him to catch the bug about pealing church bells, thrown rice, and a string of tin cans tied to the bumper of an unknown car they didn't own. But after a thirty minute pep talk they were getting nowhere.

Jian was unable to think given the enormity of his stress. As far as Becky was concerned, there was really no choice about the baby. An abortion was unthinkable. When a girl got pregnant the couple married. That's just what you did.

Over the next few weeks they whispered in urgent conspiracy, each trying to persuade the other to be happy with the decision they'd independently made; hers to get married and have the baby, and his to do no such thing. Jian's stress was so overwhelming that his thirst to fornicate had been thoroughly quenched. Besides, Becky was no longer the delightful little plaything that'd been so much fun in the basement. She was ornery and unpredictable and the very thought of having sex with her caused him to rue the day he'd ever been dumb enough to do such a thing in the first place.

15

THE MONEY SHOT FOR JESUS

REVEREND JIMMY WAS SAD for the Boynton's loss, of course he was. But he also knew there was opportunity in heartbreak if you knew where to look for it. That's why Jimmy chose the Boynton's tragedy to promote the Tower of Power.

Some thought it was in poor taste to raise money for Jesus off the hit-and-run death of a thirteen-year-old boy, that there was nothing inspirational about the tragedy which justified this unabashed cash grab. But those people didn't grasp the righteous concept that the end justified the means.

Reverend Jimmy had visited the Boyntons shortly after the accident. The visit had a dual purpose: to comfort Darlene and Earl as their spiritual leader and to get an update on his investment in the San Juan Uranium Mine. Before Bruce's death, before they were numb to the core, Darlene would have been thrilled to have the Reverend in their home. She would have propped the sofa pillows and vacuumed the carpet into perfectly spaced diamonds. But not now. Lawrence Welk could have dropped by and blown his entire wad of bubbles throughout the house and she probably wouldn't have phoned the neighbors.

Jimmy sat in the Boynton's living room in his wide-lapeled turquoise suit with white stitching. He wore brown cowboy boots that had been hand-tooled from the skin of an unknown reptile. The scent of Old Spice wafted about him. The Reverend assured them, once again, that Bruce was in heaven. Exactly where that was or what Bruce was doing up there as he loitered day after day remained an unspoken mystery.

Jimmy spotted an 8" by 10" photo of Bruce propped on an end table next to the sofa. Darlene had never been crazy about the photo but they'd paid for the sitting so she'd felt obliged to frame it. Bruce looked uncomfortable in the ill-fitting plaid sport coat that'd been a hand-me-down from Carl. And his dad's tie that he'd been forced to wear for the photo had been cinched too tight at the neck and was tucked at least ten inches into his slacks. His hair stood up in spots even though Darlene had licked the palm of her hand and dragged it over his red mop moments before the photograph had been taken.

Before leaving the Boynton's home that afternoon, Reverend Jimmy had asked Earl and Darlene to sit with him on the dais during the next Tower of Power telecast, right next to the singing PIPs. Jimmy had also asked Darlene to bring the photo of Bruce to hold in her lap for the televised service. She'd been too numb to protest.

The church service that morning promised to be a blockbuster. The studio crowd was seated in their Sunday best when the organ music began to play. Several colorful posters were propped on easels within ready view of the cameras. Written on the posters were things like, "Give for Bruce!" and "Jesus is the Balm for our Pain."

Jimmy made a last-minute adjustment to his pelt and licked his lips. Phone bank operators fussed with their hair and readied themselves to look busy taking imaginary donations. A PIP brushed the dandruff from her shoulders. The cameraman stood behind a giant camera with his arm outstretched silently counting down to airtime with his fingers. Five, Four, Three, Two, One, and then pointed to Jimmy.

"Welcome, Brothers and Sisters to another program of the Tower of Power, the Lord's ministry in action!" The applause sign lit up and people in the studio audience obediently clapped. Reverend Jimmy looked dashing. It was amazing what they were doing with synthetic weaves!

"Today we have sadness in our hearts following the tragic death of Bruce Boynton, an innocent thirteen-year-old boy who was hit and killed in a shameful act of cruelty. But Bruce no longer feels pain because he rests comfortably with our Lord and Savior!" The audience agreed that Bruce rested most comfortably with the Lord and proved it with a resounding "Amen!" *"God works in mysterious ways. He tests us with sacrifices to see if we are worthy to live with Him someday."* The PIPs, who had been practicing at the Thursday night prayer group, swayed in perfect rhythm and the audience belted out a nicely synchronized "Hallelujah!"

"What does Jesus require from us to join Bruce one day? Only that we worship Him and not the idol of money, for there is nothing more evil than the lust for money. So how can we show our devotion to Him?" Jimmy smartly allowed this million-dollar inquiry to linger. *"We show Him by sacrificing some of it to His church, for Bruce, and all our loved ones who have passed on."*

This argument was compelling and the sheep agreed they ought to surrender their grimy loot. The cameraman was a professional through and through. He was not, however, a member of the church—was not even a Christian. So, he was bound to wonder why, if the loot was so grimy, they would foist it on Jesus. What was *He* supposed to do with it? Buy a new pair of sandals? A new donkey perhaps? But the cameraman, the professional that he was, soldiered through without a smirk and only a grudging admiration for the sheer audacity of the thing.

"Bruce's grieving parents, Brother and Sister Boynton, are here with us today." The cameraman expertly zoomed in on Darlene and the photo on her lap. This was the money shot for Jesus. Darlene didn't know if she was supposed to smile for the camera, or cry.

"The Boyntons want to see their son on the other side of the veil someday. Help them spread the word of Jesus by making a pledge."

Jimmy stepped over and put his hand on Darlene's shoulder.

"Join with me and pledge a simple gift of $10 to the 'Jesus Loves Bruce' campaign. Imagine if everyone within the sound of my voice who can sympathize with the pain of losing a son like the Boyntons have, and like God the Father who lost His Only Begotten, made a simple pledge of $10?"

Jimmy had done the math. He was only $74,500 from the tip of the thermometer and this campaign would surely put him over the top. At the current pace, Jimmy would soon require a new thermometer that wouldn't cap out at a measly million— it would go to five million, its shaft throbbing with crimson magic marker.

After the program, Jimmy approached Earl who was being consoled by another church member. Jimmy took him by the elbow and led him a few feet away where they stood beneath jigsaw pieces of stained glass depicting Jesus walking on fairly choppy water toward a sailboat. Earl was still sweating from the heat of the television lights and his face and bald head were shiny. Jimmy's powered makeup was starting to run, too, and small rivulets were beginning to form at his faux hairline.

"Thanks for participating in the program today," said Jimmy. "I hope you and Darlene had some fun."

Oh, they'd had a ball all right, sitting on the stage holding a photo of their dead son.

"Listen, how's our little investment coming along?"

"Investment?" Earl was caught off guard because he hadn't expected to provide a shareholder update.

"Yeah, how we doing on the uranium mine?"

"Oh, that. Sure, yeah, that's, uh, that's coming along nicely, I think."

Earl had been derailed by his son's death and hadn't made the mine his top priority. In fact, he hadn't raised a single dime since Jesus went all in with His fifty grand.

"Well, we're counting on you," Jimmy said with a slap on the back. "Don't let us down."

Before Earl could respond, Jimmy had turned toward the phone bank for a report on the day's haul.

———

Reverend Jimmy and Betty Mae returned home to a pot roast following the church service. Betty Mae wanted to invite their son, Darrell, but worried Jimmy would be upset. Their other two children were there, however, along with their passel of children. Jimmy held the children at arm's length because a year earlier his two-year-old grandson had grabbed a fistful of his synthetic weave and yanked it off, much to the astonishment of the other grandchildren who'd never seen grandpa without hair. Jimmy dropped the child and quickly reached for the toupee, hoping to stick it back where it belonged before anyone else noticed.

"Have you heard much from Darrell," their daughter asked.

"Well, your father thinks—"

"He's confused," Jimmy cut in. "That's all there is to it. God knows I've tried to straighten him out but he won't listen."

It is true that Jimmy had tried to realign Darrell's sexual orientation. He constantly reminded him that God obsessed over whose privates Darrell preferred looking at. He even bought a *Playboy* and put it on Darrell's bed after swearing to Betty Mae that he hadn't looked at the photos, hardly even the cover. Unfortunately, this Playboy Therapy was a bust. Darrell hadn't even dog-eared a single page. So, Jimmy retrieved it from Darrell's trash can and hid it under the mattress in the spare bedroom.

Jimmy and Betty Mae knew from the get-go that Darrell was different than his two older brothers. There was the dressing up in his mom's pearls, and the fact that he liked a good Nancy Drew mystery. He'd devour the tattered *Vogues* and *Glamours* fanned on the coffee table where his mom had her weekly shampoo and set. And while other boys in the neighborhood were climbing the neighbor's elm tree with hammers and a mouthful of nails to build the hut, Darrell had been hunkered down over Betty Mae's sewing machine making the curtains.

After the episode with the sleepover, the one where he'd *allegedly* touched the other boy when they were in the sixth grade, word spread that Darrell was, officially, a homo. Even his older brother called him an uckingfay omohay during his homophobic Pig Latin phase. He was ditched repeatedly because he couldn't throw a proper spiral or name the Boston Red Sox starting line-up.

Jimmy reminded his son that he was bringing it on himself. "Listen, Darrell, it's hard to blame them if you're acting like a queer. Just try to fit in, okay? It's not that hard."

Reverend Jimmy and Betty Mae spent hours trying like mad to pray the gay away. But, alas, Darrell's iniquity was too much for even God to overcome. That's when they tried electro-shock therapy. Darrell resisted this effort because, among other fairly obvious things, it was painful. But Darrell was a pleaser so he allowed his nether regions to be hooked up to a series of electrodes before being forced to look at photos of naked pool-boys prancing. If he got an erection, or had any movement at all for that matter, he'd be given an electrical shock.

It came to a head when Darrell refused to go for a third session. Therefore, Jimmy kicked him out of the house. Enough was enough.

Betty Mae hadn't tragically lost her son like Darlene Boynton had, but she'd lost him nevertheless. And the sad kicker was that everyone rallied around Darlene, telling her how wonderful Bruce had been. They reassured her that he was in God's loving arms and Darlene would have a glorious reunion with him someday. But Betty Mae had to live with her pain in private because no one said boo to her about Darrell. The neighbors weren't blind, you know. Worse still, Betty Mae knew that Darlene's son had gone straight to heaven, spotless of sin save for a few errant dirt clods and a couple naughty dreams. But her son Darrell? So, all in all, Betty Mae's loss may have been just as painful.

At least the Tower of Power was doing well. Betty Mae had even become a quasi-celebrity herself. Her expensive wardrobe swelled with each telecast, requiring her to take up most of the closet space in the extra bedrooms, too. Jimmy also traded in her Ford Fairlane for a new Starlight Silver Cadillac because no one could picture Jesus in a Ford Fairlane. People recognized her at Sears with her tall bouffant. It seemed the more righteous she'd become, the higher her beehive rose toward heaven. The sheer number of bobby pins holding it in place was inspiring. The only problem was the wind, for neither Betty Mae nor her husband was particularly fond of it.

16

THE POLE DANCE

DR. LAWRENCE MONTGOMERY was going crazy with worry over his impending arrest. This feeling of dread bubbled just under the surface like a gurgling volcano. In fact, there was very little external evidence other than the bags under his eyes. They'd come to look like small nipple-less breasts, just hanging there with no purpose except to provide clues that he wasn't getting enough sleep, or that he'd hit a thirteen-year-old boy with his car and left him to die on the side of the road. It is also possible those eye bags carried small puddles of alcohol and traces of tonic because Lawrence had been drinking more than ever and it had to go *somewhere*. One thing was clear, however; he didn't lose an ounce of fluid through tears, not having shed a single one since the accident.

Lawrence did not drink because he was sad or to douse his guilt. Lawrence drank because he feared the exposure of his monstrous deed and the booze steeled his nerves.

It had now been five months with no suspicion in his direction and Lawrence realized his fear over the dent was probably overblown. He knew this was no time to let his guard down because the police might be circling like a shark's fin, taking his measure before slipping silently beneath the surface. But was he to suffer with a dent on his beloved Mercedes forever? He was a surgeon who'd gone to Yale and had no business driving a dented car, no business whatsoever.

He was sitting at the kitchen's built-in desk where a coffee mug was crammed full of pens and pencils next to a stack of utility bills. The Yellow Pages were opened in front of him and he thumbed through them as Jean teetered nearby with an eight-ounce pour in her hand. She, too, was drinking more.

"I think I'll take the car in tomorrow morning to have it repaired."

"I suppose you'll do whatever you want," said Jean. "Just leave me out of this."

"I just wanted you to know that I was going to fix it so we can move on with things and not have the constant worry."

"The worry is yours, Lawrence," she lied. "I've already moved on," she lied again, "because there is nothing I can do about it."

"Listen, Jean, I don't want to fight about this. Mistakes were made and I'm going to fix them."

"Mistakes were made. Right. And whose mistakes might those be, Lawrence? And how in God's name are you going to fix them?" Poor Jean had been dragged into this mess and was now forced to carry the bulky sin on her frail shoulders that were accustomed only to the weight of a silk pashmina or muskrat shawl.

"I know I can't turn back the clock and fix the boy. He paid dearly for his misjudgment and now we'll have to live with it."

"So now you're blaming the boy for your drunken mistake?" She shook her head then took a gulp of wine. "You're pathetic, Lawrence. Just pathetic."

Lawrence laughed, but it wasn't joyful.

"What?" Jean asked. "You think this is funny?"

"No, Jean, I suppose it's not." He slammed the Yellow Pages shut and stood from the desk. She took a step back toward the sink. He had never hit her but there was the look in his eye that suggested he might.

"If you'd been driving you would've called the police and waited at the scene, wouldn't you, Jean? You would have demanded a field sobriety test. You'd have said, 'Officer, I'm completely shit-faced and it was totally my fault. Sure, it was dark and the kid jumped out in front of me, but take me to jail because that's where I belong.' Yeah, Jean, that's what you would've done."

They stared at each other for a long time in a stalemate. Jean could not forgive Lawrence and he had no reason to forgive himself, for he had choreographed his version of the events to suit his self-interest and had no desire to expose himself to information that might complicate the narrative he'd created for himself. So, an odor had developed between them, lingering, settling in for the long haul. They tried to disguise it in public, but you could still smell it if you took an honest whiff.

"You're always right, aren't you."

"And you're a sanctimonious, spoiled bitch."

She turned to her bottle of chardonnay and glugged it into her wineglass nearly to the brim before taking it back to the bedroom. She slammed the bedroom door for show and some of the wine sloshed onto her hand. She wiped it on the bedspread.

———————

Lawrence slept in the spare bedroom and the next morning drove the Mercedes to Doug's Auto Body which was within walking distance of his clinic. Doug's had a cheesy logo with the smashed front-end of a cartoon car drooping down to look like a frown. A chain link fence surrounded the property where two savage-looking dogs patrolled. There was the implication that the dogs hadn't been fed.

He opened the glass door and a few bells jingled. The lobby was cluttered with boxes and spare auto parts. It smelled like rubber and burnt coffee, the culprit being a Mr. Coffee that hadn't been cleaned in months and held an inch of black sludge. Next to it were two stacks of Styrofoam cups and a handwritten sign that read, "For Customer Use Only," as if a stampede of non-customers had been sneaking in to drink it.

"Be with you in a jiffy," someone hollered from the back.

Lawrence sat on a plastic chair in front of a coffee table where an assortment of old, swollen magazines were scattered. He picked up a tattered *Car and Driver* just as a middle-aged man appeared from the back, wiping his greasy hands on an even greasier rag. "Frank" was sewn in cursive above the breast pocket of his navy-blue coveralls. Frank was the owner; Doug presumably having died, or been demoted.

"Hot out, ain't it?" Frank said as he lifted his sleeve to wipe the sweat from his forehead. "So, then, what can I do you for?"

"Say," said Lawrence as nonchalantly as he could. "I have this small dent out there on my bumper. I figured you could fix it."

"Well then, let's take us a quick look-see."

They walked out to the parking lot. Frank looked it over then crawled underneath for further inspection. "Whaddya do to 'er?" he called up from under the car. "Give 'er to your teen-ager for the night, did ya?"

"I hit a pole. Pretty stupid, I know. I wasn't going very fast. I just didn't see it and hit it. It was right there in front of me but the pole didn't budge." Lawrence chuckled nervously. "I guess I was just careless, hitting the pole like I did. I bet you see this kind of thing all the time, running into poles and things." Lawrence was usually deliberate when he spoke, carefully selecting his words because he assumed they'd all be chiseled in stone one day, so important was he. But now Lawrence realized he sounded like a complete moron as he rambled on and on about the pole.

"You got insurance?"

"Yes, but I'll just pay in cash," said Lawrence. "I'm sure my deductible's too high anyway."

"Whatever you say, boss."

Lawrence left the Mercedes at Doug's and walked to work.

———

Roger Flygare was a detective with the County Sheriff's department and the Boynton hit-and-run case was his. Flygare was a disheveled man, the sort who occasionally missed a belt loop and had a small food stain on his golf shirt. He had thick, shaggy eyebrows that had never been trimmed, giving each eye its own little thatched roof. He was a good detective though, rooting around for clues like a truffle pig. Unfortunately, he and his wrongful eyebrows didn't have much to go on.

The detective assumed the vehicle had struck Bruce with its right-front bumper because of the scuff marks on the roadway and the way Bruce had been thrown to the curb. He believed the impact would have left a dent or some other disfiguring mark on the vehicle. He'd canvassed local auto body shops a few days after the accident looking for a repair to the right front side of a bumper, but not one that involved a broken headlight because there'd been no broken glass at the scene. He'd come up empty. Now, six months later he did it again on a lark. Perhaps the unrepentant driver had waited until he thought the coast was clear. It was a longshot but Detective Flygare had nothing else to go on.

"Well, this here's the thing," Frank told the detective over the phone. "I had me some fella in here about a week ago with that sorta damage. It was a Cad if I remember right. No, I think it was a Mercedes now that I think on it. Had himself a small dent on the bumper there in the front. Guy paid in cash."

"Can you recall anything else about him? Did he say how it'd been damaged or anything like that?"

"Well, let's see, he was a big guy, dressed fancy. I remember him saying something about a pole."

"A pole?"

"Yeah, guy said he'd hit a pole and made quite a point about it, too. Must've told me it was a pole about ten times, which I thought was a bit strange if you know what I mean. Course, I don't give a rat's ass about any of that, if you'll pardon the French and all."

"Was the damage consistent with what you'd see if you'd hit a pole?"

"Well, I suppose that depends on the pole now, don't it," said Frank. "But there wasn't no paint transfer, I can tell you that."

"What does that tell you?"

"Well, it tells me he probably didn't hit another car or anything else with some paint on it. Course, most poles don't have paint on 'em either."

"Can you get me his name?"

"I suppose it'd be there in the paperwork somewheres. But Bonnie ain't here so it'll take me some time to rustle it up."

"See what you can do. I'll be by in an hour."

––––––––––

It was a startling coincidence that the Montgomery's neighbor, the obnoxious one who sat in his folding lawn chair on his driveway jotting down the license plate numbers of speeders, had placed a call into the sheriff's office a few days earlier. He'd called in to report the Montgomery's Mercedes had a small dent on its front bumper. Could this mean Dr. Montgomery was the guilty party? This neighbor's wife was embarrassed by her husband and his reputation, a reputation that did not endear them to the neighborhood. Why, they hadn't even been invited to the Drake's annual chili fest and she knew it was because of her husband's antics. "Please, do not call the police, Richard. Please don't get involved in this. Mitsy Bateman won't even look at me ever since you reported her for speeding." But Richard would not be deterred, not when lawlessness ran amok in their neighborhood.

––––––––––

Lawrence finished his afternoon round of golf at the club and changed into a clean dress shirt and tan slacks, the cuffs brushing the top of his loafers. He was in a good mood because he'd won a twenty-dollar bet with his snobbish friends who hadn't seen him kick his ball out from under a bush on the twelfth hole. He didn't want to go home and face another evening of Jean and her petty judgment, so he tarried over a whiskey sour at the club before finally going home to endure another evening of her disapproval.

He'd been home for about an hour when the doorbell rang. Jean was in the bedroom with the door closed doing god knows what so Lawrence answered it, a tumbler in hand. A disheveled man with bushy eyebrows and mustache stood on the porch.

"Mr. Montgomery? Lawrence Montgomery?"

"Yes, I'm Dr. Montgomery."

"My name is Roger Flygare and I'm a detective with the Riverside County Sheriff's office. May I come in?"

Lawrence almost dropped his glass of booze right there on the spot. What was he supposed to say? Was he supposed to take the Fifth right off the bat? Or was he supposed to deny Flygare entry until he produced a valid search warrant to inspect his bumper? Lawrence quickly composed himself and invited the detective in from the front porch.

"How can I help you, Officer?"

"Do you own a 1970 Mercedes?"

"Yes, why? Is there something wrong?"

"Several months ago, there was a hit and run accident several blocks from here up on Orchard Drive. Maybe you heard about it?"

"Yes, I vaguely remember that. A young boy was killed, right?"

"That's right."

"So, how can I help you?"

"You recently had your car repaired."

"Yes, I'd hit a pole in a parking lot down off Jackson. Why do you ask?"

"When was that?"

"Oh, golly, maybe what, two weeks ago?"

"Where were you the night of the accident?"

"What accident? Oh, you mean the night the boy was hit?"

"Yes."

"I was home that night," said Lawrence. "The only reason I remember is because the next morning my wife and I were saying how it could have happened right out front and we wouldn't have known a thing."

"You were with your wife that evening?"

"Yes."

"Did you leave that night for any reason?"

"No."

"Is your wife here now?"

"She is. Let me go grab her."

Lawrence walked back to the bedroom and knocked on the door before opening it. Jean was lying on the bed reading one of her romance novels with an empty wine glass on the bedstand. She didn't look up.

"Listen Jean, it's a detective from the sheriff's office. He's here. He's asking about the accident."

Jean did not respond, didn't even look up.

"He knows I had my front bumper repaired. I told him we were home that night. I told him I had it fixed because I'd hit a pole a few weeks ago. Now he wants to talk to you."

Jean finally looked up at him for a long moment, expressionless.

"Please, Jean," he pleaded.

She marked her place in the book with a letter opener, stood, and walked out of the room without saying a word. Lawrence trailed her down the hall and into the living room like a hopeful puppy.

"Hello," she said to Detective Flygare. "I'm Jean Montgomery, Dr. Montgomery's wife."

"Hello, Mrs. Montgomery. My name is Roger Flygare and I'm a detective with the Riverside Sheriff's Office. I was just asking your husband about any information he might have concerning the hit and run up on Orchard a few months ago."

"Oh my, that was awful. We were so sorry to hear about it."

"Your husband said you were home that night."

"We were."

"Did either of you leave the house for any reason?"

"No, we were in for the night watching television. I specifically remember because the next morning I was talking about it with some friends at the country club when another woman told me of the accident. I was shocked—we both were."

"And both you and your husband were home all evening?"

"That's right."

"And neither one of you left for any reason?"

"No, I'm certain of it. Why?"

"We're following up on any possible leads. Apparently, your husband recently had his car repaired and we wanted to be sure there was no connection to the accident."

"Oh that? Oh my goodness no. Lawrence bumped into a pole a few weeks ago. I told him I didn't think he even needed to have it repaired, but he's such a stickler about that car of his."

After a few more questions and exonerating answers, Flygare left after wishing them both a good evening. He figured the dent was an unhappy coincidence. Even if it wasn't, there was no way to prove otherwise. Even the corroboration from the nosey neighbor was not enough because this particular man was well known to the police department as an annoying, embellishing rat and the dent had been explained away in any event.

If Lawrence thought Jean's Academy-Award-worthy performance signaled a truce between them he was sorely mistaken. His first clue had been when she'd gone to their bedroom after the detective left without saying a word and he heard the click of the lock. His second clue had been when she didn't answer his knock. His third and final clue came twenty minutes later when she emerged from their bedroom with a suitcase and informed him that he would be staying at a motel until further notice.

Lawrence had been kicked out of his own home? To a *motel?* Had she no heart? But after her heroic save, he'd slinked out with the Samsonite without a fight lest she change her mind and recall that Lawrence had indeed left the house in a drunken stupor, returning a few minutes later to buff out the blood from his bumper.

17

THE CHICKEN DROP

TIMMY HAD ALWAYS BEEN A QUIET BOY who was mediocre in dodgeball and had no taste for middle-school fashion. Because of his average-ness, he'd never been embraced by the in-crowd and didn't seem to care. He'd been content to sit alone in the lunchroom if Bruce wasn't around and attend school assemblies all by himself. Preferred it even.

Bruce's death had rocked him to his tighty-whities, for death had no precedent because no one had ever died on him before, not even his grandparents. It had been so sudden and so permanent. Life had always been so reliable but now Timmy's equilibrium was off. He cried for two straight days until his parents informed him that he'd cried enough—that he'd reached the arbitrary cut-off point for mourning.

Bruce had been Timmy's only friend and now that he was gone, sad as it was, Phil and Mitsy hoped Timmy would expand his social circle. Something they didn't see coming, however, happened to Timmy while he moped around feeling sad. His contrariness was nuanced at first—he grew his hair a little longer, spent hours listening to rock and roll on his transistor radio, and hung a poster of The Doors on his bedroom wall—innocent symptoms that wouldn't necessarily portend trouble. But then his contrariness became less nuanced when he sassed Mitsy and started hanging out with the hoods who smoked Camels behind the school and skipped class.

Mitsy was horrified by this anarchy. Their perfectly tamed child had become a full-blown hood and they realized their influence over him might have expired. Why wasn't he content to play on his Etch-a-Sketch anymore? Where were the manners? She wanted him to expand his social network but surely not with marauding hoodlums. This new group of friends, however, had no requirements for inclusion and Timmy realized his parents were just like the popular kids at school with their list of conditions for determining who was worthy of them, and who was not.

It was another evening when Phil had come home late again smelling suspiciously floral-scented. He and Mitsy were in their bedroom where Phil was setting out his clothes on the bed for the next day, walking from the closet to the bed and back again.

"Phil, you need to talk to him."

"Fine," he said as he laid three different ties onto his navy pin-stripe suit lying on the bed, then stepped back and cocked his head to consider them, "but I don't see how spending time with me is going to change anything. And, for the record, I think you're overreacting."

"I am most certainly *not* overreacting."

"Yes you are."

An hour later they were in bed with the light off, their backs to each other. Mitsy was convinced Timmy's behavior was mostly Phil's fault, or at least she believed he had the primary responsibility to fix it.

"He wouldn't be this way if you were more involved in his life."

"What's that supposed to mean?"

She sat up and propped the pillow behind her, then reached for the lamp on her nightstand. Phil groaned because he knew she'd process this out loud for another half hour. He actually began listening to her five minutes into the processing when she appeared to lay the blame for Timmy's hood-like behavior squarely at his feet.

"You need to show up more often. Honestly, Phil, you care more about your job than your own son. Maybe if you were his Little League coach or something he wouldn't be so—"

"Wait, you're blaming *me?*" He rolled over to face her. "Are you being serious right now?"

"I just think you need to make more of an effort, that's all I'm saying."

"More of an effort. Got it. In the meantime, it's good to know you're busting your ass at home all day."

"That's a low blow, Phillip. Don't you dare blame me."

"Whatever," he said and rolled back to face the wall.

"Just talk to him. Is that too much to ask? You're his father and he'll listen to you."

"Mitsy, for god's sake, there's nothing I can say that's going to magically fix anything. But I'll talk to him if you'll give it a rest."

So, Phil had his little chat with Timmy to zap the hood away. Unfortunately, it didn't take root and the phone call they received a few days later from the vice-principal of Evergreen Jr. High was proof enough of that. Obviously the actual principal, that dashing, sleeveless-sweater-wearing Ray Gooding couldn't call them, not with the ugly demerit of his little fling with Mitsy wafting about.

The vice-principal reported that Timmy had been caught smoking cigarettes behind the school. Phil and Mitsy, who smoked a pack a day, worried their son was headed for the gates of San Quentin.

Mitsy scheduled a visit with a therapist when Timmy was expelled two weeks later for a prank the teachers didn't think was funny. Timmy and his new hood friends had rounded up some live chickens and smuggled them into a pep rally in the school's auditorium. (They'd tried to round up a few bald eagles because that was the school's mascot but they couldn't find any of those, so the chickens would have to do.) When the lights went out and the program began, an incorrigible hoodlum named Howard gave a low whistle which was the signal to release the chickens from the auditorium's balcony. Several boys, including Timmy, removed their live chickens from paper bags they'd smuggled in and tossed them off the balcony.

The boys had assumed the chickens would fly around the auditorium and amuse the other students with the prank. These southern California kids, however, had no formal barnyard training and didn't know chickens can't fly. Instead, the poor things fluttered and spun to the ground like fighter planes shot down over the Pacific, landing with a thud on the students seated below. That would've been bad enough, but one unlucky chicken landed squarely on Mrs. Harrow's head. Harrow was a humorless prude who taught Algebra and rumor had it that it'd been Timmy's chicken that'd lost its life on her graying bouffant.

Phil didn't think the prank was juvenile detention material; in fact, he thought it was funny. Mitsy though was completely dismayed. Her son was out of control. How could she face another parent-teacher conference? You're Timmy Bateman's mom, you say? The one who smokes behind the school and dropped a live chicken on Mrs. Harrow's bouffant?

Ray Gooding was at once thrilled and frightened by the potential confrontation with the Batemans. Mitsy would have to face him now, but so would her husband, Phil, who had yet to confront him about the wicked little tryst. And it was that likely confrontation that had Gooding on edge.

They were getting ready for bed that evening, a rare evening when Phil was home by six smelling like an ordinary lawyer—just the lingering scent of an early morning squirt of English Leather and not the florally scent of a secretary.

"We've got a big problem on our hands, Phil. A big problem."

"Will you just relax. He's just a kid doing what kids do. You were probably the same way."

"I assure you, Phillip, that I would never have disrupted a school assembly with a turkey prank situation like that."

"It was a chicken."

"Whatever, Phil. That is not the point."

"He thought the chickens could fly. I thought it was pretty funny, myself."

As bad as the chicken drop had been, however, it was learning about Timmy's shoplifting a week later that sent Mitsy into a parental tailspin. Phil had just returned from the office when they got a call from Kmart's head of security. Could one of them please come down to the store off Kensington to retrieve their son who'd been caught shoplifting a Butterfinger?

Phil arrived and was escorted through the store to a windowless back room where Timmy sat forlornly at a breakroom table surrounded by vending machines, employee lockers, and two overweight security guards. He would have preferred that his mom be the one to come fetch him because she was generally the nicer one. Then again, he could never figure her out because sometimes she would freak out over the smallest thing ("That looks like poison ivy! Call the doctor!") and other times she'd do just the opposite ("You swallowed a penny? Don't worry, it'll pass.").

"We apprehended your son as he left the facility with the stolen property," said the security guard as he waved the offending Butterfinger in the air before setting it down on the breakroom table.

Phil turned on Timmy with a stern what-do-you-have-to-say-for-yourself! look.

"I'm sorry dad, it's just that …"

"It's just that what? You have no idea the trouble you're in." Turning to the security guards he said, "I am very sorry our son has done this. It is completely unacceptable and we will not tolerate it." He turned again to Timmy. "How could you? What were you thinking?"

"Ordinarily we involve the police," said one of the security guards. "But—"

"Oh, you'll call the police all right!" said Phil. "This young man needs to be taught a lesson!"

"But, sir, I think we can release him to you with just a warning this time."

"Are you sure, because my son knows better than this and you better believe there will be hell to pay as soon as we get home."

The security guards stole sympathetic glances of pity at each other. "He made a mistake, sir, but we're satisfied he's learned his lesson. Isn't that right, young man?"

Timmy nodded.

"Are you sure?" asked Phil, staring down at Timmy with the glare of hard discipline.

"I'll pay you back," said Timmy.

"Oh, you're damned right you will!" said his father.

"That won't be necessary because—"

"Oh, yes it will!" said Phil.

Timmy had rarely seen his dad this angry. The security guards had strong conservative views about crime and punishment but also had compassion for the young man who they knew would pay dearly for his misdemeanor. When they released him to the custody of his father, they did so reluctantly because they knew the poor kid was in for a whipping.

Phil said nothing until they got in the car. When both doors were closed, Phil started to laugh. Timmy was confused.

"Listen, Timmy, you've got to be smarter than those idiots who run security at places like that. If you're going to steal something, you can't let them catch you."

"But I thought—"

"Just be smarter next time," Phil said and then reached into the pocket of his jacket and pulled out the Butterfinger and tossed it to Timmy's lap. "*That's* the way you do it, okay?"

<h1 style="text-align:center">18</h1>

LEAVING THE PANTRY

DARLENE WAS A MESS. Her depression would not allow her to find interest in anything, not even neighborhood gossip. Others were moving on with their lives but she could not. Even Earl was showing signs of renewal. He'd been able to get out of bed, go to work, and even concentrate on something for a few hours before remembering that his son was dead. But not Darlene. The grief weighed on her like the heavy lead shield the dentist puts over your chest when he x-rays your teeth. The only comfort she found was in sleep but even that refuge was interrupted by dreams of Bruce, that he was still alive, and when she woke she had to reacquaint herself with the reality of his death. Friends said she needed closure.

Darlene tried. She'd crawl out of her wilderness of grief like a mortally wounded animal, determined to go on, but then she'd see his toothbrush in the cup or his cleats by the back door. He was everywhere and nowhere—a balled-up sock behind the sofa, a baseball card under his bed. And when she found a note in his bedroom that he'd written to himself in his juvenile penmanship about her upcoming birthday ("Remember to get mom a present"), she wasn't sure she could survive another moment. Even looking at the toilet made her sad, reflecting on the absence of splashes because Bruce hardly even aimed. It was like an eraser had swiped across a blackboard leaving streaks of chalk that had been her son.

Darlene's sadness, like a fever, would eventually break, but not completely, for there would always be the symptoms—a low-grade numbing that would dull her for the rest of her days, even the happy ones.

Darlene was a prayerful woman and her belief provided comfort. Whereas before she'd merely believed in life after death, now she demanded that it must be so. She daydreamed with confidence about a joyful heavenly reunion with her son without obsessing over the details—like whether they'd be indoors or outdoors, or if they'd eat, sleep, speak English, or wear white tunics. And neither did she consider the possibility that he might be forevermore stuck as a thirteen-year-old boy with a striped T-shirt and tangled mess of red hair. She couldn't imagine lounging on puffy clouds listening to harps all day, but she could imagine a place of ultimate safety for her family.

Darlene hid from her pain in bed, eating her way through the grief. Earl and the kids tiptoed around the issue of her alarming weight gain. Never before had they seen so many Hostess products.

Earl distracted himself with home projects. He even cleaned the rain gutters, balanced on the stepladder straddling a dogwood bush as Mrs. Hobson walked by with her Pekinese straining against its leash. "We haven't seen Darlene. I hope she's well." He spent more time at the office too, working fifteen-hour days to avoid facing the sad truth that Bruce was really dead and his wife was in bed all day getting fat. Even Joy tried to have a better attitude about taking his messages and bringing him coffee, for everyone can sympathize with a heartbroken father. She didn't boast about her ailments for weeks.

Earl found comfort in talking about Bruce, but not Darlene who limited her conversations to safe and superficial topics. For example: "Are we out of potato chips?" or "How do you get grape jelly stains out of the bedsheets?"

Carl, too, was out of sorts. There were ripped shirts with drops of blood from nose bleeds and black eyes from angry fist-fights. Fury was the glue that held him together—furious with the unknown killer and furious with the cops who couldn't find him. He was able to burn off some of that fury holed up in his room, barbells clanging, but even Kent and Alejandro the Mexican were wary of his outbursts. The latest one occurred when a man filled his car with gas at the local Quik Mart and then left it parked in the gas lane while he went inside to grab a soda. When he returned, Carl shoved the poor man who wanted nothing to do with the long-haired bully in the sleeveless sweatshirt. It seemed anything was an accelerant to Carl's rage.

Becky spent her time with Jian or couped up in her bedroom lamenting in her diary about all the injustices that had been foisted upon her. She was so *tired*. She felt fat, too, but her weight gain was diluted by her pre-existing plumpness.

Earl also began pouring his energy into the San Juan Uranium Mine, an investment that'd hit the skids for a few months. Now it was time to rededicate himself to it. And what better way than to go see the mine for himself, road-trip style.

"Darlene, I think it'd be good to get out a bit, maybe take a road trip to see the uranium mine or something."

"I know you're trying, Earl, but I just don't think I'm ready for that."

"Come on, it'll be good to get out."

"I just don't think I could handle it—being away for so long." Earl wasn't sure if she was referring to being away from her bed or from the pantry.

"We could make a vacation out of it," he said. "We could stop for a night at the Golden Nugget in Las Vegas. Come on, it'll be fun."

"I just don't know, Earl. I have so many Thank You cards to write."

"People don't expect a Thank You note because of the accident."

"But who would be here to water the plants?" she asked as she wrestled with the lid on a jar of peanut butter.

"Becky could handle that," said Earl.

"I don't think we dare leave Becky here alone. She's been spending a lot of time with that Wang boy down the street."

"Don't be ridiculous. The kid's an Oriental and Becky's not interested in him. At least not in that way. Maybe that Marjorie girl can stay over with her."

Earl finally talked Darlene into the road trip. She didn't care about the mine but she went along for Earl's sake. She packed a supply of sandwiches, potato chips, and soda pop in the Coleman cooler and they'd been off. Unfortunately, the station wagon overheated before they hit Las Vegas. They pulled over to the shoulder and Earl got out, traffic swooshing by. He opened the hood and was engulfed by a cloud of hot steam before burning the palm of his hand when he grabbed the scalding radiator cap. They sat in the hot car for over an hour on the side of the road with Earl's hand wrapped in a wet T-shirt until the radiator cooled down before finally limping into Vegas where Earl promptly lost twenty dollars at the roulette table.

Earl tried to drum up enthusiasm for a dip in the motel's swimming pool but Darlene felt unmoored, pulled to the motel's bed by the undertow of grief, so Earl spent the evening sitting on a plastic stackable chair just outside the motel room door with a can of Schlitz in his hand, staring at the front grill of their station wagon that was plastered with dead bugs.

When they left Las Vegas the next morning it was already one-hundred degrees and they fought the desert mile after barren mile with the windows rolled down, the hot wind buffeting the station wagon. They were windblown and exhausted by the time they reached the Colorado Plateau in southeastern Utah where they checked into a dingy motel with a lumpy bed that squeaked whenever either of them moved. And because it was so uncomfortable, there was much tossing and turning which led to a lot of squeaking. On a bright note, the bed was so disagreeable that at least Darlene was anxious to leave it.

They'd driven southwest another forty miles the following day with the Rand McNally road atlas on Darlene's lap when they spotted a silver Airstream trailer parked off the side of a dirt road that seemingly led nowhere. The dirt road wasn't even on the map. They pulled up to the trailer dragging a tail of dust. There was no sign announcing they'd arrived at the showy headquarters of the San Jaun Uranium Mine Company, only a faded bumper sticker on the trailer that read: *It's Nixon in '60!* It was a modest main office—no, it *aspired* to be a modest main office.

A canvas awning stretched from the trailer to shade the patio, as it were. A mangy dog was tied to one of the poles supporting the awning. The dog showed its teeth and yanked on its chain causing Earl to jump back. It then stared at Earl with contempt for his inferiority because Earl needed the chain to be safe from it, and both man and beast knew it.

Harvey Pratt emerged from the trailer holding a tin cup of black coffee. He was the brains and brawn behind this enterprise that was befitting of its lofty headquarters.

"You must be Earl and the missus. I'm Harv," he said and held out his calloused hand. He wore a sweat-stained cowboy hat and a ragged DeWalt T-shirt. The outline of a thick wallet was worn into the back pocket of his dirty jeans.

"Oh, don't mind him," he nodded toward the dog. "He's all bark. Ain't ya Fang."

"It's nice to finally meet you," Earl said, giving Fang a wide berth. "I've been anxious to see the operation."

"Well, then come on inside and I'll show you some maps and what not." A cigarette hung from his mouth and bounced with each word he spoke, the ash on it long. He took one more drag and dropped the cigarette to the dirt, shifting the heel of his boot from side to side to snuff it out.

Earl and Darlene followed him up the metal step and into the trailer that tipped with their weight. There was barely room for the three of them inside, which smelled like dirty socks, mosquito repellant, stale cigarettes, and B.O. Harv cleared a dirty mess kit and deck of cards from the table top and unrolled a smudged map. He then hunched over it enthusiastically, stabbing his finger at areas where his "gut instinction" told him there was uranium.

This presentation did not inspire confidence. Maybe a nifty slideshow would have eased the concern but not this. Earl tried to muster excitement for the project but Darlene knew he just *had* to be disappointed.

"So, when do we start digging," asked Earl.

"You kiddin' me? We've been diggin' for weeks now! Got us a backhoe down where there's probably a bunch of the stuff. Come on, I'll show ya."

Harv stepped out of the trailer that rocked from his weight. Darlene caught Earl's eye but he quickly looked away because he didn't want to see the truth in her look. Instead he made a be-my-guest gesture with his hand and stepped aside.

"We can take my truck here," Harv said, pointing to an old pickup with bald tires. "Thought about buying me a new one with all the investment money, you know, but then I decided againer seems as how we're runnin' sa low on money."

Earl pulled on the squeaky passenger door and he and Darlene stepped up into the filthy cab. Harv moved a thermos, more rolled up maps, and a pair of dirty underwear (which Darlene chose not to ponder upon), and they rumbled toward their meal ticket. Fang disappeared in the dust behind them, barking and flinging himself again and again against the chain wrapped around his throat.

They crested a hill and saw a single dirty-yellow backhoe out in the middle of the forsaken badlands of southeastern Utah. When she saw the lonely backhoe, Darlene thought of Bruce's accident and was hurled back into despair.

They pulled up next to a hole the size of a backyard swimming pool. Harv opened his door and they were swamped by the trailing dust. Harv didn't seem to notice, or mind.

"Have we found any uranium so far?" Earl asked.

"Why, hell yes we have! Fact, Bob's got himself a load of ore in his Chevy right now. I'm bettin' there's a shitload of uranium in 'er."

Darlene had so many questions, none of which had anything to do with uranium and atom bombs. For example, did they both live in that trailer? Where was the bathroom? And did their combined IQ exceed 150?

"When do you think there'll be some pay-off for the investors?"

"Soon."

"Really?" Earl asked and shot a hopeful look in Darlene's direction. "You mean like soon as in a few months?"

"Can't really say on that because we got to find the stuff first. But soon after that."

"But I thought you said we'd already found it."

"Well, we just found us a little bit so far. But there's probably more where it come from. The Geiger's been beepin' like a sonofabitch. Course that don't mean uranium per se, but there's bound to be somethin' good down there."

This was not the inspiring pep talk Earl had hoped for. He'd hoped to see a thriving network of tractors, dump trucks, and perhaps a few armored Brinks trucks transporting either high-grade uranium or cash directly from the dig site.

Earl had rolled up the hem of his jeans a few inches and now stood with his hands on his hips, staring down into the hole. "How much money do you have left?"

"We got, what, maybe fifteen thou in the bank? Spent us a damned fortune on the trailer and backhoe, and all the permits and what not."

Anyone with general sobriety could readily see they'd overspent on the trailer, backhoe, permits, and the what nots.

"Do you think that'll be enough?"

"I figure we're gonna need us another hundred grand or so to get 'er off the ground."

Earl was quiet on the long drive home. Darlene tried to be cheery, her grieving temporarily replaced by sympathy for Earl.

"It might still work out," she said.

"I don't know what we're going to do."

———

Reverend Jimmy and Earl were standing in the church's foyer following Jimmy's latest discourse on turning the other cheek, a rare sermon that didn't come with a hard sell. An artist's rendition of the new church building was propped on an easel. And what a rendition it was! It even had drawings of little people milling about in the beautiful gardens to be. The easel stood next to a bulletin board where a flyer about a bake sale was thumbtacked next to an announcement for choir practice.

"So, my friend, how's our uranium mine coming along?" Reverend Jimmy asked with a slap on Earl's back.

"Well, they're working on it," Earl said. "It's slow going, but I think they're finding some uranium."

"Let's hope so. I've got fifty grand in the deal and I'm hoping to double my money." No one could say exactly how Jesus felt about His investment. Did He salivate over the prospect of more uranium or the gobs of cash it would generate? Perhaps. But He might have been so antsy about construction on the brand new building that He didn't even notice the debit from His ledger.

"It looks like they might need more money, Reverend. The equipment's been expensive."

"You think they'll run out?"

"Harvey Pratt told me they might need another hundred thousand to get it off the ground."

Reverend Jimmy was quiet. He knew this was a worrisome sign but he had too much pride to acknowledge that he may have been duped, for Jimmy was accustomed to being the duper and not the dupee.

The next Sunday's service was, by necessity, another fund-raiser. Jimmy had artfully sprinkled in the story of Jesus berating the money changers in the temple—just enough Bible talk to satisfy the spiritual requirements of the service. The remaining time was spent chastising those who hoarded their filthy rotten lucre. He finished his sermon with a flourish by hinting he might have a private investment for those who had any money left.

After the service, curious Tower of Power fans lined up to hear more about this potential money-making scheme, crowding around Jimmy like the wide-eyed disciples crowded around Jesus on the Mount. He filled them in on the gist of the pyramid scheme that was the San Juan Uranium Mine Company. He told them how it was producing uranium to make atom bombs for the good of the country. This was patriotism in action and was exactly what Jesus wanted—the mother lode of Christian virtue.

19

SAFEWAY

THE ASSISTANT MANAGER WAS HUNCHED over a glazed donut and cup of coffee on the second floor of Safeway. From his small office he could overlook the store below through a one-way mirror. He took great pride in spotting shoplifters. They were too casual as they'd roam the store like disinterested tourists. Surely there's nothing I want in *this* store. These would-be thieves had the irritating habit of not looking directly at the item they were about to steal. Instead, they'd swivel their heads to be on the lookout for potential witnesses. They just looked guilty, for nothing is so conspicuous as the attempt to be inconspicuous. There was a part of him that wanted to coach them—to tell them to go straight to the item they wanted to steal and grab it like a regular paying shopper would do. He expected the occasional teenager but what struck him were the middle-aged women with a tube of Maybelline in their purse.

He had his eye on one such woman in a baggy coat when he spotted two men in the office-supplies aisle who appeared to be in a heated exchange. One wore a starched shirt smartly tucked into a pair of expensive slacks and the other was dressed for mowing the lawn on this particular Saturday morning. Other shoppers were ogling them, keeping their distance but unable to turn away from the unfolding scene. When he saw the well-dressed man shove the other he called 911. Perhaps this was an overreaction, but he was a stickler for the absence of drama in his store.

By the time he ran down the back staircase and into the store, the fight had escalated. Unfortunately for Phil Bateman, his opponent had retaliated for the shove and Phil was now on the tile floor surrounded by magic markers and rolls of scotch tape. Ray Gooding was clearly getting the best of him. Ray had been a college wrestler and even though he was not wearing his earmuffs or the tight-fitting singlet that had snugly cupped his genitals for years, he was accustomed to tangling with other sweaty, desperate males. Phil, on the other hand, was only accustomed to suing them.

Phil would not give up easily, especially after he had been so wronged by the sleeveless argyle-sweater-wearing principal. Besides, Ray Gooding was now handicapped by the assistant manager who'd grabbed him from behind in a bear hug to break up the fight, pinning Ray's arms to his side. This allowed Phil a free shot at Ray's nose. A crowd had gathered to breathlessly watch as their grocery carts formed a parade line of fresh produce, yogurt, and cereal boxes. The sound of Phil's fist to Ray's defenseless nose could be heard all the way to the dairy section.

It was something of a surprise that Phil would find himself at Safeway in the first place because shopping was Mitsy's domain. But he'd gone to buy his own office supplies for his recently remodeled den. This, too, was something of a surprise because Phil would usually steal those supplies from the law firm. When he'd rounded the aisle and saw Ray Gooding internally debating over a set of colored pencils, he snapped.

When the police arrived, they found Ray sitting on an end cap where bags of potato chips had been twenty minutes earlier but were now scattered on the floor. He held a bag of frozen peas to his face and looked thoroughly disheveled. Phil had been kept several feet away from Ray with his shirt ripped and untucked. He was still shouting to anyone who'd listen that he was a lawyer and would sue Ray for assault, in addition to a blockbuster count for alienation of affection.

The police arrested Phil for assault and battery. After all, they had to do *something* because Ray's nose was still on his face but loosely out of position. Even though Phil had started the altercation with the shove and ended it with his punch to Ray's unprotected nose, he believed his arrest was an outrageous affront to the legal system he professed to cherish.

"But he slept with my wife!" he shouted.

There were several unhappy circumstances in the aisle that morning, but perhaps none more than the fact that Mrs. Hobson was an eyewitness to the assault and, more importantly, to Phil's public revelation that Mitsy had been sleeping with Ray Gooding. Naturally, Mrs. Hobson was dutybound to report this information to anyone who would listen, and plenty did, their mouths agape.

This was some of the best gossip in the history of the neighborhood, even rivaling the time Milton Osterloe, a fifty-year-old dentist with five kids, had been caught straddling the petunias late one night with his eye to the bedroom window of a recently divorced young woman two years earlier. And good gossip like that spreads. Phil Bateman assaulted Ray Gooding at Safeway?

Our Phil Bateman? And Mitsy was having sex with the kids' principal? You mean *that* Mitsy?

Mitsy did not know the particulars of the fight or of the forthcoming public humiliation when she drove to the jail a few hours later with the bail money. All she'd been told was that Phil had been the victim of a terrible misunderstanding and he would explain it all to her later.

Mitsy was upset that her husband had been arrested, of course she was, but she was pleasantly flattered that Phil had cared enough to hit the man she'd slept with. In fact, she'd been surprised up to that point that he hadn't been more upset—that there had been apathy in his reaction to her affair. This made her wonder if he even cared. But apparently he did! Unfortunately, any newfound affection she might have had toward Phil for protecting her honor vanished when she learned that he had publicly, and quite loudly, broadcast her sexual indiscretion to every shopper at Safeway, including that blabbermouth Mrs. Hobson.

Phil was embarrassed that he'd been arrested for assault, humiliated actually, and word of the arrest quickly spread within the legal community. Secretaries at his law firm pretended they didn't know the first thing about it but Phil noticed they abruptly stopped their whispering whenever he walked by. He was even more embarrassed, however, for having so publicly declared the underlying reason for the assault—that he'd been lacking in the bedroom and his wife had been forced to seek satisfaction elsewhere.

Timmy was embarrassed, too, but not because his dad had slugged Ray Gooding in the nose. It was because of the reason he'd done it. His mom and Mr. Gooding had been doing it?

Gross. Fortunately, he didn't see much of the principal for the remainder of the school year because Gooding had holed up in his office to nurse his nose and his pride.

In an odd way, the Chicken Drop had caused Timmy's stock to rise at school. He'd suddenly become popular. He hadn't sought it out, but it was nice when the eighth-grade girls discovered this shy boy with a daring sense of adventure. The boys, too, admired him for the prank, especially when it'd been his chicken that'd landed on Mrs. Harrow's bouffant. And now his dad had smacked the principal in the nose? Timmy's standing in the locker room skyrocketed. Come to the party Saturday night! Oh, and tell your dad he's a stud!

20

BECKY FESSES UP

DARLENE DIDN'T NOTICE HER DAUGHTER'S strange behavior that winter. She was so mired in her own grief that Becky could have grown a handlebar mustache and she probably wouldn't have noticed it. Darlene would later despair that she hadn't been there for her pregnant teenage daughter because that's what most mom's do, they despair.

Becky and Jian's relationship had been strained ever since Becky dropped the stink bomb. And the more she talked about cribs and wedding bands, the more Jian longed for the good old days when he'd been an innocent virgin—before his seed had been decisively planted in Becky's fertile soil.

The carefree months of after-school sex had screeched to a halt. Jian barely even wanted to touch her because of the impending doom she represented. Becky felt bad that Jian no longer wanted to touch her, so she cried. He felt bad when she cried, so he touched her. This convinced her that he loved her after all, so she renewed the wedding-song talk. This made him quit touching her.

They were in the school lunchroom on a Friday afternoon, poking their way through Mrs. Paul's fish sticks. Becky wore a wide-lapeled shirt that was unbuttoned two-buttons worth, which was slightly too much, so she'd split the difference with a hidden safety pin. Jian's shirt was buttoned to his neck.

"I'm going to tell my mom today," Becky said.

"Do you must tell them so soon?" Jian naturally preferred to wait until the fetus was on Medicare.

"Jian, we need to tell them. They'll be mad for a few days, but then they'll see how happy we are and support us 100%."

"You don't know my parents. I must go to college."

"You could just go to night school while I stayed home with the baby."

This was the very sort of conversation that inspired Jian to keep his hands to himself. But, alas, the touching had already been done, for the three-ounce fetus now clung for dear life to the wall of Becky's teenage uterus.

Jian lay awake at night trying to come up with a solution. What if he refused to marry her? What if he ran away? What if she miscarried? What if he could prove the baby wasn't his? He came up dry.

Becky's days were spent anguishing over telling her parents and planning a wedding, and her nights were interrupted by disturbing dreams, like being in labor limbo, or giving birth to a litter of spotted puppies.

She'd finally run out of time.

They were in the kitchen after school and Becky stood facing the opened refrigerator door. She saw a scoop of guacamole and almost barfed. "Mom, I need to talk to you."

"Is it urgent? Your father will be home in an hour and I have this casserole I need to get in the oven."

"Yeah, it's pretty important," Becky said as she walked over to the kitchen table and sat.

"Very well then, we haven't talked in a while," Darlene said as she sat at the table facing her daughter. "Are you having boy problems? Is that what this is about?"

"Yeah, I guess you could call it that."

"Oh, Becky honey, boys your age can be so silly. Why, when I was your age, we'd have sock hops and the boys were so immature. We'd stand around and—"

"I'm pregnant."

"—wring our hands because they were so . . . *What!*"

"I'm pregnant."

Darlene stared at her daughter in utter disbelief. How could this be? Becky didn't even know what sexual intercourse was! She'd never even been on a date! It seemed like only yesterday when they'd gone to the school maturation program and both of them had squirmed uncomfortably by such blatant penis and vagina talk.

"You're *pregnant?* But . . . *how?*" This question was largely rhetorical, of course, because Darlene knew the drill. She wasn't even sure she believed in the Immaculate Conception. But *Becky?*

"I found out almost four months ago," Becky said.

"Oh, Becky. You've carried this secret for *four months?*"

"I'm sorry, Mom. It just sort of happened."

Darlene burst into tears. She stood and walked around to the other side of the dinette set, holding onto the table for support. She leaned down and hugged her daughter.

"I'm so sorry I haven't been here for you."

After much crying and mutual apologizing, there were still unanswered questions.

"Becky, honey," she asked, "who is the father?"

Becky looked at her mom with a confused look on her face. "It's Jian. Who else would it be?"

"Jian Wang, the Chinese boy from down the street?" Darlene was strangely fascinated by this turn of events as much as she was horrified.

"Yeah, we're in love and we want to get married. At least that's what I want, but Jian's worried his parents will be mad because they want him to go to college."

Darlene was speechless. Becky, however, finally had someone she could talk to so she plowed ahead. "I'm thinking about a smaller type wedding after the baby is born, probably no more than a hundred people. Our apartment will be really cute and we'll have—"

"*STOP!*" Darlene held up her hands to ward off further assault. "Just stop," she said more softly as she sat back down across the table from Becky.

"So, you're telling me," Darlene said slowly, "that you are four months pregnant and you think you're going to keep the baby and marry this Chinese boy who can't support you and has never even taken you on a single date? No," she began shaking her head slowly at first and then picking up momentum. "No, no, no, that is not possible. *This* is not possible!"

"But, Mom . . . I thought . . ."

"No, this is too much. This is just too much. I'm sorry but I just can't deal with this right now." Darlene stood. "Your father will be home any minute and I need to put dinner in the oven."

Darlene had no idea what she was saying, or doing. She was simply falling back on routine, that monotonous engine of comfort in crisis. She knew that if she let her guard down she'd fall apart.

"Are you going to tell dad?"

"I'll tell him if you want me to."

"Do you think he'll be mad?"

"You know your father. He'll be very upset. But you need to remember that he wants what's best for you."

Becky retreated to her bedroom to wait it out while Darlene made dinner in her Casserole Trance. A poster of the Fab Four was thumb-tacked next to one of just Paul, the cutest Beatle. Her diary with the little lock sat on the nightstand next to her retainer and the jewelry box with the one-armed ballerina. Her last entry had been written a month earlier: *I ♥♥♥ J. Maybe get apartment by the mall??? Afraid M and D will be mad.* Clothes were strewn across her room and covered a chair that she'd never sat on—it was just there to collect clothes.

Humphrey let a long, sorrowful fart and she scolded him. She was already mad at him because he ate money, literally. It might have been the smell of paper money but no one really knew. Anyway, she'd had a dollar bill go missing and figured Humphrey had eaten it. She smiled when she recalled how mad her dad had been a few weeks earlier as he combed through Humphrey's shit pile on the back lawn with a stick trying to retrieve a five.

She heard her dad's car pull up. *Please be in a good mood. Please be in a good mood. Please be in a good mood.* She heard the car door close and then the door from the garage to the kitchen. She listened for the tone of his voice, trying to divine his temper. She then heard the dinette chairs scrape the floor and then she heard her mother crying. A few minutes later she heard them walk down the hall, pass her bedroom door, and into their bedroom. Becky strained to hear them but there was only the click from her clock radio when the numbers flipped over after each minute passed.

Her bedroom door opened fifteen minutes later. It was her dad standing just inside the doorway. His skinny tie was askew and his white shirttail was partially untucked. He said nothing, at first.

"How *could* you?" He waited. "After all we've been through, you would go and do this to us? And you expect us to *accept* it? You expect us to be *happy* for you?"

"But Dad, I—"

"You throw yourself at any boy who will have sex with you? Even a Chink?"

"Earl, honey, please." Darlene touched his arm.

"You are such a disappointment."

Darlene stood slightly behind him, head bent. She, too, was disappointed in what her daughter had done but her daughter was not a disappointment.

"Let me be crystal clear," he said. "That Oriental kid will never set foot in this house. Do you hear me!"

Jian bused tables at the Ming Chinese Café that night, wiping kernels of rice and crumbled fortune cookies from the table tops and carrying a gray bin full of dirty dishes from the dining room to the kitchen and back. He'd thought about calling Becky when he got home but he didn't know her phone number. Besides, tonight was The Night and he half expected a car to come squealing into his driveway and Mr. Boynton to come charging up to the door with a 12-gauge shotgun.

He sat at the small desk in his bedroom which was tidy and neat. A row of sharpened yellow pencils was lined up next to a perfect stack of paper. The only thing on his wall was a Chinese calendar which reminded all lookers that they happened to be living in the year of the Rat. He needed a preamble of sorts. Maybe he'd lead out with the 98% he got on the trig test. It was nearly 11:00 p.m. and his parents would be exhausted when they got home smelling like soy sauce, so he decided to stall a bit longer. It was the same feeling he had when he needed to vomit, an event he hated more than basketball. He'd lay on the sofa or bed for hours with a mixing bowl nearby, trying to tamp down the urge rather than get it over with by kneeling in front of the toilet with a finger down his throat.

———

Darlene stretched the telephone cord from the kitchen to the dining room for more privacy, head bent and a finger stuck in her other ear.

"Hi Bev, it's me."

"Darlene? What's the matter?"

Bev was Darlene's older sister who always assumed something was the matter. She was ruled by fear and nothing terrified her more than Mexicans, rock and roll, sin, and Democrats. But mostly sin, for she was churchgoing. It was for this reason that Aunt Bev had been a last resort.

"It's Becky," Darlene said as she pulled the phone cord even tighter and cupped her hand over the end of the receiver.

"Is it drugs? Is that it?"

"No, it's just that, well, it's just that Becky is pregnant."

Aunt Bev had never married and had no children. There had been whispers over the years that she was incapable of a sexual thought. So, instead of romance with any living being, she was content to be exclusive with Jesus and was constantly on the prowl to stamp out feelings that might tempt her to cheat on Him.

"Was she raped? Is that it?"

"My goodness, no. Why would you say that?"

"Because she ought to know better, that's why."

"Oh Bev, Earl is so upset and I don't know what we're going to do."

Darlene's clouds had been thick and dark, but they'd parted recently. This partial clearing made her feel guilty, as if it somehow betrayed Bruce to have a moment without grief. And now this. But at least Becky's crisis allowed her to focus on something else, for it was impossible to dwell exclusively on Bruce when her sixteen-year-old daughter was four-months pregnant.

"Anyway, Bev, I wondered if maybe, well, if maybe you'd let Becky come down to your place for the summer. I know that's asking a lot and I'd pay you and we could—"

"I suppose that would be all right. But I won't have her out gallivanting, not when she's in my charge."

"Really? You think it would be okay if she came down to Lubbock until the baby is born?"

"I need some help with the garden anyway."

"I don't know what to say." Darlene eased on the cord and moved back into the kitchen.

"Have you talked to her about this?"

"Yes, well, sort of," said Darlene. "She's just finishing her sophomore year in about a month and she's due the first week of September. We thought maybe she could have the baby down there and then come home for her junior year. She might miss the first few weeks, but she'll just have to make do."

"So who is he? The father? Don't tell me he's some Mexican."

"No, he's Chinese."

"*Chinese?* What on earth! Tell me she doesn't plan to keep it."

"Well, Becky says she wants to keep the baby, but you can only imagine how that'd go over."

Later that night, Earl was in bed watching TV on the small black and white television they'd set on top of the bedroom dresser. They had taken the television from Darlene's mother who had gone on a TV strike because television was corrupting the youth.

"So, I talked to Bev."

"Yeah, and what did she say?"

"She said she'd take her until the baby's born."

"Well, good," Earl said. "That way no one will know."

The next day Darlene informed Becky of the plan. Becky didn't know Aunt Bev very well other than she lived somewhere in Texas and had no children. She knew her dad didn't like her but, then again, her dad didn't like anyone on her mom's side of the family.

21

THE X-RAY

JEAN FINALLY ALLOWED LAWRENCE back into the house. He slept in the master bedroom, too, but there was no attempt at intimacy. Actually, Lawrence tried once but was spurned by an ice-cold shoulder. The tension between them was so thick they could barely ford their way through it.

"She'll probably sue—you mark my words," Lawrence said to Jean one evening during their nightly ritual of cocktails and indifference. "She'll go hire some goddamned ambulance chaser and try to take me for all I'm worth. She's as sue-happy as they come."

"Well," said Jean as she swirled her wine glass, "you were careless and it nearly ruined her life."

"Ruined her life, my ass. I didn't even charge for the second surgery. Not a fucking dime."

"It might be hard for you, Lawrence, but try to put yourself in her shoes."

"Jean," he tried valiantly to be patient with her, "it was a simple mistake that could have happened to anyone, okay? It was mostly the nurse's fault anyway—some new broad who doesn't have a clue."

"But you're the captain of the ship in the operating room, as you remind anyone who'll listen."

"You sound like some goddamned ambulance chaser. What in the hell has become of you?"

What had become of her was no secret. She was no longer insatiably awed by him and all his dazzling virtues. She'd come to see him as an arrogant peacock strutting around with his bow tie and collection of navy blazers with gold buttons. He could put in a stitch or hem an abdomen, it was true, but how hard could that be? It was just sewing.

The more Lawrence tried to impress her with his Latin words, words she suspected he might not have entirely understood himself, the less impressed she had become. Mens sana in corpore sano? Really, Lawrence? And if he told one more person that he'd gone to Yale, awkwardly trying to squeeze it into every conversation, she thought she would vomit. Simply put, Jean had had enough.

Cocktail hour kept creeping earlier as their faces became more swollen and corpulent. Lawrence would drive directly from work to the club where he'd have a couple before going home to face Jean, who'd already had a couple herself. They'd have a few more before Jean would retire to the bedroom to read romance novels about better men while Lawrence sat alone in the living room brooding over the fact that Jean no longer believed his talents were the show-stoppers they'd once been. The spotlight that had always been trained on his good side had now been unplugged.

This unraveling could be traced directly back to Bruce Boynton. One thing had led to another, even to the sue-happy woman who was now probably meeting with some personal injury lawyer to sue him for malpractice. After all, if Bruce hadn't flung himself into the car like he did, Lawrence would have been able to focus on Mrs. Clements's surgery.

Mrs. Clements had been referred to Dr. Montgomery for gall bladder removal. The surgery went well and she'd been sewn back up. She returned for follow-up a few days later complaining of pain in her stomach. Lawrence impatiently reminded her that post-surgical pain was to be expected.

"I know, but it's a sharp pain just under my rib cage that I've never had before. It feels like a stabbing pain."

"This is normal, Mrs. Calvin," he said, annoyed by her whining.

"It's Clements," she said.

"Yes, I believe that's what I said."

"Can't I get something more for the pain?"

"We sent you home with enough pain medication. Now, why don't you go on home and call my nurse in a few days if you think you're still having some pain."

After she winced her way out of the clinic, Lawrence wrote a cryptic note in her medical chart. *Patient presents with exaggerated pain suggestive of narcotic pain meds seeking behavior. Additional meds were denied and the patient was encouraged to adopt reasonable expectations for her recovery.* Why were patients so fragile? Why did they whine so much? Why weren't they more appreciative of his vast talents?

When Mrs. Clements returned a few days later with similar complaints, abdominal x-rays were taken and she was sent back to an exam room to wait. Thirty minutes later, Dr. Montgomery barged in. He turned on the back-lit shadow box mounted to the wall and shoved the x-rays up to the clips at the top with practiced efficiency.

The diagnosis was fairly obvious. Indeed, even that sue-happy, symptom-magnifying, narcotic-pill-popping Mrs. Clements could see the problem, for there was a large pair of scissors in the middle of her belly opened like an "X" from her kidneys to her esophagus. It looked like someone had placed an opened pair of pruning shears underneath her before the x-ray had been taken as a prank.

This was a situation where diagnosis was fairly obvious and a sincere apology would've been a prudent first step, followed by a large bouquet of hydrangeas and a Get-Well card personally signed by Lawrence and everyone else at the clinic.

"It appears a foreign object has been left within the chest wall cavity."

Mrs. Clements was speechless, for the object looked rather domestic to her.

"Unfortunately, it appears a nurse may have been careless in counting the equipment used in surgery. I assure you she will be disciplined for this breach."

The only person in the operating room Mrs. Clements had seen before she blacked out was Dr. Montgomery. She also assumed he'd been the one using the scissors.

Mrs. Clements didn't dare move for fear the tip of a scissor would puncture her heart or pop a lung. She was taken directly to the operating room, wincing with every breath, not because it hurt but because she thought it ought to hurt—an understandable form of anticipatory wincing. She was obviously displeased with the medical care and her post-op customer evaluation form was destined to be uncomplimentary, but she hadn't even thought about suing.

Lawrence snipped the stitches and went back in to retrieve his scissors before stitching her back up, sans scissors. His bedside manner improved dramatically with Mrs. Clements, but behind her back he still thought she was being overly dramatic about the whole affair.

Lawrence believed he was a good man who'd been made to suffer disproportionately for his trivial indiscretions. And now he waited for not one, but two shoes to drop; the discovery of his hit and run *and* the scissors lawsuit. And Jean, his goddamned *wife*, seemed to side with the so-called victims.

———————

Jean wanted to confide in someone, but who? She spoke to their daughter who lived in Denver at least once a week and they had a close relationship, but that would not do. It would be a lovely way to get back at Lawrence for his indulgent vanity but why burden her daughter with such an ugly truth?

Jennifer was their daughter. She and her husband, Stan, moved to Virginia about a year before giving birth to their own daughter. This was a welcome cross-country move for Stan who had grown weary of his father-in-law's relentless ridicule over his profession as a mere chiropractor.

Stan's fondness for his father-in-law suffered another blow when their son was born. Jean and Lawrence had traveled to Roanoke for the birth of their grandson but Jennifer went beyond her due date. Lawrence was upset because this delay would cause him to miss his weekly golf game back home at the club. When Jennifer failed to deliver by her due date, Lawrence flew back to southern California to make his tee time and missed the birth two days later.

Whenever Jennifer visited her parents in southern California, Stan found excuses to stay home. If it wasn't a chiropractic convention it would be a patient who needed help with her scoliosis. Stan's absence gave Lawrence unrestricted freedom to comment on his son-in-law's inferior profession. Jennifer would endure her father's preamble long enough to gently change the subject to another of his favored topics, usually having to do with the growing list of things that irritated him: Fat people. Women in spandex. People who improperly use "I" instead of "me" in a sentence. Female drivers. Foreigners. And people who shop with coupons.

22

EARL'S SHOWDOWN WITH JIAN WANG

BECKY AND JIAN STOOD in the school hallway with its rows of gray metal lockers lining the walls. The lockers lead all the way down the hallway to the school's trophy case where the Woodrow Wilson Eagles' last vestige of glory was displayed—a too-big trophy commemorating the 1962 state championship football team. Becky's locker was opened and Jian was horrified to see what was inside—scattered papers, smeared makeup, candy wrappers, and even the dried remains of a few wiped boogers. A photo of Donny Osmond had been taped to the inside of the door.

"So, did you tell them?" Jian asked Becky.

"Yeah."

"Were they mad?"

"No, Jian, they were thrilled. What do you think? Of *course* they were mad. What about your parents? Are they mad, too?"

"I didn't tell yet."

"Why not? We were supposed to do it at the exact same time, remember?"

"I will soon."

"You better hurry because my dad was really mad. He might come over to your house to talk."

Jian turned and looked down the hallway.

The romance had fizzled under the weight of their transgression. Becky's carefree afternoons of unfettered romping had been replaced by long ones filled with her mom's disappointment and her dad's furious silence. And Jian wanted out but couldn't figure out how to do it.

"You better not call me," Becky said, having casually forgotten that Jian had never once called her—didn't even know her phone number. "Because my dad would probably freak out."

She closed her locker and spun the combination lock. "So, you're going to tell them tonight, right? You just need to get it over with."

"Yeah, probably." But there was no conviction in his voice.

"Call me after you do so I'll know."

"What's your number?"

Jian didn't call Becky that night, or the night after that. He was paralyzed by inaction and his stomach lurched every time the Wang's phone rang. But, so far at least, he hadn't yet heard his mom say, "Wang wesidence . . . Oh, hewo Mr. Boy-tone . . . You want come over? Bewwy well."

They still ate lunch together at school, pretending they weren't about to become parents while the other kids talked about summer lifeguarding jobs, scout camps, and trips to the beach.

"Are you going to your graduation? You're supposed to win some award thingee, right?"

"I must work."

Jian was undeniably smart but it was mostly the result of his tireless studying, something that had been ground into him from birth, practically from the time he crowned. He didn't have the marks at Woodrow Wilson to be valedictorian but he probably would've been passed over anyway in favor of a white boy with a neatly circumcised penis.

"Are you going to college?"

"I got a scholarship at Berkeley," he said.

She slid her tray away. "So, like, are you going?"

"I think. But it depends, you know, what happens."

Earl hadn't said boo to Becky in nearly a week, for he was known to effectively wield the Silent Treatment. He'd mostly recently used it when Darlene invited her mother to stay with them for three weeks. It'd been awful—her room was too drafty, the kids were too spoiled, and she insisted everyone hold hands and pray over every meal, prayers that lasted too long and were largely dedicated to pleas that God bless Richard Nixon who was the victim of a smear campaign.

The silent treatment may have been appropriate in that mother-in-law circumstance but it wasn't when he employed it after Darlene switched from whole milk to the two percent. To be fair, Darlene had also used the silent treatment on Earl when she'd found the ticket stub to a girlie show in his pocket following an accounting convention in Las Vegas. Earl said it had probably been a colleague's prank and that he was every bit as upset as she was.

Becky wondered when her dad's stubborn silence would expire. Surely, it would have to end *sometime*. A week later it did, with a simple declaratory statement after they finished dinner.

"Come on, let's go. We're going to talk to that Wang kid."

"But, dad—"

"Why?" asked Carl. "What's going on with the Wang kid?"

"It's nothing," said Darlene.

"Doesn't sound like it."

The short ride over to the Wang's house was quiet. Earl never looked at Becky, just straight ahead with both hands gripping the steering wheel. They pulled the station wagon into Wang's driveway and Earl shoved the gear shift into park. He was already heading for the door by the time Becky got out.

Jian was sitting at his bedroom desk doing homework, trying not to think about his predicament, when he saw the burgundy station wagon with the faux-wood paneling pull into the driveway. *Shit! Shit! Shit!* He peeked through the shutters. Becky's dad looked pissed. *Shit! Shit! Shit!* He had the potent urge to flee—maybe dye his hair, grow a beard, and find a border to cross.

The Wang's doorbell was the type that played a jingle. Mr. Rhinehart had installed it a week before his wife found the love note to his secretary and threw him out on his ear. Earl and Becky now stood on the porch waiting for *Shave and a haircut—two bits!* to finish. Becky cowered behind her dad, leaning against the wrought-iron railing for support. She hoped Mr. and Mrs. Wang were still at the restaurant and Jian was hiding in a closet pretending not to be home.

Jian saw no way out. It was time to face the music. He walked to the front door like a condemned man to the gallows, the death rattle imminent. He opened the door to Mr. Boynton and the mother of his fetus. All that separated them now was the screen door with an elaborately scrolled *"R"* welded into it about waist high, something in an Old English font. This and the doorbell jingle were the only holdovers from the Rhinehart's.

Jian reluctantly opened the screen door, removing the last protective shield between him and Mr. Boynton. "You can come in but nobody is home."

Earl and Becky stepped inside.

"When will your parents be home?"

"Um, not until really late. They work at café." He felt no guilt whatsoever for temporarily wishing he was an orphan.

"Do your parents know about this?"

"Um, I maybe tell them tonight."

"So they don't even *know?* You have impregnated my daughter and your parents don't even *know?*" Earl's face and scalp turned an autumn crimson and his fists curled. Jian took a step back. Becky touched her father's arm.

"I don't want to tell them until I have to." At a minimum, Earl had to respect Jian Wang for his honesty.

"Do you have a job?"

"Uh, not too much. But sometimes I work at the café. I save my money for college."

"How much do you have saved up?"

"$250."

Earl laughed, but there was no humor in it. "$250. And tell me, how do you expect to support a child on $250?"

"Um, I'm not for sure."

"Do you think you're going to have anything to do with this baby?"

Becky, who'd been sitting on the sofa with her head down and her hands tucked under her thighs, looked up hopefully at Jian.

"Um, I don't know."

"Let me make this perfectly clear, Jian Wang." Earl pronounced "John Wang" with scorn, as if he was Earl's least favorite actor of all time. "You are never to speak to my daughter again. Do you understand me?"

"Okay."

"Never."

"Okay."

"You will sign a parental waiver if we ask, and you will have nothing to do with this again."

"Okay."

Becky was furious with her dad and crushed by Jian's willingness to walk away from her life and their love child so easily. But she said nothing in the Wang's living room that evening as she watched her life being torn apart by these two men, each wielding a club and smacking her again and again like a bloated piñata.

23

THE SEA OF GALILEE

BUSINESS WAS ROBUST at the Tower of Power. People wanted their blessings and they wanted them now. The weekly service had been picked up by other syndicates and God-fearing people were investing like mad. There was so much money rolling in that Jesus could've finally upgraded his wardrobe and that sad looking donkey he rode, even after expenses.

Speaking of expenses, the list was long. The travel and clothing budget alone were eye-poppers. Jimmy and Betty Mae had to stay on top of their shopping because Jesus's messengers shouldn't be seen in old jalopies and two-pant polyester suits. The largest chunk, however, went to the entertainment budget because the Tower of Power wanted to properly thank its largest donors. And what better way to say thanks than with a spin on *The Sea of Galilee*?

The Sea of Galilee was eighty feet long from bow to stern. It had a mahogany-paneled dining room, bar, sun deck, and hot tub. It also came with a pool table, theatre room, and four spacious bedrooms. About the only thing it didn't have was a chapel. And it was all tax deductible.

Reverend Jimmy had formed the All Saints Club in a moment of inspired philanthropy. Everyone wanted to get into the club, of course, and everyone was eligible provided they donated the fifty-grand minimum. Once they were a charter member of the ASC, they could remain in the club for annual dues of only fifteen-thousand dollars. Each member was given a special ASC gold pin for their lapel and their photo was hung in the church's hallway next to a handsomely framed print of The Last Supper.

The real plumb for club members, however, was the right to be wined and dined aboard *The Sea of Galilee*. The yacht was moored about an hour away and overnight guests could sail to Catalina Island and back. Each of the lovely staterooms came with T of P embroidered bathrobes and slippers. But even though the staterooms were all impressively appointed, they were not equal in either size or prestige. Members of the ASC were awarded the suites based on their contribution level.

The Beatitudes Suite was the nicest. That's where Reverend Jimmy and Betty Mae stayed. But the Miracle Suite wasn't too shabby. Its walls were painted with murals which paid tribute to all the miracles Jesus performed. The Gethsemane Suite wasn't too bad either, although the décor was a bit morbid, especially when you knew the ending, what with poor Jesus praying so hard and all for naught. Even the Bethlehem Suite was nice enough for an evening at sea, even though it was decorated to look like the inside of a manger. Its walls were painted with images of donkeys, pigs, and straw, and the chandelier was made from tree branches in the shape of a star. One ASC member gently complained it had the feel of a barn, which was disappointing considering his $75,000 donation.

Evenings on *The Sea of Galilee* were congenial. Jimmy would emerge from the Beatitude Suite in time for dinner wearing a white skipper's jacket and blue-silk ascot which went nicely with his jet-black toupee. And Betty Mae looked like Mrs. John Jacob Astor moments before the ship hit the iceberg. Conversation usually centered around inventive ways to raise more money for Jesus. The sheer number of potential fund raisers they'd come up with was impressive but perhaps none of them would be as lucrative as the Sailing for Jesus campaign which boasted a quick loop around the San Diego bay for only $1,000 a pop.

When they'd exhaust potential fundraisers, they could be heard bashing intellectuals and discussing conservative politics. Jimmy treated his guests to lurid descriptions of how intellectuals wouldn't stand a chance in heaven, not a chance. He deftly substituted *intellectuals* for *rich men* when talking about camels and eyes of needles because it made no sense to trash the rich when they were the ones supporting The Work.

"Earl, there's a caller on line two," said Joy, her hair stiff with AquaNet. "Says his name is James Monson."

Earl sat behind his desk combing through accounting ledgers. James Monson, James Monson, James Monson. The name sounded familiar but he couldn't quite place it. "All right, I'll take it."

"Good, that was line two. Oh, and Earl, I might need to leave early today for a doctor's appointment. My gout's been acting up."

"Earl Boynton," he said as he picked up the phone.

"Hi, Earl, it's Jimmy."

"Oh, hello, Reverend."

"Listen, Earl, I was hoping you could give me a little update on the mine."

"Geez, Reverend, I'm not sure I have much to report. I've been preoccupied with some problems at home."

"How soon could you provide me with a progress report?"

"Uh, well, let me call over to the headquarters there and see what I can find out." Earl winced when he referred to the camp trailer as the headquarters.

"That'd be great. Say, Earl, I'm going to be in the southern Utah area in a few weeks. Maybe I'll swing by the project myself to see how she's coming along."

"Well, that would be an option," Earl said. Obviously, he didn't want Reverend Jimmy anywhere near that trailer, or hole.

"Some people have suggested that I give it a blessing."

"A blessing? Give what a blessing?"

"The ground there. You know, where we're digging. I've thought about maybe consecrating the land to invite the Holy Spirit to help us find the stuff."

Earl pictured Reverend Jimmy at the dig site in a three-piece suit. Maybe he'd bring one or two PIPs. He'd be hunched over the edge of the dirt hole imploring God to bless it so it would yield more uranium for the increased production of nuclear bombs.

"Well, Reverend, let me make a few phone calls to see what I can dig up."

"All I want you diggin' up is more uranium!" he said with a chuckle. "Get it?"

Earl hung up and called Harv Pratt. No answer. He called Bob Neely next.

"Y-ello."

"Bob? Earl Boynton here."

"Oh, hey, Earl. We're out here working our tails off."

"Finding any uranium?"

"As a matter of fact we are."

"Excellent!"

"That's not the problem though."

"There's a problem?"

"Well, we're finding out the market's pretty saturated," said Bob. "The government's just not buying anymore." This was true. A year earlier, the Atomic Energy Commission announced the United States government no longer needed uranium. There'd been such a mad rush to find and sell it to the government that now they had *too* much. The boom was over before it even began for the San Juan Uranium Mine Company.

"So, like, what are you saying?"

"Well, I figure we might as well collect what we can. But the price is dropping like a rock and we've pretty much run through our reserves. I'm sick about it, Earl. Just sick about it."

Earl wasn't merely sick about it; he was on life support. His money. His mother-in-law's money. The Reverend's money, no *Jesus's* money. And now it was gone, vanished in the dirt of southern Utah.

24

THE IT

DARLENE AND EARL DROVE BECKY to the Greyhound bus terminal. Becky wasn't sad to be leaving, at least not the type of sad you see in the movies where the clinging endures until the bus driver threatens to close the door, then the looking back, face smashed to the window, waving until your loved one disappears in the distance.

After all, she wasn't leaving much behind. There was an ex-boyfriend who didn't want her or their love child, a disappointed mother, and a father who wouldn't speak to her. She'd already lost Bruce and Carl wasn't around much anymore. Her relationship with Marjorie was strained too, probably because the bulimic virgin was both concerned about Becky's salvation and jealous that she had a boyfriend. But still it was her home and she was sorry to be leaving for a few months to a strange place with a strange aunt. So, all in all, it was more anxiety than sadness.

Becky looked forward to being away from the constant lecturing. When her parents weren't reminding her about her boo-boo, they were telling her what she would do with the baby. But Becky didn't want to give it up for adoption, believing that her child would love her unconditionally. She'd heard of Lizzie Borden, and she knew that most people are in therapy because of their mother issues, but her child would be different and so would she.

The plan had been for Becky to stay with Aunt Bev in Lubbock and deliver the baby there. Darlene would come down a week before the due date to help with the pushing. Papers would be signed and Becky and Darlene would return empty-handed, just in time for Becky to begin her junior year at Woodrow Wilson. This unhappy incident would be forgotten, never to be spoken of again. This plan, however, hadn't been developed by Becky. She hadn't even been consulted.

"Will someone tell me what's going on?" Carl had said. "Why is Becky going to Texas to see Aunt Bev?"

"We just think it will be good for her to get away—maybe take a break and go somewhere new."

"Why?"

"I don't know, Carl," said Darlene. "We just do."

"Just tell him," said Becky.

"Tell me what?"

"I'm pregnant."

Darlene jerked her head in Becky's direction. "This is not something we were—"

"You're shittin' me."

"Language! And this is no one else's business."

"You're pregnant? How? I mean, with who?"

"It's not important," said Earl.

"Not important? My sister is pregnant and it's not important? What the hell is going on?"

"Jian Wang and I are in love."

"That Wang kid? What the fuck? Are you being serious right now?"

Earl slammed his fist to the table and the plates jumped. "One more word, about any of this, and you'll leave this house. Do you hear me?"

"You're seriously pregnant? With that Wang kid?"

"And that information will never leave this home," said Darlene.

Becky sat by herself for the twenty-hour bus ride. There was no air conditioning and the backs of her thighs were slippery with sweat on the vinyl seat. A young man on the bench seat ahead of her scribbled song lyrics into a notebook. There were needle tracks in the crook of his skinny arm. He shared a cigarette with a frail-looking girl who had brassy hair with four-inch dark roots.

There wasn't much to see from Becky's window, just a smattering of podunk, wind-ravaged towns. What did they *do* in these places, she wondered? Strings of songbirds squatted on the drooping power lines that stretched for miles and she wondered why the birds weren't all electrocuted.

The bus had a bathroom the size of a telephone booth which she used every twenty minutes because her bladder was squished between a variety of organs. She'd brace herself against the walls with both hands to negotiate the toilet as the bus swayed and bumped along. She stared at her sweaty face in the cloudy mirror above the sink. It was fuller and bumpier than ever.

Jian. She tried not to think about him.

When the Greyhound finally pulled into the Lubbock depot, Becky saw Aunt Bev sitting primly on a depot bench, gripping her purse with both hands.

"Well then, you're here," Bev said. "Let's have a look at you." Becky obediently stood to be evaluated.

"Keep your posture up," she said as she picked up one of Becky's bags and headed to her Buick LeSabre which bore the tell-tell signs of a hoarder. Becky considered moving the pile of old magazines from the floor to make more room for her feet but realized there would've been no other spot to put them. A cross hung from the rearview mirror along with about five old cardboard-tree air fresheners and a small picture of Saint Christopher on a chain. The drive was awkward because Bev said nothing, at least not to Becky. She did, however, have plenty to say about other drivers who had the audacity to exceed the speed limit by a few mph's. "Look at that idiot. Probably some foreigner who's never driven a car in his life."

The first thing Becky noticed when Aunt Bev pulled into the driveway of her modest home was the plastic four-point buck artfully positioned next to a wishing well that had its own small roof and a hanging bucket. Then she noticed the ceramic bunnies, turtles, and a collection of gnomes that looked a lot like the Seven Dwarfs winding their way through her overgrown gardens. But the centerpiece, the ultimate prize, was a large Easter Island head positioned among the petunias. Its head had been sawed off just above the brow and was used as a planter.

They lugged Becky's suitcases into the small house.

"This is your room. Be careful—I've spent years collecting them."

It turns out that Aunt Bev had an unhealthy fetish for Madam Alexander dolls and stray cats. There had to be at least forty of the dolls displayed on shelves in the guest room. This was disturbing—all those dolls just staring at Becky without blinking.

Even when she got up to pee in the middle of the night they stared. She squeezed her things into the closet after shoving Aunt Bev's collectibles out of the way, including a cardboard box of Christmas scrap which included a nativity set with two wise men, a shepherd with a broken staff, and a three-legged donkey.

And the cats. Becky counted four of them. I like cats, Aunt Bev had told her. "I was going to get another one, but five cats is too many."

Dolls and cats were not the only thing Aunt Bev collected. She was a yard sale junkie who could not resist a bargain— doilies, coffee mugs, shot glasses, and anything made of porcelain. Mostly, however, she appeared to be in the market for anything with a Christian angle which made the house feel like a Jesus shrine. Paintings of Jesus, charcoals of Jesus, and woodcarvings of Jesus. And the crosses! Some were handsomely carved with a desperately pained Jesus wearing only a twisted loin cloth, his head lolling. Those creeped Becky out as much as the dolls did, especially the ones with barbed wire wrapped around his little head and miniature nails through his wrist and feet. Other crosses were vacant but there was the clear implication that Jesus had once been nailed to a facsimile.

Becky lay on the bed to rest her throbbing legs. There was a framed photo of her family on the nightstand and she picked it up. She remembered when it had been taken the summer before. They'd been at the community park just off Orchard Drive for the Fourth of July. Her mom had asked a stranger to take the family photo with their new Kodak Instamatic.

They'd all looked so happy in the photo. Darlene's arm was around Bruce and Earl's hand rested on Carl's shoulder. She was kneeling on the grass in front of Bruce. Now she closed her eyes and tried to remember the feel of the cool grass and how the blades, like tiny sabers, had indented the skin on her knees. What a happy little virgin she'd been. So much had changed since the camera captured that split-second in time.

That first evening, Becky dove into the spaghetti before Aunt Bev reprimanded her. "I don't know what they teach you at your house but around here we say grace." She then grabbed Becky's hand and pled with the Good Lord to bless the food. When she finally wrapped it up, she crossed herself. Becky would come to learn that Aunt Bev prayed and crossed herself before every meal. She didn't bother, however, with snacks or any type of liquid. It may have been wise to bless the meals with such rigor, and maybe even the snacks, because Aunt Bev was a terrible cook. If it couldn't be made in her new Amana microwave then it probably wasn't worth bothering with. The microwave fascinated Aunt Bev who had learned to embrace the benefits of modern technology while simultaneously rejecting basic science.

Aunt Bev was churchgoing and Becky was required to accompany her to services every Sunday morning where the preacher preached sin, and more often than not, the sin of sex. Becky told Aunt Bev that it made her feel bad to hear that her misdemeanor would doom her heavenly prospects. "Well," said Aunt Bev, "if you feel bad, that's how you know it's working."

Becky was homesick and Aunt Bev and her look of stale disappointment made poor company, unless you enjoyed hearing how the country was going down the tubes. If it wasn't a sobering lecture on the dismal state of the nation, it was a discourse on the virtues of Christianity. Unfortunately, Becky had quickly exhausted her scant knowledge of the atonement and had, consequently, run out of things to talk about. At least back home she had the company of Humphrey who had taken a liking to Becky from the start because she allowed him to lounge on her bed where they both farted in peace. Maybe that's why Earl always referred to Humphrey as Becky's dog, as in "Becky's dog shit on the driveway again. Check it for money."

The days passed slowly in the muggy heat. What she needed was an advent calendar for the birth countdown, preferably one with jumbo Snicker bars behind each numbered day because she had thrown in the towel on her weight, and Aunt Bev was good to remind her of it.

Back home, Darlene and Earl rarely spoke of Becky and her condition. To Earl, the baby was simply an It. He figured the local adoption agency would cart It away for display at the It Store until a young couple from the suburbs with a beagle and station wagon strolled through the aisles of Its shopping for a cute one. He did not dwell on the possibility that there would be no takers. And neither did he consider the effect of this abandonment on It whose maternal grandparents pretended didn't exist and whose paternal grandparents didn't even know that It was an It.

———

They picked Darlene up from the airport a week before the due date to help with the pushing. Becky waddled down the terminal with swollen ankles and a cotton summer dress that hiked up in front. Darlene was struck by how big Becky was—her grandchild nearly ripe and ready to drop.

"You can share the guestroom with Becky," Bev said.

"Oh, that would be lovely. I mean, if that's okay with you, Beck."

"Sure, but it seems like she's up all night so I haven't been getting much sleep."

"She?"

"My baby. I have a feeling it's a girl."

No one had speculated about the baby's gender and neither had anyone said boo about baby names. Earl regarded the ill-planned pregnancy as a temporary condition to be overcome by surgical removal, like a malignant growth. And it's rare to name a malignant tumor.

Darlene and Becky went through their usual beauty routines before crawling into bed that first night, routines that appeared to be producing limited results. Darlene smeared Ponds on her face and Becky rubbed castor oil on her stomach because she'd heard it helped prevent stretch marks. "I think it's working," Becky said as Darlene pretended not to see the purple streaks.

It was late summer and muggy but Aunt Bev refused to turn on the air conditioner because of the cost. There was a rotating fan perched on a stool in the corner of the guest room and they also opened the bedroom window to allow the warm breeze that smelled of tamarisk and freshly cut grass to stir the air. Becky rolled her head to look at the family photo on the nightstand. Her baby was a part of that family. How could she give it away? When she rolled her head back, the pillow was slightly cooler, the light sweat on the cotton having chilled a few degrees. It was quiet except for the occasional bark or revved engine.

"Mom," Becky whispered, "I want to keep her."

Darlene was quiet for a few moments.

"Beck, you're not even halfway through high school."

"But, Mom . . ."

Darlene rolled onto her side to face her daughter. "We only want what's best for you."

"But this is what's best for me."

"I know this is tough, but in the long run you'll have babies of your own that you'll raise in a family."

"This *is* a baby of my own and we already belong to a family."

"But, Beck, realistically, how could you possibly manage?"

"You and dad could help me. We could live with you and you could watch her when I went to school."

"You know how your father feels about this."

"But you could talk to him. He'd listen to you."

———

Her water broke on the afternoon two days before her due date and all hell broke loose. Darlene was especially frantic. "Are you hurting?" "Are you sure it was a contraction?" "How sure?" "When was the last one?" "Quick, Bev, time it!" "Where's the hospital suitcase?" "Bev, where'd you put the suitcase? I can't find the suitcase!"

Aunt Bev nervously embraced her newfound civil disobedience as she sped to the hospital at five miles per hour over the posted speed limit. Becky had been told virtually nothing about the birthing process because only five people knew she was pregnant, and two of them were men, another was a childless prude, and the final one was a teenaged bulimic virgin who only had a vague notion about how babies were made. So now, on the way to the hospital, Darlene crammed it all in as quickly as she could. "Don't worry." "Breathe." "You'll know when to push." "Stay calm!"

If Becky thought she'd waltz in and have the hospital staff fall all over itself for this unique, once-in-a-lifetime event, she must have been sorely disappointed. She was put in a waiting room and told to report when her contractions became more consistent. She'd been tempted to fake an enormous contraction, one so grand they'd think she was having quadruplets all at once. But, as most mothers know, it's tougher to fake a contraction than an orgasm and no embellishment is necessary when they come.

For six long hours Becky toiled in labor before she was finally placed into the stirrups. She hardly recognized her mom who looked like the Pillsbury Dough Boy with her hospital gown, shower hat, and mask. Darlene held Becky's sweaty hand that squeezed tight every three minutes. She *had* to push. This was not something she needed to be told. "We just need two more good pushes," the doctor said. We? *We?* The head emerged on their first push, and the shoulders and body were liberated on their second.

Becky's red, blotchy face was covered with tears and sweat. Darlene was bawling, too. After all the tears of sadness, these were finally happy ones. The nurse wrapped the bundle in a pink blanket and laid it on Becky's chest.

25

THE BOONDOGGLE KEYCHAIN

THE MONTGOMERY'S MARRIAGE had deteriorated to the point that it was nearly bone on bone. At first Lawrence had been hurt when Jean demanded a trial separation, but then he became angry. She was going to make him move to an *apartment?* After all he'd been through? After all he'd done for her?

"You're the one who wants to separate," said Lawrence, "so why don't *you* move out?"

"Because this is my home. This is where Jennifer and the kids come to visit."

"It's my home, too. In fact, I paid for it. And as much as it may gall you, Jennifer is also my daughter and I adore Chelsea."

"So much that you wouldn't even stick around for the birth."

"You have blown that completely out of proportion. She repeatedly said the due date was June fourth and that's what I committed to."

"Lawrence, she was born on the sixth."

"Precisely my point."

Jean waited in the living room where she could hear Lawrence from the bedroom muttering loudly enough to be heard over the sound of hangers sliding on the metal rod and masking tape coming off the roll. "Goddamned bitch" and "my own house" were phrases she heard more than once. He emerged with a few cardboard boxes stuffed with clothes, toiletries, and a few kitchen appliances. "You'll regret this," he said before slamming the front door.

Apartment 3F at The Heritage Estates had thin shag carpet and bent venetian blinds. There was also a large yellow stain on the asbestos ceiling in the living room. The cupboards were bare except for a few plates, cups, a box of Rice Chex, and a fifth of Johnnie Walker.

How had it come to this? He didn't belong in a crummy one-bedroom rental. He was a doctor, for god's sake. He'd gone to Yale. His beloved Mercedes was parked in the single parking spot reserved for 3F, flanked by an old Ford Fairlane in 3E with a flat tire and a faded-red landscaping truck in 3G. It could fairly be said that Lawrence was the only tenant at The Heritage Estates who wore a bow tie.

Adding insult to injury was the fact that the woman in 3B had been a patient and had a mouth on her. "Dr. Montgomery? Is that you?" What was he supposed to say? He mumbled something about how his home was undergoing a remodel, then barricaded himself in the apartment and sat on the vinyl sofa drinking the Johnnie Walker from a plastic cup.

He brooded and seethed. How dare Jean kick him out of his own house. Didn't she know he sat on the board of the largest hospital in southern California? Did that mean *nothing?*

The picture in Lawrence's mind was a bleak and dreary one. First, Jean would divorce him and take his money. Then, just to be spiteful, the ungrateful bitch would probably rat him out on the hit and run. And then what? He'd go to jail. He'd lose his job and be stuck in the rental forever, hiding out in shame, fearful of being recognized as the drunken doctor who'd left an innocent boy to die in the gutter. She'd turn Jennifer and his granddaughter against him, too. And Alan, his chiropractor son-in-law, would likely gloat.

Lawrence hit a new low when the sue-happy patient in the scissors case filed a lawsuit against him and his malpractice rates doubled. Her lawyer was the one on all the billboards—the obnoxious one with a goatee and a smirk. "One call, that's all!" Lawrence started drinking earlier in the day and washed himself into bed in the furnished rental with a mattress that felt like a box spring.

It was on such a night when he first considered killing himself. He wasn't afraid of death, per se, or at least he wasn't afraid of being dead (the actual dying part was not something he looked forward to, however). There was even some egotism in his logic, for he believed he would go out at the top of his game, an Ivy League doctor forevermore remembered as a young and vibrant scholar who'd been unfairly maligned.

Lawrence hoped his suicide would cripple Jean with guilt. This was something she deserved for having breached her marital vow to worship him. And now he was left to pay the price of that breach. Jean's moral superiority would soon be exposed for what it was; haughty and naïve. Her once cushy life would end and she'd have to get an actual job. His only regret was that he wouldn't be around to see her suffer.

He thought about overdosing on pills but decided that was too clean. If a principal motivation was to repay Jean, it needed to be grisly—something that would haunt her—the lasting image of what her disloyalty had wrought. Therefore, he decided to shoot himself in the head.

Lawrence owned a rifle but hadn't actually shot it since he and a friend had bagged a deer at the bottom of a ravine ten years earlier. They decided to leave it to rot after dragging it fifty yards because the damned thing was too heavy. But at least he had photographic evidence of his conquest—Lawrence in an orange hunting vest kneeling next to the dead buck with one hand gripping an antler. It was jarring to see him without a bow tie, or a blue blazer with gold buttons, or one with leather patches on the elbows.

A pistol would've been handier because he could aim it squarely at his temple but he didn't own one and was too cheap to spend the money now on something he'd only use once.

He drove from his apartment to retrieve the rifle from a cabinet in his garage. Jean wasn't there, thank god. He figured she was probably out strategizing with some sleazy divorce lawyer. He couldn't have known at the time that she was holed up at the Marriott Suites with Phil Bateman. The lovers would normally rendezvous at Jean's home but they were celebrating Phil's birthday with a bang. Lawrence now walked through his house one last time to admire all the trappings that had defined him. He grabbed a bottle of gin on the way out. Lawrence didn't even like gin but he knew Jean did, so he took it. Let her assuage her guilt by marinating in a bottle of something else.

He found a box of bullets on the garage shelf next to a grimy can of motor oil. He put the rifle into the trunk of his Mercedes and backed out of the garage, then manually pulled the garage door down. It creaked and moaned before finally succumbing to gravity and slamming to the concrete floor.

After leaving his home on Orchard Drive, he drove by the scene of his undoing. Lawrence had polished his version of the accident so often in his mind that he'd come to believe he'd done nothing wrong. He'd been drinking, yes, but that alone should not amount to a crime, at least not a crime so heinous that he should be locked up. Besides, he could handle his liquor and was an accomplished drunk driver. Even Jean would have to acknowledge he could ably drive drunk.

He drove to the office for a few scheduled appointments. Lawrence didn't particularly care about these whiny patients and their goddamned acid refluxes but he wanted to establish for the record what a martyr he'd been—the devoted doctor's final act of selflessness on the day he was to die!

His office was a shrine unto himself. Diplomas had been hung behind his desk to be admired by his patients but there were so many that it diluted what he'd been going for. Jean had recommended, for example, that he not display the certificate for attending a half-day seminar on Managing Medical Records but the swirly calligraphy from a distance promised a more substantial achievement, as did his certificate from the local Kiwanis Club.

Lawrence's diploma from Yale was the real keeper. It was hung separately on its own wall, a testament to its stature and to Lawrence's, too. Lawrence had been slightly disappointed when he'd been awarded the diploma because, even though it was embossed with an elaborate YALE, it was too small for his taste. Therefore, he had it framed with an extra-large matting to give it more heft. On the wall below The Yale there was a bookcase filled with a set of hard-bound Readers Digests that looked, at first glance, like priceless leather-bound tomes. Jean had picked them up at a yard sale because they looked impressive and were "good filler."

He dispatched his few patients that morning with admonitions to lose weight and follow-up in two weeks, making sure his chart notes were thorough and legible so the physician who replaced him could see what a fine doctor he had been. He then removed a bottle of single-malt scotch from the bottom drawer of his desk, poured an inch into a crystal glass designated exclusively for this purpose, and leaned back in his leather wingback.

"Excuse me, Doctor Montgomery." It was Fran, the office manager. Lawrence had promoted her from receptionist to office manager seven years earlier out of default, and because of her deep cleavage. Fran, however, had been plagued with an insatiable appetite ever since the promotion and the remainder of her body had caught up to (and may have surpassed) the plumpness of her bosom.

"What do you need? Can't you see that I'm busy?" Lawrence rarely engaged with the staff at the Mid-Valley Medical Clinic, except perhaps for the new receptionist who looked like Fran had in the days of yore.

"I'm just following up on my request for a raise. It's been three weeks now."

"Yes, but now's not a good time. Can't you see that I'm extremely busy," he said as he tried to hide the glass of booze behind a stack of overdue medical charts.

"Can we schedule a time to talk?" she asked.

"I'll let you know in a few days. Now, if you'll excuse me."

Lawrence finished his drink and poured another one, then pulled a blank piece of paper from his top drawer and laid it on the sheet of glass that covered the top of his desk.

Dear Jean,

When this letter finds you, I will no longer be available to pay for your extravagant lifestyle. I wish you luck with your high school diploma and track record of never having earned a dime.

Ever since that kid ran out in front of me you have treated me like dirt. Sure, I'd been drinking, but I didn't think he'd live regardless of what medical aid I might have given him. As I said, I did it for you. But you have punished me for it ever since. What did you want me to do? Confess? Is that what you wanted? No, of course not. You didn't want to be smeared as the poor wife of a "monster" (your words, not mine). So, you covered for me when the police came, but you didn't do that for me. You did it for yourself.

I hope you'll tell Jennifer that I loved her. I could not always be there for her because I was working to support all of you. That support has now come to an end.
Lawrence

He folded the letter and put it in a plain white envelope. On the outside of the envelope he scribbled *"Important"* and tucked it under a glass paperweight on his desk where his heartbroken fans would find it. He pushed himself up from his chair with a stubborn determination to end his misery and walked out the back door of the clinic without telling the staff he was leaving.

He sat in his car in the parking lot for a few minutes, fingering his keys that were held together by a boondoggle keychain Jennifer had made for him in Girl Scouts years earlier. The keychain was loaded and he spent a melancholy reverie with each key. There was the one to his dream home. He remembered the day they'd moved in; so full of satisfaction at having finally arrived.

There was the key to his office, a key he'd used almost every day because he'd usually be the first one to arrive in the morning and the last one to leave at night.

There was the key to his locker at the country club. He was tempted to go there now and walk through the men's locker room one final time, to smell the Old Spice and Barbasol and run his finger over the felt card table where the boys sipped bourbon and reminded each other of their superiority. Maybe he'd say hello to Mel, the old Negro shoe shiner. What was it with Mel anyway, he wondered? Why in god's name was he always smiling? He wasn't even allowed to play the golf course, even on Employee Day, because of the club's "No Coloreds" policy. All that smiling made no sense to Lawrence—it even annoyed him.

There were other keys, too, and each one reminded him of tortured pleasantness. Take, for example, the key to the garage where he stored his boat. It was a good boat but from the moment he bought it he'd wanted a bigger, faster, flashier one. Same thing with the cabin. He'd been happy with it until some rich lawyer built a nicer one next door, and he'd done it, Lawrence knew, simply to show off. When Lawrence complained about roofing materials blowing onto his property, this arrogant lawyer threatened to sue him for harassment. Lawrence wasn't known for his pettiness but this neighbor had no one to blame but himself when Lawrence defecated in the cabin's unfinished basement.

It was muggy and hot and the back of his shirt was wet on the leather seat as he drove without a specific destination in mind. He looked for a secluded spot, but not out in the middle of nowhere where his body might not be discovered for days, all congealed and smelly. Lawrence wanted to be found and he wanted it to be messy, but he didn't want to rot. He came upon a vacant lot at the end of a cul-de-sac in a low-priced subdivision. How appropriate, he thought, that he'd find himself on a dead-end road at this moment. While Lawrence hoped to leave an enduring legacy, and thought he'd earned it, he also conceded the remote and deeply sobering possibility that he might be destined to oblivion.

He parked the car then got out and retrieved the rifle and box of shells from the trunk before returning to the driver's seat. An adolescent boy on a skateboard looped around the end of the cul-de-sac, staring at Lawrence suspiciously through the windshield. After fumbling with the box of shells with sweaty hands, he removed a single bullet from the box and put it in the chamber. He slid his seat back and reclined it a few inches before bringing the end of the barrel to his mouth, the butt of the rifle resting on the floorboard. Soon Lawrence would be gone, swept away like a rabid bat in a gust of wind.

The barrel was oily and had a metallic taste. His hands were shaking and the barrel clicked against his teeth. He thought he may have chipped a tooth and then realized such a vain concern was absurd when his head was about to be blown off.

He didn't put his finger on the trigger just yet because he wanted to enjoy a few more moments of contemplative self-pity—to recount, again, the many injustices that had been foisted upon him, not the least of which had been the unfairness of his role in the hit and run. No one understood. They would crucify him, and Jean would make sure of it out of retribution for . . . for what?

He removed the barrel from his mouth and rested it on his shoulder. The boy on the skate board made another loop in front of his car but could not see the rifle's barrel.

It was his narcissism more than his cowardice which caused Lawrence's hesitation. This primitive view of his self-importance had been the bedrock of his life. It is only a slight exaggeration to say he thought his handsome countenance should be on a postage stamp one day.

Maybe he'd been too hasty. Maybe Jean wouldn't rat him out. She was a bitch, to be sure, but she was a proud bitch and would have to know that if she tattled on him the police would nail her for obstruction of justice. Not only that, but her friends would smear her for the mere association—for having slept with a devil. No, he knew Jean would cling to her station in life with her manicured nails for as long as she could.

What had he been *thinking?* Why should *he* be the one to pay the ultimate price? No! Hell no! His secret was safe because Jean was too egocentric to snitch. He would take back the house he'd paid for! Fuck the apartment. He'd wear his scrubs and drink his vodka. And if she left him? All the better because then he could upgrade to a younger model who knew what it meant to be with a board-certified surgeon.

He started the car and pulled out of the cul-de-sac, glaring at the boy on the skateboard as he passed. The boy flipped him off and Lawrence slammed on his brakes. The boy, however, was fast and disappeared between two houses separated by a chain-link fence with the skateboard under his arm.

Lawrence eventually found his way to Grand Avenue. The street had been misnamed by the city planners in a fit of giddy optimism—unless an ugly string of Chinese restaurants, laundromats, and nail salons met your core definition of grand. His secret was safe and he felt so much better! A block later he was passing through an intersection on a green light, fantasizing about the look on Jean's face when he marched in to reclaim his house, when he saw the greenish blur to his left.

The crash was horrifically loud and violent.

———

It was all so confusing. He'd been in an accident, Lawrence knew that, but he kept drifting in and out of consciousness. He was lying on his back on the hot pavement, the sun stabbing his eyes. People were hovering over him, their voices mumbled. His memories were only fragments. He recalled the ambulance door slamming shut and looking up at the white corrugated ceiling. A paramedic in a black uniform sat next to him. He remembered being wheeled into the ER on a gurney and the airy hiss from the pneumatic sliding door.

He awoke a few hours later in his hospital room. The pain in his leg was sharp and he was still fuzzy in the head. When the doctor realized Lawrence was awake, he began talking down to him the way Lawrence talked down to his own patients. "I set the tibia with a rod and screws. You should be fine but you'll need to be patient. So, if there's nothing further . . ."

Just who in the hell did this arrogant sonofabitch think he was talking to? Where was the professional respect? Didn't this idiot of a doctor know he was talking to an important surgeon with good insurance?

———

The timing of the accident had been poor, at least from Jean's perspective. She was sorry Lawrence had been hurt, but not so sorry that she let him back in the house with a good attitude. It was only a broken leg. Jean was simply there out of marital duty, a fact that was plainly felt by both of them.

The day following his surgery, he called his office and spoke to Fran, the fleshy office manager who was overdue for a raise.

"How *are* you, Doctor Montgomery? We're all concerned for you." This was partially true. No one wished Lawrence harm but there were no plans in the works for balloons and a Get-Well card signed by everyone at the clinic.

"The fracture was quite serious," said Lawrence, "but I'll be up and walking with crutches soon."

"Well, you let us know if there's anything we can do for you."

"Yes, actually let me ask you to bring me my mail. And bring Margaret Johnson's chart note while you're at it. It's on my desk. Oh, and there's an envelope on my desk which you might as well bring as long as you're there. I've labeled it *'Important'* because it concerns my granddaughter's private schooling."

Lawrence didn't care about his mail, and even less about that whiny Margaret Johnson and her chart note. All she needed to do was smear a daily dab of Preparation H, and he'd told her so quite emphatically. It was the suicide note he needed to destroy.

Back at the clinic, Fran collected Lawrence's mail and then stepped into his office to grab the chart note and envelope he'd requested. The envelope labeled *"Important"* was unsealed and she couldn't resist a little peek. She looked over her shoulder, then carefully removed the handwritten note and began to read. She was confused, for it had nothing to do with his granddaughter's school.

She read it again. My god, she thought, this was a *suicide note!* Not only that, but Dr. Montgomery was apparently the one who'd hit and killed that little boy the previous December! Fran would've been less surprised had it been a handwritten letter penned by the Founding Fathers asking Dr. Montgomery how to treat dysentery. She steadied herself with a hand on the glass-topped desk and then sank to his chair.

This was unbelievable. It'd been *Dr. Montgomery?* And now he was going to kill himself? She knew this bombshell might come in handy so she made a copy of the note and placed the original back in the envelope. She buried her copy at the bottom of her purse.

Fran was still reeling in disbelief on the drive over to the hospital. *Dr. Montgomery?* And his wife knew, too? When she arrived, she found Lawrence propped up in the hospital bed smoking a cigarette, his bandaged leg elevated in a sling.

"Just put the mail and the other papers over here by the phone," Lawrence told Fran. "And did you remember Mildred Johnson's chart?"

"Yes, I picked up *Margaret* Johnson's chart for you, and I also picked up that other envelope you'd requested. It's all in the stack of mail here."

"Thanks. Now, if you don't mind, I'm not feeling well so you can leave." And, for the love of God, do not ask me about your goddamned raise.

As soon as Fran left, Lawrence fumbled through the mail and found the envelope. He hadn't sealed it which had been foolish, but he'd figured it didn't matter because he was supposed to be dead by now. Besides, it'd been clear from Fran's reaction that she hadn't opened it. He removed the note from the envelope and ripped it into several small pieces and then lit each one on fire in the ash tray next to his bed so as not to attract the attention of the nurses with a small bonfire. When the entire note was safely incinerated, he was finally able to relax.

He leaned his head back onto the pillow. His mind drifted to the car accident and the idiot woman who'd run the red light. He'd take her to court for all she was worth. Goddamned women drivers.

26

IF ONLY HE'D FONDLED
A PIP INSTEAD

REVEREND JIMMY HAD A NOSE for business and his predatory snout could smell the decaying prospects of the San Juan Uranium Mine Company. He needed a way out. Fortunately, Brother Wendell Johnson, his erstwhile clerk at the Tower of Power, was as gullible as he was loyal. And loyal gullibility spelled trouble when facing a salesman with the moxie of Reverend Jimmy Monson.

Brother Johnson tapped on Jimmy's office door after Sunday services where Jimmy had given a moving sermon on the perils of greed.

"Come in."

"Reverend, I'm concerned that our funds are running low." Brother Johnson was a timid soul who treated Reverend Jimmy like the Pope. "I know they'll bounce back, but there's a lot of overhead tied up in *The Sea of Galilee*."

This wasn't new information. Jimmy was obsessed over the books so he knew *The Sea of Galilee* was gobbling up the widow's mite. But he loved that boat so much.

"Thanks, Brother Johnson. It looks like we'll need some short-term capital to keep promoting the Word."

Jimmy leaned back in his leather wingback and looked up to the ceiling in thought. Meanwhile, Brother Johnson took stock of Jimmy's office. How he wanted an office like this! There was a diploma on the wall behind Jimmy's desk. Jimmy had applied for the mail-in certificate declaring him to be an official Reverend and for an extra thirty dollars they'd included the elaborately scrolled diploma, presumably in compensation for its lack of any merit. A print of Jesus feeding the five thousand with a loaf of bread and a few trout hung on another wall.

Jimmy finally spoke. "I've got a personal investment that's probably going to make me a bundle," he said, "but it doesn't do me any good right now—not when we need the money to thank our donors in the All Saints Club."

"Well, let's just keep praying the work can go forward," said Brother Johnson.

"Yeah, that investment's a darned good one," said Jimmy. "I wish I could keep it but I might have to let 'er go."

"Well, I hope it works out for you."

"Yeah, I wish I could hang on to it but I might need to sell it to someone."

"Okay then, I'd best be leaving now," said Brother Johnson. "Myra's got dinner on."

"Yeah," said Jimmy, "if I knew somebody smart enough to come up with $50,000, maybe take out a second mortgage on their house or something, they'd luck into quite an investment."

"You'll think of someone," said Brother Johnson who was a darn good clerk but generally clueless about the scars of the marketplace.

"Hey, wait a second," said Jimmy, suddenly leaning forward. "I just had a thought. What about *you*, Wendell? Maybe *you* ought to take over this investment of mine. I hate to let it go, but the Lord's message takes priority over my personal financial interests."

"Gosh, Reverend, I don't have $50,000."

"I suppose you could take out a second mortgage."

"You think that's a good idea?" he asked hopefully.

"Well, any investment has some risk to it," said Jimmy. "But I got into it, didn't I?"

"So, what's the investment?"

Jimmy filled him in. For a mere fifty grand, Jimmy would sell his stake in the flailing uranium company. Brother Johnson was flattered that Jimmy would let him in on the deal and arranged to get the money.

Five and a half weeks later, the shareholders of the San Juan Uranium Mine Company, including Brother Johnson who was now the largest shareholder, received the following letter:

Dear Shareholder,

It is with great regret that I announce the dissolution of the San Juan Uranium Mine Company. Our expectations of securing uranium at the site were met but the demand has largely evaporated. The U.S. Military has recently informed us that its stockpiles of uranium are significant. Therefore, it is no longer profitable for us to continue under present market circumstances.

There remains approximately $20,000 in our operating account. We believe that should be returned to our shareholders proportionate to their investment. However, there will be attorney fees and other costs associated with dissolution which must be paid from the money on hand.

We apologize for this unfortunate turn of events. We appreciated your confidence and trust in this project.

Sincerely,

Harvey M. Pratt

President & CEO of SJUMC

Brother Wendell Johnson was floored. He read it again. Surely there'd been a mistake. He called Reverend Jimmy who didn't answer. Wendell was frantic. When he finally reached Jimmy, he'd hoped for a different response than the one he got.

"Yeah, geez, Brother Johnson. Sorry about that. I had no idea things were so rough there. I thought you'd make a bundle. But at least you're going to get *something* back, maybe $5,000 or so."

"But, Reverend, I—"

"I know, I know. Investments are tricky that way. I thought this would be a big winner but, dammit, that's the way the cookie crumbles."

"But, I . . . it just seems like, well, it just seems like I shouldn't have to, you know, lose all my money. Can't you maybe . . . can't you repay me. I mean, it was your investment, Reverend, and I relied on your word."

"I'm pretty broke too because I've put everything I've got into The Tower. But who knows, maybe it'll bounce back."

"But, Reverend, they're dissolving the company. You know that."

Over the next few days, Brother Johnson thought back to the Tower of Power's Christmas party the previous December. It had been a grand affair. Reverend Jimmy had substituted his toupee for Santa's hat and cotton beard and sat in a large, red-suede chair while the kids approached him one by one to grovel.

Brother Johnson's ten-year-old daughter was named Jackie. She'd asked Santa for an Easy Bake Oven and he'd come through. Wendell now recalled, however, that on the drive home from the Christmas party that night, Jackie had said that Santa had "tickled her in a funny place" while she sat on his lap begging for the Easy Bake. He hadn't given it much thought at the time— it'd probably been a simple misunderstanding and Jackie hadn't seemed too troubled by it.

Brother Johnson had now come to believe, however, that Reverend Jimmy had fondled his daughter and should be punished. Because the fondling had been so egregious, he believed the damages should amount to $50,000. He called Jimmy and told him of his daughter's accusation which had now morphed into a formal, lurid allegation by Jackie who'd actually said nothing further about it since the ride home from the Christmas party several months earlier.

"I didn't touch your daughter, Brother Johnson, and I resent your accusation. This is an attempt to extort money from me because you made an unwise investment. Making a charge of child molestation is a crime, and if you think I'm going to sit back and take it, why, you've got another thing coming!"

"Why would my daughter lie, *Reverend?* She doesn't even know what extortion means. It's my daughter's good name that I care about, and I'll not have you going around fondling her!"

"So, what exactly do you want, *Brother* Johnson?"

"I want my daughter to be compensated! You have ruined our lives with your child molestation!"

"Let me guess, *Brother* Johnson. You want $50,000."

"That wouldn't be nearly enough, *Reverend* Monson. But, yes, I would consider it. Otherwise I'll go public with this."

Jimmy decided he needed a break from the stress, so he and Betty Mae took a short spin on *The Sea of Galilee* where he sat in the plush Beatitudes Suite, ruminating. Maybe if he'd touched Sister Fleming, the bustiest PIP, it'd be understandable. Bad to be sure, but not like *this*. No, this would be very bad for business.

While Jimmy lounged in his lair stewing over his dilemma, Brother Johnson was busy persuading both himself and his ten-year-old daughter that she'd been sexually assaulted.

Jackie didn't want to disappoint her father, so her memory improved with his suggestion. Brother Johnson was so upset about losing the money that he did not consider the effect on his daughter by willingly subjecting her to the growing knowledge that she'd been savagely assaulted on Santa's lap. And not by just anyone, but by the Reverend—someone who used his religious power as a shield to insulate himself from the scrutiny of his flock. And, adding insult to injury, it'd been Santa Claus. Who gets molested by Santa Claus? Christmas might never be the same.

The potential damage to the Tower of Power could not be exaggerated. This was unfortunate because everything about the program had been upgraded since the beginning. The early PIPs had been culled for comelier versions, and the men and women sitting at the phone banks were the best-looking people in the entire congregation. They'd even brought in ringers; attractive actors who weren't even church members. One handsome man with white teeth and a dimpled chin was even an atheist. And the way Jimmy spoke so lovingly about the All Saints Club made it difficult to remain unmoved.

As the scandal unfolded, Jimmy's citywide fame caused the entire family to be lashed to him, yanked down into the muck, especially his son Darrell. It was an open secret that Darrell was gay and now the most pious among them assumed this was credible evidence of an odious family-wide trait—that the entire family was queer. Darrell called his mother when the ugly accusation was leaked. Betty Mae assured him the rumors were untrue. "Besides," she said, "your father doesn't blame you for any of this." For what exactly, Darrell wondered.

The mangy affair had a terrible impact on the Tower. Some church members lined up with the Johnsons, and some with the Reverend. But it was actually Jesus who was taking the brunt of it even though he hadn't fondled anyone at all. Donations were down nearly fifty percent. Jimmy needed to do something, so he reluctantly called Brother Johnson.

"Listen, Wendell, I feel terrible about what has happened," he said. "I didn't abuse your daughter, but I can see how it might have looked. What if I paid you $50,000? Would that end this ill will between us?"

"Well, we've had a lot of suffering," said Brother Johnson. "But I think that would help with our healing. Let me talk it over with Myra." Still nothing about Jackie. She'd been told for weeks how bad it'd been and now she'd be told it was all better and she needed to get over it.

The Reverend wrote a check for $50,000 from the Tower's account. The check was made payable to Brother Johnson and not Jackie.

As a final stipulation to the settlement, it was agreed that Brother Johnson would join Reverend Jimmy on the podium for the following week's televised broadcast. Brother Johnson would tell the viewers and studio audience that it'd all been an unfortunate misunderstanding. The phones started ringing again, slowly at first, and then picking up steam.

Ten-year-old Jackie sat on a pew next to her mother wearing her pigtails and a pink cotton dress. Her mother looked down on her with a reassuring smile and patted her hand. There was confusion on Jackie's freckled face as she looked up at her two abusers on the dais who had their arms around each other singing praises to the Lord.

27

THE PRINCIPLE OF THE THING

THE LETTER EARL BOYNTON received from Harvey Pratt, President and CEO of San Juan Uranium Mine Company, put him on the ledge with his toes hanging off. This latest blow wasn't as crippling as Bruce's death or even Becky's out-of-wedlock pregnancy, but it was definitely worse that Carl's hippie heresies and it would gut his retirement.

Then there was the question of his mother-in-law's investment in the mine. She'd probably have to move in with them, which was a horrifying thought. This was the same woman who constantly reminded him that Darlene's first boyfriend had been in pre-med and that his kids were too spoiled. Therefore, he decided he wouldn't tell her for a while—he'd stall until she was senile or, god willing, dead. She'd nearly reached the actuarial zone anyway.

Darlene didn't care about the money. She would've felt the same way if the investment had gone the other way because she was not a showy woman. Let Mitsy Bateman and Jean Montgomery down the street have their furs and country clubs.

It was barely a pleasant surprise, therefore, when Darlene opened the letter from Colonial Life Insurance Company and found the check for $15,340. The accompanying cover letter was so painful to read that she would've given the money back not to have read it. "Dear Mr. and Mrs. Boynton," it began. "Attached please find a check in the amount of $15,340 for the death of your son, Earl. We regret the unfortunate passing of your loved one." They hadn't even gotten the name right.

The timing of the letter was unfortunate because Darlene's days barricaded in her bedroom with half the pantry had been winding down. She was making a comeback. She still cherished her solitary sessions with Bruce's scrapbook though. It was red and bound on the left by a gold rope with tassels. There was the official documentation of his birth, his baptism certificate, the ink imprint of his tiny feet, and all the polaroid photos stuck to the black, construction-paper pages by triangular stickers on each corner.

Earl, on the other hand, was pleased with the check. His pleasure was not a reflection on the monetary worth of his son, of course, but he'd forgotten about the life insurance policy so this was found money—like pulling on a pair of pants you haven't worn in years and finding a twenty-dollar bill in the pocket. He'd taken out the policies when his children were younger and hadn't given them a thought since. He'd done it for the investment and what an investment it'd been!

He figured his insurance agent must've made the claim on his behalf, so he called him. "Say," said Earl, "I got this check here from the life insurance."

"Yeah, I saw you hadn't made a claim," the agent said, "so I went ahead and made it for you. I hope that's all right."

"Well, sure, thanks. It's just that we hadn't thought about getting money off our son's death."

"Then I probably shouldn't tell you there's also other potential coverage if you want to make a claim."

"Like what?"

"Well, you could make an uninsured motorist claim. Seems it was a car accident, and we don't know who the driver was, the coverage would probably kick in from your auto policy. They'd presumably consider it an uninsured loss."

"How much is that?"

"It's also $15,000."

This was another windfall Earl hadn't planned on. But a windfall? What was he supposed to do with the money? Buy a motorhome? Re-carpet the basement or splurge on a cruise or a new boat? On the other hand, it made no sense whatsoever for the insurance company to keep the money.

Darlene was quiet, almost repulsed by the news. Blood money for her son's death? Repugnant. Earl collected the two checks and put them in the bank without a celebratory toast or Macy's shopping spree to mark the occasion. It was just another formal acknowledgment that their son was really dead.

A few weeks later, Darlene broached the subject of the money for the first time. She was propped up in bed with a magazine on her lap. Cold cream was smeared on her face and a hairnet trapped the sponge curlers in her bob. Earl stood at the bathroom sink brushing his teeth. He wore only tighty-whities and a white-sleeveless tank. The tank was several years old and fit snugly around his midsection.

"Earl, what did you do with the insurance money?"

"I put it in the bank. It pretty much paid for the money we lost in the uranium investment."

"I don't want to spend any of Bruce's money."

"But, Darlene," he said as he tapped his toothbrush on the sink and wiped his mouth with the hand towel, "it's not his money. We ought to use it for the family. That's what Bruce would want."

"I can't enjoy that money. You know that. How are we supposed to spend it? Huh? Go on a family trip without him? It's wrong, Earl. It's just plain wrong."

"Why is it so wrong?"

"It just is and you know it."

"I don't know it. That's what insurance is for."

"Well, I'll be darned if I'm about to start living high on the hog over his passing."

"So what do you think we ought to do with it? Burn it? Come on, Darlene, be reasonable. I'm not saying we should throw a big party or anything but maybe this will take some of the financial pressure off."

"Then I think we should reimburse my mother. Whatever's left we can donate to charity."

This isn't what Earl had hoped to hear. "Charity? Like what?"

"I don't know. Maybe give it to the March of Dimes or something. Or we could give it to the church."

Earl held no grudge against the March of Dimes but he had soured on the Tower of Power. He knew that Reverend Jimmy had foisted his uranium investment onto Brother Wendell Johnson. That, even more than the alleged child molestation charge, struck Earl as so cold that he could never look at Jimmy the same way again. No way would Jimmy Monson get Bruce's death money. No way.

"I'm sure we can find a charity that would appreciate a small donation," Earl said, wisely setting modest expectations.

Darlene picked up her magazine and then put it back down again.

"And what about my mother?"

"What about her? She put $10,000 into a risky investment and she lost. We all did."

"No, Earl, *you* put her money there."

"Because she told me to."

"Because you twisted her arm."

"I didn't twist her arm. Besides, she doesn't even know she's lost it yet. We don't even need to tell her. What would she do with it anyway?"

"It's the principle of the thing," Darlene said.

"Darlene, please. I'm not trying to cheat your mother. But we'll pay her back if you insist." He went back to flossing. "I just wish somebody would pay *us* back."

"I don't think I could live with myself if it ever got back to her that she lost her life savings in your failed investment."

"Even though she doesn't need it?"

"What does that have to do with it? It's her money, not ours. And she has nothing in reserve."

"Well," he countered, "she's got the Hummels."

Darlene's mother was proud of her Hummel collection and routinely boasted it was worth a fortune. The value grew with each successive boast, too. Earl had heard about their inestimable value for so many years that he finally asked a pawn shop dealer what they were actually worth. The dealer told him he could probably count on forty dollars for each figurine. There were twelve of them.

"She'd never sell them," said Darlene. "Besides, they're going to Aunt Bev."

Aunt Bev had arbitrarily reminded everyone many times over that, as the oldest, the collection of figurines would go to her. And so would the hutch they were displayed in.

"But, Darlene, the life insurance money doesn't belong to her. It's money that came to us because of all the premiums we've paid. This money has nothing to do with the uranium investment."

"I'm done talking about this."

"Do you think for a second your mother would have given us her profit if the investment had gone the other way?"

"All I know is if the shoe was on the other foot, she'd pay us back. That's all I'm saying."

Darlene picked up her magazine and pretended to be reading but her mind was searching for one more unimpeachable zinger that would end the debate for good. Earl was searching for the same thing.

This might have been a good time for Earl to remind Darlene that her mother was a stingy prude who hadn't said boo about paying for the damage to their garage door when she'd crashed into it five years earlier. Or, perhaps he could have mentioned how his mother-in-law never repaid them for the money they'd loaned her to get a new furnace. She hadn't even surrendered a single Hummel to them.

"All right, then we'll pay her back if you insist. But maybe she can pay for her own bus ticket next time she comes for a visit."

28

THE PINEAPPLE DO

THE LORD'S BUSINESS WAS PICKING UP. The economy was in good shape and people were focused on their salvation, zeroing in on the donations that would put them over the top. Regrettably, however, the Good Lord was now under attack—not by the forces of darkness, but by the IRS. Yes, the United States Treasury had become suspicious of the Lord's ministry. And as His spokesman, the federal government also had its sights set on Reverend Jimmy. No one knew for sure why the IRS was suddenly sniffing around Jimmy but they had to wonder what Brother Wendell Johnson may have leaked to them.

Despite Jimmy's payment to settle the sexual molestation claim, Brother Johnson never got over the original injustice and the other congregants knew it. They knew it because Brother Johnson would not shut up about it, trashing the Reverend's good name at every conceivable opportunity. That's why they suspected it'd been Brother Johnson who'd leaked the financial irregularities to the IRS. He denied it, of course, like any faithful church member would. Why, he and Sister Myra Johnson had even spent a carefree night in the Bethlehem Suite aboard *The Sea of Galilee!* Now Jimmy rued the day he hadn't upgraded them to the Gethsemane, or maybe even the Miracle Suite.

The tax man put Jimmy in a real bind but you could never count him out, for just when it looked like he was finished, Jimmy would come firing back like a trick birthday candle that keeps reigniting. This capitalistic resiliency was borne out of desperation and nothing brought him back like a good old-fashioned fundraiser.

This final moneymaker promised to be a blockbuster. The television studio seats were filled to capacity and the upgraded phone-bank operators were ready. Jimmy had even subbed out Sister Holmgren for a stunning unemployed actress who'd never stepped foot into a church. Sister Holmgren had been a proud phone-bank operator from the get-go and after Reverend Jimmy gave her the boot, she stomped out in the floral dress she'd borrowed from her sister-in-law. Betty Mae tried to stop her on the way out but Sister Holmgren kept walking. "You tell that husband of yours that wasn't very Christ-like!"

The cameraman counted down with his fingers: Five, Four, Three, Two, One, and then silently pointed to Jimmy. The PIPs began sashaying, slowly at first, and then with gyrating hips. The upgraded soundtrack was mesmerizing—music designed to lure the gullible into the chronic Donation Trance.

"Welcome to the Tower of Power! Praise the Lord!" The audience dutifully praised the Lord on cue. *"Woe be unto them at the End of Days who are not charitable for that day is nigh upon us!"*

Betty Mae had now made her way to the stage after her brief conversation with Sister Holmgren and stood next to the PIPs. She exuded confidence that she'd be ready for the Big Day and God's forthcoming rage directed toward the stingy. Her hair was normally stacked high but she'd used extra pins and pipe clean-ers on this special day to make it taller and stouter than ever. It looked like she'd taped a pineapple to the top of her head.

"Brothers and Sisters, I have something important to share with you." Jimmy paused before lowering his voice to signal the magni-tude of his next dramatic statement. The faithful craned their necks and cocked their ears. *"The Lord has made manifest to me that He will call me home if we do not raise five million dollars before October 15th."* Jimmy bowed his head to acknowledge his will-ing martyrdom as the sacrificial lamb whose very life was now on the line. The crowd murmured. God would call him home? As in he'd be *killed?* It was now abundantly clear that God was no longer playing games—October 15th was only six weeks away! This had now become deadly serious and none of the faithful wanted to be caught at the End of Days with Jimmy's bright-red blood smeared all over their greedy hands.

29

THE COLANDER

JUST WHEN JEAN THOUGHT THEIR SEPARATION had taken root, Lawrence went and got into the car wreck. Now she'd have to let him move back into the house and wait on him hand and foot or be shamed for her callous indifference. Therefore, she did so reluctantly and without the cheery commitment that "in sickness and in health" implies.

"Jean, bring me an ice pack." "Jean, hand me the pain pills." "Jean, hold still." "Jean, get me another pillow." She counted the days until he was well enough to return to the rental.

Lawrence hobbled into the clinic on crutches a week after his accident. They hadn't forgotten what a big deal he was at work because He of Yale would not let them. As soon as he settled in at his desk, Fran appeared at his door.

"Knock knock. Do you have a moment?"

"This isn't the best time," he said. "I'm reviewing medical charts."

"I know you're busy but I just wondered if you've had time to consider my raise."

"As a matter of fact, I haven't," he said as he shuffled a few office charts around and didn't even bother to look up at her. "I'll remind you that I was in a serious automobile accident and your annual salary review hasn't been my top priority."

"It's just that it's been five months."

"Well, I haven't had time. But I'll tell you what; give me a few weeks and then maybe we can talk."

This was the wrong thing to have said to a woman who had a copy of his written confession in her purse.

"No, Doctor Montgomery, I'll tell *you* what," said Fran. "I want a twenty percent raise by the end of the week." She paused, impressing even herself with this flash of attitude. "And if I don't get it, you'll regret it."

"What in God's name? You don't just barge into my office and tell me what I will and will not do! I've been extremely patient with you on this subject but you'll be fired immediately if you annoy me with this again. Have I made myself clear?"

"Perfectly clear, yes. But let me make myself clear, too. If I do not have a twenty percent raise within a week, I will quit and you will regret it, Doctor Montgomery." She stared him down. "You really will."

She stomped out of his office before he had a chance to fire her on the spot. Lawrence was outraged. Who in the hell did this woman think she was? She must certainly know that a raise was unthinkable at this point and it would give him great joy to fire her as soon as he had a chance to speak to the other physicians in the group who shared her mediocre services.

But if it was so unthinkable, why would she have behaved so outrageously? The gnawing possibility that she'd seen the note wafted to his consciousness like a lingering fart. Is *that* why she'd been so bold? He doubted it but rather than hobble over on his crutches to talk to his partners, he decided to think about it for a day or two.

Meanwhile, Fran went home to talk the situation over with her husband.

"You need to march in and demand a raise," her husband said. "Don't take no for an answer. Show some goddamned backbone!" This was the same guy who'd licked his superintendent's boots down at the manufacturing plant for years without a whimper. Oh, he'd threatened to quit in passionate speeches, all right, but they'd all been delivered to the foggy bathroom mirror with a towel wrapped around his waist.

"Glen," Fran said to her husband, "you can't breathe a word of this to anyone."

"But holy shit, do you know what we're sittin' on here? He's the bastard who went and run over that kid! This is un-fucking-believable. You should've asked for thirty percent. Minimum."

"I've given it a lot of thought and I don't want to make any money off that poor boy's death. I couldn't live with myself. Just a raise, that's all."

"Don't be stupid. You play your cards right and you could *double* your salary!"

Lawrence didn't have the luxury of bouncing this indelicate situation off his spouse the way Fran had done. Jean knew about the hit and run, of course, but she didn't know about the suicide attempt or the note which implicated her.

Lawrence was still recuperating at home, so Jean was forced to stay in the guest bedroom, a temporary unpleasantry that only bolstered her martyrdom. She could have slept in the king with Lawrence but the way he sprawled out with the extra pillows and demanded that she hold still was more than she could reasonably bear. So, Lawrence was left alone that night to snore in spurts of interrupted sleep as he stewed over his dilemma with Fran.

The next day he summoned Fran to his office at the clinic while his bored patients impatiently waited in the windowless exam rooms where they weighed themselves and stared at the glass jars of cotton balls and extra-long Q-tips.

"Listen," he said to Fran, "I've given this some thought and I'm prepared to give you a ten percent raise, effective immediately."

Fran would have been thrilled with a ten-percent raise before she had the goods on him. But now that she could lever his cowardly corruption into a fat raise? Fran knew she had him on the ropes, bloody and staggering. How could she face her husband if she accepted the measly ten percent?

"I appreciate that, Dr. Montgomery, but I believe I said twenty percent."

"But you were only asking for a cost of living raise. This is double that! Why would we do that?"

"Because, Lawrence, I have information that you don't want me to make public."

"What are you talking about."

"The suicide note. I made a copy of it."

"The suicide note? What are you talking about? What suicide note?"

"You know exactly what I'm talking about."

"If you're referring to my personal note, I will see to it that you are sued if you release its contents to anyone. I'll have you arrested."

"Really? Is that *really* what you want, Lawrence?" She'd never called him Lawrence before and now she'd done it twice in a row!

"Show it to me. Show me this so-called 'suicide note' you're talking about."

"Trust me, Lawrence. I have a copy of it."

"So, you sit here and admit that you went through my private effects and stole a personal note and now seek to blackmail me with it? Is that what you're saying?"

"No, not exactly. See, I didn't steal the note, I picked it up at your request. But, yeah, I copied it and that was rude of me. Would you like me to call the judge and confess to using the copy machine for personal use?"

"This is blackmail!"

"I only asked for a twenty percent raise, Lawrence. You don't need to overreact."

"We'll talk tomorrow. In the meantime, I trust you'll do nothing with the *alleged* note that you believe is worth blackmailing me over."

The next day, Fran was in the small area of the clinic where the nurses drew blood and congregated to write their chart notes. She saw Lawrence hobbling down the hall on his crutches with his bow tie and white lab coat and began walking toward him. Lawrence pretended he hadn't seen her coming and veered into the supply closet. This was unfortunate because now she had him cornered, backed up against packages of tongue depressors and a ballpoint pen dangling from a string tied to a clipboard.

"Dr. Montgomery?"

"Oh, hello, I was just looking for the insurance forms." He might as well have said he was looking for the Sword in the Stone because he'd never touched an insurance form. He didn't even know what they looked like, or that Fran kept them in the bottom drawer of her desk.

"My raise?"

"You have given me no choice, illegally I might add. You can have the twenty percent on the condition that I get every copy you made of my personal note that you had no business looking at. And I will also insist that you sign a confidentiality agreement."

"Lawrence, please don't lecture me on legality." Fran, a chronic pushover, was going toe-to-toe with the great man of the suburban medical clinic!

"You have no idea about the circumstances of that unfortunate accident and yet you blackmail me for a raise you don't deserve. Congratulations. I hope you can sleep at night."

"You'll have my copy of the note as soon as I see the written authorization of my raise."

She left him with his back pinned to the stack of preprinted medical questionnaires and went to fetch the note from her purse. However, because her wrath flamed anew, she made another copy.

Later that afternoon, Fran went to lunch with Velma, Dr. Montgomery's long-time nurse. Velma saw Lawrence's bedside manner firsthand and knew it was atrocious. For example, if the patient was overweight, Lawrence would gush forth criticism from the time the ether kicked in until the patient came to. She knew he padded his bills, too, and operated when it wasn't really necessary so he could better afford his country club dues.

Fran and Velma sat with their tuna salad sandwiches in the clinic's small cafeteria.

"Dr. Montgomery can be so arrogant," Velma said. "The way he treats some of our patients is downright deplorable. He thinks he can get away with murder."

"He can," said Fran.

"No, seriously, he thinks he can get away with anything he wants, and he usually does."

"He did," said Fran.

"What are you talking about?"

"I was just agreeing with you that he gets away with everything, even murder."

"Well," said Velma, "I didn't mean *murder* murder."

"He has," said Fran.

"What on earth are you *talking* about?"

"I promised I wouldn't say anything."

"Say anything about what?"

"Nothing," said Fran.

"Wait a minute," said Velma. "You can't just say that and then say 'nothing.' Tell me!"

"I promised I wouldn't say."

"So, there *is* something. Come on, I swear I won't tell anybody and you know I can keep a secret." Fran had no knowledge whatsoever about Velma's secret-keeping abilities but she was cracking, and Velma knew it.

Fran tried to hold it in but she'd become a fleshy, middle-aged colander.

"Promise you won't say a thing?"

"I swear. What *is* it?"

Fran hesitated.

"Is it about Dr. Montgomery?" Velma asked and leaned in closer. "Is it about their separation? Obviously, you've heard that he and his wife are separated." Actually, Velma hoped Fran did *not* know this because it had been told to Velma on the sworn condition that she not tell anyone.

"It's not about that," said Fran.

"Then what is it?" Velma's voice trailed to a whisper as she leaned in even closer.

"You swear you won't say anything?"

"Of course. You know you can trust me."

"Okay, remember that hit and run over on Orchard Drive? About ten months ago? The one where the little boy was left for dead but was still alive? Remember?"

"Yeah, I remember."

"And then the boy died?"

"Uh-huh," Velma said, nodding encouragement.

"I know who did it."

"Who did what? You mean who hit him?"

"Yes."

"Who?" Velma whispered.

"Dr. Montgomery."

"No, I mean who was the hit and run driver?"

"Dr. Montgomery."

There was a moment of silence as the statement sunk in. "Wait, are you saying," Velma whispered incredulously, "that Dr. Montgomery was the hit and run *driver?*"

"Afraid so."

"No way."

"Yes way."

"How do you know?"

"He was going to kill himself and wrote a suicide note, and I saw it."

This was too much for Velma to absorb over one tuna salad sandwich. She leaned back and put both hands on the table. "Dr. Montgomery was going to *kill himself?*"

"Shhhhh!" Fran hissed. "Yeah, that's exactly what I'm telling you," she whispered, looking around the breakroom to be sure no one else was listening. A table of four conservative women sat a few feet away, engrossed in a conversation about the ERA. They collectively agreed it was bad for women.

"So, you're telling me," whispered Velma, "that Dr. Montgomery, *our* Dr. Montgomery, confessed in a suicide note that he'd been the driver and then left the scene?"

"Uh-huh," Fran nodded with barely restrained joy.

"Then why didn't he do it? The suicide, I mean?" asked Velma.

"How am I supposed to know? Maybe he was on his way to do it when he got in the car wreck. All I know is that a few days after the wreck he asked me to take an envelope from his desk to the hospital. I know I probably shouldn't have, but I peeked at it. It wasn't even sealed or anything."

"I can't believe this," Velma said and then leaned again toward Fran. "Show me the note," she whispered hopefully.

Velma, just like Fran, desperately wanted to tell someone. It was on the tip of her tongue all afternoon. She almost told RayLynn who worked in medical records but that would've gotten back to Fran because RayLynn had a mouth on her. By the time she got home that evening, Velma could hold it in no longer. Her husband had been a last resort because he didn't get worked up about things. In fact, he'd barely even raised an eyebrow after she'd breathlessly revealed the secret that his brother-in-law was cheating on his sister. But Velma really had no choice—she had to tell *someone.*

"You won't believe what I heard at work today."

"What?" her husband said as he sat in his recliner with a beer in his hand watching Walter Cronkite.

"Promise you won't say a word?"

"About what?"

"About this secret I learned today. You're not going to believe it."

"Okay."

"I promised I wouldn't tell a soul."

"Then don't tell me," he said without looking away from the TV. "I don't care."

"Okay, fine, then I'll tell you if you insist."

The secret then spewed out and he turned his attention to her for the first time all evening. "Hang on, back up. You're telling me that Dr. Montgomery is the one who killed that kid?"

"Can you believe it!" she said with inappropriate joy.

"You're shittin' me."

"No, I'm not kidding. It's true."

"Holeee shit."

Velma's husband passed it on to his friend at work who, out of civic duty, passed it on to a friend who worked for the San Bernardino Bee, a newspaper with local readership.

30

CARL'S GIG

SHE WEIGHED IN AT SIX POUNDS and measured nineteen inches long once they stretched out her skinny, bowlegged legs. Her black hair shot from her head like she'd been electrocuted. The nurse indelicately wrapped her like a butcher handling a rump roast before crowning her with a pink stocking cap. A sheet of pink paper was taped to a bassinet next to the bed. "Boynton baby" had been written on it with a black magic marker.

When the delivery nurse left, Becky looked at her mom in a way that made words unnecessary.

"I just don't know, Beck."

"But, Mom," she said as she looked down at the swaddled bundle on her chest, "how could I?"

The phone next to Becky's bed rang and Darlene picked it up. "Hello?"

"Is this Becky Boynton?"

"No, this is Darlene Boynton, Becky's mother."

"Mrs. Boynton, this is Janice Stephens with adoption services. I believe we've spoken before."

"Yes, thanks for calling."

"I understand your daughter had the baby and is doing well."

"She's exhausted but, yes, she and the baby are well."

"We know how difficult it can be, but a quick transition is in everyone's best interest. That's why we'd hoped to have a family ready but we've run into a small delay. I'm sure it can be resolved within a day or two but there are a few extra considerations with a mixed-race child."

"We appreciate all you're doing," Darlene said, "but we're re-thinking our decision to give the baby up."

Becky didn't hear the rest of the conversation, only her mom saying, "I see," and "Yes, uh-huh, we're aware of that." When Darlene hung up, she and Becky broke into simultaneous tears. They blubbered "Are you sure?" and "Are we doing the right thing?" followed by, "I'm positive," and "I've never been so sure of anything in my life." Aunt Bev, who was also in the room, only huffed.

Becky decided her baby looked like an Amy. Therefore, the pink sheet of paper was replaced by one that read: "Amy Boynton, female."

Darlene called Earl an hour later to report that Becky had survived the ordeal and both she and the baby were doing well. He asked if the adoption agency had placed the baby yet. Darlene told him they'd run into a snag. "Well, I hope they get right on it," Earl said as he stood in the kitchen opening and closing cabinet doors looking for something pre-made to eat. "There's no sense dawdling."

For the rest of the evening, Darlene fretted over what she would tell Earl. They had already decided, emphatically even, that the baby would not establish residency in Riverside, CA. So, it was with stomach-churning dread that Darlene placed the long-distance call to Earl later that night. Earl was in bed slumped over a Louis L'Amour, trying to finish a chapter before falling asleep. He'd re-read the last paragraph four times, his head jerking back again and again when the phone rang.

"Hi, Honey," she said. "Sorry to call so late but I just wanted to tell you that things are going well and we should be home in a few days."

"How's Becky handling it?"

"She was magnificent. She was strong and feels great."

"And what about the adoption? Hopefully it was quick, before she had a chance to bond with it. They say that's the best way to do it."

"Well, Earl, that's why I'm calling."

Earl woke up all at once. "Was there a problem?"

"Becky loves the baby so much, Earl. She's carried this baby for nine months and they have already bonded. Please, Earl, it's all she's got."

Earl's silence prompted Darlene to hurry on, filling the silence with what she had to work with. "It's just that . . . if you'd been here . . . I mean, she's the most beautiful little girl you've ever seen."

More silence.

"And this has to be Becky's choice. Right? I mean, if we make her give it up, she'd resent us for the rest of her life. Can't you see that?"

Darlene could hear Earl breathing into the phone. "I can help her, Earl. I can watch the baby during the day and Becky can finish high school. Maybe she can get on at Uncle Wayne's plant. She could work the swing shift. I know it's not ideal, but the choice to give it up was impossible, too. I know you'll feel differently when you see her."

Earl had heard enough. "I can't believe we're having this conversation. We've discussed this. What in the hell are you thinking!"

"But, Earl, it really isn't our decision to make."

"The hell it isn't!"

"But Earl—"

"Don't you 'but' me. She's *sixteen*, for god's sake! How does she intend to support it? This will ruin her life and you know it!"

"She's young, I know, but I really think this was meant to be. "

"Listen to yourself, Darlene!" Earl shouted over the phone. By now he had stood and was pacing in the bedroom in his underwear. "This is crazy! We can't raise a child! And what do you propose to tell the neighbors? Huh? That our sixteen-year-old daughter got knocked up by some Chinese kid? This is unbelievable. I can't believe this is happening—that we're even having this conversation."

"Earl, I know you're angry but—"

"You're damned right I am!"

"But, please, this is our daughter we're talking about. And whether we like it or not, this is our granddaughter. It's not a perfect situation, I know that. But what would you have me do?"

"I can't believe this," he said.

"That's what Becky has decided and I think we need to support her decision."

"So you think you're bringing it *home?*"

"We'll get through it, Earl. We've gotten through worse things. Please, I'm begging you. Tell her you love her, please, because I know how much you do."

———

Carl smoked a lot of pot. It calmed him down and also made him horny. And his good looks and lean, muscular body were advantages when he was calmly horny.

He was a budding but unsophisticated capitalist and the single marijuana plant in his bedroom wasn't enough, not when he'd come to be known among his friends as the go-to guy. So, he'd parlayed the mother plant into two more which he planted in the corner of the yard flanked by a similar looking cranberry hibiscus. His dad had distracted himself from the trauma of Bruce's death and his sister's teenage pregnancy with home projects, including yardwork. Therefore, Carl was both relieved and upset when his dad trimmed both the marijuana and hibiscus plants. Notwithstanding his dad's trimming, however, the plants flourished.

Carl's customer base was modest, at first. There was only Kent and Alejandro the Mexican. But word of Carl's cache spread and soon he was going through his mom's zip-lock sandwich bags to beat the band. The first purchase from his profits was a top-of-the-line 8-track stereo. He then set his sights on a car to put it in. Within two months he had enough to buy the used souped-up Firebird which further enhanced his ability to attract girls. Other than his mom's sandwich bags, his only overhead consisted of his dad's pruning shears and a water bucket. The profit was rich.

It was never his intent to become a dealer, a real dealer with tenacles stretching countywide, and he pledged to grow only enough for himself once the Firebird was paid off. Unfortunately, one kid left a sandwich bag of buds in his pocket. His mom found it when she picked up his jeans from a heap on his bedroom floor to wash them. Worse still, the kid's dad was a cop. After grilling their son over where he got the weed, the cop vowed that Carl

Boynton, that embryonic drug lord, would be prosecuted to the full extent of the law.

Carl was arrested for possession and intent to distribute. Kent lied to the cops when asked if he'd ever bought marijuana from Carl but Alejandro the Mexican was too principled to obstruct justice, even though he felt terrible when he confessed that Carl had sold him an ounce. Carl didn't have much of a defense either, not when the police found the plants flanking the cranberry hibiscus in his backyard, and he was sentenced to thirty days in jail.

Darlene and Earl were mortified. Earl would've been an accessory to the crime by carefully trimming the plants if only he'd known what they were. It was bad enough that Earl looked awfully foolish, but now their own flesh and blood had been arrested for dealing drugs? Right under their noses? And soon he'd be required to report to the freaking county *jail?* Darlene was hurtled back into despair.

The jail was small with only a handful of inmates. The security was lax too, especially with only one surveillance camera from Radio Shack and a sympathetic night-shift jail worker named Theresa, a buxom twenty-five-year-old. Theresa was ill-suited to work in the jail because she was an occasional pot smoker herself and thought incarceration was rather unnecessary. She was also smitten by the newest jailbird's good looks.

31

THE SPIN CYCLE

THE CALL WAS ROUTED TO ROGER FLYGARE, the lead detective on the case with the thatched-roofed eyebrows.

"Detective Flygare here."

"Yes, this is Randall Jaworski from the San Bernardino Bee. I'm calling to confirm you've identified the suspect in the fatal hit and run accident from last December."

"Sorry, I didn't catch your name."

"Randall. Jaworski. From the Bee."

"I'm not prepared to discuss the results of our ongoing investigation." But please, I'm begging you to tell me what you know.

"Oh, sorry, detective," said Jaworski. "I heard from an anonymous source that you've identified someone who has confessed. Someone fairly prominent I'm told."

"I'm curious, Mr. Jankowski, just who did your 'source' say it was?"

"It's Jaworski. My source told me that Dr. Lawrence Montgomery has confessed. Can you confirm that? I'm about to write a story on it."

Dr. Lawrence Montgomery? Wasn't he the guy whose name had come up from the auto body repair shop? Flygare had checked into it, but Montgomery's wife had given him an airtight alibi. "I can't confirm that one way or the other, Mr. Warenski."

"It's Jaworski."

"Yes, I'm sorry. Who's your source? I'd like to control what's being reported so we can contain potential misinformation," Flygare said. "I'd hate for your newspaper to face defamation charges on this deal."

"I'll tell you my source if you promise to keep me in the loop. I know you've got to do your job, but I want to be the first to report the story."

"I don't ordinarily make deals with the press, but I'll do what I can."

Jaworski gave him the name of the friend and Detective Flygare unpeeled the layers of gossip until he'd come to the original source: Fran, the full-figured office manager. He called her and learned she had a handwritten note—a suicide note of some kind. The detective was at her house within the hour. Before he got there, however, Fran's husband registered his unhappiness with this development.

"How does this cop even know about this anyway?" he asked as he paced in the kitchen, cracking his knuckles. "Did you tell somebody?" He was upset they'd lose their leverage with Dr. Montgomery once they arrested the stingy bastard. Poof, there goes the twenty percent raise.

"I can't remember if I told anybody."

"You can't *remember?*"

"It's not my fault. The police have their ways of finding these things out. I'm as disappointed as you are."

Detective Flygare demanded to see the note as soon as he arrived. Fran looked at her husband and then took the crumpled piece of paper from her purse and handed it over.

"How do you know this is his handwriting?" asked Flygare.

"Because I work with him every day," she said. "I picked it up off his desk. He was pretty upset when I told him I had it."

"What did he say?"

"He demanded that I give it to him," said Fran. "He even threatened me."

"He threatened you?"

"Yeah, he said it was blackmail."

"That doesn't sound like a threat, ma'am."

"Well, that's what it felt like."

The detective frowned. "And when was that?"

"About a week ago."

"A week ago? Why didn't you immediately come to the police with this information?"

"Uh, it's just because I thought he was being unfair with my raise."

"I don't understand. Are you telling me you kept the note for leverage with Montgomery so you could get a *pay raise?*"

Fran's husband looked at her like he was every bit as shocked and disappointed as the detective was.

"That sounds bad, I know," said Fran. "But it wasn't really like that. See, Dr. Montgomery kept promising me and then lying about it. I was going to tell the police pretty soon."

"Pretty soon," said the detective as he stared her down. Fran looked down and brushed some invisible lint from her skirt.

"Did Montgomery admit to you that he was the driver that hit the boy?"

"Yeah, pretty much he did."

Lawrence was two vodka tonics into the evening when the doorbell rang.

"Jean! Someone's at the door!"

Jean was in the laundry room, toiling away with his sheets and dirty underwear. She was counting down the hours until her Florence Nightingale routine could end. "Just a minute!" she yelled back to be heard over the washing machine's loud spin cycle.

Jean was plainly irritated as she made her way to the door. She'd just about had it with Lawrence. Yes, she was going to divorce him. At least she thought she would. Phil Bateman had intimated he'd do the same thing with Mitsy so they could finally be together, although so far Phil had only wanted to shag her. Jean hadn't seen a divorce lawyer yet or breathed a word of it to her friends at the club, but she spent hours rehearsing in her mind how she'd spring her divorce demand on Lawrence—the look on his face and then the stammering. "But, but, I thought . . ."

When Jean opened the front door and saw the detective on the porch, she had the overwhelming urge to flee.

"Mrs. Montgomery, I'm detective Roger Flygare. We've met before. May I come in?"

"Who is it?" Lawrence yelled from the back bedroom where he'd set up shop. He even had a bell to ring when he wanted Jean to perform an additional Til-Death-Do-Us-Part duty.

"Excuse me, Detective, but my husband is incapacitated in the back bedroom. He recently had an unfortunate accident."

"Would you prefer I speak to him in there, or should I wait for him to join us in the living room?"

"Us?"

"Yes, Mrs. Montgomery, I'd like to speak with you as well."

Jean walked back to the bedroom, numb. She noticed a family portrait in the hallway was crooked and she straightened it. What am I doing? she thought. She hadn't followed her instincts and now she was on the verge of being arrested for perjury, harboring a criminal, providing false information to the police, and probably an array of additional crimes she couldn't even pronounce. And all this because of Lawrence and his goddamned ego.

"It's the detective," she said flatly when she entered the bedroom. "So get up and get your crutches because he wants to talk to us again."

Jean turned and walked into the bathroom and stared at the mirror. What would she say? Would she come clean, or dig in? How much did the detective know? He obviously knew *something*. But what? Hopefully he'd tip his hand before she had to commit herself to another treacherous lie.

"What are you going to say?" Lawrence asked her. He wore a white terry-cloth bathrobe, loosely tied, and stood in the bathroom doorway with his crutches tucked into his armpits. He hadn't shaved in three days.

"I don't know, Lawrence," she said and walked past him and down the hallway into the living room. Lawrence limped in behind her, grimacing with embellished pain for whatever mercy that might grant him at this trying time.

"Mr. Montgomery," Flygare began, "I have a copy of the note you wrote."

Jean jerked her head in Lawrence's direction. A *note*? What note?

Lawrence leaned over his crutches and looked down at the slipper on his one healthy foot. The bow of his leather shoelace had come undone and he stared at it.

"Would you care to look at the note to refresh your memory, Mr. Montgomery?"

"No," he said without looking up.

"What note?" Jean asked. "I don't know what you're talking about."

Detective Flygare looked at Lawrence. Oh my god, he thought. Did she not know her husband had planned to kill himself? The detective figured Jean must've known that Lawrence was the hit and run driver and had lied to protect him. But, then again, maybe she didn't, in which case she was about to learn her husband was the degenerate who'd left the child for dead in the gutter and had planned to kill himself, too.

"May I have a moment with my wife?"

"Sure, I'll just step outside," Flygare said. "Let me know when you're finished." He stepped out onto the front porch, leaned against the wrought iron railing and lit a cigarette, then shook the match out and inhaled deeply. He actually had compassion for Montgomery who must have known this day might come. Well, maybe not compassion, but pity.

Inside the living room, Jean stared at the top of Lawrence's head which hung low. He finally dared look up at her. "I hit rock bottom when you kicked me out. Living in the apartment, and being sued, and this misunderstanding over the boy who ran out in front of me . . . I guess it was all too much and I considered suicide. I wrote a note and drove to a secluded spot to shoot myself because I just couldn't bear to be a noose around your neck any longer."

She stared at her husband as her life was swirling down the toilet in real time.

"I was doing it for you, Jean. Don't you understand? Our secret would've died with me so you'd never have to worry about it again. But then I realized that we could recover, so I changed my mind. The note was lying on my desk at work and I was on my way to retrieve it, to destroy it forever, when that idiot woman ran the red light and hit me. My office manager must've found the note and given it to the police."

"What did it say?"

"It just said that our troubles seemed to begin with the hit and run. The cop must've figured out it was me, especially when they'd already suspected me because of the repair to my bumper."

They both stood in the living room, him with his head down, defeated, and her glaring at his thinning bald spot.

"What were you thinking?"

"I was doing it for you, Jean. You've got to believe me. Everything I've done since that kid ran out in front of me was for you—for us."

When the detective came back into the living room, the three of them sat. It was confession time. Lawrence admitted that he'd written the note. He said the accident had been Bruce's fault, but he'd been drinking a small amount—not nearly enough to be intoxicated of course, but enough for people to leap to the conclusion that he'd been drunk, which wasn't the case at all. Not at all. He left Bruce there because he thought the poor kid was already dead. In fact, he'd been shocked and devastated to learn the boy had survived for a short time.

The detective then directed his attention to Jean. "When I came by several months ago you provided an alibi for your husband. Were you not aware that he'd left the house?"

"No, Detective, I had no idea."

"You had no idea he'd left the house?"

"No idea at all. We'd been watching a movie. This is all news to me. And, quite frankly, I'm disgusted to learn it was my husband who did such a thing."

Turning to Lawrence she said, "What on earth were you thinking!" She stood and glared at him, pretending to be truly shocked to learn that the man she slept with was capable of such barbarism and deceit.

Detective Flygare was suspicious of her story but she'd told it so well and with such conviction! He couldn't prove she was lying and he was prepared to let her go.

That is, until Lawrence repaid Jean's months' long alibi and sacrifice with a dagger to her back.

"Jean," Lawrence said. "I've told the truth to the detective. I realize it's been a mistake to hide what I did, even though it wasn't my fault. Maybe it's time you told the truth, too."

Jean stared at him with unrelieved contempt. She might have killed him right then and there if a law enforcement official hadn't been an eyewitness to the slaying.

FATAL HIT AND RUN CASE SOLVED

INVESTIGATION >> Responsible Driver charged

with drunk driving in connection with fatal hit and run collision.

By Randall Jaworski San Bernardino Bee

RIVERSIDE, CA >> SEPTEMBER 1, 1971. The driver who was allegedly responsible for the hit and run accident that took the life of a thirteen-year-old boy has now been identified. Dr. Lawrence C. Montgomery of Riverside was charged in connection with the fatal accident. He was apprehended when his failed suicide plot was foiled. Authorities discovered a note Dr. Montgomery had written wherein he acknowledged his role in the homicide.

The case inflamed the community months ago when it was learned the boy, Bruce Boynton, 13, survived the collision but was left on the side of the road. He died at the hospital several hours later as a result of his injuries.

Authorities initially suspected Montgomery of the crime based on damage to his bumper. He was cleared, however, based upon the alleged alibi of his wife, Jean Montgomery, also of Riverside County. According to the lead detective on the case, Montgomery has now admitted he was the driver responsible for the collision and young Boynton's death.

Montgomery was taken into custody yesterday evening but has since been released on bail. Final disposition of the case is pending. Neither Lawrence nor Jean Montgomery could be reached for comment.

Lawrence's façade had been scalped, right down to the blood and bone. And he'd done it to himself—an ugly self-mutilation—and soon they would know his every shame. People would scatter from him the way they do when someone vomits and they don't want to be splashed on.

It was Jean who moved out after he posted bail because she would not, simply could not, be seen living with Lawrence. And especially after he'd thrown her under the bus like he had.

32

A SOFT THUD AND SHORT SKID

WALLY PEPPER AWOKE TO THE SOUND of his alarm clock at 5:00 a.m. He mixed a scoop of Malt-O-Meal into a glass of milk and stirred more than was necessary because he hated the clumps. He quietly opened the door and found his bike in the carport, an old Schwinn with a large wire basket mounted to the handlebars. He pedaled to the grocery store where he picked up his allotment of newspapers and began his paper route. He was too young to care about the cover story that morning in the San Bernardino Bee.

It was still dark that early in the morning. Sprinklers watered the lawns with the slow and steady *click, click, click,* followed by a machine-gun series of rapid clicks, and then resuming the slow and steady *click, click, click.* Otherwise it was quiet. He pedaled down Orchard, tossing newspapers to his right and left. They landed with a soft thud on the cement driveways and then skidded a few feet. Soft thud, short skid. Soft thud, short skid. Kitchen lights turned on and people were sleepwalking through their first cup of coffee. Some opened their doors as soon as he passed to collect the morning news.

Earl had always enjoyed the pre-dawn quiet with a cup of coffee and the morning paper. He was an accountant and routines were important to him. Always a splash of cream and one cube of sugar. Always one Geritol. He knew his routine might now be confiscated if Darlene and Becky refused to think clearly. They would both be returning home later that day from Lubbock, and hopefully empty handed.

Detective Flygare was rather pleased with himself for having solved the hit and run mystery even though he really hadn't solved it at all—it'd been handed to him on a silver platter thanks to Fran stumbling upon the suicide note. He boasted to others in the department about his stellar detective work but had forgotten to notify the Boyntons.

Earl opened the front door and stepped onto the porch in his bathrobe. He held his cup of coffee and surveyed the quiet neighborhood. The cement porch was cool on the bottom of his bare feet. He saw Wally zig-zagging down the middle of the street on his bike. He bent down, picked up the Bee that was wrapped with a rubber band, and went back into the house.

It was Earl's routine to read the sports section first before turning to the front page because he liked how men in sports were in contest, if not conflict, and that section, he believed, celebrated man's achievements while the remainder of the newspaper celebrated his failures. He read about the Dodgers win streak courtesy of Don Sutton and the scores from the first week of college football.

He finished with the sports section and set it aside, then spread out the front page. FATAL HIT AND RUN CASE SOLVED. *The driver who was allegedly responsible for the hit and run accident that took the life of a thirteen-year-old boy has now been identified. Dr. Lawrence C. Montgomery of . . .*

He hadn't been prepped to ward off the blow and was assaulted before he had time to brace himself. Dr. Lawrence Montgomery? Earl stared at the print. *Lawrence Montgomery?* The realization that a physician had done it, someone who could have helped Bruce survive, caused an outrage that kept building through breakfast and on his drive to work.

When he arrived, his secretary was eager to greet him. "Earl, aren't you happy about the arrest?" Joy had spent the morning gossiping about it in the breakroom with Margie and LouAnn.

"We're so happy for you," said LouAnn.

"Yeah, congratulations!" said Margie.

Congratulations? *Congratulations?* For what? He was asked to comment all morning long but didn't want his anger interrupted so he stayed in his office with the door closed to wallow. Colleagues asked Joy if he was okay. "He just needs some alone time. I'm the only one he wants to talk to about it."

Earl hoped Darlene wouldn't find out about the arrest until he picked her up at the airport later that afternoon so he could break the news to her in person. He arrived at the airport early and waited just inside the terminal wearing his short-sleeved white shirt and skinny tie with the clip below his ribcage. He watched the passengers emerge from the plane and walk down the portable steps. He first saw Becky who held a wad of blankets to her chest. When she reached the bottom of the steps, she waited for Darlene to catch up before walking across the tarmac to the terminal door.

Carl was surrounded by testosterone in jail. Not a single inmate was polite or deferential. Thirty days was doable, but it was still thirty days. Darlene and Earl (especially Earl) were convinced a jail stint, sad as it was, might be the spur Carl needed to get his life in order. Carl disagreed. All he'd done was grow a small garden and sell his produce to a few friends.

Most of the employees at the Riverside Correctional Facility had become hardened cynics and lacked a sense of humor or community. They made no effort to befriend their charges who came and went—the drunks, the drug offenders, and the petty thieves—generally harmless and misguided souls without accounting degrees.

Carl struck up a conversation with the night attendant on his first night there. Ordinarily Theresa would have dismissed an inmate but this was Carl Boynton and young women were loath to dismiss him. Carl would have also ordinarily dismissed a jailer who was an extension of "the man" but this was Theresa and young men were loath to dismiss her. They felt an equal pull to hook up once Carl was liberated from this largely unjust incarceration.

Two nights later, they flirted for the majority of Theresa's night shift. After exchanging phone numbers, Carl asked for a special favor.

"Listen, I know this is asking a lot. But I've got this guy who wants to buy my new stereo. Problem is he's now telling me the deal's off if I don't deliver it to him by this Thursday."

"Do you want me to go get it for you?"

"That would be awesome, except it's installed in my Firebird. I could unhook it and get it to the guy within an hour."

"So, like, what are you saying?"

"Like I said, I know this is asking a lot but is there any way you could let me sneak out for an hour, like at two o'clock in the morning or something so no one would know? I'd be back within an hour."

"Are you serious? I could get fired."

"No one would find out. I could run over, get the stereo and deliver it to the guy Wednesday night. If I wasn't back within an hour you could report I'm missing and call the cops or whatever. But, obviously, I'd be right back."

Theresa would not have considered this request from any of the other inmates, not even for a second. But she and Carl had become instant friends with the promise of romance. No one would find out. And he certainly wasn't a threat to the community. And he'd only be gone an hour.

33

BETTY MAE'S UGLY INDISCRETION

IT BEGAN WITH ABDOMINAL PAIN and Betty Mae was eventually referred to Dr. Lawrence Montgomery for possible gall bladder removal. Ordinarily, she and Dr. Montgomery would enjoy a traditional doctor/patient relationship—one that did not involve both of them winding up naked at the Holiday Inn.

Lawrence's relationship with Jean had soured to the point that he felt no guilt cheating on her. Besides, he smelled mischief between Jean and his good friend, Phil. He had no proof but there was an odorous suspicion wafting about. And Lawrence wasn't a man of faith, so he knew virtually nothing about the Tower of Power, believing as he did that preachers were often crooks. Therefore, he'd never met Betty Mae's husband—didn't even know who he was, and didn't care. This little fling of theirs was only meant to be a simple romp of lust, not love. And possibly retaliation, as least on Lawrence's part.

Betty Mae, on the other hand, was not a casual cheater. Truth be told, she had never cheated on Jimmy in her life—had hardly even had an errant sex dream, so focused was she on her eternal hopes. This feverish hope made a violation of the seventh commandment, the thou-shalt-not-commit-adultery one, a top priority. But Betty Mae had barely graduated high school and was far too impressed with Lawrence's stature as a genuine surgeon. She had also grown weary of Jimmy and his get-rich-quick schemes and had come to believe he'd lost track of Jesus and the true meaning of Christianity. She also hated the way he treated their son, Darrell, which caused additional fissures in her marital vows. So, her discontent with Jimmy had begun to metastasize but still she was besieged by guilt and would be the first to acknowledge that none of this justified her spending a naked afternoon with Dr. Montogomery.

Their one-time fling occurred a week before Dr. Montgomery's accident and Betty Mae was shocked like the rest of the community when Lawrence's crime was exposed a month after their little romp. She tried to call him but hung up when Jean answered the phone. Should she pray for him? Should she testify about his moral character or provide some sort of mitigating circumstance? If so, what? And how? But the larger question was why, for she believed Dr. Montgomery's actions that night were egregious ones and considerably more evil than a simple roll in the Holiday Inn sheets.

Phil and Mitsy Bateman were also shocked to learn of Lawrence's crime. The Montgomerys were their friends! They dined at the country club together and gossiped about less fortunate people over fancy wine! My goodness, they'd even talked about going on a cruise together! The cruise had largely been Phil's idea with Jean Montgomery's eager encouragement, for who knows, maybe they'd be able to squeeze in a quickie on the lido deck.

———

Darlene was appalled to learn about Lawrence Montgomery's arrest. She knew that people made mistakes, and she could have forgiven him if he'd done all he could to render aid. But leaving Bruce to die on the side of the road was more than a mistake, it was a premeditated act of cruelty that she would never recover from.

Darlene was a church-going woman with a robust belief in the power of prayer. When she reflected on the events of the past year or two, however, her faith had been shaken. How could God allow Bruce to be taken from her when she'd prayed her guts out? How could He inflict the pain of her sixteen-year-old daughter becoming pregnant and her nineteen-year-old son to be in jail for drugs when she regularly went to church and paid her tithing? And her husband? Earl was so pissed about all of it that he withdrew his belief completely.

Speaking of Earl, he had reluctantly allowed Becky to move back in with her infant daughter, Amy, but not without another ugly fight with Darlene.

"You've given me no choice. You go down there and bring the baby back when you know damned well that is not what we agreed to. So what am I supposed to say? Huh? You know I can't kick her out now."

"Won't you give her a chance?"

"I'm done talking about this. You and Becky can raise that kid but just don't ask for my help."

This left Darlene on edge whenever the baby cried, worried that Earl would erupt. So, she and Becky tried to hide the child from him, or at least the messy parts of her. His stubbornness would not allow him to admit to it, but Earl had actually become smitten with Amy. Darlene caught him winding the mobile over the crib and then whispering to the sleeping child. When he saw Darlene watching him, he grunted that the baby would not stop crying and stomped out of the room.

Becky was back at school for her junior year. Still no one at Woodrow Wilson High knew she had been pregnant, or had a baby waiting for her at home after school. When someone leaked it (Becky assumed it had to have been Marjorie even though the bulimic virgin steadfastly denied it), word gushed down the school's corridors.

"Becky Boynton has a kid?"

"Who's Becky Boynton?"

"You know, that one in Chadwick's class? The one with zits? Sits by Sherry Herbert?"

"No way, *her?*"

No one fessed up to having contributed the sperm. Jian had enrolled at Berkeley and wasn't around to arouse suspicion. But now it was time for Jian Wang to fish or cut bait. Becky couldn't force his involvement but she knew he should at least be given the chance to see what the injection of his little swimming minnows had created.

She arrived at the Wang's house after school, hesitating on the sidewalk in front. She thought Jian might be away at college—at least that's what he'd said the previous spring when he'd bailed on her, folding like a cheap suit in front of her father.

She rang the doorbell and waited out the jingle. Jian's mother appeared at the doorway.

"Herro, how I can help with you?" She was a beautiful woman and Becky hoped Amy would look like her unknowing grandmother when she grew up.

"Is Jian home?"

"No. He away at college. You pretty girl who come when we move?"

"Yes, that's me," Becky said.

"Oh, yes. Thanks to meet you."

"Do you know when he'll be coming home?"

"Yes, two week."

Two weeks later, it was time to settle this, alone, without her dad. She wasn't expecting sparks to fly, but she hoped an ember still smoldered somewhere in Jian's heart, or, failing that, at least down near his loin. She left Amy in her stroller at the base of the cement steps leading to the Wang's front porch. She rang the bell and waited. *Shave and a haircut, two bits!* She thought Jian might spy through the door's peephole, so she scooted to the side so he wouldn't try to duck her.

Sure enough, Jian peeked through the spy hole and saw half of Becky's face and straight ahead, at the bottom of the steps, there was a baby stroller. Not good. Not good at all. He thought about pretending not to be home but figured he might as well get it over with. At least his parents weren't home.

He opened the door and then the screen door with the fancy *R* welded into it.

"Hi, Jian. I brought our baby by so you could see her."

"Oh. Is it a boy or girl?"

"It's a her. Her name is Amy. She looks like you."

"But, uh, I thought . . ."

"Yeah, I was going to give her up for adoption, but I just couldn't do it."

Jian was holding the screen door halfway open with his right arm. He had thought surprisingly little of Becky and her pregnancy. And when he did, it depressed him so he thought about more pleasant things, like re-organizing his dorm room that was already so organized it was weird.

"I think we need to talk," she said.

"Maybe we could go for a walk. Okay?" Jian wanted to have this conversation anywhere else, lest his parents come home to see this . . . this . . . whatever it was.

He stepped over the threshold and let the screen door slam behind him. Whatever affection he'd once had for Becky had evaporated. There was nothing about this situation that inspired eroticism. Absolutely nothing. He walked down the steps and past the stroller, hardly even slowing to peer into the bundle of blankets.

"Don't you want to see her?" Becky asked. "She's so beautiful. Everybody falls in love with her." She bent over the stroller and lifted Amy up for Jian's personal inspection. He only did a quick once-over because he was nervous as hell standing in his front yard in broad daylight with Becky Boynton holding up a Chinese baby for his personal inspection.

If Becky was discouraged by Jian's awkward response, she didn't show it. She'd steeled herself for whatever he might say, good or bad. She'd spent so many days and nights thinking about this moment and now realized she didn't love this boy anyway. If he'd dropped to a knee right then, having been to Zales earlier that day, she would've had only marginal interest, and then only for her daughter's sake. This realization was an unexpected relief.

They walked single file down the narrow sidewalk until they got to a school playground where Jian finally felt safe enough to look into the stroller. When Becky handed Amy to him, he held her out in front of him like she was a wet puppy about to shake the water off.

"She looks good," he said and quickly handed her back.

"I know my dad said you couldn't have anything to do with us. But that's not his choice."

"Oh."

"So, I guess what I'm saying is do you want to be her dad? Because if you do then that would be great. I'm not saying we need to get married or anything, unless you want to. All I know is that I'm going to keep her and we're going to live with my parents until I finish high school."

"My parents kill me if they find out."

Six months earlier, Jian's preoccupation with what his parents' thought had crushed her, but now it just disappointed her. She was neither mad, nor inconsolably sad. She had Amy and together they would get through this, one way or the other.

It was quiet in the empty schoolyard except for the clank of a metal ring against the school's flagpole. She waited for something more from him.

"I go to college now and have low money. My parents don't know."

"I don't want to force you to do anything. If you don't want to then we'll just get by, that's all."

"I want to, but I don't think I can."

Becky looked at Jian a long time. She wasn't waiting for him to change his mind, she was simply absorbing what she knew was a critical moment in her life. She had once thought Jian was so vital and so smart but now she realized he was nothing special. She could live without him but she couldn't live without her daughter. So, it would be his loss. She wouldn't grovel for his love and she wouldn't do it on behalf of her daughter either. To hell with Jian Wang.

Darlene had watched Becky push the stroller down the street to the Wang's house to confront Jian. She had a pit in her stomach because she feared he would reject her daughter and the baby once again. Becky had gained strength in the last few months but Darlene knew her heart was still as tender as any girl's would be.

Amy was growing so fast that Becky could practically hear the creaking and groaning of her daughter's tiny cells. But Amy still had none of the Boynton family look. Then again, neither had Bruce. His flaming red hair had come out of nowhere, or so they'd all assumed. You see, Darlene, seemingly impervious to sin, had a secret of her own that she would carry to her grave.

It'd been a mistake, a one-time fling with the red-headed manager of the produce section at Ernie's Grocery Store. Darlene had two kids with Earl and was on the cusp of matron status. The produce manager's attention had been flattering and Earl's had not. Of course, this wasn't Earl's fault and she wouldn't have the audacity to blame him for her dalliance.

The fling was exciting and different because it was so out of her character. They met at the Fairway Motel twice. When she became pregnant, she'd assumed it was Earl's. But when Bruce was born she knew immediately from his hair. Not a doubt in her mind. She never went back to Ernie's Grocery Store again. The red-headed produce manager had never known, and neither had anyone else.

Earl had been a good father and Bruce had been his son, albeit not his biological one. Darlene had been surprised that no one had wondered where Bruce's crop of fiery hair had come from. Oh, there'd been some innocent speculation, but no one suspected a thing. Darlene? Nah. Not Darlene. No way. When Bruce was about two-years-old she'd been relieved to hear Earl say that his Aunt Fern had bright red hair, so it was "in his family."

Therefore, Darlene had more perspective than Becky imagined. Perhaps it was only fitting then that, one generation later, Amy's natural father was also largely unaware of his child; a child who also looked more like him than her own mother.

34

ASSAULT & BATTERY

IT WAS QUIET EXCEPT for the faint wail of a distant siren and the chirps of crickets in their diligent mating ritual. The dogs were all asleep. It was a cloudy night so it was even darker than usual which made driving without headlights difficult, especially on the tree-lined residential street.

He parked two doors down in front of a tall, unmanicured hedge. After grabbing a baseball bat from the passenger seat, he got out and closed the car door as quietly as he could. He knew it was unwise not to wear gloves but had no time to get a pair, for time was of the essence. He'd just have to be careful not to touch anything and be vigilant to wipe it if he did.

There was the flickering glow from the window of the first house he passed and he wondered who in their right mind was watching television at three o'clock in the morning. Perhaps they'd fallen asleep with it on. There were no lights from any other house on the street, and specifically not the one he was focused on.

He was not a thief. In fact, he did not consider himself to be a criminal at all, not even a petty one. The absence of a savvy criminal mind was evident too, for there had been virtually no plan. The plot had been hatched in a hurry and without the appropriate deliberation of risk.

He crawled over the fence on the side of the house and found himself in the backyard which was secluded from the neighbors. No dog, thank god. He figured he would break in through a window but first checked the sliding glass door off the backyard patio. It was unlocked. What an idiot this guy was, he thought. He slid it open about a foot, slowly, slowly, and stepped inside. His shoes had damp mud on them from the garden, just enough to leave a footprint.

He waited, holding his breath. There was no sound. He stood motionless a few moments more. The refrigerator motor in the mini-bar kicked on causing his heart to race like an overwound toy. The house was larger and fancier than his own but followed the same basic floor plan of all the homes in the neighborhood so he knew the general direction of the master bedroom. It was dark inside but there was enough light to find the hallway and he crept down it to the bedroom. The bedroom door was open and he heard breathing, breathing that sounded labored or perhaps gurgled.

The man in the bed was large, and he was alone. He lay on his side with his back to the intruder. The intruder touched him on the shoulder to roust him and when the man didn't move, the intruder pulled him from his shoulder onto his back. The sheets, blanket, and pillow case were covered in blood. The intruder stepped back, shocked at what he saw. He turned and ran from the bedroom, down the hall, and out the patio door he'd come through, sliding the glass patio door closed behind him.

———

He lay in bed later in the early morning hours trying to make sense of it. He replayed the events and tried to remember what he'd touched. There was his hand on the man's shoulder, but could they get a finger print off the guy's shoulder, he wondered? Oh, *shit* there was the sliding glass door handle. And the cops now had his fingerprints on file. He hadn't hurt the guy but how could he prove it if they ever caught him? But surely they wouldn't catch him because he had a perfect alibi.

35

REVEREND JIMMY'S NEON CROSS

REVEREND JIMMY'S MOST RECENT FUNDRAISER, the one where he told his flock that God threatened to call him home unless they donated like crazy, had been a big hit. No one who watched the program every Sunday morning on Channel Five wanted the Good Lord to call Jimmy home. So they donated. Even though Jimmy had only raised four million dollars by the October 15th death-deadline, a cool million dollars less than the bounty God had initially demanded, Jimmy had presumably been granted a reprieve with a generous grace period.

Betty Mae didn't want Jimmy to be taken, of course she didn't, but she knew Jimmy was prone to making things up. And the more audacious his made-up claims, the more his flock believed him. How could they be so gullible? How could they keep donating? It was a remarkable thing to behold. The crack in both her faith and marriage was small at first but had widened. She wasn't even sure she believed in God anymore. Oh, she said she did, but did so with private reservation. This emerging disbelief was not, however, the root cause of her little one-time fling with Dr. Montgomery.

Jimmy used the grace period God had granted him rather gracelessly. He'd become obsessed with a custom-made electric neon cross he had personally designed. This, he believed, showed his commitment to the Tower. The cross was enormous, standing eight feet tall with the arms and torso a foot wide and six inches thick. It was intended to hang directly behind the pulpit at the Tower of Power. Once plugged in, it would light up with a reddish hue, subtly pulsating where Jesus' hands and feet would've been nailed.

Jimmy's original design included a battery-powered, remote-control device that allowed him to regulate the glow. He could change the color and adjust the brightness depending on the sermon. For example, if he was lecturing his flock for their miserly donation levels, it might glow a fiery red. If he was talking about Jesus' mercy, he might choose a softer shade. And for the Christmas season? The torso lit up in a festive neon green and the arms in a cherry red.

Jimmy had commissioned the cross from a local electrician shortly after God imposed the audacious October 15th death deadline, confident that he would survive beyond that date. It might have turned out differently if the electrician had come when he'd promised or if Jimmy hadn't been so eager to fiddle with the remote control. But that's all second guessing.

The three-hundred-pound cross had already been securely hung, so all that was needed was to splice a few wires and attach them to an electrical outlet. Jimmy was so eager to see the neon glow that he decided to do the electrical work himself. He retrieved the wooden step ladder from the storage shed behind the church and hauled it to the podium, then trudged up the ladder feeling quite magnanimous for his selfless toil on Jesus's behalf.

The ladder felt sturdy under his weight. He found the black and white wires from the wall socket that had been cut into the sheetrock next to the neon beauty. The two wires stuck out a few inches from the wall like rogue hairs from a mole. He set his pliers on the top step of the ladder and grabbed the wires. He'd be done in a less than a minute.

Unfortunately, in his haste to experiment with the mood lighting, Jimmy got careless. Invisible current ran through the wires, and even though the wires didn't actually touch each other, they got close enough to arc. The resulting shock wasn't lethal but it buzzed Jimmy with enough voltage that he lost his balance and fell off the ladder, striking the pulpit with the side of his head on the way down.

It was the janitor who found him. Jimmy was out cold. The janitor called 911 and then called Betty Mae. No answer there. After the ambulance took Jimmy to the hospital, the janitor kept calling her with no success. Two hours later, Betty Mae finally showed up for choir practice at the Tower when the janitor informed her that poor Jimmy was battling for his life at St. Lukes Hospital. This was a breathless exaggeration because Jimmy had only been left with a nasty, ten-stitch cut and significant goose egg. Betty Mae felt terrible about Jimmy's accident and she felt even worse over why she hadn't answered her phone when the janitor kept calling. She rushed to the hospital to be by his side, passing the Holiday Inn where she'd been holed up two hours earlier with He of Yale.

It was a month later when the news broke about Dr. Montgomery's arrest for the hit and run. That's when she'd called Lawrence and hung up when Jean answered.

"Who were you calling?" Jimmy had asked Betty Mae as

he lay propped up in bed at their home with his head elaborately turbaned, a pink spot having formed on the gauze near his temple. He could have changed the gauze but the spot was a reminder to all who witnessed it that Jimmy had endured significant trauma in service of the Lord.

"Oh, that? It was nobody."

"Nobody?"

"Well, obviously it was *somebody*, Jimmy. But I didn't think you'd be interested in overhearing my conversation with the florist."

"Then why didn't you speak to them?"

"The line was busy."

Jimmy sensed something fishy but he did not expect that Betty Mae had been holed up at the Holiday Inn.

"Mel said he tried to reach you repeatedly for two hours after I fell," he said as he reached up and touched the spot of pink followed by an unnecessary wince. "Where on earth were you?"

"Just out shopping."

"But you told Mel you'd been getting your hair done when you finally showed up to choir practice."

"He did?"

"Yeah, he said something was off about you that afternoon."

"Off? I don't know what he's talking about. Personally, I think he's the one who's a little off. He's not a good janitor. You saw the way he left the mop and bucket within the television camera's view. I was mortified. It might be time to change janitors."

The news that Dr. Lawrence Montgomery, recently arrested and released on bond, had been found beaten in his bed caused all sorts of speculation over who'd done it. It was unclear whether the assailant had tried to kill him or simply beat him senseless, but Lawrence survived and was recuperating on the third floor of the hospital with broken ribs, jaw, forearm, and head wound as the police scurried for motive and opportunity.

Once again Jean was pressed into her reluctant spousal duty. Everyone knew how angry she was with her husband, or at least they highly suspected it, but no one seriously considered her to be a suspect in his beating. Besides, the coincidental timing between Dr. Montgomery's arrest and the beating he took a week later could not be overlooked. Afterall, the police found no evidence of theft and Lawrence had been found in bed so they didn't believe he'd startled a burglar. Therefore, it was presumed to be connected to the cowardly hit and run.

Carl Boynton had to be a potential suspect because he was known to have threatened vengeance over his little brother's killing. But Carl was in jail so it couldn't have been him. Earl Boynton perhaps? Unlikely, for he was a rather timid accountant. Darlene? No way. How about Becky? She was awake during those crucial early morning hours but she'd been breastfeeding. Fran his office manager, or perhaps a disgruntled patient like the scissors victim? Also unlikely.

The police combed the house looking for clues and took fingerprints from the bedroom and beyond.

The Boyntons had mixed feelings about the assault. Carl was happy to learn of it and so was Earl whose anger had ballooned in the days following Lawrence's arrest. Darlene though believed he should be punished under the law and did not endorse vigilantism. "Whoever it was must have had their reasons, but the law is the law."

36

THE INVESTIGATION

REUBEN FLORES WAS A CHRONIC THIEF who'd been arrested for stealing stereos, televisions, and Black & Decker products from garages in the area. Flores would steal anything, even if it was something he didn't particularly want. Even things that had no particular value. His was a level of kleptomania rarely seen. The justice system had largely given up on compulsory therapy for Reuben—it simply resolved to keep him in jail.

The jail where he was kept was relatively small. Another unique feature was that the individual cells had no doors—inmates could roam from the main living area to their cells at their leisure, and they had plenty of leisure. The jail's intimate nature made it a haven for Reuben who, in addition to his ability to steal things and only get caught occasionally, had rabbit ears and liked to talk.

Caleb Benjamin was the top-notch investigator assigned to the Lawrence Montgomery assault case. The police department would never formally acknowledge it, but they put their best man on the case because the victim was a notable physician, and a recent notorious one at that. They would have investigated the case if the victim had been an unemployed plumber, or a sex worker, but without their ace as lead investigator, and likely without the same enthusiasm.

Benjamin had a slew of fingerprints from the Montgomery home to work with. Naturally, most of them belonged to Lawrence and Jean, who had only recently moved out. Jean could not be eliminated as a suspect but, honestly, they didn't believe she had it in her. Perhaps if Lawrence had been slowly poisoned or pushed off a cliff, but not this type of brutal beating.

There were several fingerprints on the nightstand and a box of tissues in the master bedroom that belonged to someone else. That someone was Phillip T. Bateman, a prominent lawyer who had been required to provide fingerprints twenty years earlier when he'd been admitted to the bar.

Phil knew his fingerprints were on file with the police department but he didn't yet know that his world was about to be rocked. He'd worn a condom on those blissful afternoons with Jean in her bedroom but, regrettably, he hadn't worn gloves. So, there was some explaining to do. Obviously, Phil's intimate relationship with Jean now made him a suspect in the assault of her husband, to say nothing of the assault on their two rocky marriages.

When Detective Benjamin first contacted him, Phil adamantly denied ever being in the Montgomery's bedroom and certainly denied any role in Lawrence's beating. He said they were good friends and there'd been no reason to harm him. In fact, he was appalled they would even suggest he was capable of such a barbaric thing. When confronted with the fingerprint evidence, Phil hemmed and hawed before finally, and reluctantly, admitting to the affair. "But listen," he said, "can we please keep this between us? Come on, there's no reason to make this public. It wouldn't be fair to my wife." Benjamin had no particular interest in ruining the Bateman's marriage but he would not, indeed could not, simply keep this little secret between them. This meant that Phil's dear wounded pal, who himself was up to his neck in legal peril for the hit and run, would learn that Phil had been having sex with his wife. And in Lawrence's very bed no less. So, naturally, Lawrence would be angry with Phil, but would he finger Phil as his assailant?

And Mitsy? Oh boy. Phil was in his den when she'd answered the phone in her kitchen. Someone from the police department was calling. "Phil," she hollered, "it's for you." Phil picked up the extension in his den. Mitsy, who wasn't ordinarily a snoop, was curious why the police would be calling her husband so she hung up her extension but then quietly re-lifted the receiver to eavesdrop on the call.

This was all too much for Mitsy. Lawrence Montgomery had been nearly beaten to death in his bed at home? And the police were now questioning Phil because his fingerprints were all over the Montgomery's bedroom? They were? Why, she wondered, were Phil's fingerprints on a box of tissues in the Montgomery's master bedroom?

Mitsy had always liked Jean, or at least they'd been friends. Jean's pomposity irked her at times but it wasn't inflicted on Mitsy because Mitsy was also a beautiful member of the upper crust which made the arrogance fairly relatable. Each of them, however, knew about the other's weak spots through years of friendship. The gossipy cleaning lady they both used happily filled in whatever gaps remained. For example, Mitsy knew from Rosa that Jean lied when she claimed to buy her clothes from Nordstrom because Rosa had snooped through the Montgomery's trash and was eager to report that she'd found all the receipts from JCPenney, and Jean knew that Mitsy lied about being a vegetarian because of all the bacon and lunch meat packages Rosa found in the Bateman's trash while snooping there. This was the same cleaning lady who employed an irritating strategy of always leaving a few hanging photos a bit crooked so you'd know she had dusted.

Mitsy didn't care so much that Jean's husband had been beaten. She'd never really liked Lawrence and his condescending, sexist ways. Besides, he may have had it coming after what he'd done to poor little Bruce Boynton. But the revelation about Jean's affair with her husband, Phil? Not good. Mitsy was actually more upset over Jean's betrayal than she was over Phil's and when it came time to deliver Jean's Avon order, Mitsy left it on the Montgomery's porch without so much as a note.

"It's not what it looks like," Phil told Mitsy when she confronted him. "And since when do you eavesdrop on my phone calls? You have no right."

"I have no right? I have no right to answer the phone in my own home? I have no right to ask about your affair with Jean? Are you being serious right now? Listen to yourself."

"I'm going to work. I have a living to make."

"So that's it? You're just going to leave?"

"That's exactly what I'm going to do. In the meantime, maybe you can call Timmy's principal to see how he's doing. Maybe ask him about his nose."

Mitsy was normally a polite woman who didn't like conflict, so she would deny to her dying day that she'd been the one who'd started the rumor at the country club that Jean had a history of affairs—that she routinely came on to married men. In doing so, Mitsy hoped to punish Jean for the betrayal and perhaps dilute the impact of her affair with Phil at the same time, for she knew the Phil/Jean affair was sure to be made public soon.

———————

The police had also retrieved a partial print on the handle of the Montgomery's sliding patio door. Detective Benjamin could not be absolutely certain, but it appeared to match the prints of a young man currently being held at the county jail. If indeed those prints belonged to Carl Boynton, which was a potential but not a scientific certainty, that would make him an obvious suspect. After all, Carl had a stronger motive to assault Dr. Montgomery than Phil did.

Benjamin immediately drove to the jail to interview Carl. Carl wisely, and truthfully, denied the assault.

"Then can you explain why your fingerprints were found at the Montgomery's home?"

"It must be a mistake, that's all I can say. I mean, come on, dude, I was in jail."

And that is all Carl would say. But not Reuben Flores, his kleptomaniac jail mate. Reuben told his public defender, a young attorney who represented Reuben and about ten thousand other guilty criminals, that he had important information about the Montgomery assault and could he please lever that information into a deal?

This lawyer called Detective Benjamin who then took Reuben's statement in a small room adjoining the jail. Benjamin was a hardcore law and order guy but he often took pity on certain criminals, the ones who didn't appear to get a break at birth. Take Reuben, for example. He had a fairly severe hunchback, or kyphosis. This had, unfortunately, been a family-wide trait because his relatives looked like an evolutionary chart and Reuben would've been about second or third from the right. This genetic trait did not require him to be a thief but was nevertheless unfortunate. The relevant portion of Benjamin's transcribed interview with Reuben follows:

This is Caleb Benjamin and I am taking the statement of Reuben Flores.

CB: Will you please state your name for the record?

RF: Reuben Flores.

CB: And I am recording this conversation with your permission?

RF: Yeah. So, like, do I get a deal? Cause I'm no snitch.

CB: We can address that after we hear what you have to say. Now, I understand you may have some information concerning the assault of Dr. Lawrence Montgomery at his home last week."

RF: So, yeah, I'm in jail, you know, and I hear stuff.

CB: What specifically did you hear?

RF: This guy, I think his name is Carl. Buff guy. Thinks he's tough. Anyways, he was talking to this lady who works the night shift at the jail here. Name's Theresa I think.

CB: And what did you hear?

RF: So, yeah, he was saying something about getting let out for an hour or so to go steal a stereo or something.

CB: Ok.

RF: And this Theresa girl said she'd think about it but she didn't wanna get caught or anything, you know what I mean?

CB: Okay.

RF: And I don't sleep too good, you know because the beds suck in here. So, I was awake and heard him get up and then he wasn't here for a while.

CB: Who wasn't there?

RF: That Carl kid.

CB: And when was that?

RF: The night that doctor guy went and got the shit beat out of him.

CB: What time was it when you heard him get up?

RF: I don't know. I wanna say, like, two o'clock in the morning or something like that.

CB: When did you see him next?

RF: Maybe an hour later or so later. He wasn't gone too long, I do know that.

Detective Benjamin's next interview was with Theresa, the pot-smoking night-shift jailer who had the crush on Carl.

This is Detective Caleb Benjamin and I am at the Riverside County jail taking the recorded statement of Theresa Lowe.

CB: Please state your name for the record.

TL: Theresa Lowe. So, like, am I in trouble or something?

CB: Do you know an inmate named Carl Boynton?

TL: Um, I think I might. Is he the one who's in jail for possession?

CB: I believe so. We have information that you may have assisted in allowing him to temporarily escape from the jail.

TL: No I didn't. Who told you that?

CB: Are you saying you did not facilitate his temporary escape?

TL: No. I mean, no I didn't do anything like that.

CB: Our information suggests you let him out in the early morning hours of October 14th and he returned an hour or so later.

TL: I don't know what you're talking about.

CB: I believe there should be a surveillance camera showing that timeframe. Will you provide that to us.

TL: I'm not sure there is one.

CB: You don't know whether there is a surveillance camera?

TL: Um, I guess there might be but I don't know where it is.

Detective Benjamin tracked down the footage and found it had been erased for an hour and ten minutes in the early morning hours of October 14th. When confronted with that evidence, Theresa tearfully confessed to helping Carl. But he was only going to be gone for an hour to pick up a stereo. And he promised to come right back. That's all I know, I swear. "So, like, am I in trouble? Like, could I get fired for this?" Benjamin figured her exit interview promised to be ugly.

Benjamin formally interviewed Carl next.

CB: Please state your name.

CB: My name's Carl Boynton. Do I need a lawyer or anything?

CB: That is up to you, Mr. Boynton. I simply want to know what you were doing the night of October 14th.

CB: Like what do you mean?

CB: Did you leave the jail for any reason that night?

CB: Why are you asking me that?

CB: Just answer the question, please.

CB: I don't think I did.

CB: You don't *think* you did? Young man, I presume that is something you would know.

CB: How do you know? I mean, why do you think I did?

CB: We have witnesses who will testify that you left the jail and returned about an hour later.

Carl finally confessed to Benjamin that he had, in fact, left the jail but came right back and never hurt a soul.

CB: And did you go to the Montgomery home?

CB: Yeah, but just for a minute.

CB: Why did you go there?

CB: Because I heard they finally caught the guy who killed my little brother and I wanted to confront him, man to man.

CB: What did you intend to do?

CB: You mean, like did I want to kill him or something?

CB: Yes, what was your intention?

CB: Like I said, I only wanted to confront him. And maybe rough him up a little. But I didn't want to seriously hurt the guy or anything like that.

CB: And what happened when you broke into the house and
      found him?
CB: First of all, I didn't really break in. The door was open.
CB: The door was opened?
CB: Well, it was unlocked, okay? And I went to his bedroom
      and saw him lying in his bed and he was all bloody. I could
      tell he was still alive and all but he was in pretty bad shape
      and there was blood everywhere so I hurried and left. I
      swear to God I never touched the guy. I swear it on my life.

Detective Benjamin tended to believe him. *Tended* to. Part of
this belief rested on the fact that there was yet another fingerprint
on the bedroom doorknob that belonged to neither Lawrence,
Jean, Phil Bateman, nor Carl Boynton. He could not make an
arrest until he pinned down the owner of that final print.

37

BLOOD MONEY

THE BOYNTONS RECEIVED A CALL from a personal injury lawyer who was trying to rustle up some business. The lawyer was one of those who had started popping up on billboards and the daytime soap operas. You deserve compensation! No fee unless we win! Once again, Earl was gung-ho but Darlene was offended by the whole concept.

"I am so sorry for your loss," the lawyer said as he crossed his legs in the Boynton's living room. He wore a shiny pair of expensive loafers and his new champagne-colored Cadillac was parked in the driveway. "I know we can't bring your son back but I could probably get you something in the $500,000 range."

Darlene was appalled by the entire spiel. How could anyone possibly put a price tag on her son's life? Why, the very notion was vulgar.

"This doctor's probably got a lot of insurance, you know," said the lawyer.

"Well, we don't really—"

"He probably has a lot of personal assets, too."

The lawyer explained that Dr. Montgomery's automobile policy would probably pay its liability coverage limit, and if not they could sue Lawrence personally. Or perhaps they would do both. After all, the Boyntons deserved it. In fact, he told them it would be a miscarriage of justice *not* to sue. And don't forget, you owe us nothing unless you win.

"We could use it to help Becky, or maybe to pay Carl's legal fees," Earl said.

Darlene had little energy left to fight. And when the lawyer saw the opening, he expertly produced the fee agreement. "You're doing the right thing," he said as he straightened his Herme stripped tie and handed them a pen. "You deserve this. You really do."

Dr. Montgomery had liability insurance coverage with a $500,000 limit and his insurer knew it was wise to settle because the optics were just awful. A jury might even award the Boyntons much more than the $500,000. But the insurer balked because it was an insurance company and could not help itself. It only offered the Boyntons $350,000. Their lawyer wanted to take it and so did Earl.

"Here's the thing," the lawyer said. "I know your loss is incalculable and no one would say otherwise. But—"

"There is no amount of money," said Darlene.

"I agree. But the value of these wrongful death cases mostly depends on the survivors' economic loss when a family member is killed. That's why we probably can't get more."

"So what's that supposed to mean?"

"Well, your son was not the breadwinner and the other side will argue that you haven't lost any money by virtue of his death—it might even have been an economic windfall." He knew it was a stupid and insensitive thing to say the moment it escaped his mouth, even if it was technically true. After all, the Boyntons no longer had to pay for Bruce's food, clothes, college, or wedding. But still, you don't say that, you just don't. And he knew it.

"Excuse me?" said Darlene.

"I know," he said. "These insurance companies are heartless."

"We'll think about it," said Earl.

Darlene only seethed.

After the lawyer left, Darlene was still upset.

"This is exactly why I didn't want to do this," she said. "Exactly why."

"But Darlene, they've offered $350,000. Do you know how much money that is?"

"And do you know how much we've lost? It's insulting, that's what it is."

"But I thought it wasn't about the money."

"It's not."

"Then why don't we take it?"

"I'll tell you why not. I'll be danged if I'm going to sit here and let that crooked insurance company try to take advantage of us."

"But you didn't even want to—"

"This is totally different," she said. "I'm done talking about this."

And she was. That is until they put a pencil to Carl's legal bills and their furnace took its last breath.

"Listen, Darlene, why don't we just settle. We can replace the furnace and help Carl out with the legal costs. Maybe we set the rest aside for Becky and the baby."

Becky's future economic prospects did look shaky. She had, however, recently landed a part-time job at Kmart which would now have a new stock girl trained to organize the inflatable Rudolph's and the silver aluminum trees in time for Christmas. She'd been told she could work through Valentines Day stocking candy if it worked out. Unfortunately, it didn't work out because she tried to squeeze in a nap in the life-size manger scene. The manager found her curled up in the straw next to a paper mâché donkey.

"Fine, do whatever you want," said Darlene to Earl. "Settle it for all I care. Just leave me out of this. But I want that Dr. Montgomery to pay."

"I'm sure he'll go to jail and pretty much lose everything."

"I should certainly hope so," she said. "I'm sorry to be so harsh but that's the way I feel."

Earl called the lawyer who ultimately negotiated a $400,000 settlement. Still it irked Darlene that the lawyer received a third of it without losing his son.

———————

Carl was released from jail after thirty days on his illegal possession charge. They didn't have quite enough evidence to arrest him for the Dr. Montgomery assault, but they were perilously close. They could have arrested him for breaking and entering to keep him in jail while they tracked down the phantom fingerprints but first they wanted to shore up the evidence to add the charge of attempted murder to the B&E. In the meantime, they didn't consider Carl to be a flight risk and Detective Benjamin told him in the sternest way that he was the primary person of interest in the Montgomery assault case and that he was not to leave the area.

When Carl was released from jail and returned to his parent's home, he was slightly amused to see that his little grove of marijuana plants had thrived in his absence because his parents still didn't know what marijuana plants looked like. This, however, was about the only amusing thing in his life. He was scared shitless, waiting for the other shoe to drop. He'd had the perfect alibi but he then went and blew it by not wearing gloves. Stupid, stupid, stupid. He lay on his bed staring up at the stolen BOYNTON AVENUE street sign. He was sorely tempted to light a joint but wisely figured this was not the time. He could hear muffled voices coming from his parent's room where Earl and Darlene were sparring over issues of crime and punishment. He now realized his little jail-break stunt had been more treacherous than simple lunacy.

He called Theresa to explain he hadn't beaten anyone, that it had all been a big misunderstanding, but she didn't return his call so angry was she. After all, she'd been unceremoniously fired and informed that she, too, might be charged with aiding, abetting, and a host of other charges they might cook up. Carl Boynton was handsome, but he wasn't *that* handsome.

It would be a careless understatement to say Carl's parents were upset with him. Indeed, they were furious, frantically musing over the vast illegal drug distribution network he ran, not fully comprehending that Carl had only sold a few buds from his collection of backyard weeds to his closest friends. Kent and Alejandro the Mexican were no longer allowed in the Boynton house because Darlene now knew they smoked marijuana. So, all of that was bad enough but now their son had escaped from *jail* and may have beaten a man nearly to death in his own home? No, this was more than his parents could reasonably bear.

Carl promised his parents that he hadn't touched Dr. Montgomery. Yes, he admitted, he'd gone there with the *intention* of confronting him and probably fighting him for what he'd done to Bruce but it turned out someone else had beaten him to the punch. "You've gotta believe me." They surely wanted to—to at least hang on to the hope that their pot-dealing, draft-dodging son was not an attempted murderer.

38

THE ANNONYMOUS NOTE

SISTER MYRA JOHNSON, wife of the Tower's clerk, Wendell Johnson, had never been fond of Betty Mae Monson. The friction between them was aggravated by the way Jimmy cheated them on the uranium mine investment (which Betty Mae must have known about) and might have molested their daughter at the Tower's Christmas party. The friction began to peak the more Betty Mae put on her airs. Myra's husband was doing the heavy lifting at the Tower of Power and yet Jimmy and Betty Mae were taking all the credit. Where was the Johnson's expense account? Why weren't *they* showcased on the television program from time to time? Where were *their* keys to *The Sea of Galilee*? Sister Johnson was the smart one in her marriage and she knew that Jimmy had been taking advantage of Wendell, her gullible husband.

Oh, Sister Johnson pretended to like Betty Mae, pretended to be impressed by her new Cadillac Seville and Tiffany tennis bracelet. She even complimented her on her trademark high-stacked hair which Sister Johnson actually thought looked rather ridiculous. With a dose of rich irony, it was this very pineapple hairdo that ultimately gave Betty Mae away.

It should be fairly noted that Sister Myra Johnson was a good woman who loved her husband and had the true Christian spirit. She was the first to volunteer for soup-kitchen duty and her knowledge of the New Testament was inspiring. It should also be noted that she performed her acts of charity anonymously. The limit of her charity, however, did not extend to aiding and abetting sin. And especially not ugly violations of the adultery-focused seventh commandment.

Myra had been driving through town on her way to the soup kitchen one afternoon when she spotted Betty Mae's distinctive hairdo out of the corner of her eye in the Holiday Inn parking lot. It was Betty Mae all right and she was getting in to her Seville. A tall man wearing a blue blazer with gold buttons over a turtleneck was standing next to the car and bent down to kiss Betty Mae before she closed the car door. What on earth? Sister Johnson quickly turned into the IHOP parking lot next to the motel to spy. The man lingered for a bit next to Betty Mae's car before she ultimately pulled away. Sister Johnson took a very close look at the man.

She knew the man because he was on the board of the Riverside Country Club, the hoity-toity club that had blackballed the Johnson's petition to join the club because they were not yet A-listers in the community. Too churchy, she'd heard. His name was Lawrence Montgomery, the very man who'd bent down to kiss Betty Mae. Perhaps if she and Betty Mae had been better friends or if Betty Mae hadn't looked down her pious nose at Sister Johnson when she'd asked if maybe, just maybe, they could take a spin on *The Sea of Galilee* with their daughter and her new fiancé, Sister Johnson would have approached Betty Mae privately to admonish her to stop the tryst before someone got hurt. But no.

The anonymous note was handwritten on scented stationary and sealed in an envelope before it was placed on the collection plate with the Reverend's name on it.

39

THE GOBBLER

LAWRENCE HAD BEEN ASLEEP when he was attacked—asleep with a significant blood alcohol level—so he had no idea who the assailant had been. He'd awoken with the first strike but it was dark. The assailant had said nothing, just went about his business and left the way he'd come in. When pressed for any details about who might have done it, Lawrence could only remember the smell of tires and B.O.

Jean had come to the hospital, the second time she'd come to St. Lukes to see her ailing husband in six months. It was unseasonably cold but at least the cold snap allowed her to accessorize, the price tags tucked in for easier returns. She'd come out of wifely duty and perhaps as penance for having slept with Phil Bateman in her and Lawrence's bed, a fact that Lawrence was yet unaware of. In fact, he didn't learn about it until he was able to sit up in the hospital bed a full week after the assault when Detective Benjamin dropped by to ask him if he had any reason to believe his attacker had been Phillip Bateman.

"You mean my friend Phil Bateman from the club? Why would you even ask that?" That's when Benjamin told him they'd found Phil's fingerprints all over Lawrence's master bedroom and did he have any explanation why they might have been there? "I'm still confused," Lawrence said. "Where did you say his fingerprints were?" The detective told him they were on the nightstand next to the bed (and on Lawrence's side of the bed no less) and on a box of Kleenex there. Lawrence had gone to Yale so he was able to do some deducing.

Jean came to visit him in the hospital shortly after the detective left. She had no idea the police had found the invisible evidence of her fling with Phil and was therefore blindsided when Lawrence confronted her. An innocent explanation was not forthcoming, especially not on the fly.

She hemmed and hawed. "We were separated and I, well, I know I shouldn't have but it was Phil. And you know how he can be. He was insistent."

Lawrence rang for the nurse and told her to please escort his *wife* from the room. He refused to even look at Jean. "I trust you won't tell Jennifer and Alan," Jean said as she was leaving, "because this is just between us." Lawrence just stared out the window. "And there is no way Phil would have done this to you—the beating I mean. He likes you, Lawrence."

"Good to know. Now, please get the hell out of here and tell Phil to go fuck himself."

Lawrence was in bad shape but he would recover from the assault. It was unfortunate that he had nothing more than scabs and yellow bruising by the time he had to face the judge for the hit and run. Perhaps if the sentencing judge had seen him in the days immediately following the beating he might have shown more compassion by giving him the benefit of a time-served sort of leniency.

———————

Judge Gustav Franco was the longest tenured judge in the county, a distinction that came with the nicest courtroom. He'd been a football star in college but the ensuing years had made him fleshy. His large jowls looked like they stored an emergency cache of food—a portable pantry of sorts. There was so much skin hanging below his chin that a confused Tom turkey might try to court him. It jiggled when he spoke. Thus, Judge Gus Franco was affectionately known by the lawyers in town as The Gobbler.

The Gobbler was stern but fair. He'd seen the worst in mankind for decades but saw the unique difference between the crime and the criminal and had come to have a tolerant and weary decency about him.

His clerk was a devout woman who was even older than he was but refused to retire even though her sag was staggering. No one in the dark-paneled courtroom could see it, of course, but her nipples were nearly aimed at her shoes. She believed her tenure allowed her to candidly speak her mind to the judge in his chambers, and she did, weighing in on questions of crime and punishment like she was Solomon. Unfortunately for Lawrence Montgomery, she eschewed drunk drivers, and especially those who hit, kill, and run. The Gobbler patiently listened to her but rarely deferred.

Lawrence had no defense. After all, his own handwritten note was his undoing. He'd admitted to the crime and the drunk driving in the note so there wasn't much to argue about. Simply put, Lawrence was defenseless.

When he appeared in court next to his high-priced and largely ineffective lawyer, Lawrence wore a suit, a feigned humble expression, and a regular tie. (His lawyer had wisely convinced him to leave the bow tie at home.) Lawrence would admit that he may have erred but who among us hasn't sinned? And now he was fully repentant! The Gobbler had seen this show for years.

Lawrence had been charged with "gross vehicular manslaughter while intoxicated," a serious crime in California which carries a sentence of up to ten years in prison depending on the circumstances and mood of the judge. The circumstances in Lawrence's case were ugly. But, alas, he was deemed to be an upstanding citizen who'd never been caught committing a crime and who paid most of his taxes.

Jean was not by Lawrence's side as the supportive wife in court that day. She was home instead with an eight-ounce pour of chardonnay and the blinds drawn. Jean had been charged with obstruction of justice and her lawyer had negotiated a $1,500 fine and six months' probation. But the worst punishment was the overwhelming shame. Gone were the airs of privilege, replaced by only with the air of broken beauty.

"ALL RISE! The First Judicial Court in and for Riverside County and the State of California is now in session, the Honorable Gustav Franco presiding. You may now be seated."

When *The State of California vs. Lawrence C. Montgomery* was called, Lawrence and his lawyer stood and approached the lonely podium in the pit of the courtroom. The Gobbler pulled his mike closer and began. "Before I pronounce the sentence in this matter, is there anything the defendant would like to say?"

The old clerk stared at Lawrence, daring him to face her wrath. There were several members of the media present with their pens poised. No one appeared to notice the two people in the gallery who may have cared the most. Earl and Darlene held hands and silently prayed for justice. And what would justice mean to them? The ability to re-wind the clock perhaps? Or for this proceeding to cinch a torniquet around their bleeding hearts? Unfortunately, it would do neither.

"Your Honor, I am sorry for my actions which contributed to the tragic death of the young boy who darted out in front of me. I should have been more attentive and I've lived with the consequences of that inattentiveness every day since that night. I now realize I should have stopped but I believed the boy had already passed away and there was nothing I could do. I have always taken responsibility for my actions and I appear before you today to accept a fair sentence for my inattention."

This was not the sort of speech that inspired The Gobbler but Lawrence simply could not help himself. His lawyer put his head down with the tinniest shake to demonstrate that this was definitely not the sort of appeal he had recommended.

"Counsel?"

"Thank you, your Honor. My client is a prominent citizen in this community with an outstanding reputation. We hope you will consider the fact that his driving record is clean and he has had no prior offenses. Because of his admitted crime, he has lost his medical license and has been severely beaten, as you may know. Nevertheless, he realizes that he made a terrible, irreversible mistake and is prepared to accept whatever additional sentence this court in its wisdom imposes."

"Very well," began The Gobbler and then cleared his throat. "Mr. Montgomery, you may otherwise be a fine man who feels remorse for your actions even though your comments today do not reflect it. Your crime involves both callous indifference and cowardice. I do not believe your intention was to commit premeditated harm. For that reason, if you had mistakenly hit the boy, even while intoxicated, I could understand your behavior. I could not condone it, of course, but I could understand it. But fleeing the scene and leaving this child to die is morally unconscionable. Your choice to do so was selfish and premeditated. And you Dr. Montgomery, of all people, might have been able to save him. But rather than do so you fled in a reprehensible display of cowardice.

"I believe Bruce Boynton's parents are in the courtroom today and to my knowledge you have neither acknowledged them nor asked for their forgiveness. In fact, it is my understanding that you have never even contacted them. My sentence here today will not eliminate their suffering, but perhaps it will show them that I care, that society cares, about their son.

"You are hereby sentenced to seven years at the state penitentiary. I do not wish you ill, Mr. Montgomery, but it is my genuine hope that you will come to see the devastation your selfish and arrogant behavior has caused and that you will one day show the strength of character to humbly ask for forgiveness."

Lawrence did not turn around. He did not look down. He did not look at the clerk. He did not cry or become angry. In fact, he showed no emotion at all. This emotionless, apathetic ruse was a façade because he was overcome with fear. Seven years in prison? With those angry, ruthless, convicted felons? He was also overcome with disbelief—disbelief that he would find himself in this position. It was incomprehensible to him. But mostly it was fear. Prison. Lawrence, who had always been contemptuous of the lower crust, was now several rungs inferior to that. His vulgar belief that he was a big deal was notable only for its smallness.

Darlene and Earl drove their station wagon home after the sentencing without saying much. Besides, what was there to say? There were no celebratory toasts or chest bumps. The prison sentence didn't diminish their pain at all. Unfortunately, no effort of jurisprudence could undo their loss.

There was a new cream-colored brick rambler with dark mortar where the pile of dirt and backhoe had been. They almost passed it before realizing it was the spot where their son had been killed. Rainstorms had long since washed away the chalk on the roadway which had surrounded the location of his body and his solitary Adida shoe.

40

HAWK TUCKER AND THE LAB RAT

NINE MONTHS LATER AND STILL NO ARREST in the Dr. Montgomery assault case. Nine months with Carl Boynton and Phil Bateman still waiting for a dropped shoe. Nine months with Lawrence becoming accustomed to the bland prison food. Nine months with Becky still not having been asked out on a single date and with a child who was now pulling herself up to the coffee table. Nine months with Reverend Jimmy crushing it at the Tower of Power.

The victim of the assault did not clamor for answers from his prison cell, and even if he did, Lawrence was an unworthy victim who didn't inspire the police department to pull all its stops. And neither did Jean demand to know who had sneaked into her house in the middle of the night to bludgeon her husband. She had retreated and everyone let her, for no one wanted to be infected by her radioactive shame. Her ultimate dream to be admired with envy was now largely shot. Therefore, analysis of the unknown fingerprint languished without urgency in the crime lab. But still the case was open and Detective Caleb Benjamin had rededicated himself to closing it with a conviction.

Carl Boynton remained the most likely suspect but there was that pesky loose end of the unknown fingerprint. Besides, Carl wasn't going anywhere now that he'd enrolled in college with the embryonic goal of becoming an accountant one day, a turn of events that thrilled his parents but caused Kent and Alejandro the Mexican to instantly distrust him for selling out. And Phil wasn't going anywhere, not with a thriving law practice and Jean still giving it up on the side (although they *really* needed to sneak now that their two spouses were in on the tryst).

Alex Matsumura was a nerd at the county's forensic lab. He logged more hours staring into a microscope than anyone else in the department and made about as much noise as a lab rat. Matsumura was a scientist and not a moralist. He had no beef with the criminal element so long as they left him a clue—a drop of blood, strand of hair, or a fingerprint.

A particular challenge was a partial print. But whether he had a partial or full, it made no difference unless he had something to compare it to. Phillip Bateman had his fingerprints on file from the moment he passed the bar exam years earlier and Carl Boynton had to provide them when he'd been booked on the marijuana possession charge. But the partial print he had from the bedroom doorknob matched nothing on file.

That is where Hawk Tucker came in. It is unlikely that Hawk had been his given name but no one knew for sure, and no one really cared. His mother had died in childbirth and his sperm donor was unaccounted for, so he'd been put through the foster-care ringer until he met the love of his life who happened to be an ugly, overbearing woman.

Hawk was ugly, too. His ears were too big, his forehead bulged like a prehistoric man, and he had an unusually small chin. In short, he was an unfortunate model of human deformity. He was also an idiot. He was not an idiot for having been arrested for theft and certainly not because of his unfortunate looks. He was an idiot for having bragged to anyone who would listen that he'd stolen an entire rack of children's clothes from Kmart—just rolled it out of the store and into the parking lot for his sister-in-law's baby shower. The clothes and hangers were never returned and now his infant niece was well clad, provided an entire wardrobe from Kmart met the core definition of "well."

Hawk had been tracked down to his apartment after the Kmart theft and promptly arrested. He had no defense because there were plenty of witnesses who had been impressed by the sheer audacity of the thing. And if that were not enough, the metal clothes rack on wheels had been left in the carport space reserved for apartment 203B.

Following his arrest, Hawk was photographed in front of the life-sized ruler, fingerprinted for the first time, and spent three nights in jail where he wished to be celebrated as a modern-day Robin Hood. Regrettably, he was not.

Matsumura again ran the partial print from Montgomery's bedroom doorknob and found a probable match to one Hawk Tucker. Probable only because it was a bit smeared. Matsumara passed it on to Detective Benjamin before hunkering down over another slide from an unrelated case.

Benjamin rang the doorbell at 203B and was invited in to Hawk's filthy apartment. Take the kitchen. The sink was filled with unwashed dishes and sauce pans of congealed Kraft mac and cheese. There was a cardboard pizza box on the counter with one slice of cold pepperoni next to a plate with crumbs and the crust of toast. Next to that was a wadded-up dirty diaper. Other than the diaper, there was no evidence that a child lived there except for the stroller and play pen in the living room, Legos covering the floor, and half-empty yellow containers of dried Playdough, the remainder having been ground into the carpet. Detective Benjamin moved a binky and hair brush from a chair and gingerly sat below a black velvet painting of a Bengal tiger on the wall.

This is Detective Caleb Benjamin and I am interviewing Hawk Tucker at his home.

HT: Well, actually it's an apartment not a house.

CB: Yes, I'm sorry. Mr. Tucker, do I have your permission to record this interview?

HT: I guess.

CB: I understand you were recently arrested for theft from a local retail store.

HT: Okay, yeah. But I already done my time.

CB: I understand. Do you know a man named Lawrence Montgomery?

HT: Nope.

CB: You have never met him?

HT: Sure don't think so. Does he work for Kmart or something?

CB: No sir. He is a physician who was beaten at his home last December.

HT: Okay. So what's that got to do with me?

CB: That, sir, is what I'd like to know. You see, we found your fingerprint in his home.

HT: You did?

CB: Yes, your fingerprint was found on the doorknob to his bedroom.

HT: You sure about that?

CB: Quite sure, yes.

HT: So, like, are you saying I need to get me a lawyer or something? Is that it?

CB: Well, you certainly have that right, but I simply want to know why your fingerprint wound up there.

HT: Beats me. Maybe I did some work at their house or something, I don't know.

CB: And what is it that you do for a living?

HT: Driver.

CB: Driver?

HT: Yeah, deliveries and what not. Got my CDL.

CB: What kind of deliveries?

HT: Mostly appliances and stuff. I also deliver tires.

CB: Tires?

HT: Yeah, like to local tire stores, you know.

CB: Did you ever make a delivery to the Montgomery home?

HT: I make lots of deliveries.

CB: Do you go into the home when you make your deliveries?

HT: Sometimes, like if it's heavy and they need help.

CB: So, you don't know a Lawrence Montgomery?

HT: No. At least I don't think I do.

CB: Would you be willing to take a polygraph test?

HT: You mean like a lie detector?

CB: Yes.

HT: What if it shows up that I know him?

CB: Well, do you know him, or not?

HT: Maybe I do but I'm not a hundred percent sure on that. And I'm not answering any more questions until I get me a lawyer.

These were not the answers of a completely innocent man. Detective Benjamin liked to believe his role in law enforcement was an honest one, but it was dishonest advice to tell Hawk it would go much better for him if he just puked up all the grisly details of the crime because Benjamin knew damned well that many convicts could have avoided punishment altogether if they'd simply kept their mouths shut.

Benjamin did not have the requisite probable cause to arrest Hawk. For starters, the fingerprint was slightly ambiguous and even if it had conclusively been shown to have been his there may have been an alternative explanation for why it was there. He contacted Jean who did not recall an appliance delivery or any other delivery to her bedroom. Beyond that, she showed no interest in the topic. So, the detective decided to tail Hawk for a bit. This would not be a squad-wide stakeout, but it might lead to *something*.

Hawk Tucker did not strike Detective Benjamin as a hardcore church goer, maybe not even an Easter sort of worshipper. Therefore, he was surprised when Hawk led him to a church of all places, and on a Tuesday afternoon no less. Benjamin parked a hundred yards away and watched Hawk knock on a side door of the church which was opened to him before he disappeared inside.

He re-emerged fifteen minutes later with a middle-aged man who had thick, jet-black hair. They appeared to be arguing about something—or more accurately, the older man appeared to be dressing Hawk down, shaking his finger at him. Hawk eventually got into his old pickup and drove away. Benjamin decided not to follow him but rather wait instead to see who else might emerge from the building. Ten minutes later someone did.

The man was conservatively dressed in polyester slacks and an out-of-fashion sweater. As he was about to get into his station wagon in the parking lot, Benjamin pulled up next to him.

"Excuse me, but do you happen to work here?"

"Yes, I'm the church clerk. How can I help you?"

"My name is Caleb Benjamin and I work for the Riverside police department."

"Oh my goodness, is everything all right?"

"I just wondered if you might be able to tell me the name of the gentleman who just left here a few minutes ago."

"Brother Tucker, you mean?"

"Yes, I believe that's him. Does he work here, too?"

"Not to my knowledge. He was just here to meet with the Reverend."

"And what is your name if you don't mind."

"Not at all. My name is Wendell Johnson."

———

Detective Benjamin drove directly to Hawk's apartment.

"I'm sorry to bother you again but I saw you at the church earlier this afternoon. The Tower of Jesus, I believe."

"It's the Tower of Power and since when are you following me? Just leave me alone. I already done my time on the Kmart deal."

"Well, see, here's the thing. I'm still stuck on why your fingerprint was at the Montgomery home. I thought maybe we could chat some more."

"Listen, I don't know what your game is here but since when is it a crime to go to church?"

"No crime at all. In fact, I ought to go more often myself. It's just that I saw you arguing with a gentleman there, the Reverend I believe."

"So, what's it to you?"

"I just thought it was odd, that's all."

"Then we're done here?"

"Do the Montgomerys attend church there?"

"I don't know. Lots of people go there. Who are the Montgomerys, anyway?"

"The people whose home you were in—the home that had your fingerprints in the master bedroom."

"I already told you, I don't know anything about that. Besides, what's that got to do with me going to church? You ought to go arrest somebody who's doing something wrong, not somebody who's going to goddamned church."

Benjamin would have ordinarily agreed with Hawk's sentiment but something was off here.

"We're going to have a problem if you don't cooperate with me."

"I am cooperating with you. You're standing right here and I'm answering your questions for the tenth time."

"What's your business with the Reverend?"

"What do you mean," he said as he looked back over his shoulder and yelled at someone to turn down the goddamned television.

"Why was the Reverend upset with you?"

"Nobody's upset with me," Hawk said just as a heavyset woman with five-inch roots and a tank top came up behind him and yelled at him to turn down his own goddamned television.

"Do you work for him?"

"For the Reverend you mean?"

"Yes."

"He helps me. Gives me odd jobs to do."

"Like what?"

"Like what? Hell, I don't know. Just odd jobs and stuff."

Detective Benjamin decided to leave it there. He would follow up with Wendell Johnson who'd been pleasant enough and might shed light on what odd jobs Hawk Tucker did for the Tower of Power.

41

THE YOUNG REPUBLICAN

IF THERE WAS A BRIGHT SPOT on the horizon for Earl and Darlene it was Carl. Yes Carl. For starters, he'd cut his hair. It had been a traumatic experience to sit in the barber's chair as he witnessed his beloved locks corralling him on the tile floor. Kent and Alejandro the Mexican were certain he had lost his mind when they saw his ears for the first time and the rigid part in his hair. "Don't say a word, Earl," Darlene had said. "Just treat him the same or he might regret it." This was wise advice because Carl wasn't prone to take fashion advice from his parents who he thought were the spitting image of the American Gothic couple, only heavier set.

He also upgraded his wardrobe and began wearing shirts with sleeves attached, a belt, and the occasional permanent-pressed slack. This too caused his friends to wonder if he'd undergone a lobotomy. What next? Would he actually vote for Nixon? Was this a temporary phase, perhaps a way to redeem his image with the cops while he was still a suspect in the brutal assault case? Or was it something more sinister?

When Carl volunteered that he would join them for church, even Earl and Darlene were suspicious. Thrilled but suspicious, for they dared not let their hopes go unrestrained. And so it was that Carl began attending the Tower of Power on a fairly regular basis. When he invited Kent and Alejandro the Mexican to join him at his weekly Bible study class, the boys knew without a shadow of a doubt that they had lost their friend forever.

It was at Bible study where he met Lisa, a conservative girl who'd pledged to remain a virgin until after the rice was thrown. Lisa's parents were wary of Carl. After all, he'd been in jail for possession of marijuana. They would have forbade their precious, innocent daughter from ever seeing him again and followed it up with a restraining order if they'd known he'd temporarily escaped from jail to administer a near-lethal beating.

Kent and Alejandro the Mexican were baffled. Carl was now committed to a virgin? And he went to Bible study and was a fringe member of the Young Republicans' chapter in town? No, his friends did not know him. There was hope, however, when Carl threw a party at his parent's house. A party! Yes, we have our old friend back! But when he served only punch and invited the Young Republican chapter's president to stand and say a few words, his friends knew they'd been Trojan horsed.

Meanwhile, Becky had been given a second chance at Kmart because they needed seasonal workers for the lead up to Valentines Day. Unfortunately, they hired the wrong young woman again, for Becky had been prone to shoplift candy since she was eight, honing her craft to peak at about fifteen. But she'd been distracted by other things in the ensuing few years so her shoplifting skills were rusty. And it's difficult to hide entire bags of candy corn and Hershey Kisses in one medium size purse. The weary manager did not have the heart to call the cops after letting her go because he knew she had a baby at home, but he did retrieve the half-eaten bags of candy.

Just when it appeared Becky would eventually suck up the entire $400,000 wrongful death settlement, there came a surprising act of charity. Mitsy Bateman had rededicated her energy to Avon sales in the aftermath of Phil's traitorous fling with Jean, realizing as she did that she might soon be single. It also distracted her from the thoughts of Phil and her best friend tangled in the sheets as Phil reached for the box of Kleenex.

Darlene had reached out to Mitsy to see if there was any way she would take Becky under her wing, maybe teach her the ins and outs of Avon. And Mitsy did. They made quite a pair, Mitsy and Becky. Mitsy was more beautiful than ever, slimming down even more as a result of the potential divorce diet, and Becky had gone the other direction. This combination caused customers to buy more. Perhaps it was admiration for Mitsy for having hired Becky, or perhaps it was sympathy for Becky's physical and emotional hardships.

Two months into her apprenticeship, Becky saw a photo of herself at Amy's one-year-old birthday party, a party attended only by Earl, Darlene, Carl, Marjorie, and Mitsy Bateman. How many times had she seen her own reflection in the mirror? Surely she knew exactly what she looked like. But the photo was jarring because seeing oneself in a photograph is not the same as seeing oneself in the mirror. Am I really that heavy, she wondered? She looked at it again and then she looked at herself in the mirror. They were different somehow. The photo was more authentic— the way she must look to other people. It was a seminal moment in her life, this moment where she took an objective inventory of her face, her body, her style.

She lost three pounds that first week and three more the next. Was her face a little thinner? Did the sapphire birthstone ring she'd bought for herself at the kiosk in the mall feel a bit looser? Darlene did not notice it at first because six pounds did not make an appreciable difference on Becky's chunky frame but it had a major impact on Becky who was inspired to keep it up. Mitsy was enrolled in an aerobics class which Becky joined and she soon began eating healthy food. She felt so much better about herself! Her Avon money went to more stylish clothes (which Mitsy blessed with her approval) and she used all the products from her Avon sample collection. And when her dad said there was something different about her she resolved to keep it up.

42

WENDELL

HAWK TUCKER WASN'T TALKING, or at least he wasn't talking enough, so Detective Caleb Benjamin decided to meet with Brother Wendell Johnson again. He found out where the Johnson's lived and went by after work unannounced. Wendell's daughter, the very one who'd sat on Santa's lap, answered the door. Yes my dad's home. I'll go get him.

"Oh, hello," Wendell said when he came to the door.

"I am sorry to bother you again, but I just had a few more questions about that fellow in your congregation. I believe his name was Hawk. Hawk Tucker."

"Okay, is he in trouble? Is that it? I know he's had a string of bad luck and we've tried to help him and Sister Tucker where we can."

"Well, that's what I wanted to ask you about. Did the church just give him money or did he do odd jobs to earn it, or what?"

"I'm not really sure. I know he's not formally on the payroll or anything, I can tell you that. He worked mostly on the side with Reverend Monson who had him do a few repairs and what not around the Tower. I think he was just trying to help the guy if you want to know the gospel truth. The Reverend does things like that from time to time—you know, make-work projects so it isn't just a handout. The Reverend believes that way they'll feel better about themselves."

"Could you look into it for me? Maybe check the books to see what you can find about payments to him?"

"Sure, I could do that easy enough."

"And could we just keep this between the two of us for now?"

Wendell's wife, Myra, had been eavesdropping on the conversation and when Benjamin left she asked Wendell why on earth a police detective was at their house. Oh, it's nothing, he'd said. He was just asking about a congregant who's been down on his luck and what the Reverend was doing to help him.

"And you need the police to get into the middle of something like that?"

"Well, actually I'm not sure what's going on but I highly doubt it's anything serious."

"You know how I feel about the Reverend and Betty Mae. He's selfish and smug behind closed doors and Betty Mae, well, I know the *real* Betty Mae. So nothing would surprise me."

"Myra, that is uncalled for. Is he perfect? No, but he does a lot of good in the community and at the Tower."

"And gets paid plenty for it."

"Now, Myra."

The Johnsons were forever checking each other's pettiness because each of them sincerely wanted to be good. And, surprisingly, it did not annoy the other when confronted with a "Now, Myra" or a "Calm down, Wendell," for they had genuine respect and love for each other, despite his chronic snoring and her driving skills that had him pressing his right foot to the floor-board whenever she was at the wheel.

Detective Benjamin drove back out to the prison for another little chat with Dr. Lawrence Montgomery. Are you sure you don't know the Reverend James Monson? "Sure I'm sure." Ever attended services at the Tower of Power? "No." Okay, how about a guy named Hawk Tucker. Do you know him? "Who? The guy's name is Hawk you say? Never heard of him."

Two days later Benjamin got a call from Wendell.

"So, I went through the Tower's books like you asked me to and sure enough Hawk Tucker is not on the payroll. But there were two payments made to him. One was for $350 for a sprinkler repair and another one was for $650 to paint the fence."

"That's it?"

"Well, there was another payment that might belong to him but I can't tell for sure. It's a payment of $3,000 which I wasn't aware of, so I'm a bit confused. See, I normally do all the books but this one was entered by the Reverend directly."

"And who was it made out to?"

"Well, see, that's the thing. The ledger entry only notes a $3,000 payment for quote 'HT job LM.' That's all it says and I'll be danged if I know what that means."

Wendell had nothing at all against Sister Betty Mae but he didn't particularly care for Jimmy. He'd been defensive when Myra said Jimmy was selfish and smug, even though he tended to agree. Especially on the selfish part. One measly invite on *The*

Sea of Galilee? And all the personal expenses Jimmy ran through the Tower just wasn't right.

Wendell had an apathetic curiosity, at best. He stuck to the box with his head down and didn't question much. If the Bible said God created Eve from Adam's rib a few thousand years ago, that was good enough for him. Or if Noah had to coax two penguins to walk from the South Pole to gain passage on the ark, he didn't seem to wonder. It was this very uninformed gullibility that had prompted him to take out the second mortgage to invest in the failed uranium mine. It's not that Wendell wasn't smart, for he had training as an accountant and was a math whiz. But he was neither a prober nor a querier. His limited curiosity was piqued, however, by the police and their interest in Hawk Tucker. Something was obviously up.

Wendell was a devout rule follower, but even though the detective asked him to keep the Hawk Tucker business between them, he decided to take it up with Reverend Jimmy.

He approached Jimmy following the next church service. "Say, Reverend, you got a minute?"

"Can it wait? I'm checking on the receipts. I think I've finally convinced the Ferguson's to make a big donation."

"Sure. Just let me know when you have a moment to discuss Brother Tucker."

Jimmy flinched. "Don't leave. I'll be with you in a minute." Jimmy was so rattled that he even forgot to check on the Ferguson donation. He caught up to Brother Johnson in the foyer and ushered him by the elbow to a nearby prayer room and closed the door.

"So, what about Brother Tucker?"

"I just wanted to let you know that someone from the police department has been asking about him, something about payments to him."

"And you're just telling me this now?"

"Well, I didn't think it was necessary to mention it, Reverend. They just wanted clarification on what we paid him for odd jobs and what not. He asked me to comb through the ledgers to clear it up, that's all."

"And?"

"I told him I found the payments for the fence and the sprinkler repair."

"Anything else?"

"Well, there was a confusing entry that you made for $3,000. I didn't know if it was related to Hawk Tucker or not. It just said, 'HT job LM' so I told him about that too, just in case the HT might have referred to Hawk Tucker."

"And why on earth would you tell him that? Why didn't you come to me first?"

"What do you mean?"

"You go behind my back talking to the police about my personal business?"

"But I didn't think it was a prob—"

"That's what you get for thinking!"

Wendell was taken aback. "But, Reverend, I don't understand why you are so upset. Was that entry not related to Brother Tucker? If not, I can explain all that to the detective."

"This is a betrayal, Brother Johnson. A betrayal of trust within the Tower. You had no right to go behind my back about our ledger."

"But you're the one who—"

"After all I've done for you."

"What have you done for—"

"This is none of your business. Do you hear me? None of your business. But seems you seem to think it is, that $3,000 was for the hot tub we installed in our backyard a few months ago. I floated the money from the Tower's account because I was a bit short that month but I had every intention of repaying it. It had nothing to do with Hawk Tucker. But congratulations Wendell! You caught me floating money from the church for a short period of time."

"Then I'll just tell him that—"

"You won't tell them a thing, Brother Johnson. I've let you work here despite your attitude. But now I'm tired of your accusations. Sick and tired of them. I paid you fifty grand for that scam when you threatened to sue me over that ridiculous molestation charge. I didn't need to do that but I did it anyway. And now you go and bad mouth me to anyone who will listen."

"I'm not bad mouthing anybody. And, by the way, I saw that you used the Tower's money to repay me that fifty thousand dollars. *You* didn't pay me anything. So, what in the world is going on here?"

While the Reverend was busy chastising Brother Johnson for cooperating with the police, Detective Benjamin was driving to Hawk's house for one final showdown. He knocked on the door. A baby was screaming inside and a husky female's voice yelled at the child to shut up. Hawk opened the door.

"Let's go for a walk," Benjamin said.

"What, you have a search warrant or something?"

"Mr. Tucker, a warrant is unnecessary for taking a walk. I have no interest in searching your apartment." And indeed he didn't, at least not without rubber gloves, gas mask, and a large squirt bottle of Clorox.

Hawk stepped outside. "I've already told you everything I know."

"Have you?"

"What's that supposed to mean?"

"You were paid $3,000 by Reverend James Monson and I want to know why."

"I don't know what you're talking about."

Benjamin then lied. He told Hawk there was a $3,000 accounting entry to Hawk Tucker for a job, conveniently adding "awk" to the H and "ucker" to the T because he thought that's what the note meant.

"Listen, I painted the fence down there at the church and worked on the sprinkling system. That's all."

"So, what was the $3,000 for?"

"How am I supposed to know?"

The apartment door opened and Sister Tucker, all three-hundred pounds of her, yelled at Hawk to wrap it up because she was sick and tired of cleaning the house all day. Benjamin didn't know *what* to make of that.

Perhaps it was his wife and her relentless hounding. Perhaps it was the prospect of going back into that apartment to endure this woman for the rest of his life that made Hawk put his guard down.

"Okay, here's the thing," he said. "This is off the record, okay? But the Reverend might have paid me something on the side to rough someone up. You know what I mean?"

"No, I don't. Tell me what you did for the $3,000."

"So, see, there was this guy who the Reverend wanted to teach a lesson to."

Detective Benjamin had never met Reverend Jimmy but was anxious to do so now. He went to the Tower of Power service the following day and listened to Jimmy's sermon on the perils of same sex attraction. Benjamin's best friend was gay and, so far at least, he was pleased to report that his friend's sexual preferences hadn't rubbed off on him, or led him to divorce his wife.

He waited around for the congregation to clear before approaching Jimmy.

"It's a pleasure to meet you, sir," he said and stuck out his hand. "My name is Caleb Benjamin and I am with the Riverside's sheriff's office."

Jimmy explained to him that it was all a terrible misunderstanding. The payment, he said, had been a short term float to cover the cost of a new hot tub. When the detective did not immediately apologize for the misunderstanding, Jimmy panicked. "Just what are you accusing me of here?"

"Do you know a Lawrence Montgomery?"

"Never met the man in my life."

"Did you pay one of your congregation members to kill him?"

"What on earth are you talking about. Of course not. And I'm offended by the mere suggestion. Do you have any idea who I am?"

43

THE TRIAL (in brief)

UNLIKE THE GOBBLER who had presided over Lawrence Montgomery's vehicular manslaughter case, the judge in Reverend Jimmy Monson's trial for felony assault with a deadly weapon was new to the judiciary. She'd been a tax lawyer for years before she was elevated to the bench and hadn't yet been fully exposed to the bad in mankind, unless charging $850 per hour to create dubious tax-dodging strategies to line the pockets of wealthy clients was considered "bad."

Most of Judge Sheila Dobbs-Wallace's criminal cases were banal—habitual offenders with habitually similar backgrounds committing crimes that didn't stop the presses. Prosecutor comes into the courtroom with a stack of files he or she has barely had time to look at before the orange parade of disobedient citizens files in with their chains jingling. No press. No hype. No gallery. But not this time. It wasn't so much the crime. After all, men frequently assault each other. It was the criminal, a man of God with regional fame accused of ugly, unbecoming deeds not endorsed by the Sermon on the Mount.

Jimmy's defense lawyer, Rolfe Bastion, was a holier-than-thou atheist who was unimpressed with his client's religious vocation. Nothing new there because rarely were his clients impressive. But at least they didn't claim to be virtuous. Innocent, almost always, but not virtuous. The prosecutor, on the other hand, was a holier-than-thou Christian named Stewart Reynolds who found no corollary between the Reverend and the Good Book. He thought he knew a guilty man when he saw one.

The gallery was chock full. Most of those in attendance were Tower of Power fans who were there to support the Reverend, including Betty Mae who was on the second row to show moral support for her husband. The view of those directly behind her on the third row was partially obscured by her impressive hair stack. Betty Mae had been extra nice to Jimmy as partial atonement for sneaking off with Lawrence Montgomery who was not in the courtroom when the judge banged her gavel that first morning. Jimmy had no idea why Betty Mae was being so nice to him but allowed for it. A few of the PIPs were there, too, including both the older, less attractive originals and the newer, comelier ones. The Monson's daughter was also there but not Darrell who'd fled the community for San Fransisco a year earlier. Darrell didn't want to believe his father could be guilty of ruthlessly orchestrating such an assault, and with no apparent motive. On the other hand, his father had forced him to have his balls shocked, so there was that.

Reverend Jimmy sat at the counsel's table in a three-piece suit, an innocent citizen who had willfully submitted himself to the mercy of the justice system, content that his willful innocence would surely save the day. He looked back at his fans and confidently gave them a thumbs up, then adjusted his tie and touched his hair to be sure they were both in their proper position. His heavy gold Rolex clanked on the wooden table when he lowered his hands.

There were seven women and five men on the jury, all of whom had denied any bias and all of whom had partially lied, for how could they have no opinion whatsoever on the matter when Jimmy was such a well-known preacher? They'd either changed the television channel quickly with a huff and roll of their eyes, or they'd sat on the sofa in their donation trance ogling the new PIPs. But, alas, each of them solemnly swore to listen to the evidence, evidence the prosecution insisted was overwhelming and the defense insisted was anything but.

The attorneys presented their opening statements and the trial was underway. Reynold's first witness was Detective Caleb Benjamin who provided an efficient history of his investigation—dates, interviews, photos, the $3,000 HT ledger note, etc. On cross, Bastion tried to introduce doubt by hammering him on the two other suspects whose fingerprints were also in the home. It is true, Benjamin agreed, that there had been other potential suspects until Hawk Tucker *admitted* that he'd done it at the direction of the Reverend. Trust me, he testified, we didn't rush this investigation. But, Bastion asked, didn't this Hawk Tucker character admit it only because you agreed to give him a sweetheart deal if he said someone else had paid him to do it? Even though Benjamin had prepared for this question, he stammered.

The next witness was Alex Matsumura, the lab rat, who testified the fingerprints on the bedroom doorknob belonged to one Hawk Tucker. His cross-exam focused on the partial nature of the fingerprint to suggest it wasn't totally reliable. True, he acknowledged, but he was confident "to a reasonable degree of scientific certainty" that the fingerprint belonged to Hawk. And what about the fingerprints from the other two suspects? Yes, Matsumura agreed there were also prints at the Montgomery home belonging to a Phillip Bateman and a Carl Boynton. He wasn't a detective, however, and couldn't say whodunit, only that all three non-homeowners had been in the house at some point in time, but only one of them had confessed. And the confessor was Hawk Tucker. Matsumura was so non-partisan about the whole affair that his testimony was credible.

Hawk Tucker took the stand next. He'd been temporarily released from jail to testify and was allowed to wear civilian clothes. Unfortunately, they dressed him up *too* well because Hawk had never worn a blazer and slacks in his life, and it was somehow obvious. The following are relevant portions from the actual trial transcript:

BY MR. REYNOLDS:

Q: Did you know Dr. Montgomery?

A: No, never heard of him until I was given the assignment.

Q: The assignment?

A: Yes, you know, until I was paid to do the job.

Q: And what job was that?

A: He paid me to go rough him up.

Q: Who paid you to go rough him up?

A: Reverend Monson. I do odd jobs for him, you know what I mean?

Q: So, Reverend Monson paid you to go assault Mr. Montgomery?

A: Yeah. Said to hurt him pretty bad.

Q: Did he say why he wanted you to do that?

A: No, but I figured he has his reasons and all.

Q: Did he say how you were supposed to do it?

A: Not really. Just gave me his address, you know. Said I probably ought to do it at night so nobody would see me and so the guy wouldn't be awake to ID me.

Q: And how much did he pay you?

A: $3,000.

Q: How did you get in the house?

A: The front door was unlocked so I just went in.

Hawk then told the jury that he found Dr. Montgomery asleep in his bed and just started hitting him with a club he'd taken with him. He emphasized that he wasn't actually trying to kill him because that hadn't been the assignment. The cross-examination was next.

BY MR. BASTION:

Q: So, you admit you beat a man nearly to death.

A: If you say so.

Q: No, you said so.

A: Okay, yeah, I guess.

Q: And you knew you'd go to prison if you got caught.

A: I'm not sure how that'd work.

Q: You didn't think you'd go to prison for breaking and entering this man's house and beating him to within an inch of his life?

A: I didn't think I'd get caught.

Q: But you did get caught because your fingerprints were on the doorknob to the bedroom. And after you did, you said someone hired you to do this 'assignment' as you called it.

A: Yeah.

Q: And you were told by the police that if you cooperated with a name, you'd get a reduced sentence?

A: Yeah.

Q: And when you met with the prosecutor he showed you the $3,000 ledger note, didn't he?

A: I can't really remember.

Q: So you blamed the Reverend to get a reduced sentence. How convenient.

A: What do you mean?

Q: Mr. Monson does not even know Dr. Montgomery. Did you know that? They've never even met.

A: Who's Mr. Monson? Oh, you mean the Reverend?

Q: Yes.

A: I don't know if he knows him or not. Course I didn't know him neither.

After reviewing Hawk's rap sheet for the jury to hear what a scoundrel he was, Bastion ended his questions.

The next prosecution witness was Carl Boynton. He, too, had primped for the occasion but it wasn't as obvious as Hawk because he'd cut his hair a few months earlier and didn't have the whitewalls around his ears and neck. Carl was asked about his background and the fact that he was angry with Dr. Montgomery when he learned he'd been the hit and run driver that killed his little brother. He was also asked about his marijuana possession and his stint in jail, all the unflattering truths on the table to take the sting out of his anticipated cross-examination.

BY MR. REYNOLDS:

Q: So, you were in jail on a marijuana charge?

A: Yeah, I mean yes.

Q: And you escaped to go confront Dr. Montgomery?

A: I wouldn't really call it an escape. She just sorta let me out for a little bit.

Q: She?

A: Yeah, the girl who works there. She said I could leave for an hour or so if I promised to come right back.

Q: What time was that?

A: About two o'clock in the morning.

Q: And what did you do when you left the jail?

A: I went over to Lawrence Montgomery's house.

Q: Why?

A: I wanted to talk to him, face to face.

Q: That's all?

A: Well, I wanted to beat him up if you want the truth.

Q: Did you in fact beat him up?

A: No, because when I went in he was already in bad shape.

Q: What do you mean, he was in bad shape?

A: Somebody already got to him, like there was blood every-where, so I hurried and left. I never touched him.

There was more to his direct testimony but that was the rele-vant portion.

Phil Bateman testified next, and did so very begrudgingly. He'd called the prosecutor two weeks earlier after he'd been served with the subpoena to testify. He pled with the prosecutor, man to man, lawyer to lawyer, not to make him publicly admit why he was a relevant party to this mess when he hadn't laid a finger on his friend Lawrence. Okay, maybe on Lawrence's wife, Jean, I'll admit that. But not on Lawrence. Sorry, Phil, you still need to testify in court. I have no choice.

BY MR. REYNOLDS:

Q: I understand you were having an extramarital affair with Jean Montgomery, Dr. Lawrence Montgomery's wife.

A: I wouldn't call it an affair, no, but I do admit to seeing her at her home.

Q: When you say you saw her, do you mean you had a romantic relationship with her at her home?

A: I don't see how that is relevant.

BY JUDGE HOBBS-WALLACE:

Please answer the question, Mr. Bateman.

A: Yes, we had a very brief relationship.

Q   And you were in her bedroom?

Witness pauses.

A: Yes.

Q: Were you angry with Dr. Montgomery?

A: No.

Q: Did you have any reason to assault him?

A: No, he is my friend.

MR. REYNOLDS: Thank you. I have no more questions for this witness.

BY MR. BASTION:

Q: Some friend, huh?

A: He was.

Q: Do you commonly sleep with your friends' wives?

A: Of course not.

Q: Just this time, huh?

BY MR. REYNOLDS:

Is there a question in there or is he just going to badger the witness?

BY MR. BASTION:

I'll move on.

Q: Isn't it true, Mr. Bateman, that you and Mrs. Montgomery discussed divorcing your spouses so you could be together?

A: No.

Q: No?

After several more awkward questions, Phil was released to go home and try to mend things there, with only marginal success.

Lawrence Montgomery testified next. He'd been temporarily released from prison to appear for the prosecution. He, too, was allowed to wear something other than an orange jumpsuit with Riverside County Corrections stenciled on the back. Lawrence had lost weight in the months he'd already served in prison but what he hadn't lost was his arrogance, for even in these dire circumstances this jailbird remained a peacock.

BY MR. REYNOLDS:

Q: Did you see your attacker, Dr. Montgomery?

A: I did not. It was dark and I believe he wore a mask of some kind.

Q: Do you know why someone would intentionally harm you?

A: No, I do not.

Q: Do you know Mr. Tucker, the one who admitted to assaulting you?

A: I do not.

Q: Do you know a Mr. James Monson?

A: I am generally aware of who he is but no, I have never met the man.

After many more questions of debatable relevance, Reynolds rested his case. He did so reluctantly, for never had the light of dubious stardom shone so brightly upon him. There were even professional illustrators who had sketched him in the courtroom and the media hung on his every word. Colleagues were plainly jealous.

Now it was the defense's turn. Rolfe Bastion was an experienced criminal defense attorney who knew that putting his client on the stand was a mistake. The prosecution's case had holes they could exploit to cause doubt without calling the Reverend to the stand. For example, he could call a number of character witnesses to vouch for the Reverend's impeccable standing in the community—maybe a few members of his congregation or an original PIP or two. Jimmy agreed to all of that but he also demanded to testify in his own defense, to proclaim for all to see that he was an innocent man who would not cower! He would look the jurors in the eye and swear he had nothing to do with this illegitimate accusation.

Bastion was so convinced that calling his client to the stand would be a mistake that he threatened to withdraw as counsel. Reverend Jimmy, however, persuaded him that he was different, that he was a god-fearing man who was good on his feet and people loved him. Witnesses like that, Bastion knew, are typically the worst variety.

BY MR. BASTION:

Q: May I refer to you as Reverend?

A: Yes, please do. It has been my life's work to serve in my ministry.

Q: You have been accused of hiring a convicted felon to beat Dr. Lawrence Montgomery. Do you know Dr. Montgomery?

A: No.

Q: You've never met him? Never spoken to him?

A: That is correct.

Q: Did you or did you not hire a Mr. Hawk Tucker to attack Dr. Montgomery?

A: I did not. And, truthfully, I am offended by the accusation.

Q: But Mr. Tucker claims you hired him to carry out this assault.

A: Hawk Tucker is a disturbed young man. I have tried to help him, tried to encourage him to turn his life around. I have even given him a few odd jobs around the church to help support him and his family.

Q: Now, the prosecution has much to say about an accounting ledger entry wherein you paid $3,000 for a HT job.

A: I did pay $3,000 toward a home improvement project, but it had nothing to do with Hawk Tucker and certainly nothing to do with Dr. Montgomery.

Q: A home improvement project?

A: Yes. My wife and I put a hot tub in our backyard and I

temporarily used the Tower's account to do so. I noted it in the ledger as hot tub job and noted it was $3,000. I should emphasize that was a temporary loan which has now been fully reimbursed to the Tower.

Q: The Tower?

A: Yes, the Tower of Power.

Q: And the LM?

A: What do you mean? What LM?

Q: The ledger entry says, 'HT job LM'.

A: That just means 'hot tub job loan memo'.

Q: Loan memo?

A: Yes. I just wanted to be sure it was coded as a loan because I wanted to be clear it was something that I intended to repay.

Q: Can you see how the prosecution might have mistakenly believed 'HT job LM' referred to 'Hawk Tucker job Lawrence Montgomery'?

A: Perhaps, but it clearly did not.

Q: Reverend, did you hire Mr. Tucker to break into the Montgomery home and beat Dr. Lawrence Montgomery?

A: Absolutely not.

The Reverend was confident that his robust denial would, or at least should, resolve any doubt in the jury's mind that he was an innocent man, an innocent man with no priors who'd spent his life in the service of God. He looked out from the witness stand into the gallery where he unexpectedly saw Dr. Lawrence Montgomery who'd been allowed to remain in the gallery for the remainder of the trial. They stared at each other, neither willing to break the stare.

And then Lawrence offered the tiniest smile from the third row. Perhaps more smirk than smile.

Jimmy's cross examination did not go as planned.

BY MR. REYNOLDS:

Q: You would have us believe you are a man of God.

A: I have spent my life in His service.

Jimmy looked out again at Lawrence Montgomery who was sitting in the row behind Betty Mae and slightly to her left. Lawrence continued to stare at Jimmy with one side of his mouth raised slightly. Jimmy thought he detected the smallest huff—a man-of-god-my-ass sort of huff, or perhaps an I-slept-with-your-wife sort of huff. But more likely both—dual huffs that infuriated Jimmy.

Q: So you misappropriated money from the church?

A: Excuse me? Can you repeat that?

Jimmy had lost his concentration and his confidence, too.

Q: The money you took from the church. Isn't it true you used the church and its funds as your own?

A: No.

Q: No? You wouldn't consider using the church's money to install a hot tub in your backyard a personal expense?

A: Not really. It's just that . . . wipe that smirk off your face!

Q: Excuse me?

A: Sorry, not you.

Reynolds looked around, confused for a bit before resuming his questions.

Q: So, to be clear, you take money from the church for personal reasons.

A: That's not what I meant. It's just that . . . I said wipe that smirk off that fat face of yours!

Reynolds was stunned.

Q: Are you talking to *me*?

A: No, not you. That arrogant piece of shit behind you!

No one knew what to do. Reynolds looked behind him into the gallery. The judge reached for her gavel. Members of the gallery looked at each other. Is he talking about me? Or me? Or me? Jimmy now stood from the witness stand and pointed over Reynold's shoulder.

BY THE WITNESS:
Get him out of this courtroom!

The judge banged her gavel.

BY JUDGE HOBBS-WALLACE:
The witness will remain seated! I will not tolerate this in my courtroom!

BY THE COURT REPORTER:
Should I be transcribing this?

BY MR. REYNOLDS:
Yes!

BY MR. BASTION:
No!

BY JUDGE HOBBS-WALLACE:
Yes, please continue to transcribe this—

BY THE WITNESS (still standing and pointing to the gallery):
I said get him out of this courtroom! He is a degenerate scum!

BY JUDGE HOBBS-WALLACE:
Sir! I will not tolerate this behav—

BY THE WITNESS:
But he slept with my wife! The dirty sonofabitch slept with my
wife! Do you hear me! You piece of—

Gavel banging. Everyone staring at Lawrence. The gallery
now talking, speculating, those on the back row standing to get
a better view.

BY JUDGE HOBBS-WALLACE:
We are in recess! I will instruct the bailiff to remove this witness
immediately. Counsel, in my chambers. Now!

44

THE NEW FISH

IT TOOK CONVINCING to persuade Betty Mae to attend the final day of her husband's trial. Attorney Bastion called her at home that night. "We need you there for the jury to see you still support your husband's innocence." Betty Mae, however, was mortified about her affair becoming public and only wanted to hide out at home with the blinds drawn. Betty Mae Monson had slept with the man who'd killed Bruce Boynton? Can it be true? *Our* Betty Mae? How could she ever show her face at the Tower again?

She was finally guilted into going by Jimmy and his lawyer and immediately regretted it when a TV reporter and his cameraman saw her getting out of her Seville in the courthouse parking lot and ran over to her followed by several other eager reporters who clustered around her with microphones shoved to her face, asking the absurd questions that they knew she would not answer. She freed herself of them and made her lonely walk of shame down the corridor and into the courtroom where she sat on the second row looking straight ahead with her hands in her lap. A few friends dared wave or touch her on the shoulder but it was all so terribly awkward, for the Tower's madam had suffered a dreadful blow.

Once again the courtroom was packed. Tower of Power fans who'd been so confident of an acquittal were now on edge. The Reverend had given the prosecution a motive courtesy of Betty Mae and her ugly indiscretion.

Stewart Reynolds stood to make his closing argument. He was into his fourteenth minute of fame and made the most of it in a new charcoal gray suit. He'd tried on several ties that morning before finally settling on a solid red because he'd read somewhere that red is the power color. Now he walked to the center of the pit in the courtroom with his head bowed, a humble servant of the court seeking only justice for the oppressed.

"Ladies and Gentlemen of the jury, I humbly stand before you as an officer of this court, charged with the grave responsibility of seeing that justice is done for this brutal assault. I do so with confidence that you will discharge your sacred duty to evaluate the credible and *corroborated* evidence, and find the defendant guilty of this horrific act of violence."

He then reviewed the evidence—the fingerprints and Hawk's confession that the Reverend hired him to beat the poor man to within an inch of his life. Here is the accounting entry, he told them. "Was it just a remarkable coincidence that 'HT job LM' for a whopping $3,000 had nothing to do with Hawk Tucker and Lawrence Montgomery? The defendant knew his wife was engaged in a sexual liaison with the victim and took his revenge in the most cowardly of ways. You saw how angry he was. You saw the unrestrained temper. You saw the real Mr. Monson and not the man of God he claims to be." Means, motive, and opportunity, as they say.

"The victim, Dr. Lawrence Montgomery, is not a perfect man. We all know that. But the law has already punished him for his crime. His character is completely irrelevant here and you must not consider it."

Rolfe Bastion stood next. He didn't know if his client was guilty or not. In fact, he'd never even asked Jimmy if he'd done it. It was his job to offer Jimmy the best defense he could, regardless of guilt. His best argument would have been a lack of motive until Jimmy barfed one up on a silver platter. Bastion was still upset with himself for allowing the Reverend to testify, a decision he knew legal pundits would have a field day with. But what choice did he have? His client had demanded it.

"The Reverend, who has been a pillar in this community for many years, tried to help one of his parishioners by giving him small work assignments. He paid him to fix the sprinklers and paint a fence. Unfortunately for the Reverend, this very parishioner that he tried to help, nearly beat Dr. Montgomery to death and now blames the Reverend for his crime. And why would he do such a thing? Because by doing so he got a better deal, that's why."

Bastion reminded the jury for the tenth time that Jimmy's fingerprints were nowhere in the home, that there were no other witnesses, that there was no weapon, and that the only evidence connecting him to the crime was offered by a convicted felon to get a reduced sentence. You would believe a convicted felon over the sworn testimony of Reverend James Monson? Preposterous.

"And what about the other potential suspects? Carl Boynton was so obsessed with punishing Dr. Montgomery for his mistake that he broke out of jail to exact his revenge. He admits he broke into the Montgomery's home in the middle of the night with a baseball bat in his hand with the express intention of beating Dr. Montgomery senseless. If that doesn't provide reasonable doubt about the lack of Reverend Monson's involvement then I don't know what does. Or how about Phillip Bateman? He was in love with the victim's wife and was in the very bedroom where the assault took place. Doesn't that provide reasonable doubt, too?

"You heard plenty about the ledger entry for $3,000. But you also heard testimony that that was the price of the new hot tub. What is a more believable scenario? That 'HT job' means a hot tub job, or that it means hiring a man to kill another man?"

Reynolds had the last word and emphasized the motive belonged to the Reverend and the Reverend alone. "You saw it in this courtroom. The passion. The anger. And even though Hawk Tucker was imperfect, he didn't lie. He committed a crime and will be rightly punished for it. But Hawk Tucker didn't commit this crime alone and out of the blue. My goodness, he didn't even know who Dr. Montgomery was—didn't know him from Adam. So why did he do it? What was his motive? Money. He was paid to do it. He was paid by the defendant, Reverend Jimmy Monson."

The jury deliberated for six hours before being led back into the courtroom. Their heads were down as they filed in and none of them betrayed their verdict with a smile or a smirk. The Reverend sat stoically next to his attorney who saw the writing on the wall, for he knew from experience that the jurors would only look at the Reverend, perhaps even smile at him, if they were about to bring him tidings of great joy.

When the guilty verdict was read, Betty Mae broke into such a shoulder racking sob that it caused her stack to nearly topple over, listing forward like the horn of a rhinoceros. Jimmy jumped to his feet and yelled it was a sham, the whole thing, before the bailiff was able to subdue him.

The sentencing hearing followed the guilty verdict. Even though Jimmy steadfastly insisted on his innocence, he allowed for the fact that *if* he had told Hawk to beat Lawrence Montgomery, and he's not saying he did, but *if* he had, he'd only wanted Hawk to "rough him up" a bit. The prosecutor then called Hawk Tucker back to the stand as a rebuttal witness. Hawk testified that Jimmy had told him to "beat Montgomery to within an inch of his life." And what if he dies? Hawk had asked. To which the Reverend replied: "If he dies, he dies."

Judge Hobbs-Wallace sentenced Jimmy to three years in prison, a fairly lenient sentence that pleased no one.

Betty Mae was not there to see him off to prison. He was taken by bus along with several other unsavory citizens who'd been convicted of their own crimes. These were the new fish, a name affectionately given to all new inmates.

Jimmy's first night in prison was a long one. As a new fish, he'd been sent to maximum security for one week. This was not a reflection on the severity of his crime—all new fish start there. Twenty-three hours a day in lockdown. He was allowed out of his cell one hour each day to shower or walk around the yard, and it was usually at an inconvenient time. This first week was a period of relative safety because he wasn't forced to mingle with other inmates, something he wasn't eager to do because he'd seen all the movies.

The next morning, his first in prison, he heard the boots on the painted cement floor of the corridor at 7:00 a.m. sharp. He hadn't been provided with an alarm clock, nor was one needed, because he would hear the same boots at the same time every single morning. Then he heard the loud click when the guard pulled the electrical power switch and the bright fluorescent lights sputtered and spit on and off, warming up for the day. They illuminated a small desk, twin bed, wall calendar, and a stainless steel toilet, sans lid. The cinderblock walls had been painted Navajo White so many times they were practically smooth.

They transferred him to general population after one week where all the inmates were housed together, none of whom had attended Princeton. It was in general pop where one must make his stand or become someone's bitch. Jimmy was a coward and therefore a bitch. He received his first care package from Betty Mae—a radio, underwear, coffee mug, and a note she'd written wherein she apologized again for her "lapse in judgment." Within minutes, three tattooed inmates demanded he give it all to them. As soon as he did, he realized he would never have anything of value again in prison, for he had exposed himself as a weakling. He thought about forming a Neighborhood Watch Program, but quickly sensed the futility in it.

The days turned into weeks and then months as he slowly became accustomed to the routine of prison life and the dank, twice-breathed air inside the joint.

Only once did he cross paths with Lawrence Montgomery, a brief encounter in the prison cafeteria. Lawrence did not recognize Jimmy at first because Jimmy hadn't taken his toupee to prison. "Good seeing you, Reverend. Oh, and tell Betty Mae I said hi." Were he not such a coward, Jimmy would have lunged at Lawrence with a homemade shiv.

He had a few visitors. Betty Mae came regularly and so did his children, minus Darrell. They sat across from him in three-sided booths—the functional equivalent to a row of urinals. Dirty sheets of plexiglass with small holes separated them as bored guards eavesdropped and made sure Betty Mae wasn't passing Jimmy a lemon bundt cake with a file baked inside it. For his part, Jimmy no longer claimed his innocence, only his chivalrous justification.

Jimmy's local fame would gradually decompose far from the spotlight of the pulpit, his branch scrubbed off the tree of life that was the Tower of Power. Even the possibility of posthumous glory appeared to be a hopeless wish. The wizard of prosperity theology, the huckster who'd christened the magnificent *Sea of Galilee*, the one who'd greeted doomsday with a wink and a nod, would now begin to rot in the pit of a cell.

45

THE FINAL TOUPEE

DR. LAWRENCE MONTGOMERY would serve five years in prison. At least he gained his involuntary sobriety there, which was an unwelcome bonus. No church basement twelve-step meetings for him. The stay was otherwise unpleasant and failed to produce a repentant sinner. He worked in the laundry and dispensed a few medical tips to other inmates. The rest of his time was spent interrogating the past, ruefully at times, dishonestly at other times, eventually concluding his story with the conviction that he'd been the victim of unfortunate circumstance.

Jean visited Lawrence a few times, partially out of penance, and so had his daughter, Jennifer. His son-in-law would have loved to come, to sit smugly on the free side of the plexiglass discussing scoliosis and the finer points of chiropractic care to the former star of the Mid-Valley Medical Clinic whose license had been unceremoniously taken from him. But, sadly, Alan had not been designated as a welcome visitor.

The Montgomery's house on Orchard Drive was sold. There was the loss of income and all the legal bills to pay. Lawrence had initially refused to pay his lawyers who hadn't done a damned thing for him, but they threatened to sue him so the house was sold and the IRA had been raided. Neither Lawrence nor Jean had the appetite to live in the neighborhood anyway as Pariah Number One and Number Two. The Century 21 sign hammered into the front lawn had stood as a sentinel to their ignominious undoing.

The weight of betrayal had wrung the joy from their lives. There was not even the energy to divorce. They figured, without expressly saying so, that they were better off together, as dreary as that prospect was. Besides, who would have them? So, Lawrence made up his story and Jean retreated to her booze, but even the tall tale he told himself and the fog of her inebriation could not overcome the devastation wrought by the chance collision of lives near that tractor on Orchard Drive.

The Batemans tried to stay together, for Timmy's sake, but Mitsy had finally had enough of Phil and his handsome jawline. The divorce was contentious and messy. Phil was a divorce lawyer so he thought he had a leg up. He contacted every good divorce lawyer in town to prevent Mitsy from hiring anyone decent. The lawyer she finally got was a dud in court but a whiz in forensic accounting. He found a few accounts Phil had fraudulently hidden. This lawyer was also prone to gossip so he made sure everyone in the legal community heard that Phil was a dumb cheat. So, in the end, Mitsy came out on top.

Timmy bounced between his mom's new house and his dad's condo where he met a string of his dad's girlfriends who fawned over him during their three-month stints with Phil and promptly dumped him when his dad dumped them. All the while he patiently endured his parents' spite for each other. He would eventually adopt the grown-up name of Tim and finished school with the hope of following in his dad's footsteps as a lawyer. The pocket knife, swollen *Playboy*, and forty-seven-card deck of worn Hoyle's that he and Bruce had stashed in their tree hut would remain unremembered in the crotch of the neighbor's maple.

Darlene would never outlive her grief. Time was helpful, to a point, but her grief would only age over time, not go away. Earl's anger would also endure. All the talk about closure eluded them. But at least their two other children were doing well, a prospect that seemed unlikely for a few rough years. Take Carl, for example. Who would have thought he would enter the realm of politics, and for conservative causes no less? But it is true—Carl had become the chapter president of his local Young Republicans group, the same group which espoused strict penalties for drug use and promoted aggressive military spending.

Becky got her own apartment. It wasn't much—a one-bedroom furnished with sticks of used furniture that'd been cobbled together from local consignment shops and donation centers. But at least it was hers. And because it was hers, she cleaned and organized it like it was Versailles, scrubbing the oven and rousting out the cockroaches with aerosol cans of Raid. It was a forgone conclusion that she would take Humphrey with her.

She upgraded to a condominium after she made Medallion status at Avon. She'd become a wild success after finding her tribe of Avon customers, most of whom did not look like Mitsy Bateman or Jean Montgomery. They were normal women, women who might have been less attractive or overweight and preferred doing business with a young woman they could relate to.

Becky never heard from Jian Wang again. Never did he ask about the daughter he had spawned. She'd gone to the Ming

Café a time or two, hoping perhaps to run into him but never did. She remained a single mom until she met Ernest who'd done some carpet cleaning at her condo. She fell for him because he was kind, he adored Amy, he tolerated Humphrey and his various stenches, and he was her only suitor.

Betty Mae Monson was mortified that her one-off at the Holiday Inn had been made public, and in such a dramatic way. But she'd also been flattered that Jimmy cared enough to take such aggressive action to re-claim her. After the public outing, Betty Mae had racked her brain over how Jimmy had learned of her fling with Lawrence Montogomery because she hadn't told a soul. Did Lawrence tell someone, she wondered? And then she found it while busying herself with a deep clean of the master bedroom closet. It was folded up in the small wooden bowl Jimmy used to hold his tie clips, spare change, and shirt-collar stays. The anonymous note wasn't anonymous to Betty Mae. "Your wife is having an affair with Dr. Lawrence Montgomery. I have proof." The distinctive handwriting belonged to Sister Myra Johnson. She was certain of it.

The Tower of Power telecast had been temporarily taken off the air following the trial in favor of *The Lone Ranger* re-runs but had since resumed its weekly slot. Betty Mae kept tabs on the Tower, she and Jimmy's love child, sneaking into the back of the church with flattened hair beneath a scarf. She wore inconspicuous clothing and even the PIPs did not recognize her. Brother Wendell Johnson had been elevated to head preacher a week after Jimmy's conviction because it would no longer do to have Jimmy's countenance be the face of the church. Brother Johnson gradually mastered the remote control to manipulate the mood lighting on Jimmy's large neon cross.

Most people assumed Brother Johnson would continue fleecing the sheep, barely even pausing to sharpen the shears. His first act of responsible stewardship, however, had been to sell *The Sea of Galilee* because it was sucking up too much overhead when the money could be put to more charitable use. So, the handsome vessel was sold with all the furnishings right down to the silverware and bed sheets with their exorbitant thread counts. They used the money to build a homeless shelter. Reverend Jimmy was overcome with emotion when he heard the news from prison. A homeless shelter? When they could own a yacht? Unfortunately, despite the new emphasis on genuine charity, the Tower of Power was never quite the same. Donations tanked ever since the Johnson's axed the All Saints Club and refused to bribe donors with fanciful spins around Catalina Island.

It was a month after he was released from prison that Jimmy was diagnosed. Prostate cancer. The bad kind that wasn't caught soon enough. This sad diagnosis helped to mitigate his shame because everyone can find sympathy for a dying cancer victim.

After the service, the shiny black hearse drove slowly through Riverside. The hole at the cemetery had already been dug and a granite gravestone, standing a modest six-feet-tall, had been prominently placed. It simply read:

James R. Monson
Born June 3, 1930. Died November 1, 1979.
"Dedicated His Life In Service To The Lord."

Jimmy's life was better remembered like this, in brief synopsis, without rooting out the grimy details. Besides, who thinks it just to be judged by a single error, or even a grubby collection of errors?

Thus, unwanted if not unmourned, he was laid to rest. When the final mourners had drifted away, a cemetery employee drove up in a dirty yellow front-end loader, just like the one on Orchard Drive, and shoved the pile of dirt on top of the casket. Once the hole was filled with dirt, the employee grabbed a piece of turf and tamped it down into place, like a final toupee on top of Jimmy.